BRILLIANCE

BRILLIANCE

Rosalind Laker

This first world edition published in Great Britain 2007 by
SEVERN HOUSE PUBLISHERS LTD of
9–15 High Street, Sutton, Surrey SM1 1DF.
This first world edition published in the USA 2007 by
SEVERN HOUSE PUBLISHERS INC of
595 Madison Avenue, New York, N.Y. 10022.

British Library Cataloguing in Publication Data

Laker, Rosalind
    Brilliance
    1. Motion picture industry - France - History - Fiction
    2. Love stories
    I. Title
    823.9'14 [F]

    ISBN-13: 978-0-7278-6509 - 0   (cased)
    ISBN-13: 978-1-84751-011-2   (trade paper)

All Severn House titles are printed on acid-free paper.

Typeset by Palimpsest Book Production Ltd.,
Grangemouth, Stirlingshire, Scotland.
Printed and bound in Great Britain by
MPG Books Ltd., Bodmin, Cornwall.

To Inge, Susan, Iain, Paul, Nancy, Jenny and Dan,
all very special to me.

One

A lone in a first class carriage, Lisette sat forward tensely and watched as Victoria Station, a familiar sight, came into view. Once again she was back in London after yet another journey from France. In her late thirties, she had fine facial bones that would carry her beauty through to the end of her days. Her generous mouth, although unfashionable at this time when rosebud lips were expected of any silver screen goddess, had never been a disadvantage in her career. Poised, sophisticated and, through her acting ability, able to hide her innermost feelings, nothing in her composed expression hinted at the heart-tearing apprehension she was suffering at this present time.

When the train stopped she rose to her feet and took a deep breath, gathering her strength in readiness for all that awaited her. Then she stepped out of the carriage into the noise and bustle of the platform. A porter hurried forward, pushing his trolley.

'Porter, missus?'

She shook her head. 'No, thank you. I have no luggage.'

With homes in both England and France she had no need to transport anything, except when she had been shopping in Paris and had purchases from the Houses of Paquin or Worth, her two favourite haute couture designers. This time, after the urgent cable she had received, she had not delayed her journey even for a day and yet she was still terribly afraid that already she might be far too late to have any influence over the dreadful crisis that had arisen.

It was a warm June evening and still light as the sun had not yet gone from the rooftops and spires of the city. As her arrival was not expected there was no one to meet her and she made her own way to the taxicab rank. As she went by there were the usual sharp glances in her direction, motivated by her Parisian elegance, for the clothes of this summer of 1914, although still ankle length, had a new slim line that suited her slender figure. Her waist-hugging jacket was cream silk velvet as was her skirt, and, set straight on the blonde luxuriance of her hair, her hat was trimmed with ribbons and a single yellow rose. Today, as often happened, some glances in her direction changed to surprised recognition, but she took no notice as she hurried on her way.

In the taxicab she sat back and closed her eyes, dreading anew the trouble ahead. All she did know was that she would fight whatever was ranged against her. Yet she felt as confused and vulnerable and desperate as if she were eleven years old again when her world had fallen into pieces around her for an entirely different reason. She could visualize all that had happened then as clearly as if were yesterday, for she had left the same surroundings of her childhood in Lyon early that morning.

Then, on a similar day of anguish, she had sat perched on a chair after the funeral, feeling that she was being suffocated by the black bombazine and taffeta of the mourners rustling about her. Tragic-faced and pale with grief, she was finding it impossible to come to terms with the bereavement that had taken away the person she loved most in the world. Then suddenly a plate with a slice of gateau had been thrust under her nose.

'You must eat something, Lisette.' It was the crisp voice of a well-meaning guest. 'It does no good to starve yourself. It is not what your late grandmother would have wished.'

For a few moments she had stared in revulsion at the offering, its cherries slipping sideways in an ocean of cream. Then, with a gulping sob, she thrust it from her and sprang from the chair to rush from the room with the speed of a young lizard. Another of the mourners, Monsieur Lumière, saw her leave and shook his head in pity. Then, after a quiet word in his wife's ear, he followed her. In her flight she had left open the glass door of the garden room, which showed him the way she had gone.

He found her lying face downward on the lawn under a tree, sobbing desolately, and lowered himself down on to the grass beside her. Regarding her sympathetically through his pince-nez, he took his freshly laundered handkerchief from his pocket and handed it to her. She took it blindly and pressed it to her eyes.

'*Merci*,' she mumbled wretchedly.

Antoine Lumière waited patiently for her sobs to ease. A happily married man himself with two outstandingly clever adult sons, a younger one and three beloved daughters, he pitied any child denied the inherent right to a happy family life. Lisette's widowed grandmother, Madame Decourt, had given the child a home with love and security, trying to make up for the selfishness of her only son, who had shown no interest in his newborn daughter after his wife had died giving her birth. Now Lisette's world had been turned upside down again through another bereavement, her devoted grandmother having died quietly in her sleep just ten days ago.

Lisette knew who was sitting beside her. The handkerchief had a faint and pleasant fragrance hanging about it. Expensive and masculine with a hint of Cuban cigar. Antoine Lumière was an eminent photographer in Lyon and throughout her childhood she had had her photograph taken by him at his studio on the rue de la Beurre. He also had a thriving factory making photographic plates to meet a worldwide demand. Being a kind-hearted man, he was always concerned for the welfare of his workers and had introduced savings schemes for them that were entirely for their benefit. Her grandmother had always spoken highly of him, although admitting that his two sons with their exceptional scientific achievements were the brains behind the business.

Her grandmother had known the Lumières ever since they had moved to Lyon from eastern France some years ago. They were a musical family and an invitation to their home was always a highlight, for there was laughter and animated conversation and impromptu concerts with Madame Jeanne-Josephine Lumière, a gracious, smiling woman, presiding over the proceedings. Lisette knew how much she would miss those occasions, but then she was about to miss everything that mattered dearly to her. Soon she would be leaving Lyon in the company of her father, whom she knew only from rare visits.

Slowly she sat up and raised her tear-glazed eyes, more violet than blue, to meet Antoine Lumière's sympathetic gaze through his pince-nez. He had a splendid moustache and neat dark hair. The words stumbled from her.

'I don't want to leave here with Papa when he has finished settling Grandmother's affairs. I've been told that she had bequeathed this house to me and nobody will listen when I say that I want to stay on here. Madame Carmet, our house-keeper, would look after me and I could continue at my school.'

He shook his head with a sigh. 'Madame Carmet is only remaining until she has supervised the closing of the house, which will not become yours until you are twenty-one or if you should marry before that day. In any case she is too elderly to have sole responsibility for you and, through your Grandmother's generous bequest to her for long service, she is now able to retire. Even if somebody else came to take her place just think how lonely you would be with a stranger in charge and without your grandmother in the home where you have always been so happy.'

She considered his words for several minutes before answering. She respected his judgment, even though inwardly her whole being cried out against it, but she saw clearly for the first time how impossible it would be for her to stay on here. Nobody else had put matters simply and intelligently enough for her to understand. She had failed to see that she had no choice but to accept the arrangements that had been made for her.

'Yes, you are right, Monsieur Lumière,' she answered reluctantly on a deep sigh. 'Nothing would be the same with somebody else in charge that I didn't know.' Then, shaking back her curly hair, she tilted her chin and added on a new and determined note, 'But I shall come back here to Lyon and to this house as soon as I'm grown up!'

'Well said!' He rose to his feet and, after a moment's hesi-tation, she sprang up beside him, drying her eyes once more. She returned the tear-damp handkerchief to him before slip-ping her hand trustingly into his.

'I'm ready to go back indoors now, Monsieur Lumière.'

'Good girl! Look on the future as an adventure! Soon you

will be seeing Paris for the first time since you were a baby. Think of that!'

In the house most people had gone and his wife was waiting. Madame Lumière took affectionate leave of Lisette, having known that her husband would say the right words to comfort the bereaved child. He seemed to have a special rapport with young people, always seeing the best in them, which was why their adult sons could remember the date and hour of the only time in their childhood that he had ever reprimanded them. It had long since become a family joke.

'I wish you well, my dear Lisette,' she said, her hand resting lightly against the child's upturned face. 'Although this is a sad time I'm sure much happiness awaits you in the years to come.'

Lisette nodded bravely. She was resolved that she would shed no more tears, buoyed up on the promise to herself of a return and the new aspect of finding the change in her cirucmstances an adventure. Yet as she left the house two weeks later it felt as if her heart was breaking.

'Comfortable?' Charles Decourt asked his daughter when they were settled on the train in a first class compartment, specially reserved for them, and had taken seats opposite each other. Apart from a brief greeting each morning when they had met at the breakfast table he had scarcely spoken to her, being busy all day settling his late mother's affairs and answering letters of condolence.

'Yes, thank you, Papa.'

He nodded. 'There's nothing to worry about, you know. Your stepmother is ready to do everything possible to help you feel at home with us. She has also found you a fine school to attend. Does that sound all right to you?'

'Yes, Papa.'

'Good.' He shook open his newspaper and proceeded to read.

She had brought a book with her, for she was rarely without one, but for a while she sat gazing through the window as the train carried her away from the last of the city streets and then into the surrounding countryside until all that had been familiar to her had slipped away. Then she looked across at the newspaper that was screening her father. She understood fully why he had wanted a son instead of a daughter when she was born, for the family château and estate were entailed to the next male in line. His new wife, whom she had yet to meet, was only thirty-five, so perhaps there was hope of an heir before long. She felt cheered by the prospect of a half-brother to love in surroundings that would be new and strange to her, for she had never seen the family château. She had been born sooner than expected in her parents' Paris apartment and a few days later had been taken away to live with her grandmother.

When Charles finally put aside the newspaper his daughter was reading a book and he turned his gaze to the passing scenery. He was unaware of sharing his daughter's hopes that he would soon have an heir. He detested his nephew, who would otherwise inherit the château and all the land appertaining to it. Maybe he should have remarried earlier in his widowhood, but none of the women he had enjoyed for a while, even though many of them had been intelligent and charming, had been a match for the wife he had loved and lost.

Then recently, when he was fifty-five, he had met Isabelle, a widow, beautiful and enchanting, whose late husband had left her well provided for, which meant she had had no mercenary aims towards him as had been the case with so many others that had crossed his path. She had been like a light coming into his life, although at first he had not recognized it as falling in love for only the second time in all his days. It was still a wonder to him that she cared nothing for the twenty years between them and had agreed to marry him when he proposed only six weeks after their first meeting. After all, he was not the man he had been in his youth. His hair, although still fair in colouring, was thinning fast and his enjoyment of good living had added jowls to his jaw and a burgundy hue to his cheeks. Worst of all, his once-trim waistline had thickened to a paunch. Fortunately his tailor was a master of the flattering cut to a waistcoat and Isabelle never stopped praising his distinguished appearance. He smiled to himself in anticipation of seeing her again.

Already wearied by the monotony of the journey, his spirits lifted when the train halted at a station and he recognized an amiable business acquaintance, accompanied by his tall son, about to come on board. He tapped on the window and attracted their attention.

'Monsieur Bonnard!' he said heartily as they entered the compartment. 'And Philippe! How are you both? This is an unexpected pleasure!'

Lisette was introduced and she moved up to let Monsieur Bonnard sit opposite her father in the window seat and the two men immediately started talking together. She and Philippe sat across from each other, he idly watching the station disappear. She guessed he was at least eighteen and did not expect him to be friendly. Youths of his age thought themselves too important to notice little girls. There was a superior air about him, his hair thick, blue-black and well groomed, and he had the kind of lean good looks and dark-lashed eyes that made her think of a prince in a storybook illustration.

She had not realized she was staring at him or that he was aware of it until he turned his head suddenly. Regarding her quizzically with very clear, dark brown eyes and a wide grin of amusement, he caught her completely off guard.

'So where have you sprung from, wide-eyed Lisette?'

She blushed with embarrassment. 'Lyon.'

'Why there? Have you been on holiday?' He obviously thought she lived with her father at the château.

She explained briefly, thankful that he did not look bored at what she was telling him. 'So from now on I'll be with Papa at the château. He also has an apartment in Paris. That's where I was born. So I'm hoping to visit there sometimes.'

'Lucky girl! Paris is the only place to be.' He compressed his lips bitterly. 'I'd not live anywhere else if the choice were mine.'

'Why can't you?' She thought he looked as though he could conquer the world if he so wished.

'I'm about to go abroad to one of our colonies in West Africa. The Ivory Coast of all places! A stinking fever hole and I'm to oversee the shipping out of the tusks of murdered elephants! What a fate for them and for me! But my father thinks it's time for me to learn how to take over his business interests there.' Privately he knew that was not the only reason. He had become involved with a girl of whom his father had not approved and this was a way of ending the liaison once and for all.

Lisette supposed that with such resentment over leaving France churning within him he found it a relief to let it out to a congenial listener, but she was enchanted by his opening up to her as if she were his own age. School lessons had taught her about France's colonial territories and until he had mentioned those poor elephants Africa had seemed like a magical continent to her with all its wonderful animals living in forests or roaming the plains. But then it was still wonderful away from the cruelties of mankind.

'It's always hard to leave home,' she said consolingly. 'I know, because I've just done it. But perhaps you will like Africa more than you expect. There will be so much that is exciting to see.' She remembered what Monsieur Lumière had said to her. 'Such a change will be an adventure.'

He had shot an angry glare in his father's direction, but at her encouraging words he looked back at her with an indulgent smile that seemed to warm her through. 'You're a kind little thing, Lisette. Pretty, too. Nobody else has attempted to understand my feelings or tried to help me see things in a better light.' Then mischief danced in his lively eyes. 'Maybe when I return from Africa, grey haired and burnt to a frazzle, you'll take pity on me again and marry me.'

She blushed like a sunset, suddenly shy in the knowledge that he was teasing her, and was saved from making any reply by her father turning to address him. After that he was caught up in the male conversation for the rest of the journey and she took refuge in her book.

It was not until farewells were said in the hissing, steam-billowing atmosphere on the platform of the Gare du Lyon that Philippe spoke to her again.

'*Au revoir*, Lisette. Wish me luck.'

'I do!' she answered fervently. Then, to her delight, he took her hand and bowed over it as if she were grown up. At her father's side she looked over her shoulder at him as they went their separate ways, but he did not look back and she knew he had already forgotten her.

Outside the station it was pelting with rain, but her father's carriage and pair was waiting for them and their luggage was soon strapped on to the back of it. Lisette could not see much of Paris apart from sodden awnings and deserted cafe tables as they were carried away through the city. Now and again her father pointed out places of historic interest, but the rain slashing across the windows impaired her view. Eventually the city was left behind as they drove into the countryside. By the time they arrived at their destination the evening sun had come out from the clouds for the last hour of daylight. It bathed the pale walls of the château with a watery glow that cast diamonds into the many windows and across the wet lawns. The château was not the grand edifice that she had expected, but to her delight was a charming mansion set among trees and formal flowerbeds with a welcoming air about it. A sense of excitement rose in her, for she was sure that something of her mother's presence would still linger in the rooms she was soon to explore.

As soon as Charles entered the portals of his home he could tell by the buzz of voices coming from the Blue Salon that his wife was entertaining again. Handing his hat, gloves and cane to a manservant in the spacious entrance hall, he sighed deeply. He was tired from the journey and had hoped for a peaceful hour or two alone with Isabelle after her meeting with his daughter. Unfortunately Isabelle thrived on being surrounded by company, never tiring of parties and balls and soirées, involving him in a social round that never ceased. Yet he had learned early in their marriage that it was best to go along with her plans and not to cross her, for her displays of temper – never revealed before their marriage – were hard to bear and hurt him deeply.

Lisette, having removed her coat and hat, composed herself for the meeting with her stepmother, hopeful that everything would be as her father had promised. As double doors were opened for them she noticed how he straightened his back and added a certain jauntiness to his step as if to throw off his years as he entered the silk-panelled salon. She followed in his wake. At least a dozen people were present, every one of them nearer his wife's age than his, and yet it was apparent immediately from the greetings that he was well acquainted with them all.

Isabelle had sprung up from her chair at the sight of him, a delighted expression on her face. With a rustling of her taffeta gown and a swing of pearls she rushed towards him with a radiant show of affection.

'Charles! What a wonderful surprise! I wasn't expecting you until tomorrow!'

She was of medium height, full-breasted, with a narrow waist and the clear ivory skin that so often complements dark red hair, hers being glossy and abundant. Her slim hands, sparkling with rings, fluttered about him like joyous little birds as she kissed him in greeting.

Lisette observed his doting expression. She wondered if her presence was forgotten, but he turned to draw her forward with his hands on her shoulders and kept a gentle hold as he addressed his wife and everybody else in the room.

'It gives me great pleasure to present my daughter, Lisette.'

Isabelle arched her back prettily as she flung out her arms, effusive in her welcome. 'Darling child! Welcome home!'

Lisette could see that she was meant to go forward into that waiting, bosomy embrace, but somehow found herself remaining rigidly where she stood as if glued to the floor. She sensed that the woman's display was entirely for the benefit of the onlookers and knew intuitively that there was no warmth in it for her. Then her grandmother's training in good manners came to the fore and she bobbed a curtsey, voicing an adequate acknowledgment.

'I thank you for your kind words, *Belle-mère*.'

Yet the damage had been done. Isabelle had caught the child's wariness and her vanity was deeply offended. Everyone said she could charm a bird out of a tree, but embarrassingly this unwanted newcomer had failed to respond and in front of everyone present!

With her smiling expression unchanged, Isabelle came forward to put an arm about Lisette's shoulders and parade her around the room for a greeting and a word or two with everybody. Yet it was not long before the housekeeper was summoned and Lisette was given into her care.

'Do you remember my mother?' Lisette asked eagerly as the housekeeper led her up the wide staircase.

'No, I was not here when your mother was still alive. I came here when the present Madame Decourt employed all new staff after she and your father returned from their honeymoon.'

'I'd like to see the room that was my mother's.'

'Then you must ask your father about it. I don't know which one it would have been.'

Lisette found that her own room, which was a good size and wallpapered in pale green stripes, was light and airy with windows that gave a view of the château's tennis court and a wooded glade. There was a desk for her studies, shelves for her books, and a comfortable chair with cushions. A mahogany wardrobe offered plenty of space for her clothes. A half open door revealed a marble bathroom, which was an individual luxury that she had never encountered before, for her grandmother's house had been comfortably old-fashioned. The housekeeper did not stay, having sent for a young maid named Berthe.

'I'm your personal maid, *mam'selle*,' the girl said upon arrival, her frilled cap framing a neat little face that matched her appearance. 'I'm new here, but I'll do my best. I'll start with the unpacking and from now on I'm to see to your clothes and any mending and brush your hair and so forth.' The words had all come in a rush and her cheeks had flushed scarlet.

Lisette was nonplussed. She had never had her own maid before. Her grandmother had thought she should grow up learning to do everything for herself. 'That's nice,' she said awkwardly. Then they smiled at each other and the tension melted away.

While Berthe unpacked the trunk Lisette arranged her own books and set out the keepsakes she had brought from Lyon, including a photograph of her grandmother that had been taken by Monsieur Lumière. Aristocratically featured, Madame Decourt sat in a high-backed chair with her graceful beringed hands resting in her lap. Her hair was as smooth as if painted on her head, with an arrow-straight parting in the middle, and she wore a black lace gown designed by

Monsieur Worth, with pearls in her ears and ropes of them around her neck. Lisette suppressed a sigh.

When two menservants had carried away the emptied trunk and valises, Berthe unbuttoned the back of Lisette's bodice and left her in her petticoats until it was time to dress for dinner as she always had done with her grandmother.

With her arms folded under her head, Lisette lay on her bed and thought about her stepmother. There was something smooth and catlike about Isabelle. Although normally very fond of cats, she felt that it would not take very much for her stepmother to show claws and fangs if displeased, and for her father's sake as much as for her own she wanted to avoid that. She was not sure why she felt such an urge to protect him against any possible upset, but she had the feeling he had had to overcome Isabelle's opposition in order for her to come here. Then her thoughts turned to the youth on the train. She hoped with all her heart that he would be happy in Africa.

Although she put on one of her best velvet dresses, Lisette ate a lonely meal downstairs as her father and Isabelle had gone out to dine with friends. That night she cried herself to sleep, overcome by a great wave of homesickness as she yearned with a deep and desperate aching in her heart for her adored grandmother and their time together that had gone for ever.

In the morning Lisette found that her query to the housekeeper about her mother's room had been passed on. Isabelle explained matters well out of her husband's earshot.

'The whole château was quite dreary when I paid my first visit here, Lisette. So I persuaded your papa that bathrooms should be installed for every bedroom in the new fashion and decorators move in while he and I were away in Italy after our wedding. It's why nothing is left as your mother would have known it. As for her bedroom and boudoir, those are mine now, but you may view them whenever you wish.'

Lisette thought how pointless that would be since every sign of her mother's presence had been eliminated.

'Now I'll tell you about your new school,' Isabelle continued. 'It is an exclusive boarding academy for young ladies. The headmistress prides herself on its high educational standards and, since she hopes for all her pupils to make good marriages, practical instruction on the running of a great house from bookkeeping to knowledge of cookery is included with everything else. Unfortunately the school is quite far from here as it lies just outside Bordeaux, but you can always come home on vacation, even though weekends will be out of the question. So hasn't a splendid choice been made?' Isabelle clapped her hands together in one of her extravagant gestures as if she expected Lisette to follow suit.

'Yes, *Belle-mère*,' Lisette answered truthfully. She had supposed that she would attend a local school as she had done in Lyon, but this was much better as she would be well out of her stepmother's way. 'When shall I leave?'

'I thought at the end of the week. Your papa will escort you.'

Later in the day, Charles frowned when his wife told him the departure date. 'It's rather soon, isn't it? I wanted you two to get to know each other, and I had planned that Lisette should meet some of the local young people and begin to strike roots.'

But he knew the matter was settled. His wife's mind was made up.

Isabelle waved prettily with a lace handkerchief from the steps of the château as Charles and his daughter departed on their way back to Paris, where they would take a train to Bordeaux. Although it was impossible, Lisette wished that Philippe could have appeared again, but he had probably embarked already for a destination that would be as new to him as hers was about to be to her.

Two

Lisette's schooldays passed pleasantly. Learning came easily to her. Although she was sometimes in trouble through getting into one scrape or another, it was never for anything very serious and after some minor punishment was duly forgotten. Although she got on well with most of her fellow pupils it was an English girl, fluent in French, who became her special friend from the very first day.

'My name is Joanna Townsend. I'm new here, Lisette.'

They were facing each other in the dormitory where they were to sleep with six other girls. Joanna had an impudent little face with a turned-up nose covered with freckles and smiling hazel eyes, her hair a tangle of bright, coppery curls.

'Me, too,' Lisette answered. 'How did you know my name?'

'By the label on your trunk. Let's be friends.'

Joanna's father had business interests in Paris where he lived with his wife and daughter, but in summer he took a house on the Brittany coast where Lisette was invited to stay and which Isabelle encouraged. The two girls swam and explored and picnicked with the young of other families until another summer was over and they travelled back to school together again.

As time went by Lisette found that whenever she was at the château for any length of time she drew closer to her father in a way that once she would never have believed possible. He liked her to stroll with him through the château park or accompany him on a carriage ride. It was as if he had a need to talk quietly with someone content to be with him on his own away from the constant ebb and flow of company at the château.

'How are you getting on at school?' He would ask, as

grown-ups always did, but he seemed really interested. The two of them had outings to Paris, where he took her to important exhibitions at the Louvre and elsewhere, staying in his spacious apartment on the rue de Fauberg St Honoré. Isabelle had redecorated there too, but she was never with them and happily Lisette was able to sleep in the room where she was born.

These cultural visits were always the second time around for Charles, for he and Isabelle attended every prestigious preview.

'So many people on those occasions are there to be seen instead of to see,' he confided, refraining from saying that Isabelle was one of them. 'It's much better to come later as we are doing and look around at leisure.'

He also took her to magic lantern shows, puppet plays, concerts and, best of all, to the theatre. It was never to matinees, but to evening performances as if she were fully grown up, opening her eyes and her mind to the magic and drama of the stage. Being out at night also meant she glimpsed the Paris she was not yet old enough to visit. The lights shining out of the Moulin Rouge, its sails rotating against the stars. The dancing in the open-air cafes under rainbow-hued paper lanterns, the women's skirts swirling, the men with their hats at jaunty angels. The sparkle of diamonds as wonderfully gowned women entered exotic nightspots with their escorts. She thought Paris was like a jewel in itself, dazzling and glorious, and Philippe's words often came back to her about it being the only place in the world in which to live.

She had never forgotten him. His smile and kindly attention at a time when she was desperately unhappy had made a lasting impact on her that might otherwise have faded from her memory as swiftly as he had forgotten her. But it was as if he lingered at the back of her mind like a wisp of melody from a half-remembered song and would not go away.

It was a few days after Lisette had celebrated her fifteenth birthday with a party at the château that she heard Philippe Bonnard's name again. She sat at breakfast with her father and Isabelle on the morning of her departure for the new school term after being home for Christmas and New Year.

'I hear that young Bonnard has arrived back from Africa,'

her father remarked to Isabelle, who was pouring him a second cup of coffee. 'It was a tragedy that he should lose his mother before he had even reached his African destination.' He shook his head sympathetically. 'There was no coming back for him then, but now his father has gone too, it has necessitated his return. I think his aunt should have delayed the funeral for his homecoming.'

'I'm sure Mademoiselle Bonnard did what she thought best,' Isabelle replied, her disinterested tone showing she held no opinion on the matter either way. 'I met the young man briefly at the Villemonts' recently. Madame Villemont told me how upset his mother was when he was sent away. It was as if she had had a premonition that she would not see him again.'

Lisette thought how tragic it was that Philippe should have been doubly bereaved when away from home. 'The poor young man,' she commented quietly.

'Don't waste your sympathy on him,' her father advised, giving her a sharp nod. 'From what I've been told, mourning isn't keeping him from the nightspots and the gaming tables.'

'You should not be so censorious, Charles,' Isabelle remarked leniently. 'It's to be expected that he should wish to have some pleasure after being stuck in the back of beyond for such a long time. I think we should invite him to our next ball. We always include the younger group. There will be those among them whom he will know and it will help him to settle down again in society.'

For a moment or two Lisette wished she could be at that ball, but then she thought it would be pointless as Philippe would not remember her.

She went back to school and her own interests the next day, travelling with Joanna. They talked all the way as if Lisette had not spent more time at her friend's home than she had at her own.

Some while ago Lisette had begun performing in school plays and latterly had been given leading roles. Charles, taking no heed of the distance he had to travel, always came to see her perform. Even when it was Shakespeare, which normally sent him to sleep, he was wide-awake in his delight at watching his daughter as Titania, Juliet or Rosalind and was quick to applaud. He also saw how unusually lovely she was becoming, although he doubted that her beauty would ever match Isabelle's, but she was lithe and graceful and vivacious and her hair when loosened was a shimmering fair-gold cascade. He could tell she was exceptionally talented, but – mercifully to his mind – she had never spoken of any desire to go on the stage, being more interested in art, although it was Joanna who showed every sign of becoming a true artist.

When Isabelle was forty-one she gave birth to a son, who was named Maurice. Lisette's six months with Joanna at a finishing school in Switzerland ended in time for the two of them to be back in France in time for the garden party held to celebrate the christening. Never before had either Lisette or Joanna seen a baby draped in so much silk, lace and ribbons. His angry little old man's face was red as a tomato as he wailed lustily while being jogged around by his nurse, his mother preceding him, as he was shown off to guests. It was to everybody's relief, including Isabelle's, when his wailing faded from earshot as he was finally carried indoors.

Over a hundred people were present on an extremely hot day. There was a sea of top hats, parasols and wide-brimmed, flower-trimmed creations in pastel colours. Champagne flowed and long tables were set for luncheon with crystal and silver on white damask under the green awnings.

'Your stepmother has managed to make this occasion one of the social events of the season,' Joanna remarked with amusement as she glanced around. She and Lisette were now seventeen. Both of average height and wearing white dresses, they complemented each other's good looks, Joanna with her flame-red hair and Lisette with her honey-fair tresses pinned up in the same fashionable style under a similar shady hat. Close as sisters, they spoke each other's language with equal ease.

'I think it's the proudest day of my father's life,' Lisette replied, 'although I know he would have preferred a quieter celebration. He looks worn out already.'

On the lawn Charles was moving among his guests. Not all of them had been at the church and he was welcoming new arrivals. He was not feeling well, finding the heat of the day exhausting. Although in spirit he was proud and happy, as well as more than relieved that Isabelle's temperamental displays during pregnancy were at an end, he had not forgotten Lisette. Whenever their glances met he nodded smilingly to convey his equal pride in her.

She had wondered sometimes if he regretted the years that they had missed together since all would have been different if her mother had lived, but decided that was not the case. Before his marriage to Isabelle he had not needed her in his life. Now she had his long delayed paternal love to which she responded wholeheartedly and which made them such good companions.

Side by side she and Joanna wandered about the lawns, greeting those whom they knew and stopping to chat with others who were frequent guests at the château. Although some among them were married couples, Isabelle had a penchant for good-looking young bachelors and they had come on this occasion simply because she always gave good parties and the reason was immaterial.

Leaving Joanna in conversation with one of them, Lisette moved on. Then she paused abruptly, her gaze caught by a new arrival coming down the stone steps from the château's terrace. In spite of the years between she had recognized him immediately. Well-dressed in a light grey suit and top hat, he was looking around for his host and hostess. It was Philippe Bonnard!

He glimpsed Isabelle first and smiled to himself as he made his way towards her. Ever since her first invitation he had been a frequent visitor to the château with others of his age group. She was such a party-loving person and fun to be with, for age was of no consequence when a woman was pretty, witty and, as in Isabelle's case, voluptuously attractive as well. He had been told in confidence by two of his friends that while he was in Africa each had had an *affaire* with her, but neither her husband nor anyone else had ever suspected that she was not a faithful wife.

Lisette waited until he had greeted both her father and Isabelle. Then she became impatient in her eagerness to speak to him as other older people trapped him into conversation, giving her no chance to greet him on her own. When finally he broke away and hailed some of his friends she darted forward across the lawn and into his path before he could reach them.

'How are you, Philippe?'

Surprised, he gazed with pleasure at the girl who had suddenly appeared in front of him. Young and smiling, violet-blue eyes dancing as if in on some secret joke, she was on the brink of becoming extremely beautiful. He racked his mind as to whom she could be, but was completely baffled. 'Mademoiselle! A pleasure!' he answered automatically.

She laughed delightedly. 'I knew you wouldn't remember me, but I'm not in the least offended. It was so long ago that we met on the train from Lyon just before you left for West Africa. I'm Lisette Decourt.'

His host's daughter! He decided to be honest, shaking his head with a grin. 'I have to confess I still don't remember that meeting, but I'm very glad to meet you now, Lisette.' He took her hand in the conventional manner and bent over it. 'Perhaps we can get to know each other all over again.'

'I should like that very much,' she responded with equal frankness, fired through with happiness. He was as handsome as she remembered, but matured now with a man's face and physique. It seemed to her, with a thought as heady as champagne, that she had been waiting all those intervening years for this reunion with him today. She introduced him to Joanna and others joined them, the time passing merrily.

It was as Philippe watched her laughing and chatting that he wondered why he had not met her before. She must have been home at times when there were balls and other social events at the château. Yet he could guess the reason. Somehow Isabelle had managed to keep her out of the way, not wanting her own mature beauty to be overshadowed by her step-daughter's fresh young loveliness. Yet perhaps by now Isabelle had realized that she had charms enough to dominate any scene for an admirer.

It was as Charles Decourt stood up at the central table to make a short speech at the end of the luncheon that the celebratory atmosphere of the day was shattered. With all eyes on him he started well by expressing his pleasure that so many had been able to celebrate this very special occasion with him and his wife, and then he faltered, his colour changing. Even as a doctor among the guests started to rise to his feet, Charles clutched at his chest, falling back across his chair and down on to the ground. People exclaimed in dismay and confusion reigned.

Lisette, who had been seated a little distance away with Philippe and friends, had sprung up with an anxious cry. Instantly she darted in her father's direction, but found her way blocked by the sudden crush of guests also on their feet in alarm. Her way was completely blocked.

'Please let me through!' she cried desperately. Although they were quick to part she was too late. She reached him to find Isabelle, ashen-faced, standing motionless as she gazed down at the prone figure of her husband. The doctor was kneeling by him, but although he had loosened the fallen man's collar and was trying to revive him it was obvious already that it was to no avail.

Tears burst from Lisette's eyes as she flung herself down on her knees beside her father, throwing herself across his chest.

'No, my dear papa! No! No!' she sobbed.

The doctor stood to take Isabelle's limp hand in his. He was deeply distressed, for Charles had been both friend and patient for many years, and he spoke compassionately to her.

'My deepest regrets, Madame Decourt. Let your husband be carried into the château at once.'

Wordlessly, she handed her filmy chiffon stole to him and he folded it over the dead man's face.

A shocked silence had fallen over the whole gathering. Lisette was barely aware as somebody gently disengaged her to hold her close while Charles was lifted up by three of the footmen. As he was carried across the lawns and up into the château, Isabelle followed with her head bowed and Lisette, feeling stunned and still being supported, went too. Joanna had run forward to take her hand in sympathy and kept pace with her. Behind them the company began to disperse, everybody with grave expressions and many of the women weeping.

Indoors Lisette turned to nod her tearful acknowledgement

to her escort and saw that it was Philippe, his expression concerned, but he spoke to Joanna.

'Take care of her,' he urged.

'I will.'

The following days went by in semi-darkness with blinds closed and a cascade of letters of condolence. Lisette received a personal letter from Philippe, which she appreciated since his name was also on the list of those who had written to her stepmother too. Isabelle was dignified and composed in her mourning, not once shedding a tear. At the funeral she was elegant in a new black gown designed by Monsieur Worth and an exquisite hat, its veil fine enough not to completely hide her gently grieving face.

Lisette went through the funeral in a distressed daze. The church was packed with mourners, for Charles Decourt had been liked and respected by all and had many friends. Philippe was there and when he spoke to Lisette outside the church after the service she thanked him for his assistance on the afternoon her father had died.

He shook his head dismissively. 'There's no need for thanks.'

She studied him gratefully for a moment. 'It was the second time in my life that you stepped in to help me when I was shocked by bereavement and desperately sad.'

He looked surprised. 'Was the first time on the train where you say we met?' When she nodded he added, 'Perhaps one day you'll refresh my memory.' Then he stepped back, for other people were waiting to speak to her.

During the following weeks Joanna was Lisette's constant companion. Other people mostly stayed away out of respect during the conventional period of intense mourning. Isabelle, although she thought she looked particularly elegant in black, spent most of her time ordering new clothes in purple and various shades of lilac for when she could once again emerge into society with the outward trapping of the later stages of mourning.

Lisette was on her own one morning, sketching a particular rose in the circular sunken garden where a fountain played in a goldfish pond. She was missing her father deeply, not fully able to believe yet that he had truly gone from her. She kept thinking of things she would have liked to tell him and was unable yet to stop expecting to hear his footsteps coming in search or her or the echo of his laugh, for they had laughed a lot together.

She looked up under the brim of her hat. Somebody was coming along the path to disturb her peace, but it would not be Joanna, for she was going elsewhere today. Then she felt her heart give a leap of pleasure. Philippe had appeared on the steps, clad in a well-cut linen jacket and white trousers, swinging his straw boater in his hand.

'There you are!' he exclaimed in smiling greeting, coming down to her. 'Let me see what you've been doing.' He took her sketchpad from her and studied her drawing. 'This is good.' Then he flicked through the other pages to study her watercolours. 'You are very talented.'

'I doubt that you are qualified to judge,' she remarked dryly, taking her work back from him.

He sat down on the seat beside her, crossing one long leg over the other. 'Your stepmother told me where to find you. Now I've seen a sample of your work I fancy having my portrait painted.'

'By me?' She burst out laughing before realizing poignantly that it was the first time she had laughed since before the tragedy at the garden party. 'Now you are being absurd!'

'You would not agree?'

'Of course not!'

He sighed in mock regret. 'I would have liked gazing at you for hours on end while you put my likeness on paper.'

Suddenly she felt unsure of herself as well as of him. She and Joanna had flirted often enough, but it was almost as if there was a greater depth than was usual in what he was saying to her.

'I'm pleased to see you again,' she said quickly, 'but why are you here in the middle of the week? Shouldn't you be at work? There must be many things needing your attention.'

'I've sold the business.' His face became serious. 'I was not cut out for the career I was forced to follow. For the first time in my life I'm a free man. So I hope we can see each other often.'

She hoped the same. 'How are you filling your days? Do you find them long?'

'Not at all. I've been playing tennis, meeting friends, going to concerts and plays. I've taken up golf, which is becoming extremely popular with many of my friends.'

His words made her realize how closely she had been confined since the funeral, Joanna and other girlfriends being her only visitors until today. 'Is it difficult to learn?'

'Not the basics. The skills are a different matter.' He paused for a moment. 'I had a talk with Madame Decourt up at the château before coming to find you. I wanted to know if I had her permission to invite you out one day. She agreed on condition that we're not on our own, but as you're still in mourning she thought it would not be appropriate quite yet.'

She answered levelly. 'My father has left a gap in my life that can never be filled, but he would not have wanted either my stepmother or me to shut ourselves away just because we grieve. He loved life too much himself. Already Isabelle has resumed her shopping trips.'

He knew where Isabelle went on those shopping trips. Returning with a few small parcels covered everything.

'And,' she continued, smiling, 'I see no reason why I shouldn't come to watch you play golf. I'd enjoy it and perhaps have a try myself.'

He clapped his hands down on his knees triumphantly. 'Then be ready tomorrow morning. I'll come for you at half past ten.'

When Lisette went back indoors for lunch Isabelle was already seated at the table.

'So, Lisette,' she said, unfolding her napkin and laying it delicately across her lap. 'You have your first suitor.'

'I would hardly call Philippe that,' Lisette replied, taking her chair. She did not want to discuss him with Isabelle. 'He's just a friend.'

'He asked my permission to call on you. That has only one meaning. He hopes eventually to make you his wife.'

Lisette caught her breath. 'But he hardly knows me!'

Isabelle cast her a sly glance, a secret smile on her lips. 'He told me that the two of you first met six years ago when you were with your father on the train. That obviously gave weight to his request, which I granted.'

'I was only a child then!' She wished Philippe had not

told Isabelle about that meeting, which was now quite special in her memory.

'I realize that, but he is an entirely suitable young man well worthy of your consideration. Polished. Well-educated. Plenty of money. He is remarkably good-looking and a fine figure of a man.' She could have added that being married to wealthy elderly men – and she had had three such husbands – had its disadvantages, and to have somebody young and virile as well as rich was a bonus beyond measure.

In spite of Lisette's intense joy that Philippe had such strong feelings for her she shook her head in denial. 'I don't want to think of marriage for a long time yet.'

A light lunch of fish in a delicious cream sauce was being served and Isabelle waited until the servants had left the room at her dismissive gesture before she spoke again. 'Nonsense! There'll be a stream of suitors wanting to call on you before long. Your grandmother made you heiress to her fortune and your father's will has added to your coffers again for when you marry or come of age, whichever comes first.' Then just before she put a forkful of the fish daintily to her mouth, she added, 'Be thankful that Philippe has no need to concern himself with your money when he has more than enough of his own.'

Lisette frowned angrily. 'I certainly won't marry anyone who thinks first of my money and then of me!'

'Then keep Philippe in mind,' Isabelle advised sagely. 'You could not do better.'

If anything, Isabelle's advice would have finished any romance with Philippe before it had even begun, but she liked him far too much for that and did feel now that he had been an intricate part of her life since that meeting on the train. She wondered with a private sense of joy if they were indeed destined to be together until the end of their days.

Three

It was not long before Lisette realized that she was as deeply in love with Philippe as he seemed to be with her. Unbeknown to her, other would-be suitors did ask her stepmother for permission to call on her and, in spite of what Isabelle had said, none of them had mercenary motives. They saw Lisette as a lively, pretty and intelligent girl to whom they were genuinely attracted, admiring her for many reasons, not least for radiating her own happiness that drew others into its glow. But Isabelle refused their requests.

For reasons of her own she had decided that Lisette should marry Philippe and nobody else. Fortunately her stepdaughter appeared to be set on the same idea. Philippe would also benefit from the marriage, for although he had money of his own she had heard he had been gaming recklessly over past months. She truly believed that marriage to Lisette would divert him from further excesses. She smiled with satisfaction.

The first time Philippe kissed Lisette was in the arbour of a conservatory where they had slipped away during the interval in a concert being held in the home of one of her stepmother's friends. Instantly she clung to him ardently, surprising and delighting him with her passionate response.

'I love you, Lisette!' His voice throbbed with desire.

'I love you too,' she answered joyously. 'I think I've adored you ever since you first spoke to me on the train.'

He laughed softly in his pleasure. 'What a romantic little thing you are, but I love you all the more for it.' They kissed again and then he drew her across to a seat by some potted palms before he went down on one knee. 'Will you marry me, Lisette? I swear I'll love you all my life!'

For her it was a dream come true, but she did not answer

him at once. It was not in her forthright nature to keep him on tenterhooks, but she had to be sure that he truly meant the magical words he had spoken. She took his face between her hands to look deep into his eyes. The truth of his declaration shone in them. She no longer had any doubts. He would love her until his last breath.

'Yes!' she said softly, her face bright with happiness. 'Oh yes, Philippe!'

He sprang up to sit beside her and produced a small box from his pocket, which he opened for her. A beautiful diamond and sapphire ring sparkled dazzlingly at her. She watched almost in disbelief that this should be happening to her as he slid it on to her finger. Then he kissed her again and she linked her arms about his neck as he pressed her to him in a close embrace. When they drew apart she laughed joyously in her happiness and he grinned, rising to his feet and taking both her hands to draw her up with him.

'Let's tell your stepmother the good news,' he said exuberantly.

'Shouldn't we wait until the concert is over?' she queried.

He shook his head. 'No, let's do it now. I want the whole world to know!'

Isabelle was just returning to her chair with others who were drifting back after the refreshments that had been served. Then she waited as she saw Philippe and Lisette coming towards her, guessing instantly from their happy faces what they had to tell.

'We are engaged to be married, Madame Decourt!' Philippe said at once. 'I trust it is with your blessing.'

Her green eyes, holding a glint of triumph, narrowed on a long smiling look.

'Indeed it is.' She turned to Lisette. 'I'm so pleased, my dear,' she said, kissing her. Then she turned once again to Philippe, giving him her hand, which he bowed over and put to his lips. 'My warmest congratulations.'

Momentarily Lisette thought Isabelle looked like the proverbial cat that had got the cream, but forgot it again as those who had been within earshot came forward to offer best wishes and congratulations. Their host announced the engagement of Philippe and Lisette to everybody before the second half of the concert began and the news was applauded. The two of them held hands throughout the rest of the evening.

During the days that followed when everybody else approved of the match only Joanna showed any misgivings. She expressed her doubts one morning when they were resting on the grass in the shade of a tree after playing tennis together on the château's court.

'Philippe is nearly eight years older than you and knows his own mind, but you and I are only seventeen, Lisette. How do you know you're not going to meet somebody else you like better in a year or two?'

'That could never happen,' Lisette answered confidently. 'Don't forget how long it is since I first met him.'

'That doesn't count at all. I just think we should enjoy this time of being young and free. I'm not marrying anyone until I'm thirty at the earliest.'

Lisette sighed. 'You always have weighed up everything before making a decision. In any case Isabelle has refused to let us marry until next June when the year of official mourning for Papa is over. So I'll be well over eighteen by that time, but if anybody else wants to come into my life before my wedding day then he'll have plenty of time to do it.'

Joanna knew it was highly unlikely that would happen, for from now on Lisette and Philippe would be invited everywhere as an engaged couple.

Winter passed with many social events. Bicycling had long since become the latest craze with people of all ages, Lisette having first learnt under the instruction of her grandmother who, in plaid bloomers and with a veil anchoring her bicycling hat, had been an enthusiast of what she considered to be a very health-giving sport. Now Lisette and Philippe often set out on their machines with twenty or more of their friends on bicycles too. Magic lantern shows were also popular with people of all ages, performances usually held in a hired room or public hall, and often lanternists gave the entertainment of the evening at parties. It was whispered that 'naughty slides' were sometimes shown at private all-male gatherings, but nobody among Lisette and Joanna's girlfriends knew for sure. Not even the boldest among them would ask any of the young men in their circle, and those with brothers old enough were either told to shut up or to mind their own business.

Lisette liked dancing best of all. Although she would have a number of different names filling every space in a little dance programme dangling by a ribbon from her wrist, she always saved the supper dance and the last waltz for Philippe. They came together with secret smiles of reunion and he swept her away to the music.

At New Year Lisette's eighteenth birthday, being so early in the month of January, became a combined celebration with the arrival of the year 1894. Isabelle had allowed Lisette, because of her youth, to emerge from mourning clothes into paler colours for the past six months, although in her own role as widow she had felt compelled to follow convention. But this evening, unable to endure mourning black any longer, she had put away her jet jewellery and appeared in the first of her purple gowns, this one of satin that flattered her figure and from which her bosom rose in creamy splendour to display her most colourful jewels. By the time the wedding drew near she would be in shades of lilac, but on the day itself she intended to look glorious in cream silk ornamented with gold beading. She saw herself outshining the bride and everyone else, making the impact of her coming out of mourning as sensational as Venus rising from the sea. She was as happy as a prisoner seeing the day of liberation ahead.

It soon became apparent to Lisette that Isabelle intended to make the wedding a great social occasion with many guests, which was why she had wanted the period of mourning to be over first. Philippe lent a sympathetic but amused ear to Lisette's exasperated comments.

'She has allowed me to choose my own bridesmaids, but that is all. Fortunately dear old Monsieur Worth listened to me when I said I just wanted a simple wedding gown with a lovely line to it, because Isabelle had picked out the fussiest of designs that would not have suited me at all. People are coming to the château all the time to talk to her about floral decorations indoors there and at the church. Droves of caterers and other suppliers are appearing all the time. There's to be an orchestra on the lawn and then to end the day an open air ball with Chinese lanterns and everything else. How I wish we could just elope!'

He laughed. 'So do I, but that would create a scandal for your stepmother. We couldn't inflict that on her.'

'You're right,' she agreed resignedly.

They were to have a honeymoon cruising on Philippe's new yacht in the Mediterranean. As it had a crew they could spend all their time together and he planned to take her ashore to see various places of interest. Afterwards they would live in his Paris house just off the Champs Elysées where decorators were soon to finish their work.

The first time Philippe took Lisette there Joanna was with them, for Isabelle would not allow them ever to be on their own. Lisette, although she often privately resented the presence of a third person, thought it was probably just as well. Being so much in love, she could not be sure if she would be able to resist any amorous persuasion from Philippe if ever the right circumstances prevailed. More than once in a shadowed alcove or if they were hidden by a conservatory's palms he had managed to slip his hand into her décolletage and she had thought she would swoon in sensual pleasure as he fondled her breast while his lips travelled deliciously over her throat.

She had wanted to like her future home and was sure that she would when all the protective dust sheets were removed and the decorators' ladders and paint pots and pasting boards were cleared away. Unfortunately not even bright sunshine made it feel welcoming at the moment and the unsmiling portraits of Philippe's ancestors on the wall following the grand staircase seemed to glower down at her.

'Are those portraits going to stay there after the redecoration of the hall?' she asked.

Philippe glanced in their direction. 'They are a gloomy lot, aren't they? I'm so used to those paintings that I don't really see them any more. But if you like we can shove them all into the gallery. There's plenty of hanging space. Now let me show you upstairs.'

She beamed at his thoughtfulness as she and Joanna followed him. There was nothing he would not do for her happiness.

The week of the wedding came at last with all the long-standing arrangements beginning to fall into place. Isabelle, who was in full control, told Lisette to spend the last week before the ceremony at home.

'Philippe must keep away now until you meet him again at the altar.'

Lisette agreed, for there was much she had to do. Three of her former schoolfriends, coming from a distance, would be arriving soon to be her bridesmaids and she wanted to spend some time with them. Joanna was in England on a visit with her mother, but would return the day before the wedding in time to be chief bridesmaid.

On the eve of their temporary separation, Lisette and Philippe went with friends to the last performance of a travelling magic lantern show. There had been posters advertising it everywhere for the past two weeks:

> Monsieur Daniel Shaw is proud to present his
> greatly acclaimed MAGIC LANTERN SHOW
> for a limited period.

Lisette and her friends had heard good reports of the performance and were eager to see it. Apparently the lanternist was English and had sound effects to some of his slides that made them entirely realistic. An elderly cousin, addressed as Cousin Madeleine, who had already arrived to stay at the château for the wedding, was persuaded by Isabelle to go with them as chaperone, she herself having neither the time nor the inclination.

Philippe, who had obtained the tickets, organized everybody into their carriages and then Lisette sat beside him in his handsome crimson gig as he took the reins. He signalled with his whip.

'Here we go!' he announced. Then they all set off together from the château to ride the short distance through the countryside to the outskirts of Paris where the performance had been playing to packed houses in a rented hall.

There was a great deal of chatter and laughter as they all took their seats on benches. The lanternist was a tall, strongly shouldered young man in his mid-twenties with thick, brown hair, chiselled features and a very worldly mouth. His clear grey eyes under peaked brows were alert and intelligent. He bowed to his audience and spoke in faultless French.

'Welcome, ladies and gentlemen. It gives me great pleasure to welcome you all here this evening to my last perform- ance in Paris for this year. I have been touring the suburbs, but later tonight I'll be setting off for a wider tour that will last throughout the rest of the summer. I trust you will enjoy this performance enough to make you want to come back for an entirely new show next year.' He bowed again to the applause. 'Now I ask those gentlemen seated at the end of a bench if they would be kind enough to lower the wall gas lamps and then the show can commence.'

As this was done he went to stand behind his lantern and the first slide was projected on to the screen. A superb entertainment followed. Much of it was entirely new to the audience, and an assistant behind the screen arranged the much-heralded sound effects, such as setting off exploding caps as a background to the slides of fireworks, each magi- cally changing colour. When the slides depicted a burning building, the flames glowed red and seemed to flicker, a rustling behind the screens giving the effect of a conflagra- tion really taking hold with increased intensity. A clanging bell announced the arrival of the horse-drawn fire engine accompanied by the clop of galloping hooves, drawing spontaneous applause from the audience. Amusing slides of clowns, a grimacing pop-eyed washerwoman and an angry gendarme had everyone laughing.

A sequence of slides, which brought even louder gusts of laughter, followed the antics of one of the new horseless carriages as it rebelled against its owner, who floundered about in his goggles, cap and long dustcoat. He had to chase it through many hilarious scenes until finally the two of them disappeared into the distance. Other sequences followed, but the one most popular with Lisette and the other girls was a romantic one showing a soldier having to leave his sweetheart to go bravely off to war, followed by battle scenes with thunderous cannon fire in which he could be seen fighting until finally falling as though killed. Several of the young women in the party wiped their eyes in sympathy with the weeping heroine when a messenger delivered the news. But all was well at the end when the hero reappeared with a bandage around his head to take her into his arms once again. A patriotic slide of the president and the national flag closed the performance.

There was enthusiastic applause that seemed as if it would never stop. The lanternist came to take a bow and then held up his hand for silence in order to make an announcement.

'When every seat in the hall was taken this evening I had to close the doors on a number of people wishing to come in. However, I said that if they could be patient, I would delay my departure long enough to put on an extra late night show to accommodate them.' He smiled at the applause for his magnanimity. 'Word must have been passed around, because my assistant has informed me that the number of those waiting has trebled. So, ladies and gentlemen, I request that you all leave by the side door to avoid a crush at the main entrance. Thank you.'

Philippe escorted Lisette and the chaperone back to the château, the others in their party going their separate ways. As Cousin Madeleine went indoors, Philippe stood facing Lisette, looking deeply into her eyes. There was a full moon and its intense silvery light illumined their faces as they gazed at each other.

'Next time we meet it will be to become husband and wife,' he said quietly. They exchanged a long and loving kiss. Then Cousin Madeleine, realizing that she had not been followed, called shrilly for Lisette to come in at once.

She obeyed, but stayed framed in the arched entrance of the doorway to watch Philippe drive away before turning into the marble-floored entrance hall. Cousin Madeleine, who had waited, bade her goodnight from the stairs. The château was very quiet and Lisette guessed Isabelle had already retired.

As she mounted the stairs a footman went to bolt the doors, which was his last task for the day. In her bedroom Berthe was waiting to help her undress, but she did not feel like going to bed yet. She was so full of excitement and happiness that she would never be able to sleep.

'You go to bed, Berthe,' she said. 'I can manage on my own. I just don't feel at all sleepy yet.'

'Very good, mam'selle.'

The maid left her and she was glad to be alone. The window was open and she went across to lean her arms on the sill and breathe in the warm still air. It was not a night for sleeping with the moon like a luminous ball and the park full of gentle, velvety shadows. With such pent-up restlessness in her she yearned to wander along its peaceful, winding paths until she felt calmer and she could return to collapse on to her bed in instant sleep.

She would do that! Swiftly she opened her bedroom door and listened. All was silent. She made no sound as she tiptoed down the grand staircase, although two or three of the stairs creaked and she made a mental note to avoid them on the way back. Leaving the hall, she went along a corridor that led to a side door. To her surprise it was not bolted, which was a serious oversight by the footman on duty, but she threw it open to step outside.

Not wanting to risk a chance sighting from the château, she kept to the shelter of box hedges until she came to her favourite paths. The night was full of little sounds. Rustling and scuttling from tiny night-time creatures. By the lake frogs were croaking and the floating flowers seem to cup the moonlight in their depths. Everything looked so beautiful. On the grassy bank she leaned forward and could see herself reflected on the mirror-like surface.

Then she straightened quickly, hearing other sounds, which she had never heard before, coming from the summerhouse. She turned along the path that led to it. Then her heart exploded with pain and she stood immobilized by shock at what she saw there.

Isabelle, her hair in disarray and her opened bodice revealing her ample breasts, was lying on the cushioned seat, her gartered, black-stockinged legs thrashing wildly amid the flurry of her lacy petticoats while Philippe ploughed himself into her again and again. His grunts and her ecstatic moans mingled together discordantly.

Lisette flung the back of her hand across her mouth on a terrible, dry sob that wrenched from her throat. Neither of them heard it or her running away across the grass to come blindly down the steps into the sunken rose garden. There she flung herself down on the stone seat, her face in her hands. Her teeth were chattering from shock and her brain felt numb, making it impossible to think of anything except what she had seen. Wave after wave of horror swept over her, making her feel nauseous.

Gradually her thoughts began to gather again and slowly she sat up, trying to decide what she should do. How could Philippe betray her so cruelly! He knew how much she loved and trusted him! And he loved her! Nothing could shake her conviction that all he had said to her in tender words over past months had been true. It could only be that treacherous Isabelle was to blame! Somehow she had seduced him. She must have chosen her moment carefully and waited in the shadows for him to come along in his gig on his way home down the drive. Suddenly she would have stepped from the shadows into the moonlight. Surprised, he would have alighted at once. Then her seductive voice in the sultry night, her perfume and the temptation she offered would all have overwhelmed him.

Suddenly Lisette clenched her fist and thumped it down on the arm of the seat as white-hot fury seared through her. But how weak he was! What trust could she put in the marriage vows that he would make to her?

Then she caught her breath. The whisper of gravel told her that they were coming along the path, but the rose bushes were thick enough to block any view of her. They were talking quietly together and once they laughed. He was obviously escorting Isabelle back to within sight of the château. Then, as they passed by, just a snatch of Isabelle's words reached her like a soft purr.

'Remember your promise not to prolong your honeymoon *chéri*. I shall miss those afternoons we spend together until I'm in your arms again.'

'We'll also meet here whenever an opportunity presents itself,' he replied softly. There was a pause as if they had stopped to kiss before they moved on again.

Lisette closed her eyes tightly in anguish. Already in shock, she could scarcely comprehend such treachery, but fury was sustaining her. They thought her too young and gullible as well as too infatuated with him to ever suspect what was going on between them. With her out of the way at the Paris house they would use her father's home for their liaisons!

Then let them have each other. She never wanted to set eyes on either of them again! She would not spend another night under the château roof and neither would she ever return. She would leave now!

Then she realized she would have to get back into the château before Isabelle, who would lock the side door again. Springing to her feet, she took the flight of steps opposite the path and left the sunken garden to run as fast as she could through the trees. Then, well hidden by the box hedges, she reached the door and plunged through it. She was just in time. As she reached her bedroom a tell-tale creak told her that Isabelle was beginning to ascend the grand staircase. Silently she closed her door and locked it.

Briefly she leaned against it to get her breath and listened intently until she heard Isabelle's door close. Then she sprang into action and darted into her dressing room. Her satin wedding gown, which was exactly how she had wanted it to be, was hanging on a special frame, a white cloth covering it, and her veil was a filmy froth suspended from another stand. She avoided looking at them and also at the trunks that were already packed with new clothes for her honeymoon. Instead, she grabbed up one of the valises that had yet to be filled and began to push in everything she would need for the next week or two. The rest of her belongings could be sent on to her when the wedding date was over and Isabelle would no longer care where she might be. A purse full of francs, ready as a lavish amount of honeymoon pocket money, went swiftly into her coat pocket.

The valise was heavy when she picked it up, but that was not important. All that mattered was to get as far away as possible before her absence was discovered. Once again she crept down the stairs to leave by the side door. There she hurried to the stables and into the tack room where her bicycle was stored. Hers had a place for a small picnic basket behind the seat and, snatching down a strap from a collection hanging on a hook, she secured her valise to it. A minute later she was cycling away down the drive, wobbling a little at first, for she had never had any extra weight to carry along before, but by the time she sailed through the gates she had become used to it.

She was grateful for the moonlight as she sped along the country road. Although it was not yet midnight, there was nobody about, for local farming folk went early to bed. She knew exactly where she was going to avoid being traced. It was as if her brain, after being temporarily numbed by shock, had begun to work with lightning speed, her thoughts totally clear.

The fields and meadows began giving way to residential areas. She had almost reached her destination when a cat streaked across her path, causing her to brake too sharply. Tossed to the ground, she saw her bicycle spin away to crash against a lamp post. Exasperated, she scrambled to her feet and rushed to it, only to discover that the collision had done some damage to the front wheel. With an exclamation of fury, she unbuckled her valise and then thrust the bicycle into a hedge. Fearful that her escape plan would go awry if she lost any more time, she snatched up her valise and set off to cover the remaining distance at a run.

Soon the hall where the magic lantern shows had taken place came into sight and it looked dark and deserted. Then to her relief she sighted the lanternist's horse and bright red market cart, which had *Shaw's Magic Lantern Show* painted on its sides. It stood in the yellowish glow of one of the street gas lamps outside a bistro. The horse was munching on a nosebag, but was Daniel Shaw also having a meal?

She ran up the stone steps of the bistro to lean over the side railing and gaze searchingly into the window. There he was! Seated alone at a table, he had obviously finished his meal and was emptying the last drop of wine from a carafe into his glass. She should not have long to wait.

When Daniel Shaw emerged from the bistro, he thought himself alone as he paused contentedly on the top step to breathe in the clean air of the night and gaze up at the stars canopying the whole of Paris. The blended aromas of garlic, wine and bouillabaisse wafted out after him before the door swung shut again.

His sense of well-being was only partly due to the excellent supper and wine he had enjoyed. He was content, feeling as much at home in France as he did in his own country across the Channel, and for that his French mother was responsible. Although she had married an Englishman she had always preferred to speak her own language whenever possible and he had been bilingual from the cradle. His tour of the Paris suburbs away from competition in the heart of the city had brought him packed houses all the time and now the rest of France was his to entertain. By the autumn he should have enough funds to continue his particular line of research into perfecting a camera that would make pictures move, and for that he needed money.

'Monsieur Shaw!'

The lights from the bistro fell full on to the girl in a green silk coat and a stylish hat, who had stepped forward, leaving a tapestry valise on the pavement by his cart. Instantly he recognized her as having been with a party of well-dressed people at his show earlier that evening. His gaze had lingered on her more than once, for she had fine features and her long-lashed eyes had sparkled excitedly as she had watched the screen. Now she looked taut and anxious and almost plain, but most of all he thought how extraordinary it was that she should be waiting here in the street at this time of night. He supposed she had companions waiting for her somewhere nearby.

'Yes, mademoiselle?' Leisurely he descended the steps. All his lantern equipment was already stowed away in the cart under its protective tarpaulin and he wanted no delay now to his departure. 'Is there something you wanted to ask me about the slides?'

'No, it's not that. I knew from what you said at the end of your show that you would be moving on tonight and I want to ride with you to your next destination.'

His face did not change expression. 'Why should you want to do that?' he enquired coolly.

'It's for a very urgent reason that I can't disclose. All I can say is that I need to get away from Paris tonight. Now!'

'Are you running from the police?' he questioned with private amusement.

'Indeed not!' she replied indignantly. 'Nothing like that! I just don't want others to know where I have gone.'

'How did you get here?' he asked, regarding her steadily. In spite of himself his curiosity was aroused and he took a guess at what the reason for her flight might be. Trouble with her family? A lovers' quarrel? 'Did someone bring you?'

'No. I cycled until I fell off and something happened to the front wheel.'

'Never mind. There are plenty of trains at the railway stations,' he said, 'and I never take passengers.'

'What about your assistant?' she challenged triumphantly. 'You take him!'

'He was local help hired for the duration of performances at the hall.'

'But I can't take a train! A ticket purchase could be traced!'

'Good night, mademoiselle.' He had no intention of breaking his rule of solitary travel for anyone. As far as he was concerned the matter was closed and he turned his attention to his horse, patting its neck before removing its nosebag.

'But I'll pay! Whatever you ask!' Her voice was becoming increasingly desperate.

He did not turn his head and tucked the nosebag away under the tarpaulin. 'Your money is of no interest to me. As I said, I always travel alone.' Stepping up on the seat of his cart, he gathered the reins into his capable hands.

She caught at his coat and held it. 'Wait! I implore you! You're my only chance of getting away without trace! Nobody would ever think that I might be travelling with you!'

He looked down at her. Although that evening he had not announced his next destination, a list of venues on his circuit was always available from a table at every performance, for many people liked to notify friends in other towns to make sure to see it. But why was she so frantic to get there?

His thoughts went back to the young man with her at the performance. Nobody in an audience realized how much he saw as he stood in the darkness behind his magic lantern. Although there had been an elderly chaperone presiding over the party, the couple had exchanged stolen kisses and had been holding hands surreptitiously all the time. They had looked too much in love for any quarrel to sever them in the short time since the performance. Was it possible that plans for an elopement had gone awry and they had decided to meet in the next town by different routes?

'Go back home, mademoiselle,' he advised sagely. 'Readjust matters and your travel arrangements tomorrow.'

He flicked the reins and his horse went forward. Instantly the girl caught her breath in a blaze of fury and frustration. To his surprise, she swung her valise to hit his cart hard as it passed her.

'Go then!' she cried. 'I'll walk!'

The next moment he heard her utter a whimper of dismay and shake her valise as if afraid that she had broken something in it, but all seemed to be well, for she set off in his wake.

It was his custom always to travel at least part of the night when he needed to cover a considerable distance. It meant he could arrive at his destination in good time to put up his posters and set up his equipment in his prebooked venue.

He had not gone far when out of curiosity he glanced back. The girl was trudging along and was pushing her bicycle with its wobbling front wheel. It was awkward for her and he saw her pause to adjust her valise and make it more secure before setting forth once more. With a shake of his head, he continued on his way. Yet he could not get her out of his mind. After all, she was young and foolish and desperate enough to accept help from any scoundrel who happened to drive by. Once again he looked back, but now a curve in the road had hidden her from sight. He gave a sigh and drew up to wait for her.

She did not start to hurry forward as soon as she saw him, which he had expected, and he supposed she was afraid of being rebuffed again. He sprang down from the driving seat to await her. As she drew near, her expression wary and defiant, he held out his hand.

'Give me your bag, mademoiselle. I'll stow it and your bicycle away in the cart.'

Her face flooded with relief. '*Merci*, Monsieur Shaw,' she said quietly.

While he put the valise away under the tarpaulin and lifted in the bicycle she took her place swiftly on the seat as if afraid he might change his mind. As he took up the reins again he glanced sideways at her. She was looking stiffly ahead, her hands clasped over her purse lying in her lap.

'You know my name,' he said, 'but what is yours?'

She told him. He nodded, but made no attempt to start a conversation and she was grateful for it. She needed time now to think about the future, for she had closed a door for ever on the past. How quiet the night was! Yet in the heart of the city there would be lights and music and crowds enjoying themselves while here she was changing the whole course of her life, not knowing when she would see Paris again.

Four

They drove on through the moonlit countryside. Now and again Daniel glanced at her, but she did not relax, continuing to sit rigidly straight-backed and looking ahead. She spoke only once and that was to ask him the name of his horse.

'His full name is Prince of the Hills,' he replied. 'I've no idea why, except that he is high-stepping at times as if he has known grander days. I purchased him in England and brought him with me when I came to France two years ago.'

She gave a nod, but made no comment. After a while her head began to droop and, although she struggled against dozing, eventually she slept, sinking against his shoulder, which tilted her hat askew. He tried not to disturb her, but after he had driven for three hours he drew up, needing sleep himself.

Instantly she awoke with a start, blinked at her hat, which was half covering her face, and snatched it off to glance around nervously. 'Where are we?'

'In a lane just a short way from the main road. I want to sleep for a while. You can lie down on the seat if you like. I'll give you a blanket.'

'Where shall you be?'

'Just on the ground here nearby.'

She seemed reassured. He released Prince from the cart and tethered him to a tree on the grass verge. Then he took a red and blue striped bag from the back of the cart and took out a blanket and also a cushion, which he normally used as a pillow, and handed both to her. Afterwards he spread another blanket on the grass and lay down. Sleep always came easily to him and in a matter of seconds his eyes were closed.

It was different for Lisette, although the leather seat was padded and the cushion was soft. She felt as wide-awake again as she had done when going from the château to wander in the grounds with such a disastrous result. Earlier, before dozing, she had formed a plan for her immediate future and now she reviewed the situation. She knew that as soon as her disappearance was discovered, together with a valise and belongings gone, Isabelle would be frantic. An extensive search would be set in motion. It would not be out of Isabelle's concern for her stepdaughter's well-being, but because she would be terrified of the scandal that would result if the runaway bride failed to return within the week that remained before the wedding. As for Philippe, he would be bewildered, unable to understand why she should have taken such an unprecedented action. Yet she was certain that later, when she failed to return, he would become furious, his male ego deeply affronted, for as a jilted bridegroom he could become a laughing-stock among friends and enemies alike.

She remembered the time when her father had clearly regarded Philippe as someone lacking finer feelings and had warned her quite sharply not to waste any sympathy on him. What else had her father known or suspected? Joanna had never said anything against Philippe, but she had never been enthusiastic about him either.

Lisette remembered now how once in a corner at a party she had come across Philippe quietly settling a gaming debt with a friend, who pocketed the notes while advising him good-humouredly to know in future when a game had turned against him for the night.

'You're too reckless, Philippe. Remember that many a château has fallen to the turn of a card.'

Philippe had not known that she had overheard and, in any case, she had thought nothing of it then, for all the young men she knew enjoyed gaming. Yet now she wondered if the fact that she was eventually to inherit substantially had influenced him in his courtship of her? He enjoyed money and living a life of leisure. Then there was his long-standing affair with Isabelle. How they must have congratulated themselves! No doubt they had been confident that the innocent simpleton he was shortly to take as his wife would eventually accept Isabelle as his mistress and all would be well.

Anger seared inside her and she wanted to fuel it with more and more thoughts of Philippe's deviousness, for she feared that when the onslaught of it faded into despair she would not be able to bear the agonizing heartache that he had inflicted on her.

She kept her thoughts busy. It was likely that after a day or two Isabelle would concoct a story that her stepdaughter was ill, which would give more time for her to be found. Neither Isabelle nor Philippe would have any idea at first as to why she had disappeared. Last minute nervousness would probably be blamed. But perhaps with time it would finally dawn on both of them what she had discovered.

Her allowance from her late father's estate, which he had arranged for her after she left school, could be drawn from any branch of her bank and would keep her in modest comfort, but she realized now that for some time to come she could not draw on it in case her whereabouts should be traced that way and neither could she send for any of her possessions. If her whereabouts were discovered Isabelle had the legal power to drag her back under the château's roof at any time until she came of age.

Only on that special twenty-first birthday would she be free to finally return to Lyon and the house that she had loved so much. She would go back there now if it were possible, but it was one of the areas where Isabelle would think she was likely to be found. That was why she could not contact Joanna or any other friends she felt she could trust, at least for a while. She would not let them have to lie as to her whereabouts if questioned.

Raising herself on an elbow, Lisette looked down at the sleeping lanternist. She had taken a great risk in riding away with this complete stranger. He could have robbed, raped or even murdered her if he had been so inclined. So obviously he was just an ordinary hard-working man and she had nothing to fear on the rest of the journey. She smiled. He did not know it yet, but he was not going to get rid of her in the morning.

Once again she settled her head on the cushion and this time she slept soundly.

* * *

It was already light when Lisette awoke. She sat up, momentarily dazzled by the early sunbeams penetrating the foliage overhead where birds in the branches were in full throat. Then the anguish of yesterday renewed itself with an onslaught that made her wonder why her heart did not stop. How was it possible that she remained so starkly dry eyed?

'How did you sleep?' Daniel Shaw had appeared at the side of the cart with his shirtsleeves rolled up above his elbows.

'Better than I expected,' she admitted, self-consciously pushing back the flow of her hair, which had tumbled loose from some of its pins in the night.

'I've repaired your bicycle. It was easily done, and so you can take off on it again after we get to town.' He swung up her valise and dumped it on to the seat beside her. 'I suppose you need this. It's half past five now. I'd like to be on the road by six. There's a stream that you can wash in just through those trees.' He jerked his head in its direction. 'I'm going to fry eggs, tomatoes and slices of ham for breakfast over a campfire, which I've already started, so be as quick as you can.'

When she opened her valise it was her first chance to check if she had cracked the glass of her grandmother's photograph when she had banged it in temper against the cart. There had been no tell-tale tinkle when she had shaken it afterwards, but she was still relieved to find it intact. Taking her washbag and a hairbrush she went to the stream, which was icy cold but refreshing.

She had heard of the English fried breakfast, but she had never expected to eat one with such relish, being much hungrier than she realized. She ate three slices of thick bread with it. Even his coffee was good and she drank it appreciatively from a white, slightly chipped enamel mug.

When they were on the road again she told him what she had decided. 'If you would oblige me a little more, I'd like to continue travelling with you for a while longer. Two weeks at least. Maybe three if you would allow it. That should completely cover my tracks.' Then she added quickly, 'I'd pay all my own expenses, of course.'

He shook his head. 'As soon as we get to town you must

make your own arrangements from there. I don't intend to
be arrested for abduction or to be accused of any other crime
that your family might fling at me.'

'Whatever do you mean?'

He glanced cynically at her. 'How old are you? Eighteen?'
He could tell by her silence that he had guessed correctly.
'You're not wearing a wedding ring and so that means you
are still under parental control. You are elegantly clothed,
well spoken and – as I know from your attendance at the
performance last night – you are normally chaperoned. I also
saw some of your contemporaries and none was short of a
franc or two. I thought at first that you and your amorous
beau had made some botch up of a plan to elope, but now
your talk of staying on with me has made it clear that it
must have been another reason altogether to made you take
flight in such a ham-fisted way.'

She frowned at his bluntness. 'That was because I had to
leave home on an instant decision, but I could never tell you
why. As for being accused of kidnapping me or anything
else, you need not fear that! My stepmother will go to any
lengths to save a scandal. Although she will probably set a
horde of private detectives in search of me, only one other
person will be informed that I have gone.'

'Who's that? Your father?'

'No, he died last year. It was somebody I was going to
marry in six days' time.'

'So it was just a lovers' tiff.' He shook his head dismissively. 'The sooner you return home the better. You and he
will have forgotten all about it tomorrow.'

'Never!' she declared so fiercely that he looked at her
again.

'Was it that bad?' he asked more sympathetically, seeing
how white-faced she had become on recalling whatever it
was that had happened.

'Worse than anything you could imagine. It has split us
apart for ever.'

There was silence between them for a while. She was in
too much anguish to speak any more, an image of the two
in the summerhouse all too vivid in her mind. There should
have been balm in the peace of the sunny morning and the

vistas of ripening corn and flower-sprinkled meadows
spreading out on either side of the dusty road, but torment
continued to tear at her. Another half an hour had passed
when Daniel broke into her thoughts.

'Have you any other relative or a friend who would give
you a roof over your head for the time being?'

'No,' she answered bleakly. 'This is something I have to
do on my own without involving anybody else.'

'Did you leave any clues as to your intention to find me?'

'No. That's why I retrieved my bicycle from the bushes.
If it had been found it could have set someone on my trail.'

'In that case you shouldn't have anything to worry about
for the time being. I assume by your offer to pay for yourself that you're financially secure for the foreseeable future.
Am I right?'

'Yes. Eventually I'll settle somewhere far from Paris and
take an apartment.' She turned eyes full of appeal on him as
she voiced her plan for the immediate future. 'If you'll agree
to my travelling with you I could take the place of any hired
assistant. Nobody would see me. I'd be out of sight behind
the screen. I'm sure I could soon learn how to do all those
sound effects and, if there should be a piano, I could play
appropriate music for the sequences.'

He raised a thoughtful eyebrow. Background music would
be a novelty. Perhaps as audiences arrived for a performance
and when they left again. The idea appealed to his sense of
showmanship. He had been hampered at times by taking on
local, muddle-headed assistants, whom he hastily trained,
and she should be better than any of them, but on the down
side of the idea he did not want to be encumbered by a
pursued girl who could only bring trouble in her wake.

'No,' he said firmly. 'You could be recognized by chance
at any time and anywhere. You'll take off on your bicycle
as soon as we reach town.'

She was not going to give up. 'But I could wear a hat-
veil by day and a mask for the shows! I've made them often
enough for parties. Then if I happened to be glimpsed in the
shadows by the audience it would only add to the magical
atmosphere created by your magic lantern. If you'll agree to
my idea I'm willing to buy one of those folding screens

normally used against draughts, which would keep me out of sight at a piano. Naturally I wouldn't expect any wages.'

He cast a deep frown at her. 'I'd pay you what I normally pay an assistant.'

She caught her breath. 'Then you'll let me stay on with you?'

'I was simply pointing out that I would always deal fairly with anyone I engaged to work for me, however temporary the employment!'

He looked grim. Wisely she did not pursue her plea, but sat in a high state of hope for the rest of the journey. He could feel it emanating from her like an electric current. It would be entirely against his better judgment if he let her remain with him, but the veil and a mask would hide her identity just until she was safe from pursuit.

When they reached the first town along his route it was already astir. Shops were opening, streets being swept and waiters in long white aprons were setting out tables and chairs under faded striped awnings. Daniel stopped only to buy a local newspaper, which he scanned through until finding what he had been looking for on an inside page. It was an advance notice of his forthcoming show in the next town together with complimentary quotes from various reviews, plus his usual advert for a temporary assistant.

When they arrived later in the morning Lisette was interested to see that the venue for his show was a large room above one of the cafes, which was rented out for private parties and other functions. It had its own side entrance and a brightly coloured poster for the show was already pasted up on the wall beside it. Behind the building was a stable into which Daniel, after making himself known to the proprietor, settled Prince. Then he turned to Lisette.

'I'm here for a week, but it's time for a parting of the ways. I advise you to take your bicycle on to a train to the destination of your choice, but,' he cautioned, 'wherever you go don't think you can sweep into the best hotels, because if the search for you extends widely those are the first places where private detectives would expect to find you.'

Angry colour gushed into her face. So he thought he could cast her off! She would do the casting off when the time came!

A new determination had risen in her since leaving the château, a resolve to make things go her way, and this lanternist should be the first to learn of it! 'I'm not going anywhere until I travel on again with you! I've told you that I'll work and,' she added fiercely as if playing a trump card, almost stamping her foot, 'you promised me the same wage as any other assistant! If you are a gentleman you can't go back on your word!'

He stared at her incredulously, throwing up his hands in exasperation. 'I didn't promise you anything!' Then his eyes began to dance as his sense of humour overcame him and he threw back his head in a great bellow of laughter, showing a mouthful of white teeth. There was no malice in his laughter, only a highly amused appreciation of her incongruous demand for a worker's rights. She was taken aback by his mirth, but was not in the least offended, realizing what had caused it. She might have smiled if there had been any smiles left in her, but in her current state of distress her face remained stark as if set in a mould she could not break.

'In that case,' he said, still grinning at her, 'you had better look for accommodation for yourself and get whatever you need to make a mask.' He took a piece of paper from his pocket on which were two addresses with street directions. 'The cafe proprietor has written these down. So inquire at one or other of these places. Neither is what you are used to, and you'll probably look down your nose at them, but I've been assured that both are clean and respectable.'

She took the slip of paper from him, realizing that although he had given her a last chance to travel on without him he had been fully prepared since their arrival in town to let her stay, even to gaining addresses for her. 'Shall I take a second room for you, Mr Shaw?'

'No, I'm having a garret room above the cafe. Later I'll need to instruct you on how to handle all the sound effects. I'm going now to check that posters have been put up and to distribute leaflets. Come back here when you've secured a roof over your head for a week's duration.'

'What about the folding screen to stand by the piano?'

He shook his head. 'Let's take one step at a time. I have to find out first if you can carry out the tasks for which I am to pay you.'

There was still amusement in his voice, but she pretended not to notice and took her valise which he had unloaded for her. With her head high, she set off.

The first address was in a long row of tall houses that opened straight from the narrow street. Not liking the location, she went on to the next address to find it even less inviting, but this time the house had window boxes full of red geraniums that gave it a cheerful look. She took a deep breath and knocked on the door.

A dark-haired woman, neatly dressed and in her early thirties, opened the door and looked Lisette up and down.

'Yes?' she queried suspiciously before Lisette could speak.

'Madame Brousais? I need a room for a week. I'm with the magic lantern show that's come to town.'

Immediately the woman relaxed and moved aside for Lisette to enter. 'Oh, you're an artiste as stage folk like to call themselves. That explains it! Your clothes are so fine that for a moment I thought you were one of those charity ladies from the church and they can be a pest. Not that any of them are ever as elegant as you. Follow me.'

The hall was narrow, but tidy, and there was a vase of fresh flowers on a ledge. Madame Brousais led the way up a narrow staircase. As Lisette followed she realized from what the woman had said that she was more conspicuous than she wished to be in her Paris clothes. That needed to be changed without delay. She had learned to embroider and sew at school, but since leaving there everything in her wardrobe had come from haute couture houses. In any case she would have no spare time to make anything for herself now.

'Could you recommend a local seamstress?' she asked. 'I need a new dress or two.'

The woman looked back over her shoulder as they continued mounting the stairs. 'There's Madame Monclar two doors away. She's quite good, but her skills couldn't match anything you're wearing now.' They had reached the landing and the woman threw open a door. 'This is the room and the privy is outside in the courtyard. I will do your laundry at a reasonable charge.'

The room, which was smaller than any servant's room at

the château, was as clean as everything else Lisette had observed on her way upstairs. It had a single bed, an iron washstand in the corner with a china ewer patterned in pink roses and a row of wooden pegs on the wall. The rent of the room with breakfast included was so low that Lisette almost offered more, but decided that would be out of character for someone working with a magic lantern show.

With payment settled in advance Lisette went at once to call on Madame Monclar, who was thin, tall and sharp-eyed. She agreed to make two cotton dresses, a skirt and a jacket within the week, saying that her daughter, also a seamstress, would help her finish everything in time. As Lisette was measured it was settled as to how much material would be needed for each garment.

Although at the château her disappearance was probably only just being discovered, nervousness made Lisette acutely aware of the glances that she was receiving as she swished along in her silk coat among the shoppers. To add to her embarrassment a wagon driver whistled at her as she went by.

At a draper's shop she chose quite plain materials for her dresses before selecting a hat-veil and what she wanted for her mask. She found among some bargain offcuts a length of filmy black lace and another of black velvet. At the haberdashery counter she bought a sewing kit and a piece of fine canvas as stiffening for the mask, which would be lined with a scrap of silk she purchased very cheaply. In another shop she bought a shawl, more underwear, some extra stockings and a few other items she had forgotten to pack in her hurried departure. Lastly she purchased a larger, more cheap looking valise than her own to hold her new belongings and whatever else she might buy in the near future.

Back at her lodgings after delivering the fabrics to the seamstress, she sat on her bed and made her mask, attaching to it a fall of the delicate lace that would hide the lower half of her face. Well-pleased with the result, she returned to Daniel's venue. He was outside, talking to the cafe owner, and he nodded that she should go in and up the stairs. In the upper room, bare of everything but chairs, she saw that he had already set up the lantern on its stand and also the screen. Putting on her mask and tying its ribbons at the back of her head, she went across to the lantern to study it with interest, having barely given it a glance when she was at the show with Philippe.

It was the tallest lantern she had ever seen, its polished wood gleaming and its brass-work highly burnished, and it was unusual in having three lenses spaced out one above another, each with a brass shutter and corresponding slots for slides at the sides. At the back were a curved pipe and a little door, which she opened to see the prongs within what was clearly a thickly insulated interior.

Daniel grinned at her as he entered the room. 'I like the mask.'

Now that he had seen it she took it off. 'This is a fine lantern, isn't it? I've never seen one like it.'

He came to stand by her side. 'I bought it from a Liverpool company and it is the best available anywhere.' He took up a small cardboard box beside the lantern and opened it to reveal what looked like short, grey square candles. 'These are called limelight illuminants.' He stuck one on to a prong within the lantern. 'It gives a full force of light to any lantern. It is said that one of these illuminants lit in Scotland can be seen as far away as Ireland.' A smile touched the corners of his worldly mouth. 'But who conducted the experiment I've no idea.'

'Why are there three lenses, Mr Shaw?' she asked with interest.

He narrowed his eyes at her. 'I think it's time we used Christian names, Lisette.'

'Very well. Daniel,' she replied.

Just for a moment his gaze held hers and then he turned back to the lantern. 'The three lenses enable me to create certain effects with two or even three slides showing at once, such as varying the colours of a fire. I can also make one scene fade into another by opening and closing the shutters in turn. I'm quick enough to have the top slide ready before I fade out the bottom one.' He moved towards the screen. 'Now I'll show you what you have to do.'

Behind the screen everything that would be needed was neatly arranged in rows on a folding table, which she had

seen in his cart, and now a black curtain was hung at the
front of it to hide the feet of the assistant. Patiently he showed
her how to crunch up some special paper to simulate the
devouring flames of a burning building and there was a hand-
bell to ring for the arrival of the fire engine interspersed with
the speedy clop of two coconut halves for horses' hooves.
Two wooden mushrooms, which she had only ever seen kept
in a sewing-basket for darning holes in socks, were covered
in padding and could be used to convey the sound of heavy
footsteps. A tin whistle as well as another for police slides
lay with a rattle, a pair of castanets, a motor car horn, a reed
pipe and a small drum. Lastly he demonstrated how a metal
sheet could be shaken to convey thunder. She tried out everything before he gave a nod.

'Now I'll run through some slides,' he said, 'keeping to
the programme that you've already seen, and we'll see how
you manage.' He went to pull curtains above the two windows
to darken the hall before taking his place behind the lantern.

The glow of the slides through the screen gave her plenty
of light to see everything laid out before her. She soon realized that speed was essential. At first she made mistakes and
was sometimes too slow, but he was patient and did not shout
out in exasperation as she had feared. As the rehearsal went
on she became more proficient, but it was a relief when he
called a halt.

'You've done well,' he said approvingly. 'Normally I have
to interview several people before I find one alert enough to
cope with what I want. Sometimes I have to make do with
very few sound effects on the first night. We'll go into the
cafe now and have a meal. Then we'll rehearse again.'

She ate well, being hungry, and over the meal she asked
him how he had learned to speak her language as if he were
French born. He explained, adding that the holidays he had
spent with his grandparents during school holidays had given
him a love of France as great as that he felt for the country
of his birth.

'I suppose that explains why you're touring here?' she
questioned.

He shook his head. 'No, it's out of consideration for my
one and only employer, an English photographer named

Friese-Green. I grew up fascinated by photography and I went to work for him as an apprentice. I knew he was conducting experiments in some advanced work and I wanted to learn everything he had to teach me.'

'Did you?'

'Well, first of all in taking and developing photographs of babies, family groups, wedding couples and so forth.' He refilled her wineglass and then his own. 'But best of all for me, he was working on his invention for a camera that would take moving pictures and he allowed me to work with him.'

'Moving pictures!' she repeated incredulously. 'Could that ever be?'

'They are on the way.'

'But how is it possible?' she persisted.

'It's simply that photographs are taken consecutively on long strips, which are being made of celluloid now, and when projected at speed through a lens on to a screen there is an illusion of movement.'

'That's fantastic!' she exclaimed admiringly.

He shrugged. 'There are still many problems to overcome, such as jerking, blurring and so forth. There are various prototypes appearing all the time, but none of them has been successful yet, although I read that an American named Edison has been making considerable progress with his invention, which he is calling his kinetoscope. But it is yet to be seen and tried. I have a small apartment in Paris where I've made one room into my workshop. That's where I've been working on my own moving picture camera all winter. My summer tours finance me through the winter months.'

'So you came to France because you didn't want to compete with your former employer?'

'That's right. It would not have been fair to remain on his ground. In any case, my ideas differed from his and I wanted to go my own way with my invention. We parted on good terms. He's a brilliant man and I'm sure that eventually he will reach his ultimate aim of gaining colour too.'

'Do you mean hand-tinted moving pictures like the slides?'

'No, capturing colour as the photographs are taken. But that is still over the horizon even for Friese-Greene.'

'Nevertheless, I can see you believe it will come one day.'

Raising her glass, she held it towards him in a toast. 'But in the meantime, here's to your success!'

He smiled, taking up his glass. 'And to yours this evening!'

They returned to the room upstairs to rehearse again. This time she felt more confident and only made two mistakes. After that she rearranged several of the items to be quicker to hand when she needed them. As time for the performance drew near she put on her mask and waited out of sight behind the screen. Daniel unlocked the entrance and returned upstairs to sell tickets as those who had been lining up began to arrive. At first it was a trickle, but soon the room was full. Daniel made his customary announcement and she stood ready for the show to commence.

All went well. Several times she was too late with the sound effects and wisely let them go by. People laughed when she tooted the motor horn at exactly the right moment, but laughed again for the wrong reason when she blew a musical whistle in error while the policeman was in pursuit of a criminal. She made a mistake again, causing more mirth, when she gave a young woman heavy footsteps instead of making a tap-tap sound for her heels. When the performance came to an end with enthusiastic applause she sank down on to her chair, realizing how tense she had been the whole time and thankful that it was over.

'So, Lisette?' Daniel said with a raised eyebrow when the last person had gone.

'I wasn't perfect,' she exclaimed apologetically. 'Far from it!'

He grinned. 'I didn't expect you to be. Worse blunders have been made by others before you. Come now. I'll walk you to your lodgings.'

There she slept almost at once on the thought that she would do better at the two performances on the morrow.

Five

Lisette became increasingly competent with the sound effects as the days went by. When by public demand the number of daily shows was increased to three and, on the last two nights, to four, she was no longer making any mistakes or missing any cues. Yet she was so tired after the final performance that she often fell asleep as soon as she got into bed or had taken her seat on the cart if they were moving on. It would be morning before she awoke.

It was the beginning of a routine to which she soon became accustomed. Two and then three weeks went by. As full summer arrived she wore one or other of her new cotton dresses, having packed away all she had worn on the night of her flight. She had also put away her fashionable hat, wearing instead a straw one, which she had bought in a marketplace to shade her face from the sun. Always she was conscious of the need never to draw attention to herself, except when confidently masked at the performances.

Whenever there was a piano available in a rented hall she now played for the arrival and departure of patrons. She would also play if there was a long sequence of slides when music would help to convey the mood of what was being shown. Daniel always made sure that she took a bow at the end of a performance and she was always enthusiastically applauded. By now she had made a variety of masks in the same style and wore one in a different colour for every day of the week.

She had followed Daniel's advice by staying in cheap lodgings. These places were not always as clean as she would have liked, but sometimes she had to make do with whatever was available. She paid all her own expenses and shared the cost of the meals that they ate together in inexpensive places. As a result, she still had plenty of funds in her purse, supplemented by the wages that he paid her every Saturday night, which he had raised after she had proved her worth. It meant that she was still able to avoid drawing anything from her bank account, which she was afraid might be traced in some way by Isabelle's spying detectives. More than once she thought she was being followed, but each time it was a false alarm.

She knew Daniel had been making some adjustment to his projector, working on it whenever he had time to spare, but when he finally showed her the result she was amazed. He had fixed several slides in such a way that by moving them through swiftly he made the full face of a baby change from crying, showing two teeth in the lower gum, to a radiant smile and back again.

'That's wonderful! It's so real! Just as if the baby were there in person instead of on a screen. Only the noise of bawling is missing.' She shot him a wary glance. 'You're not expecting me to do that, are you?'

He laughed. 'Do you think you could?'

Her sense of humour triumphed. 'I can try, but for the happy pictures I'll have to coo. I don't think I could manage a baby's chuckle.'

They tried it out that evening on the first audience. Immediately there were exclamations of dismay from the women.

'That poor baby! What's happening? The child shouldn't be exploited like that!' Several rose in their seats until baby's happy cooing caused them to sit down again as it dawned on them it was some trick of the magic lantern and laughter resulted.

The baby slides were a continued success, although on one occasion a woman tried to hit Daniel with her rolled up parasol, accusing him of having the baby squashed into the magic lantern itself.

Lisette had been four weeks with Daniel and they were travelling on to a new venue one morning when they were held up briefly by a village wedding. The young bride and groom had emerged from the church to be followed by a swarm of merry guests, who completely blocked the road, some appearing to have started their liquid celebration early.

Daniel grinned and raised his whip in salute to the approaching bridal couple, who looked up with radiant faces at Lisette and him in the stationary cart. 'Good luck to you!' he called.

'Every happiness!' Lisette echoed with a wave, but at the sight of the loving looks the couple gave each other when they passed, he snatching a kiss, she was struck with such an explosion of heartache at what might have been for herself and Philippe that her carapace of numbness was shattered. For a matter of seconds she felt as if she might die from the pain of it. As if fighting her way out of an abyss of despair, which she had managed to keep at bay until now, she uttered a defiant and bitter statement as Daniel drove on again.

'I'm never going to marry! I've recently had a lucky escape, no matter that it's torn me to pieces, because it would have meant total unhappiness with someone unable to be true to me. I realize now that marriage is the end of freedom for a woman. Mine would have been a hateful trap! I hope that bride will be more fortunate than I ever would have been.'

Daniel listened keenly. He had gained more information about her reason for running away in that fierce declaration than from anything else she had ever said previously. It was more or less what he had guessed, but her bitterness had never before shown itself with such force. He turned his head calmly and met her fierce gaze.

'I share your hope for the bride,' he said evenly, 'but personally marriage is not for me. There was someone once, but she married my best friend and so that was it as far as I'm concerned.'

She sensed that he wanted no expressions of sympathy. 'Then we each have our own reasons for a single life,' she answered quietly.

He nodded. 'You weren't the first woman wanting to ride out of town with me, Lisette, which was why I refused you at first. I have turned away quite a number holding romantic notions about the life that I lead.' He did not add that these were usually women he had bedded or with whom he had had some dalliance. 'I only relented in your case because

you had reasons of your own for departure that had nothing
to do with me personally.'

'I'm so grateful that you did.'

She could understand that women found him sexually
magnetic with his strong good looks and fine physique. Once
she had glimpsed him changing his shirt and seen how his
muscles rippled. At the end of the show there were often
two or three young women – and others not so young –
lingering with an excuse to chat with him. It was satisfying
to know that she and Daniel were two independent people
holding the same attitude.

Yet for her the incident of the wedding had done its damage
and although she still remained totally dry eyed she could
no longer keep at bay the terrible anguish that had been
waiting to engulf her. Not being able to weep only added to
her torment. She, who had been so easily moved to tears for
her own or another's sorrow in the past, could not find such
relief in present circumstances.

Soon work was not the antidote it had been, for thoughts
of Philippe came unbidden all the time. It was as if her
memory had shut out that image of him with her stepmother,
and now she could only remember the happy, loving times
they had spent together. She began questioning whether the
fault could have been hers. Should she have surrendered to
him? Would that have put a stop to any affair with Isabelle
before it had time to develop? Had she not convinced him
how good life would be with just the two of them together
for always? Perhaps in spite of all the tender words they had
exchanged, he had never realized how fully she had loved
him since that first meeting on the train.

One evening she was masked as usual and playing the
piano while people took their seats when a tall young man
entered. He was so like Philippe that her hands fell from the
keys and she thought for one wild, heart-stopping moment
that he had tracked her down to implore her to return to him.
Then he turned his head and the likeness was gone. White-
faced with shock, she resumed her playing, realizing with
dismay that she might have run into his arms if the stranger
had proved to be Philippe.

Daniel soon became aware of the change in Lisette. She

rarely spoke and her normally healthy appetite waned. He guessed that abject misery had taken over from the anger and outrage that had sustained her until now. He decided to talk to her more than he had done before and hoped it would help to bring her through her present trauma. She was too lovely a girl to pine away for a lecher who did not deserve her. Her beauty was unusual, for she had a curiously fascinating face, even though now it had become wan, causing her cheeks to hollow, but her bodice swelled invitingly over her full breasts and her waist was a hand's span. She also seemed totally unaware of how sensuous was her walk. Her long skirts tantalized him with thoughts of her slim legs and pale thighs. It amused him that she considered herself to be inconspicuous in her humbler clothes, for any full-blooded man would turn his head to look at her even if she were in sackcloth.

'You've never told me where you were born or where you grew up,' he said conversationally one morning after she had rehearsed the sound effects for a slight change of programme that evening. They were drinking coffee at a marble-topped table under a cafe's green-striped awning. 'All I do know is that it's certain you were born with a silver spoon in your mouth, as the saying goes.'

She was surprised, for except for those few minutes when they had briefly opened up to each other at the village wedding they had only ever talked about their work, topical events reported in the newspapers, things that had amused them during the day and anything else that was not on a personal level. He had never before shown any interest in her as an individual.

'I suppose I did,' she answered with a faint smile. 'My mother died very soon after my birth and my father did not want me. He had hoped for a son. My dear grandmother in Lyon took charge of me until I was eleven and then I lost her too. After that I went to live with my father and stepmother in the family château, except when I was away at school. The best to come out of it all was that Papa and I became very close as father and daughter. It was as if the gap of my childhood years had never been and, as a bonus for him, my stepmother gave birth to a son not long before he died.'

'That was good. You've certainly had some changes in your life. Mine ran along a more even plane in some ways, in that I grew up with three sisters in a large house in the heart of London. Unfortunately my relationship with my father was never good. He was a banker and highly respected in the City, but very set in his outlook and in his ways. It meant that he always saw me as a rebel and I never fitted into the mould of the son he wanted me to be. So, needless to say, we differed strongly over my choice of career. I moved out of the family home and only visited my mother and sisters there afterwards. Eventually he fell sick after losing her and we made up our differences not long before he died.'

'Do you see your sisters often?'

He shook his head. 'The family home was sold when my eldest sister, Angela, married a Scot and went to live in Edinburgh while the other two emigrated to Australia with their husbands.'

'How scattered you all are now,' she commented. 'I've only one relative to care about, and he is my little half-brother, Maurice.' She had become very fond of him, for he was an endearing baby, although she wondered now if he was indeed her father's child. 'He'd just started taking his first steps a few days before I came away. Now I shall never see him again.'

'Maybe you'll meet him in the future when he's grown up.'

'I should like that very much. I do hope so.'

They both found everything became easier for them after that conversation and she no longer felt any strain in Daniel's company. Yet she was aware all the time of her true self being deeply buried in wretchedness and supposed he thought her a dull creature who had forgotten how to relax and to laugh. Maybe she had and would never feel anything but this tearing heartache again.

The magic lantern show had reached Rouen when one morning Lisette paused to raise her veil as she looked in the window of a bookshop, for she loved to read and liked to keep abreast of the latest titles. She did not know she had been recognized by somebody within the shop until the entrance door burst open and her name was called.

'Lisette!'

She spun about in consternation and saw her friend from schooldays, who would have been one of her three bridal attendants. 'Yvonne!' she exclaimed in dismay. 'What are you doing here? You don't live in Rouen!'

'Of course I don't! I've become engaged to Claude and we're staying with his parents at their town house here.' She giggled. 'They're getting to know their future daughter-in-law. Claude and I are to be married in the autumn. But it's you I want to hear about! Why on earth did you run off like that? I travelled with Violette and Sophie as arranged and when we arrived at your home everything was in turmoil.' She glanced about her. 'We can't talk here. Let's go into the cafe over there.'

She hustled Lisette across the street, talking all the time. In the cafe she ordered a pot of coffee and then rested both arms on the table, looking across at Lisette expectantly. 'Now tell me everything.'

Lisette had no intention of telling her anything. They had always been good friends since first meeting at school, but Yvonne found it difficult to keep secrets in spite of good intentions.

'There's nothing much to tell,' Lisette answered guardedly. 'I just decided that I didn't want to marry Philippe after all.'

'Why didn't you just tell him? He was so upset!'

'Upset or angry?' Lisette queried dryly.

'Both, of course. What did you expect? As for your stepmother—' Words seemed to fail Yvonne and she threw up her hands expressively.

'I can guess. She was hysterical with rage.'

'You're right. I've never seen anyone so violently angry.' Yvonne sat back in her chair while the coffee was served and then leaned forward again. 'She swore us to secrecy immediately, saying that if you failed to return within the next twenty-four hours an announcement would be made that the marriage would not be taking place.'

'I thought she would have said that I was ill or indisposed to give more leeway for me to reappear.'

'She did not dare take such a risk. Suppose people had

seen you or knew where you had gone? In any case Sophie and Violette agreed with me that by the time evening came she and Philippe seemed to have gained some idea between them as to why you had vanished so suddenly. We all knew how besotted you were with him and you would never have given up marrying him so suddenly unless something very untoward had occurred.' Her face was consumed by curiosity. 'So do tell! Why did you run away?'

'I've given you a reason. It was a sudden decision, that's all I can say.'

Yvonne sat back in disappointment. 'It was very foolish of you. I think you panicked. Now I'm sorry to have to tell you this, but Madame Decourt has declared that she will never receive you at the château again. The doors will always be closed to you. But perhaps if you apologized to her—'

Lisette shook her head determinedly. 'I have no intention of ever going back there. I have begun a new phase in my life and soon I hope to have a small home of my own until I inherit my grandmother's house in three years' time. I also feel well equipped to start a career.'

Yvonne was torn between admiration for such resolution and despair that her friend was being so headstrong. 'I have to accept your explanation, but I still think you've turned your back on a man who'll always love you.'

'You believe that, do you?'

'Yes, I do!' Yvonne replied forcefully. Her glance flickered from Lisette's cheap straw hat to her plain cotton dress. 'I can see by your clothes you're in desperate straits already, no matter what you say. I'm going to lend you some money.' She would have dived into her purse, but Lisette gestured quickly to stop her.

'No, Yvonne! I don't need anything. My father provided a lifelong income for me. I'm dressed like this to be as inconspicuous as possible. I knew my stepmother would set private detectives on my trail.'

'Well, she's not done that, so you can stop looking like a dairymaid. She said she had other means with which to curb your flight, but what those can be I've no idea. But I'm certain Philippe will not give up so easily. If you could have seen how desperate he was you would know that he truly loves you.'

Lisette felt a knife-like twist of painful yearning, but reminded herself sharply that it could have been because he had lost a fortune because of his runaway bride. 'It makes no difference.'

Yvonne sighed deeply. 'You'll live to regret it, but I can see that you won't be persuaded. You must promise to write to me.'

'I will when the time is right,' Lisette replied.

'Speaking of time—' Yvonne looked hastily at her dainty fob watch and sprang to her feet. 'I'll have to go! I was supposed to meet Claude ten minutes ago. He'll be frantic!'

Lisette also rose to her feet. 'It's wonderful to know you're so happy with Claude. I hope all goes well for you both.'

'You must come to our wedding. Claude has six horrible nieces I'm obliged to have as my attendants, or else I could have asked you.' Yvonne embraced Lisette fondly. 'We're leaving Rouen today for two weeks with his parents at their château, so I can't meet you again now. Promise me you'll take care of yourself. *Au revoir*, my dear friend.'

She would have dashed away, but Lisette caught her hard by the wrist. 'I trust you not to tell anyone you've seen me! Please, Yvonne! I need time to be by myself.'

Yvonne looked at her sadly. 'Very well. But don't be lonely. I know I would be.'

She darted out of the cafe. Lisette resumed her seat and poured another cup of coffee from the pot and stirred it absently as she thought over that unexpected meeting. It was kind of Yvonne to express a wish that she could be a bridesmaid and also wanting her to be at the wedding, but Yvonne's parents would not allow it after the scandal she had created by running away. As for Philippe, it sounded as if he had been overcome by remorse, he and his mistress having divined why she had fled the château that night as she had done. Perhaps a questioned servant had glimpsed her re-entering the château or from a window had seen her wandering out in the moonlight. Remembering the look she had seen deep in Philippe's eyes when he had first declared his feelings, she wondered if she would remain the love of his life. It was odd that Yvonne, who was not very bright, had come to that conclusion.

Six

As one week followed another, Daniel became increasing concerned about Lisette. She had told him that she had met a schoolfriend by chance, but nothing more. Yet it was since then that she had become extremely tense and anxious again, more so than ever before. She was forever looking over her shoulder and kneading her hands nervously in her lap. In addition, she started making foolish mistakes with the sound effects, which she would never have done except under stress. He began to fear she was heading for some kind of breakdown and decided it was high time she unburdened her troubles instead of keeping them to herself.

He chose a time when they were between venues and picnicking well away from the road in leafy shade on the edge of a golden cornfield. It was a warm, sultry afternoon in mid July and they were having some leisure time before moving on to the next booking, which was not far away. She had eaten hardly anything when she began repacking the picnic basket. He was in his shirtsleeves, lying propped on one elbow, and he waited until she had closed the lid.

'What did you learn from your schoolfriend that has put you into such a nervous state?' he asked quietly, catching her by surprise. 'I think you ought to tell me.'

For a few moments she was silent, her violet eyes holding a look of shock at his unexpected directness. Then she answered almost inaudibly.

'I believe my former fiancé is looking for me.' Her voice faltered and almost failed her. 'I'm afraid if I see him again I'll forget all the hurt and betrayal and be unable to resist going back to him. Yet I know it would destroy my life.'

She gulped in her throat and it was then that her tears, which she should have shed long before, broke forth in a gasping torrent that she could not control. Deeply moved, he went to sit by her side and put a comforting arm about her. He had never before heard such a devastating outpouring of torment and sorrow. Automatically she turned her face into his shoulder, soon soaking a patch on his shirt with her tears, and clinging to him as if she would never let go. He folded her into a close embrace, intensely aware of her whole body pressed against him. The fragrant bouquet of her filled his nostrils and desire for her, not for the first time, rose sharply in him. She must have sensed the change in him, for her arms closed about his neck with a vibrating eagerness that was an invitation in itself to abandon all restraint. As he tilted her chin upward her lips parted eagerly to meet his devouring mouth.

As their kiss continued she arched herself against him, driving her fingers into his thick hair, her kissing as passionate as his own. He began to unbutton her bodice and she made no protest, yearning towards him even more. An erotic shudder passed through her as his caressing hand found her breasts and her nipples rose hard against his palm. When he bent his head to continue his exploration with his lips she gave a soft moan of pleasure.

Knowing she was ripe for him he no longer expected opposition when he freed a hand to ease up her skirts and stroke at last the lovely curve of her thighs, higher and higher, until his fingers reached gloriously the most secret part of her. At first she uttered a little cry at his invasive fingertips, but lost herself almost at once in a renewed surge of ardour as his lovemaking turned to an even more intimate delight of which she had previously been entirely innocent. She was totally possessed by passion and when finally he took full and glorious possession of her she received him ardently.

For a long while afterwards they lay quietly, her head resting on his arm. Although no word passed between them, he stroked back tendrils of hair from her face and kissed her closed eyes and her temples. Neither of them spoke, almost as if to utter even a whisper would destroy the extraordinary golden happening that had overtaken them both. After a while he believed she slept and he kissed her soft, moist lips once more before he surrendered to sleep himself.

When he awoke it was late afternoon, the shadows had shifted and Lisette was no longer lying on his arm. He sat up and looked about him, but could not see her. Springing to his feet, he called her name.

'Lisette! Where are you?'

There was no reply. Picking up the picnic basket and slinging his jacket over one shoulder, he returned to the cart, expecting to find her there or nearby, but she was nowhere to be seen. Neither were her valises still in the cart. Now he became worried and ran into the road to look both ways for her. Although it was straight and narrow in both directions as far as the eye could see there was no sign of her. Yet once again he shouted to her, this time on a note of desperation. She could not have gone far with those two heavy valises, which meant that she must have taken advantage of some vehicle that had come by.

Without hesitation, he ran to Prince and released him from his tether. For the next few hours he searched for her, riding bareback to cover the way they had come, for he guessed she would not make for the next venue in case he overtook her. Several times he asked passers-by and workers in the fields if they had seen her, even inquiring at wayside cottages and farmhouses, but without success. Then he wheeled Prince around and galloped back, hoping that she would have thought better of leaving and returned to the cart. His frantic hope proved to be in vain.

He felt devastated when hours later he drove away from the site where so much had happened between them. On the road ahead he would continue to make inquiries. His worst fears had come true. He had allowed himself to become emotionally involved, which was a mistake he had never intended to make in any circumstance. Without acknowledging it, he had been drawn to Lisette from the first moment of seeing her. He realized now that it was why he had taken her on board against all his better judgement. Whether he was in love with her or not was beside the point. He just knew that he would have no peace of mind until she was with him again. His hope was that he found her before her erstwhile fiancé discovered her whereabouts.

* * *

Two days later, Lisette left the widow's cottage where she had taken refuge. It was not far from where she and Daniel had lain together, but she had realized that he would soon have discovered her if she had kept to the road. So she had told the widow truthfully that her former fiancé was pursuing her, not mentioning Daniel, and she bribed the woman not to give her away if he should come to the door. From the small upper window of her room she had watched him gallop past like a madman and much later she heard him ride back again. This time she did not look out. But when he hammered on the widow's door she listened intently from the head of the stairs and heard him turned away.

It saddened her that she had parted from him so abruptly, but it was the only way, for they could never have recaptured the easy companionship that had previously existed between them. She hoped that with time he would understand and forgive her seemingly harsh departure.

After twenty-four hours she had walked back to the site and seen the flattened wheelmarks in the grass where the cart had stood, but did not return to where Daniel had made love to her. Yet it had been a revelation. He had given her such exquisite pleasure, sending sensations through her that she had never known existed. The reason why she had turned to him with such abandonment was that she had wanted him to drive Philippe from her heart and her mind and, during that ecstatic time, he had done it. In losing her virginity she had thrown off the past completely, her girlhood gone and everything appertaining to it. She felt wholly liberated and more than grateful to the tender, passionate man who had brought it about.

Nevertheless, she did not want to meet Daniel again. The ecstatic encounter between them had been a beginning and an end. He must have had many such amorous moments with other women and would soon forget it had ever happened. Yet she accepted that it would be a lasting memory for her, for she had heard it said that no woman ever forgot the first man that made love to her, and Daniel had been a lover beyond all her expectations.

Next morning the widow's son drove Lisette in his gig to a nearby market town, which was not on Daniel's route. She was wearing her green silk coat again and fashionable hat that she had worn for her escape. Her plans were made and she thought them over again on the way. From the market town she would travel by train to Lyon. There she would find an apartment and, after a few days, start to settle her career. She would enjoy looking for suitable premises for a little shop, preferably with accommodation above. The fact that Isabelle considered her banished for ever was a great relief and if Philippe should come looking for her there it would no longer be of any consequence, for Daniel had been instrumental in driving a wedge between them that could never be dislodged.

At the railway station she found a late afternoon train she could take to Lyon, changing in Paris. The widow's son, whom she tipped generously, carried her valises to the left luggage office to await her departure. She then made her way to the branch of her Paris bank in order to withdraw money from her account. It would be for the first time since she had left home. Until now the wage she had received from Daniel had supplemented her funds. The bank clerk was very courteous and studied the draft she presented, then he asked her to wait a few moments. He disappeared into the manager's office, but soon returned to show her in there.

'Good morning, Mademoiselle Decourt,' the manager greeted her. 'Please sit down.' Then he cleared his throat and regarded her steadily through his pince-nez from across his wide mahogany desk. 'I regret having to tell you, but your account was closed some weeks ago.'

Lisette stared at him in disbelief. 'But that's impossible! My late father arranged matters for me to withdraw from it at any time.'

'I cannot offer you any explanation since I only have the instruction circulated to all our branches, but – if you will pardon my observation – I believe you to be under twenty-one. Therefore anyone in authority over you has the right to govern your finances.'

He remained unmoved by her stricken expression, having seen many others in similar distress for a wide variety of financial anxieties.

'It could only be my stepmother!' Lisette exclaimed, thinking how cunningly Isabelle had used her power. 'Surely

something can be done to counteract her inexcusable inter-
ference in this matter!'

'Not unless you get authorization from her yourself.'

'That is impossible!' Lisette rose to her feet immediately.
'Good day, monsieur.'

Outside the bank again she was trembling with shock at
the news she had received. How devious of Isabelle to use
such a weapon against her! She went to sit on a bench among
flowerbeds in a nearby park. There she checked with nervous
hands the contents of her purse before sitting back and consid-
ering what her immediate plans should be. She had enough
cash to see her through the next three weeks if she took
cheaper lodgings than ever before, and she would not starve,
but after that there would be nothing. She had a few little
pieces of jewellery with her, but none of it was of any real
value, except a string of pearls that her father had given her
and that she would never sell. More valuable pieces, which
she had inherited from her mother and grandmother, had
only ever been worn on special occasions and were still in
the safe in what had been her father's study. She had given
them no thought in her flight.

The long train journey she had planned to Lyon would
have to wait. The ticket was more than she could afford at
the present time. She was sure the Lumières would be the
first to offer help if she arrived almost without funds on their
doorstep, but she had no intention of being a burden to anyone.
She must get some employment here in this town and save
every sou until she was more secure financially to make the
journey.

Without wasting any more time, she left the park and
found a newsagent's shop where she bought a local newspaper. Taking it back to the park bench she sat down again
and read all the situations available. Most of them were for
domestic servants, but there was a vacancy for a saleswoman in a milliner's shop, an opening for a well-read
person in a local private subscription library, an assistant
in an ironmonger's and a temporary teacher in a school for
young children. She tore off the page and tucked it into
her purse. Then she set off first for the milliner's shop only
to find that the post had already been filled. At the library

the woman who interviewed her seemed satisfied by her reading background, but raised cool eyebrows when Lisette admitted to having no references.

'Then I regret that without any such information I cannot find you suitable, Mademoiselle Decourt. You see, we have very expensive antique volumes on the premises and have to be most careful about whom we employ.'

Lisette flushed angrily that any doubt should be cast on her honesty and she swept out of the library. Her next call was at the school. There she would have been accepted, it being an emergency since a teacher had been taken ill, but again as she had no references she was politely shown the door. Finally she tried the ironmonger's, thinking that perhaps he would be less pernickety, but there she was told that a male assistant was required.

She realized soberly that she had little chance of gaining good employment anywhere without references and decided as a desperate measure that she must write them herself. After buying two kinds of good quality writing paper, she went to the post office. There she used a different pen and paper for each reference and, disguising her handwriting, wrote two separate letters commending herself as honest, reliable and efficient. On the envelopes she wrote 'To whom it may concern' and sealed them. Now she would look for somewhere to stay and buy another newspaper in the morning.

Retrieving her valises from the railway station, she set off down the meaner streets until she came to a lodging house and took a room, which was papered horribly with yellow and brown daisies. Nowhere she had stayed in before had been as bad as this place, and from the sounds in the neighbouring rooms she was not at all sure that it was a respectable house after all. Her last thought before she slept was of Daniel, who would have been dismayed by her present straits. It made her realize how protective he had been. Momentarily her breasts seemed to ache for his caress, but she folded an arm across them in a dismissal of yearning.

There were two quite suitable vacancies advertised in the morning newspaper and she decided to apply first for the one that appealed to her most. It was for a saleswoman in the large emporium located in the main street. On her way to the bank the previous day she had paused to look at the top quality goods displayed in the windows.

She went there immediately. Although the emporium had only just opened its doors she was not the first to be there for the vacancy. Three other young women were ahead of her, seated side by side in a waiting room. She took a fourth chair and soon afterward two older women seated themselves. Nobody spoke, but Lisette became aware of the cold looks directed at her fashionable clothes, which she had decided to wear again, hoping it would raise her status in an employer's eyes. She thought to herself that these women had no idea that if she did not get employment soon she faced destitution.

Then the interviews began to take place behind an office door with opaque glass panels. Two applicants left immediately afterwards, but a third returned to her chair to await a final decision. Then it was Lisette's turn.

She came face to face with Madame Fabignon, the owner's wife, a thin-faced woman with gimlet eyes and a mouth that seemed permanently pursed in disapproval.

'What sales experience have you had, Mademoiselle Decourt?'

Lisette was fully prepared for the question. 'I have sold porcelain and china,' she answered truthfully, thinking back to the help she had given at a stall of donated, mostly expensive knick-knacks at a charity sale that Joanna's mother had organized annually in her rose garden. 'Also,' she added, thinking of another stall at that annual function, 'I had a spell of selling small antiques.'

Madame Fabignon had taken notice of this young woman's expensive attire and wondered if she was morally all that she should be. Shop girls were not able to afford such clothes. Yet in the young woman's favour were her educated speech, her poise and the spotlessness of her white gloves. There also an elegant air about her. She preferred to believe she was from a family which had fallen on hard times.

'Where were you employed?'

'In Paris.'

'Were the establishments as large as this one?'

'No, but quite exclusive.'

The woman seemed to digest this information quite favourably. 'You are quite far away from Paris now. Why did you leave?'

'Both my parents are dead. I had nothing to keep me there.'

Madame Fabignon decided that she had been right about this girl's background. A well bred family, but no money. She held out her narrow hand, snapping her fingers impatiently. 'Give me your references.'

Lisette handed them over and watched anxiously, almost holding her breath, as they were read through, but all seemed to be well. There was an approving nod.

'I find you suitable, Mademoiselle Decourt, and you may start work here tomorrow. As you will know, it is quite customary with an emporium of this size that all female employees of single status are safely accommodated. Here you will live with all the other young saleswomen in the premises adjacent to this building. It is under the supervision of Mademoiselle Valverde, who is both housekeeper and guardian. Shall you take kindly to discipline?'

'Yes, madame. I can understand that some rules are necessary.'

'Mine are very strict and breaking them can mean instant dismissal. There is a nightly curfew of eight thirty with the concession of nine o'clock on Saturdays. On Sunday the emporium is closed, which gives you the day to spend as you wish after attendance at church. You will have a respectable roof over your head and three meals a day – breakfast, a light lunch of rolls and cheese or soup, and always a hot dinner in the early evening. Alcohol and cigarettes are forbidden, also dalliance with the male staff, who have their own quarters. Have I made myself clear?'

'Yes, madame.'

'Good. You will move in with your belongings today.'

Lisette, who was feeling jubilant at not having to pay for accommodation elsewhere, was taken aback when in the next moment she was told the pittance that her wages would be for a twelve-hour working day. Yet when she left the office her spirits had lifted again, for Madame Fabignon had spoken of an eventual rise in wages and the chance of promotion if she proved herself to be a hardworking and conscientious employee. Until then, Lisette decided, if she were truly miserly, even small coins would mount up as time went by.

Seven

An hour later Lisette, a valise in each hand, was admitted by a young maidservant into the house where she was to stay. Immediately a large, full-bosomed woman came into the hall from a study and her cold eyes sharpened under heavy, dark brows as she looked the newcomer up and down.

'Mademoiselle Decourt?' she said before Lisette had a chance to speak. 'You are from Paris, I've been told. I'll warn you now that I don't tolerate any big city laxness of behaviour here. In the shop you'll work hard at whichever counter is allotted to you and in my domain you'll obey without question all the rules of the house, which you can read for yourself on the wall of your room. Do you have your own black dress for work?'

'No, I don't.'

'Then you shall have two on loan for the six weeks of your trial period. After that, if you are taken on to the permanent staff, two dresses will be specially made for you in the dressmaking department.' She glanced down at Lisette's two valises. 'When you have unpacked come downstairs to me again.' Then she snapped her fingers imperiously at the maidservant. 'Marie! Take Mademoiselle Decourt up to the wardrobe room. Then to the third floor where there's a spare bed in the north-facing room.'

Lisette, heaving her valises up the stairs in the wake of the girl, thought that Mademoiselle Valverde seemed to be even more of a martinet than Madame Fabignon, but that did not bother her. She could manage to live within the rules, however restrictive they might be, until she had enough money saved to suit her purpose.

The wardrobe room on the second floor was full of black

dresses on hangers that were suspended from rods. She set down her luggage and looked around dubiously.

'They don't smell musty, but are they clean?' she asked.

Marie was quick to reassure her. 'Don't worry! Every garment goes to the laundry before it's put ready to wear again. There's a selection of separate white collars and cuffs that you can choose from, but these have to be starched and spotless at all times. You have the use of the laundry for washing and ironing.'

Lisette picked out two dresses in her size and then the three sets of collars and cuffs that she was allowed. She had chosen those trimmed with lace. Marie carried these garments and accessories up to the next floor, for the newcomer could not carry everything.

'This is where you'll sleep,' she said, going ahead into a room located under the eaves.

Lisette followed. There were five beds, each with a chest of drawers beside it. Everything was very neat and tidy, a pair of slippers by the foot of each bed, under which there was the gleam of an individual chamber pot. A cheval glass stood in a corner, giving Lisette a full-length reflection of herself as she passed it, and pegs along one wall were hung with clothes. Two were spare and Lisette guessed those would be hers.

'This is your bed,' Marie said, dumping what she was carrying on the bed nearest the door, but farthest from the window. 'Over there on the wall is the list of rules.' She nodded in its direction. 'You'd better read them, because Mademoiselle Valverde will question you.' Then she left the room and went pattering down the stairs.

After Lisette had unpacked she read the list on the wall. Some rules dealt with personal hygiene, others with tidiness, promptness for meals and similar matters. There was also the dire threat of instant dismissal if any employee brought a man on to the premises.

She found her own way downstairs. As the maid had predicted, Mademoiselle Valverde questioned her about the rules, and she was able to answer correctly. Afterwards she was led through a pair of communicating double doors that opened into the emporium.

'You'll come to work this way every morning with your fellow saleswomen,' Mademoiselle Valverde said over her shoulder as she strode ahead. 'I've had a word with Madame Fabignon and you are to be at the shawl and cape counter. When a customer shows a preference for one or another of the items, Madame Fabignon wants you to drape it around yourself and walk up and down to display it to full effect. But never, never pressure a sale and, provided there is no damage, always exchange merchandise willingly. In the case of any doubt or trouble always remain polite, but call the floorwalker, Monsieur Giraud, who will take over the matter.'

A young salesman, named Pierre, was in charge of the shawl counter. As soon as Mademoiselle Valverde had left he expressed his relief that Lisette had arrived. 'I had to take over this counter a couple of days ago after somebody was sacked on the spot for theft, but my place is on gentlemen's ties and cravats. I'll show you where everything is and then leave you to it. Ah, here's a customer coming now. I'll not desert you yet.' Then he bowed to the well-dressed, middle-aged woman approaching the counter. 'How may I be of assistance, madame?'

'I need a shawl. Silk, I think. Blue tones or maybe red. Perhaps a pretty shade of green,' the customer said indecisively as she sat down on one of the chairs provided.

Lisette watched as Pierre took shawl after shawl from the shelves, opening each with a flourish of colour until the counter was almost covered by them, but still the dithering customer seemed unable to make up her mind. When one of the shawls, which had been rejected, slipped to the floor Lisette retrieved it and swirled it over one shoulder in a flurry of silken fringe. Immediately the customer showed interest.

'Now that shawl is more stylish than any other I've been shown!'

Immediately Lisette left the counter and walked slowly up and down for the woman's benefit. A sale was made. After Pierre had packed the shawl and arranged for it to be delivered he turned to Lisette, standing with his hands on his hips and a wide grin on his face.

'Whatever prompted you to do that?' he asked.

'I was following instructions from Madame Fabignon.'

'But nobody has ever done that before! Carry on with the good work. You should clear the shelves of shawls within a week!'

They laughed together. By a pillar Madame Fabignon, who had observed the whole incident, congratulated herself as she moved away. Any accessory or garment would look its best on that elegant young woman. It promised to be a wise appointment that she had made.

Lisette soon came to know the four fellow saleswomen who shared the bedroom. They were all in their early twenties and, apart from an occasional squabble now and again, were remarkably tolerant of each other in such cramped conditions. Mademoiselle Valverde was their common enemy, for without exception they all hated her and this bound them together.

'She listens at keyholes,' Claudine, the oldest of the girls, warned Lisette.

'Yes! And she inspects our room on her own, poking into everything,' another, who was named Blanche, declared indignantly.

'She even found my beau's letters hidden under my underclothes and read them!' This was Elyanne, her face flushing resentfully. 'I know, because the blue ribbon around them was tied differently.'

'That's right,' Celestine, a redhead, endorsed bitterly. 'The jealous old cow pokes about in the other girls' rooms too. She gives us all the creeps.'

Lisette was thankful there was nothing among her possessions that would give away all that had happened to her. Daniel was now a secret memory that she had come to linger over more often than she had expected. Yet it was a closed period in her life that was entirely hers and always would be. Now she was about to begin a new existence.

It began at seven o'clock each morning when breakfast was served and presided over by Mademoiselle Valverde. There were two long tables full of chattering women, mostly in their twenties and thirties, but a few older ones of senior status sat at a smaller table on their own. When the meal was over all would line up two by two and, at a signal from Mademoiselle Valverde, they would set off through the double doors into the emporium where they would branch off at their individual counters. It reminded Lisette of her school days when she and all the rest of the pupils went to their classrooms after morning assembly. She had soon learned that here the others called it the Noah's Ark parade.

As one week followed another Lisette became expert in her sales technique, for by now she could recognize instantly the indecisive customers as well as those who wanted the impossible or, not knowing what suited them, had to be steered in the right direction. There were also the dominating mothers with timid daughters longing to make their own choice, and it was a point of pride with Lisette that they rarely went away disappointed.

One Saturday evening she went with two of her room companions, Claudine and Elyanne, to a magic lantern show that had come to town. She had not known that they were meeting two of the young salesmen, who worked in gentlemen's footwear, and that they had brought a third young man for her, who was a bank clerk.

'I'm Henri Casson,' he said, raising his straw boater and introducing himself. He was freckled with bright smiling eyes. As the evening progressed he proved to be good company, but she drew her hand away when he tried to hold it as soon as the gaslights were lowered at the magic lantern show. Although he and the others all enjoyed the show immensely, laughing their heads off at the comical slides, Lisette watched the whole performance with a critical eye. She soon realized that she had worked with a master of the craft, and this lanternist could not compete with Daniel in any way. It was no wonder that he had always had a packed house for his shows.

When they all said goodnight Henri wanted to see her again, but she made an excuse, careful not to hurt his feelings. She had no room in her life at present for any man, not even for occasional meetings, and certainly never again on a permanent basis.

It was not long afterwards that she awoke early one morning to a slight feeling of nausea. She dismissed it, but was thankful that it was not yet time to get up, and turned over to sleep again. A few minutes later the sensation of sickness overwhelmed her and she almost fell out of bed to grab her empty chamber pot and vomit into it as if she would never stop. In the neighbouring bed Claudine stirred, sat up and then sprang out of bed to kneel at her side.

'Are you all right?' she whispered anxiously, not wanting anyone else to wake.

Lisette nodded weakly, reaching for a handkerchief from the bedside chest of drawers to wipe her mouth. 'I have felt a little sick for the past few mornings, but nothing came of it. I must have eaten something that has upset my stomach, but now I've vomited I should be better.'

Claudine looked dubious. 'Are you sure there isn't another more likely reason?'

Lisette looked puzzled. 'What could there be?'

The reply came bluntly. 'Are you in the family way?'

Slowly Lisette's expression changed from incredulity to one of horrified doubt. 'No! That's impossible!' she protested.

Claudine became practical. 'Get back into bed and think about it,' she urged, picking up the chamber pot. 'I'll empty this before anybody wakes.'

Lying back on her pillows, Lisette lay in fear of what might have befallen her. She was late in her cycle, but had given it no thought, for it had happened at rare intervals. No, it couldn't be!

Claudine returned with the clean chamber pot and sat down on Lisette's bed as she thrust it underneath. 'Well?' she whispered.

'But it was only once,' Lisette gulped. 'It doesn't happen as easily as that!'

'I'm afraid it can, my poor innocent. Will he marry you, do you think?'

'No! He's completely against marriage for himself.'

Claudine smiled cynically. 'Some men always are.'

'In any case,' Lisette continued, scarcely hearing what Claudine had said, 'I don't know where he is and if I did I'd never go to him. But I still can't be sure that I am – pregnant.' The enormity of this possibility seemed to have stunned her and her words stumbled from her. 'Within a few days I'm sure I'll know for certain that my nausea was only a bilious attack.'

Claudine looked unconvinced, but patted Lisette's arm reassuringly. 'Let's hope so.'

Next morning the sickness came again. This time she was prepared and flew at once down the stairs to the second floor where she reached the lavatory just in time. It became a pattern that continued until eventually the vomiting began to wane. Her monthly cycle had not resumed and she faced a future even more unpredictable than it had been previously. Only Claudine knew about it and was kindly keeping it to herself.

'Nobody is going to notice any change in you for quite a while yet,' she said one day when she and Lisette were alone in one of the stockrooms. 'But if you want to get rid of your present trouble there's a woman in this town who would do it for you. I got her address from somebody else who works here and had the same problem.'

'No, I could never do that!' Lisette exclaimed almost before Claudine had finished speaking. 'I've decided that I must leave here before my pregnancy is noticed and then Madame Fabignon should give me a good reference. Several times, because of the increase in my sales, I've had a nod and a smile from her whenever she has passed my counter.'

'So what shall you do after you've left the emporium?'

'I'll move on to another town some distance from here and say that my husband is in the navy and at sea. Then there will be nothing against anyone employing me.'

Claudine frowned doubtfully. 'Do you want to be saddled with a baby?'

Lisette's eyes flashed. 'Of course not! Not now or at any other time since I don't intend to marry. But I wasn't raped or seduced and the baby will be the result on my own actions. I have to bear that responsibility.'

'You're a strange girl, Lisette,' Claudine said wonderingly with a shake of her head. 'But good luck to you and don't forget to buy yourself a wedding ring.'

'I'll do that,' Lisette replied quietly.

It was another two weeks before Lisette was able to get to the marketplace on her own. So often one of the other girls would catch her up to walk and chat with her. This time she went straight to one of the jewellery and trinket stalls where she saw what she wanted. The plain rings were not gold and had a brassy gleam, but they were cheap and would pass for a marriage band.

Swiftly she glanced about to make sure nobody she knew was nearby and then tried on a few rings in quick succession until she found one that fitted her. The vendor put it into its own little box and handed it to her without a flicker of interest. Obviously she was far from the first single woman to have made the same purchase from him for a similar need. In her own mind she thought such deception was a sad business, but she had to keep her head and do whatever seemed best for herself and her child.

Eight

For the next few weeks Lisette's pregnancy continued to go undetected. Madame Fabignon granted her a slight increase in her wages when her sales of shawls and capes continued to rise. Yet her savings were still piteously small and she found it hard to find further ways in which to economize.

She wished she did not have to leave the emporium soon, for she was enjoying the work, had a good friend in Claudine and liked most of the other employees with whom she came into contact. Since she never spent a sou without consideration she was grateful for the newspapers that Pierre passed on to her after he had studied the racing news. When she had glanced at the headlines she always turned to the 'Situations Vacant' page.

It was her intention to apply for the position of a housekeeper, having decided that if she made herself indispensable to her employer she might be able to stay on with her baby after the birth. In preparation she wrote some more references for herself as to her bookkeeping and other domestic capabilities, all of which she had been taught at school. She wrote these references on the same good writing paper that had done so well for her with Madame Fabignon and which she would have ready when needed.

When two seemingly suitable housekeeping posts were advertised she applied for both, one with a retired judge, who lived in a nearby town, and the other with the mistress of a château in the same area. She gave both prospective employers the date after which she would be available for interviews. Both her letters were answered, approving her application, although each warned that the situation might not still be vacant when she reapplied. It was what Lisette had expected, and even if these situations were lost to her, the response had shown her that she stood a good chance of getting the work she wanted.

Then, quite unexpectedly, everything went awry a month before the date that Lisette had decided should be the limit of her present employment. It was Madame Fabignon herself who inadvertently caused it. She had decided that since Lisette's natural elegance could sell shawls so well, then how much more she could do for sales in parading the new gowns with the other mannequins in the dressmaking salon.

'But I like selling shawls!' Lisette protested.

'Don't be foolish,' Madame Fabignon retorted. 'Can't you see that I'm promoting you to a higher position? There will also be commission on all that you sell.'

Knowing Madame Fabignon's parsimonious ways Lisette did not expect the commission to amount to very much, but even a little more money would be a help to her before she left. She had not yet begun to make anything for her baby's layette and as her pregnancy advanced she would soon need some new clothes when those she possessed no longer fitted her. So far the corset she wore had kept her secret very well.

'Very well, madame,' she said. 'When should I start?'

'Today. Celestine can be your replacement on the shawls and capes.'

Lisette went up the wide curving staircase to the salon, which was conducted like a haute couture salon in Paris. There a *vendeuse*, named Mademoiselle Boileau, sat at a Louis VI desk from which she would rise to greet the emporium's richer customers who were able to afford the garments in her domain. She was writing at the desk, but looked up as Lisette approached.

'You are the new mannequin?' she stated sharply. 'I was told to expect you. Go through that far door. One of the dressmakers will measure you.'

In the dressmakers' room Lisette knew an anxious moment when a tape was whipped around her waist, the result checked, and then she was measured a second time.

The dressmaker frowned, looping the tape measure back over her neck. 'You'll have to lace yourself in a bit tighter, but otherwise you have a good figure, a straight back and a chic air about you. There's a parade of gowns for a client later this afternoon, so I'll get one of the other mannequins to show you how to walk and what to do.'

Lisette lasted only a week in the salon. During that time she received commission on three gowns and a coat, but the dressmaker had become increasingly suspicious about the new mannequin's waistline and mentioned her concern to the *vendeuse*.

'Thank you for bringing the matter to my attention,' Mademoiselle Boileau replied, her gaze becoming fierce. 'But not a word to anybody else.'

She chose her moment carefully, throwing open a door on Lisette when she was virtually naked while changing after the day's work had ended. At the giveaway sight of her figure in loosened corset laces the *vendeuse* threw up her hands in outrage.

'You sinful, deceitful creature! You're with child! Finish dressing and then go at once to Madame Fabignon. I'm going downstairs this second to inform her that you are not fit to be with decent people in this salon!'

Lisette sighed as the woman left and continued dressing. Her chance of a good reference from Madame Fabignon was lost and it would have been very useful to have had it in hand.

When she faced Madame Fabignon in the office it was what she had expected. Instant dismissal for immorality as a single woman bearing a child. What was owed to her was thrown down on to the desk, some of the coins bouncing to the floor for her to gather up. To add to her humiliation Lisette was prevented from saying goodbye to anyone. Madame Fabignon marched her out of the office and through the emporium where all the sales assistants, even those serving customers at their counters, turned their heads to watch as the two of them went by. It was obvious to them all from Madame Fabignon's furious expression that Lisette was in great trouble.

Only Claudine guessed the true reason, having known that it could only be a matter of time before her friend's condition was discovered. Dismayed, she gave a sympathetic little wave of farewell, which was returned with a grateful smile

from Lisette as she followed their employer through the
double doors into the house of accommodation. There she
was denounced to Mademoiselle Valverde.

'This immoral creature is in the family way! Make sure
she has her belongings packed and is off these premises
within twenty minutes!' Turning on her heel, Madame
Fabignon stalked back into the emporium.

Mademoiselle Valverde glared at Lisette. 'Get going!' she
snapped. 'We don't want your kind under this roof a moment
longer than necessary!'

To Lisette's annoyance the woman followed her upstairs
and then stood with folded arms to watch her change out of
her black shop attire into one of her own dresses. Without
the whalebone corset, which she set aside, Lisette found that
her dress was extremely tight and she had difficulty in
fastening some buttons. A side glance in the cheval mirror
showed her that now indeed she did look pregnant, but it
was high time the baby gained room to grow.

Although throughout her packing Lisette kept a dignified
silence, her cheeks flushed with anger as Mademoiselle
Valverde took spiteful pleasure in checking everything she
packed as if she were a possible thief as well as an unmar-
ried mother-to-be. Then, taking up a valise in each hand,
Lisette set off downstairs again. The thump of the woman's
footsteps followed her.

'Never dare to come near this emporium again!'
Mademoiselle Valverde spat out as Lisette descended the
outdoor steps into the street. The door was slammed after
her.

Lisette did not linger, but took stock of her position as
she walked away without a backward glance. It was a sunny,
early September afternoon, the sky a clear blue, which in
itself was an inducement to optimism and in any case she
was not in the least despondent. The time had come to leave
this town and start afresh. In her purse she had the two replies
to her application for the position of housekeeper.

Now she would just turn up at these two addresses and
hope for the best. If neither position was still available she
could always look for some other domestic work in that area.
She was not too proud to sweep and dust and scrub floors

if it would ensure a roof over her head until she found something better suited to her abilities.

At the railway station she boarded a train where she sat down on one of the wooden seats. In the past she had only travelled in first class comfort, but those days had gone for the time being. Being alone in the carriage, she opened her purse and took out the false wedding ring. When she had put it on she spread her fingers wide and regarded it without expression. Now to the world she was the wife of a seaman.

After replacing her glove she fingered the ring for a moment or two through the soft leather before sitting back and letting her thoughts drift. Not for the first time she remembered Monsieur Lumière's advice to look on change as an adventure. It was strange how his wise words had stayed with her throughout the years.

As the train began to move her thoughts continued to wander in a curiously contented way. Eventually the time would come when her grandmother's house in Lyon was legally hers. She would find it full of memories and what a pleasure it would be to see the Lumière family again! Then an unhappy thought struck her. But it could not be the same, for she would be a social outcast with an illegitimate baby. No respectable home would receive her. Neither should she expect it to be otherwise.

Her thoughts turned to Daniel. He had been immensely kind to her throughout the time she had been with him. It could be said he had been too kind in that eventually he had comforted her with such ardour that she carried a child within her who would always remind her of him.

Until now she had not thought much about the baby, except as a terrible complication to her life. She had had no privacy in which to start preparing a layette, except for a few small garments she had purchased one day in the market and hidden away in a drawer. Mademoiselle Valverde had given a contemptuous snort when she had glimpsed them being packed. For the first time she began to wonder with real interest whether she would give birth to a boy or a girl. Thinking back to that passionate interlude in which Daniel had brought her soaring to such ecstasy she could only think that most surely she would have a son from those handsome and powerful loins.

Unexpectedly she caught her breath at the memory. Although she was no longer alone in the carriage the man reading a newspaper in the corner seat had not noticed and neither had the woman opposite her, who was fussing with a fractious child.

Other passengers came and went at various halts throughout the journey. Then she was at her destination and alighted on to the platform. She had decided to go first to the old gentleman's address since the other was out of town. A porter took her baggage and led her to a waiting horse-drawn omnibus where the conductor confirmed that it went past the head of the street that she wanted. She stepped aboard. It would soon be getting dusk and she hoped her destination was not far away, because if she failed to get the position it would mean starting to look for somewhere to stay.

After about ten minutes of the omnibus picking up and putting down passengers it came to a halt again. 'That's the street you asked for, mademoiselle,' the conductor said, pointing the way.

Halfway down the avenue of some very fine houses she came to the address for which she had been searching. Large double gates opened to the driveway of a grand mansion where lamplight glowed from several windows. She supposed she should go to a servants' entrance, but she could not carry her heavy valises any longer. Taking a deep breath on the steps of the marble portico she rang the doorbell.

A serious-looking manservant in his fifties opened the door, his greyish hair so slicked back with Macassar oil that it shone like a billiard ball. 'Mademoiselle?' he inquired politely.

'I'm Madame Decourt,' Lisette replied, 'and I hope I'm the new housekeeper.'

His expression lifted and he snatched up the handles of her luggage to swing it indoors. 'Thank God for that! Come in. I'm Gerard, valet to Judge Oinville and nurse when needs be.'

She entered and looked about her at the spacious hall with its black and while tiled floor and a great crystal chandelier suspended from the ceiling. 'I'm not expected,' she warned.

'On the contrary,' he replied, having closed the door after her. 'You were supposed to be here three days ago, but never mind about that. You're here now.'

Immediately Lisette realized with an acute sense of disappointment that another housekeeper had already been appointed. 'Then there's some mistake. You're expecting someone else. I haven't even been interviewed yet.'

He sighed in exasperation and snapped questions at her as he ticked them off on his fingers. 'Are you honest? Have you good references? Do you cook? Can you supervise? Is your bookkeeping accurate? Would you have plenty of patience with a cantankerous old man?' Then after Lisette had answered all his questions in the affirmative, he gave a nod. 'As far as I'm concerned you're the new housekeeper even if you are in the family way. What's your name?'

She told him, but continued to protest. 'You have no authority to appoint me. I must see the lady of the house!'

'There isn't one, except Judge Oinville's bitch of a daughter-in-law, who comes in once or twice a week to find fault and fling her orders about. The judge can't abide her, because he knows she wants him gone in order to get hold of his money and this house and all its contents. I pity her husband, because he must have a hell of a life. Now I'll present you to the judge.'

He turned on his heel to lead the way, but Lisette caught at his sleeve. 'You really must understand that if another housekeeper is expected I can't possibly take over!'

'Don't worry about it. It's highly unlikely she'll show up now. The departing housekeeper had recommended her, but perhaps also told her enough about your new employer to make her think twice about coming here and she has decided to stay away for ever. You probably won't stay either, but at least give it a try.'

With trepidation Lisette followed him along a corridor and through a finely furnished salon where open glass doors led into a garden room. There she paused for Gerard to announce her.

'Permit me to present the new housekeeper, monseigneur. Madame Lisette Decourt.'

Gerard stood aside for her to enter and then left. The

garden room was large, but the warmth of the day had been captured and held. Oil lamps on elegant stands had been lit among the potted palms against the fading glow of the setting sun, which cast sparkles into a decanter and glasses on a silver tray placed on a side table. She had been expecting to see an ancient invalid from Gerard's mention of being both valet and nurse, but a distinguished looking, white-bearded old gentleman, his hand resting on a gold-topped cane, sat comfortably in a cushioned wicker chair, a very lively look about him. He beckoned her nearer and regarded her keenly with steel-grey eyes. Then he grunted with satisfaction.

'You are most welcome, Madame Decourt. Thank God you're pretty! In fact, you're quite a beauty. I can't abide ugly women and they usually smell.' He looked her up and down. 'If my eyes don't deceive me, you're with child. Am I right?'

'Yes, monseigneur,' she answered firmly. 'Does that make any difference?'

'We'll discuss that in a minute. So you're here to take charge. Sit down opposite me.' He continued to talk as she seated herself. 'I warn you there won't be much to eat until you get someone in the kitchen who knows how to cook. Gerard has been doing his best, but kitchen work is beneath his dignity. My daughter-in-law could have sent her fancy chef to prepare a meal or two for me, but she does not have a generous nature.'

'I don't understand,' Lisette said. 'Are there no servants other than Gerard in the house?'

'They all walked out three days ago. A clean sweep to my mind! No servant ever stays long anyway, so it's of no consequence. The menservants steal my cigars and gulp down my best wines and the silly women cry when I shout at them.'

Lisette caught her breath at his bluntness. 'You'll not shout at me, monseigneur!' There was such a resounding threat in her voice that the old man's bushy white brows shot up. 'Neither would I allow pilfering all the time I'm in charge here! Is that understood?'

'I can see you're a woman to rule the roost,' he taunted in reply, enjoying himself. 'Your husband must have a lot to put up with. Has he deserted you? Is that why you're here?'

'No. He's at sea.'

'At sea, is he?' The old man's quizzical smile puzzled her. 'When do you expect him home on shore leave?'

'Not for a long time. He has only just sailed.'

'And when is your baby due?'

'Next April.'

'Then he's unlikely to be back when you give birth. Tell me, does he even exist?'

Lisette turned ashen, all her pretence falling away, and she sat back in her chair, gripping the arms. 'How did you know?' she asked in total dismay.

'I didn't, but during my years in court I have had many a female in the dock, accused of some petty crime, who has made the well-worn pretence of being the wife or widow of a seaman to retain some shred of respectability.'

Lisette sprang her feet. 'I'll leave at once,' she said shakily. 'I apologize for trying to deceive you.'

'Wait!' the judge shouted, for she was already on her way. 'Have I said I wanted you to go? I'm a judge of the law, not of morals, and there's always two sides to everything. I've never believed that the woman should always be subject to censure and the man escape scot-free.' Impatiently he thumped his stick. 'For God's sake, come back and sit down again, young woman!'

Slowly she resumed her seat, uncertain what was to come. 'Am I to stay then?'

'Why not? You haven't come to scrub floors or carry heavy loads that might harm your condition. You're here to give orders and manage my house efficiently. If you fail in that task I'll tell you to go, but otherwise you'll stay and be well paid for it. Then when the baby comes – providing you keep its bawling out of my hearing – you shall remain as my housekeeper for as long as it suits us both.'

She felt overwhelmed by his magnanimity and wanted to be completely honest with him. 'There's something else I have to tell you. Although I applied for this housekeeper's position I'm not the one who was expected three days ago.'

He shook his head dismissively. 'Who wants to employ someone who cannot even arrive on time? I don't! So what does that matter now? I know a strong character when I see

one and you're not going to pawn my silver or drink yourself senseless as some have done before you.' He shifted in
his chair and waved a hand towards the decanter. 'Pour me
a stiff cognac and then see if you can find enough food in
the kitchen to make me a hot dinner. I'm tired of Gerard's
cold collations.'

Lisette left the garden room almost in a daze that such
good luck should have befallen her and found her way to
the kitchen where Gerard was waiting for her. 'Did all go
well?' he asked.

'Yes, I'm here to stay.'

'I thought you would be. I've put your luggage in the
housekeeper's apartment. 'It's just along the passage.' He led
the way, speaking to her over his shoulder. 'How did you
get on with the judge?'

'I stood my ground when the need arose.'

'That's the way to deal with him. He is used to browbeating
everyone as he did in his days in court and if everything
doesn't go as he likes it he roars with temper like an old bull.'
He opened a door. 'Here are your rooms.'

The apartment consisted of a pleasantly furnished salon
with a desk for her paperwork, a small dining alcove and a
bedroom with an adjoining bathroom.

'Everything is very clean and tidy,' she commented, 'seeing
that the previous occupant left so abruptly.'

'The daily woman who washes and polishes floors wasn't
here when the great bust-up took place and so she was not
affected by it. So she put things to rights in here. Old
Madeleine is an honest old soul and she's been coming here
for years. I'll leave you now. You'll find me in the kitchen.'

'The judge has asked me to cook dinner for him this
evening.'

'Good! I shopped for a few items today. Make sure you
cook enough for us too.'

'I intend to do that.'

When she went to the kitchen Gerard showed her where
to find an apron.

'Why did you say earlier that you were both valet and
nurse sometimes?' she asked, tying the apron strings at her
back in a bow.

Gerard perched on a stool in readiness to watch her at work. 'The judge has an unsteady heart. He has suffered a couple of minor strokes and gets spells when he doesn't feel well. Even though his son calls in the best of doctors and nurses at these times I'm the one he always wants in attendance. I've been with him for a long time and he trusts me.'

She began glancing about. 'What do we have in stock and where shall I find everything?'

'The departing servants looted most of the foodstuffs from the store cupboards when they left.'

'They must have been an extremely dishonest bunch! Did you know what was going on?'

'Not for a while until I noticed that a couple of small antiques were missing from the judge's dressing room and a Sèvres clock was not in its usual place. When I made inquiries none of these items could be found. I also began to suspect that somebody had made a duplicate of my key to the cellar.'

'What did you do?'

'I alerted the old man and he surprised them all by suddenly appearing in the kitchen quarters to check his fine old wines in the cellar. When he found what was missing he exploded with wrath, shouting and hitting out with his cane, and that's when he swept out all the staff, guilty and innocent alike. I was afraid he would have a seizure afterwards, but I gave him the powder on his tongue that the doctor left for any emergency. Then I managed to persuade him to rest. Thankfully he suffered no serious ill effects.'

'That must have been a relief to you.'

'It was indeed. But I have noticed that he is sitting about more during the day than normal and he is going to bed earlier. I believe he hasn't fully recovered from the upset of it all.'

'I'm not surprised.' Lisette shook her head sympathetically. 'Now, let me see what you have bought today.'

There was fresh fruit, a salad selection, mushrooms, some tired looking vegetables and a rather scrawny chicken, which she would not have chosen, but she had to make the best of what was there.

'Get a bottle of champagne from the cellar,' she said, beginning to cut up the chicken. 'I'm going to make a dish with this bird that my father liked so much *Poulet au champagne et aux champignons.*'

While the chicken cooked she prepared the vegetables and made a tasty soup, dressed up the salad and soon had ready a dessert of fresh fruits. While Gerard had been in sole charge he had served the judge's meals on a tray, but Lisette insisted that a place be laid in the dining room. At the right moment Gerard announced to the judge that dinner was served and then proceeded to wait on him.

The judge enjoyed the meal and ate heartily before sending his compliments to Lisette. After she and Gerard had eaten they shared the clearing and the washing-up. Then, when Gerard was about to help the judge upstairs to bed, Lisette went out into the hall to bid the old man goodnight, a custom she was to adopt on a regular basis.

'You did well, madame,' the judge replied courteously. 'Make sure you hire a chef that can match you.'

Later, when she had finished unpacking, Gerard took her on a tour of the house in order for her to become familiar with it before she hired staff the next day. Everything was of the best quality, with elegant antique furniture, fine tapestries, gilded clocks, an abundance of beautiful silver and much delicate Sèvres porcelain. That night she enjoyed the luxury of having a room to herself again and slept well.

Next morning after breakfast and wearing her green silk coat, which would no longer button up comfortably, and her fashionable hat, which had suffered a little from its packing, Lisette set out to visit the domestic agencies that Gerard had listed for her. At each one she arranged for suitable candidates to be interviewed that afternoon and also the following morning. By the time she returned Gerard had shopped for everything from the list she had given him and placed her orders for other foodstuffs that would be delivered.

Removing her hat and coat in her own rooms she thought how fortunate it was that she had come to this mansion. Now at last she could begin to save for her baby and face the future with well-founded optimism. Her thoughts went to Daniel.

'I'm going to be all right, Daniel,' she said softly. 'All is well.'

During the afternoon and the following morning Lisette appointed a full staff and so it was a footman who opened the door to the Judge Oinville's only son, Alain, a prosperous architect.

'You're new,' he commented to the footman, handing over his hat and gloves.

Lisette, coming from the judge's presence, had been told by Gerard that Alain Oinville often called in at this time and she went across the hall to him. 'Yes, monsieur. We are all new on the staff now.' Then she introduced herself.

He was tall and stern looking, dark-eyed and with a straight stance, but he had a smile of considerable charm and Lisette received the full benefit of it. She gained the impression that he was quite a womanizer as she had come to believe the judge had been until his health had begun to fail.

'So you're the new housekeeper,' Alain said dryly, his gaze sweeping over her. 'Prepare for a visit from my wife tomorrow when she hears of the changes here. Is my father in the salon?'

'Yes. Did you wish to dine with him?' she asked, thinking that a second place could be laid.

'Not this evening, madame.' He went striding off to the salon and before he closed the door completely she heard him say, 'You've gained the best-looking housekeeper I've ever seen.'

He stayed about half an hour, but she did not see him go.

Lisette was with the judge next morning when his daughter-in-law arrived. He had told her to sit down with him in the library and tell him something about herself. She had spoken about living in Lyon and was telling him about Joanna and their schooldays with no mention of the grandeur of her background when Stephanie Oinville swept into the room. Exquisitely clothed, slender and beautiful in her mid-thirties, she descended on the judge to kiss him effusively on both cheeks.

'How are you, *Beau-père*? I think you look well. I've come to see that everything is all right here.'

He did not look at all pleased to see her. 'Of course it is,' he answered irritably. 'Why shouldn't it be?' He indicated Lisette, who had risen from her chair at Stephanie's entry and drawn back. 'This is my new housekeeper, Madame Decourt. She was just telling me about how she owes her cooking skills to her schooldays.'

Stephanie flashed her a piercing, assessing glance from under the brim of her large hat. 'Indeed? Yes, we all know that girls at charity schools are trained for domestic service.' She moved gracefully into the chair that Lisette had vacated, dismissing her with a sweep of her hand. 'I do not require any refreshment.'

Lisette would have left the room, but the judge, with a glower at his daughter-in-law, called after her. 'Wait a minute, Lisette. I'd like a glass of wine.'

Lisette smiled to herself. The judge had seen how his daughter-in-law had snubbed her and had not liked it. Until this moment he had not called her by her Christian name and probably would not again unless Stephanie was present. Leaving the room, she sent a footman into the library with the wine and went to the desk in her study where she did some bookkeeping. She was not surprised when Stephanie sent for her before leaving.

Stephanie was waiting in the crimson salon and she turned from the window as Lisette entered.

'I just want to have a few words with you for your own good, Madame Decourt,' the woman said, taking a few steps forward. 'You're young and attractive and – as you have probably discovered already – your employer is susceptible to a pretty face and figure, although in your case – as I can see – the latter attribute does not apply at the present time. He is a generous man, often foolishly so, and I just want you to understand that under no circumstances are you to play up to him with flattery and other nonsense for gain. It will not be tolerated.'

Lisette was consumed by anger and her voice shook with it. 'You insult me, madame! I'm here to work and to run this house in a smooth and orderly fashion. Nothing more! But I shall never refuse to sit and talk to Judge Oinville whenever he asks me, because I know that often elderly people are lonely, even when they live with every comfort and have a family that cares about them. Put your fears away, madame. I am not an adventuress!'

Stephanie narrowed her chill, inflexible eyes. In that second Lisette saw that this woman would seize the first opportunity to get her removed.

'You're very outspoken, Madame Decourt.' Stephanie's voice was creamy. 'But at least now we understand each other. Good day to you.'

After the woman's departure Lisette remained in the salon for a few minutes to let her anger subside. She felt drained and exhausted by the unpleasant exchange, but realized that Stephanie probably thrived on emotional upheavals.

As she turned for the open door Gerard appeared and rested his hand on the knob. 'So you've met the dragon.'

'She seemed to think I would try to get money out of the judge!' Lisette's voice rang with renewed outrage.

'I told you that the only reason she comes here is to make trouble. She can't forgive him for not letting her have his late wife's diamonds, which he gave to a niece, and there's a sable cloak upstairs that was never worn, because Madame Oinville was taken ill before she could wear it. So Madame Stephanie has her heart set on that too and has been seen trying it on, but the old man won't let her have it. She's afraid that because you're young and pretty he'll be too generous with you.'

'But her husband is a successful architect and can surely give her anything she wants.'

'But she wants so much! There's no satisfying her. So he's landed with an extravagant wife and also a loving but demanding mistress with two children that are his, which means he has their education to pay for and all else too.'

She was astonished. 'But the judge told me that he has no grandchildren!'

'He does not know that they exist! It's a great disappointment to him that Madame Stephanie has never wanted children, and it's another bone of contention between them.'

'Yet he has two grandchildren fathered by his son that he doesn't know about! Since you have been his faithful servant for such a long time couldn't you let him know about them in a tactful way?'

'Oh, no!' Gerard shook his head fiercely. 'Surely you can imagine the trouble that would ensue! The old man wouldn't object to his son having a mistress, because he has had some of his own in the past, but he would be wild with rage that he had been kept in the dark about the children for over seven years. It could estrange him from his son and also Madame Stephanie would find out about her husband's infidelity, because the judge would want to see the children and have them come here.' He gave his head a shake again. 'So I couldn't take on that responsibility. It could destroy the family and, as I've told you before, the judge's heart is only ticking over.'

Lisette gave a long sigh. 'What a sad state of affairs.'

'I agree, but there's nothing you or I can do about it.'

She nodded, full of pity for the old judge.

Nine

The days settled down into weeks. An ancient cot was brought down from the attic at the judge's suggestion and it was placed in her bedroom in readiness. Lisette had also added gradually to her baby's layette, all the small garments neatly folded into a drawer. She was not feeling well at times in her pregnancy, often tired almost to exhaustion, and although the doctor was reassuring, saying only that she needed rest, which was impossible anyway, she hoped desperately that all was well with her child.

Apart from that worry, she would have been almost happy if she had not feared Stephanie's hostility, knowing that her dismissal was high on the woman's list of priorities if ever the opportunity presented itself. During Stephanie's visits fault was found with everything, even to the menus of the dishes that Lisette discussed with the chef and supervised whenever the judge held dinner parties for old friends, which she had encouraged him to resume after a lapse before she became housekeeper.

As yet Stephanie was not aware that Lisette would keep her baby after the birth, but assumed that the child would be fostered. Judge Oinville did not enlighten her. He did not consider it to be anything to do with her, thinking she caused enough disruption in his household with her unwanted visits without giving her further cause for argument. He supposed she had heard by now that he sometimes took Lisette to a concert or a play, but had chosen not to mention it, knowing he would not listen to her anyway. Lisette's company was a pleasure to him, for he found no enjoyment in going out alone and without her sharing an evening with him he would not have stirred from his chair. Her beauty pleased his eye and he liked her intelligent conversation and comments, for she kept up with world affairs and they were able to have lively discussions.

One morning Lisette was in town on a shopping trip for herself when she noticed with a casual glance that a large poster had come away from a hoarding, probably through the recent heavy rains, and several old scraps of posters were revealed underneath. Then she halted abruptly, catching her breath. One was for Daniel's magic lantern show, but the dates showed that it was not this year that it had been pasted there.

When she walked on she wondered how he was progressing with his moving picture camera and hoped that all was going well. Whenever there was a mention in the newspaper of some hopeful inventor's latest step in this great competition to be first with animated pictures she cut it out and saved it, hoping that she was also keeping pace with Daniel's advance. The process had been mastered to a degree, but was still far from being the final perfect product. Only the other day she had read somebody was using a fixed plate camera to take pictures of figures in motion and last month a man named Hughes had patented an improved choreuto-scope, which was being regarded with interest in the field, although what it did she had no idea. She knew by general conversation that few people believed that an invention to make pictures move naturally was possible. Most declared themselves to be perfectly satisfied with photographs in a frame or a book or through a hand-held gadget into which views of everything from sporting activities to foreign places were slotted and was then held up to the eyes against the light.

The new year of 1884 brought snow and wind well into March and the bitter weather did not ease until the days of the month ran out. Lisette was eight months pregnant and feeling far from well. Whenever she had a little time to spare she would rest by the fire in her apartment and put her feet with their swelling ankles up on a tapestry footstool. Therefore when Judge Oinville invited her to a gala evening at the theatre she felt reluctant to go, even though she did not want to disappoint him.

'I have the tickets for tonight,' he announced cheerfully,

waving them in his hand as he stood leaning on his cane. 'Gerard managed to get them for us and it's a performance not to be missed. Get ready now and we'll go and enjoy ourselves.'

Her heart sank. 'It's a very cold night.'

'We'll be all right in the carriage with warm rugs. Don't you worry about that.'

As she went from the room he saw her shiver as she hugged her arms briefly and he frowned with concern, thinking to himself that she had been looking tired and pale recently. He supposed that was why she was feeling the cold at this time. Immediately he made a decision and, with his cane thumping the carpet as it supported him, he crossed the room and tugged the bell-pull. A maidservant came almost at once.

'Tell Gerard to go upstairs and fetch that sable coat from my late wife's boudoir. I want Madame Decourt to wear it this evening. She has need of it.'

Lisette was astonished when Gerard brought the coat to her door. 'I can't wear it!'

'Of course you can. Think yourself honoured. The judge wants you to be warm when you're out this evening.'

She wore the coat and was grateful for it. They had the best box in the theatre and for a short while she forgot her worries in enjoyment of the show. Then, as they were leaving the theatre, they came face to face with Stephanie and Alain in the foyer. The woman's face froze with rage at the sight of the sable coat, although Alain, totally unaware that anything was amiss, smiled and talked as the four of them moved out of the theatre. Stephanie did not utter a word.

It was mid morning when she made her appearance, storming into the house and going straight to the salon where her father-in-law sat comfortably in his chair, enjoying a hot drink laced with brandy and reading the newspaper. He was feeling tired after the late night and intended to doze when he had finished the last page. Then Stephanie was in the room, slamming the door shut behind her and advancing on him like a goddess of vengeance, her chiffon scarf floating from her throat.

'How dare you let that servant wear the sable coat!' Her

voice was shrill with temper. 'She was flaunting it as if she were your mistress! No doubt that is what many people believe! I haven't said anything before only because Alain asked me not to do so, but your cavorting with a servant has been a source of acute embarrassment to me!' Briefly her expression was that of anguished martyrdom before it contorted into rage again. 'You don't realize how I've had to make excuse after excuse for you when people have commented on your being seen together, but those who saw her last night will take you for a joke and know you as a disreputable old rake!'

He let the newspaper drop to the floor and rose to his feet with difficulty to face her, gripping his cane. 'You have said enough,' he warned dangerously.

'Enough? I haven't even started! Don't you care anything for the good name of Oinville? Think of Alain! Consider his career! Even a breath of scandal could make clients go elsewhere!' She began pacing about in her fury, her hands agitated. 'I knew there would be trouble as soon as I set eyes on that young housekeeper. Personally I doubt there was any marriage, but I know your penchant for lame ducks and in your senility you can't accept that you're being fooled. I saw at once that she was out for her own ends and that you would be an easy target, lusting as you do from the helplessness of old age!'

'She's young enough to be my great-granddaughter!' he roared, his whole frame shaking. 'I'm eighty-eight and respected in this community by all except my own daughter-in-law! Who in his or her right mind would think such evil other than you? My house hasn't been run better for years and her company has been a comfort to me at times when boredom would have otherwise set in, and I've had too many hours on my own since I lost my good health.'

Thin-lipped and with bright spots of rage colouring her cheeks, Stephanie waved her hands in a crossing movement in front of her face to dismiss all he had said. 'I demand that you get rid of Lisette Decourt at once!' she spat viciously. 'I have every right for Alain's sake to command it. It was bad enough that she came here pregnant and the sooner she has gone the better!'

'She's not going! Neither you nor anyone else shall tell me what to do in my own home! Her baby shall be born here and I intend to do everything I can for the child. It will be like having my own grandchild around, something that you have always denied me.' Then, to deflate her further, he shouted with all the force of his lungs, 'I might even make the infant my heir!'

It was then that she screamed as if she would never stop.

Gerard was the first to reach the salon, followed by a footman with Lisette hurrying after them. She gave a cry when she saw the judge collapsed on the floor and would have rushed to him, but Stephanie, sobbing and with a handkerchief pressed to her mouth, came running from the room, giving her a great thrust out of the way. Lisette staggered back against the open door, but managed to regain her balance by clutching the doorknob.

Gerard, who had flung himself down on his knees by the judge, shouted at the footman, 'Run like hell for the doctor!'

Instantly the man turned on his heel with a swirl of his dark coat-tails. Lisette rushed forward. Gerard had started pulling away the judge's cravat and collar. 'Upstairs, Lisette! There are pills by the judge's bedside! Get them!'

She was clumsy on the stairs these days, but she gathered up her skirts and made the best speed that she could. Never before had she been in the judge's bedroom, but beside the great mahogany bed she could see the bottle and snatched it up.

Yet when she returned to the salon with it she saw it was too late. Gerard knelt dejectedly, holding the judge's hand, and his voice was choked with emotion. 'He's gone, Lisette.'

She covered her face with her hands and wept.

The next few days took on the proportions of a nightmare, all the staff knowing that the prospect of dismissal was hanging over them like a cloud. Gerard, who had formed his own opinion over the judge's death, confided his thoughts to Lisette.

'I believe the bitch hit him in her rage. She may even have jerked away his cane and struck him, because why else was it lying half across the room as if it had been flung away?'

Lisette gasped. 'That's a terrible accusation!'

'Yes, but it seems to me that is why he fell as he did and the shock of it all was too much for him. There was still a flicker of life when I first reached him and he murmured something, but I couldn't catch what he said.' He shrugged unhappily. 'Of course there's no proof, but that is how I'll always believe the judge died.'

Stephanie, wearing black from head to foot and totally recovered from her hysterics, seemed to be everywhere in the house. Oddly, she ignored Lisette completely, addressing all questions to Gerard and calling on him constantly to do her bidding in one way or another, mostly in the listing of certain antiques and other valuable pieces that she wanted for herself. The sable coat had been removed by her on the first day.

Lisette discussed her own plans with Gerard. She intended to set her path for Lyon at last, but not to cover all the distance at first. Anxious for her baby's well-being, she wanted to give birth in the care of a highly recommended midwife, Madame Marquet. She had met the woman, whom she had liked immediately and who had declared herself willing to attend her. Then there had come disappointment when the woman had moved to live near her daughter in Nantes. Yet now that presented no problem.

'I shall take a very small apartment in Nantes and have my baby there,' Lisette confided to Gerard. 'Afterwards I'll travel on to Lyon and make it my home town again.'

'Good luck to you,' Gerard said approvingly.

After the funeral Stephanie actually had a smile on her face. To her great relief there had been no recent changes to the judge's will, which was what she had feared. Alain had inherited all his father's estate, except for certain bequests to some good causes, and Gerard had been well rewarded for his years as a faithful servant.

Lisette, fully prepared for what was to come, had already packed when Stephanie sent for her. The woman was in the library and turned from scanning the bookshelves as Lisette entered.

'I want you out of this house in the next five minutes, Madame Decourt,' Stephanie stated sharply. 'Your wages are up to date.' She indicated a packet of money lying on the library table. 'Don't expect a reference, because in my view there is absolutely nothing to commend you. Now go!'

Lisette picked up the packet. 'Goodbye, madame,' she said with dignity. Then she left the room.

Gerard was waiting in the hall. 'Is it now?' he asked sympathetically.

'Yes,' she said sadly.

'I'll send for a cab.'

Her two valises and a small trunk were loaded on to the vehicle. She had said goodbye to the rest of the staff and it was Gerard who helped her into the cab. He was ready to leave himself, his packed luggage already on the doorstep.

'Take good care of yourself,' he said as he closed the cab door. He did not say to keep in touch, because with the bequest he had received he was going to visit his brother in America and maybe find a valet's position there. He waved to her as the cab carried her away.

An hour later she was in a corner seat on a train to Nantes, her valises on the racks overhead and her trunk safely stowed in the luggage van. Overcome by exhaustion after all the turmoil of recent days, she was unable to keep from dozing and welcomed the relief of it. She awoke once to find a change of passengers. A bearded man in a bowler hat had gone, as had two other men and a woman with a baby. A young couple was now seated opposite her. Neither looked particularly clean, but the girl gave her a smile, which Lisette acknowledged before she dozed again.

The train had arrived at a halt, one of several on the journey, and the carriage was empty when she sat up, tidying back a tendril of her hair. Physically she felt no better for the rest, but fortunately all she had to do when she arrived in Nantes was to take a cab to an overnight address that Madame Marquet's daughter had provided. Tomorrow she had only to find the temporary accommodation that she required where she could settle like a broody hen to await her baby's arrival. She smiled to herself at the comparison and sat back comfortably to stay awake for the rest of the journey. It was then that she saw that the strings of her purse were no longer wound around her gloved wrist.

A quake of shock went through her. It must have slipped

off as she slept and was on the floor! Heedless of her immaculate skirt, she fell to one knee and peered under the seat, but there was no sign of her purse. Heaving herself up again, she looked upwards in panic at the racks and saw her valises were no longer there. A porter had opened the door, but seeing no baggage he had hurried on.

'I've been robbed!' she cried from the open doorway, her suspicions going to the young couple who had been alone with her. Stepping down from the train, she looked searchingly about her for sight of them among the milling passengers, but they were nowhere to be seen. For all she knew they could have left the train two or three halts ago. In desperation she caught hold of the sleeve of a passing porter.

'Yes, madame?'

'I fell asleep and woke up to find I've been robbed!' she exclaimed, her voice shaking. 'My purse! My hand luggage!'

He was not unsympathetic. 'It happens, madame. It's best you report the theft to the police straight away.'

'But my destination is Nantes.'

'You can continue your journey afterwards.'

'I have a trunk in the luggage van.'

'I'll get it. Give me the ticket for it.'

She answered faintly. 'It was in my purse.'

'I'll see if it is still there.' He led her to a seat and then went off to the luggage van. Doors were slamming and last minute passengers were hurrying to get on. Even as the train started to move he was back to her, shaking his head.

She covered her eyes with a trembling hand. She had lost everything! Not only her savings in a thick roll of notes in her purse, but all her possessions, including the baby clothes that she had made or bought over the past months in the judge's employ.

'Madame? Your name, please.'

She looked up to see a moustached gendarme, who looked genuinely concerned for her and she supposed it was because of her obviously advanced pregnancy. In halting tones she told him what had happened and he wrote it all down in his notebook, including her description of the young couple. 'They may be entirely innocent,' she concluded wearily.

'There are a couple of young thieves working the trains,

but they've not been on the Nantes line before. If it is them and we find where they are, there's a chance we can retrieve some of your possessions, although don't expect to get your money back.'

'I've been left totally destitute. Even my train ticket has gone.'

'There's a convent in town where you can go for the time being until you're able to contact your husband or another member of your family. I'll take you there myself on my way back to the police station to make my report.'

The gendarme left her at the door of the convent. Located in the main street, it was a very old, stark-looking building of grey stone with the time-worn figure of a saint in a niche above the entrance. The elderly nun who opened the big door had a kindly, wrinkled face and her expression became one of concern when she saw Lisette's stricken expression.

'Come in, child,' she said at once. 'I'm Sister Delphine. Whatever is the matter?'

Lisette entered the whitewashed hall and suddenly it began whirling about her. She slipped without a sound to the stone floor.

Ten

When Lisette recovered from her faint she was lying on a wooden bench with Sister Delphine wafting smelling salts under her nose. Standing by was another, younger nun, who was holding a glass of water in readiness and regarding her with interest.

'What is your name?' Sister Delphine asked gently, helping her to sit up.

'Lisette Decourt.' She took the glass for a welcome drink. 'Thank you for looking after me.'

'This convent is a refuge for women of all ages in distress.' Sister Delphine's tone was compassionate. 'Now, if you feel well enough, Mother Abbess wishes to see you.'

Lisette nodded and stood up. The younger nun, who said she was Sister Martine, took her along a stone-floored passage to the abbess's study. After tapping on the door and entering to announce Lisette the nun left again.

The abbess was seated at a large desk. She was a severe-looking woman with sharply observant grey eyes and a firm mouth, her complexion almost as white as her starched coif as if she never saw the sun.

'Sit down, Lisette. Why are you here?'

Lisette took the chair indicated and spoke brokenly. 'I was robbed of everything I possess on the train to Nantes. I have only the clothes I am wearing. I reported the crime to a gendarme and when he knew I had nowhere to go he brought me to your door.'

The abbess's concentrated gaze did not leave Lisette's face. 'You're still a long way from Nantes. What was the purpose of your journey?' When she had heard Lisette's explanation she gave a nod. 'So you would like to stay here overnight before getting in touch with your husband?'

'I'm not married and I have no family who would help me.' There was no point in keeping up the myth of a marriage now that she had come here.

The abbess's expression did not change. 'You have friends?'

'Yes, but none I could call upon in my present circumstances.'

'Then how do you see your immediate future?'

Lisette passed the fingertips of her right hand across her forehead. 'I don't know, Mother Abbess,' she said wearily. 'I haven't had time to think.'

The abbess sat back in her chair. 'I can see you're still in a state of shock. It would be pointless to discuss matters now. You may stay here tonight in a room we keep for short stay visitors. Tomorrow morning we can talk again and decide what is to be done.'

After a supper of soup and bread Lisette went to the privy where she was on the point of throwing away her false wedding ring, but remembered in time that she would need it when she left this place again. Instead she put it in her pocket and washed away the green mark that it always made on her finger. Then Sister Martine, who was waiting for her, led her through a great domed dormitory where thirty women of all ages were preparing for bed. Some were pregnant, others gaunt-looking and skeletal-limbed and most seemed too tired even to converse with one another, falling into bed and pulling the covers up to their chins. Stares of intense curiosity followed Lisette all the way to a cell-like room at the far end of the dormitory.

'Bolt your door,' Sister Martine advised quietly before leaving her with a candle, 'or your clothes and the jewellery you are wearing might disappear in the night.'

Lisette followed the nun's advice. Then she unrolled the cotton nightgown that she had been given, which was the same as those she had seen some of the women putting on. It was clean and smelled of carbolic soap as she pulled it over her head. The bedlinen was patched, but just as spotless, and crisply ironed. She supposed laundry work was one of the tasks carried out by the inmates. When she climbed into bed the mattress proved to be as hard as the pillow, but she was thankful for the shelter she had been given.

She blew out the candle and saw the strip of light under the door vanish when the nun on duty extinguished the dormitory lamps. But silence did not follow, for she could hear sobbing, deep sighs and plenty of snoring.

Inevitably she lay awake, contemplating what she should do to struggle out of this terrible and unforeseen crisis. She thought how fortunate it was that she had been wearing the only pieces of jewellery she possessed, including the pearl necklace that her father had given her, or else she would have lost them too. When removing her cape she had found a few francs in its inside pocket and that had been like finding buried treasure in her present financial plight.

Her thoughts moved on to her baby's birth. She would have to trust herself to the care of the nuns. This did not cause her any anxiety, for in this refuge they would have delivered many babies and would be skilful in their task. Even when she had entered the building earlier this evening the presence of nuns had seemed to offer comfort and security. She had already chosen her baby's name. If a boy he should be Charles after her father and, if a girl, Marie-Louise, which had been her mother's name.

In the morning breakfast was eaten at long tables in a chill and raftered room of such height that the log fire in the wide fireplace could not be felt on the far side of it. Lisette helped to clear away afterwards and in the kitchen some of the women were beginning to wash up. She would have taken up a cloth to start drying the crockery, but Sister Martine came looking for her. The abbess was ready to see her again.

'By your speech and manners you obviously come from a good background, Lisette,' the abbess began when Lisette had seated herself. 'By rights you should not be here at all, because I'm certain there must be people somewhere who would step in to save you from your present straits. Have you thought of anybody since we last spoke?'

'No. The situation is exactly as I told you yesterday evening. There's nobody. My parents are both dead and my former home is closed to me. No help would be forthcoming from there and indeed I would never ask for it. I have been severed from the past and at the present time I'm as destitute as any other woman given shelter here.' She paused and then leaned forward in her chair as she spoke again imploringly. 'Please allow me to stay and give birth here in the convent! I've nowhere else to go and, as you can see, my time is very near.'

The abbess frowned. 'If I grant your request it means that you will have to obey all the rules here. You must also subject yourself completely to my authority as regards to your well-being and whatever is considered best for your illegitimate child. Is that what you want?'

'Yes, because I feel safe in your hands,' Lisette replied trustingly.

'This is not a prosperous convent. We have a few rich patrons, who are generous to us, but the drain on our resources is constant. We feed the hungry – any man, woman or child who begs at our door – and there are heavier demands in that we take in old, infirm and homeless women on a perma-nent basis. Younger women and girls, who are able to make a fresh start in life, have to move on as soon as possible after giving birth or whatever other cause made them seek shelter here. We give whatever assistance we can to set them on a new path and it will be the same for you.'

'I shall always be grateful,' Lisette said, thinking to herself that when she came into her inheritance she would give a large donation to this convent in appreciation of all that was being done for her at this time.

'Everyone who stays here,' the abbess continued, 'unless ill, has to take part in the daily routine of washing dishes, working in the laundry, sweeping and dusting and scrubbing floors or – if physically unable to carry out such chores – there is always mending and darning and other such tasks. I'm told you made a start this morning by clearing tables.'

'Yes. I'll continue to do whatever I can.'

'I see you are wearing jewellery, which is not allowed. The temptation to steal is ever present among those who have nothing. You trinkets will be kept in a convent safe and given back to you the day you leave.'

'I had intended to pawn my earrings and buy a few clothes for my baby in case those that were stolen are never recovered.'

'There is no need. We have plenty of very good baby clothes given to us by well-wishers. It is better that you save your jewellery for when you leave here. Selling them would help supplement a charity purse, which is given to every female when she leaves here. So you will not be turned out totally penniless into the world again.' The abbess shook her head slightly. 'Unfortunately there are those who go straight to the first wine shop, but I do not believe that of you.' She folded her elegant, thin-fingered hands on the desk. 'Have you given thought as to what you will do after your child is born?'

'I hope to work as a housekeeper again, which was my last employment. My ultimate aim is to return to Lyon where I grew up. That's where I'll really start my life over again.'

'Ah, the City of Silk. So, after all I have said, do you still wish to place yourself completely into the convent's total care?'

'Yes, I do,' Louise confirmed fervently.

'Have you decided on names for a male or female child?'

'Yes, I have.'

The abbess nodded and reached to open a drawer in her desk and take out a file. From it she took a printed form, which she placed in front of Lisette. 'Read this through very carefully before you sign it.' Then she rang a little bell on her desk and a nun, whom Lisette had not seen before, came from a neighbouring room used as an office. She was to witness Lisette's signature.

Lisette read the form through carefully. It covered all that had been put to her. She was fully aware that from the moment of signing this form she would be completely under the authority of the abbess, but she had no qualms whatever. Taking up the pen that had been placed ready for her, she dipped it in the inkwell and filled in her age and other minor details as well as the alternative names that she had chosen for her baby. There was also a space for the father's name if known and she filled in Daniel's full name. Their child had the right to know his or her full parentage. Then she signed the form.

After the nun from the office had added her signature as witness, the abbess returned the form to the file.

'Now, Lisette,' she said, 'go and find Sister Delphine,

who will give you a change of underwear from our charity store and any other basic needs. She will allot you your domestic chores and also tell you which day you may have a bath. We believe in the old adage that cleanliness is next to godliness.'

Lisette left the abbess's study and was on her way to find Sister Delphine when without warning the floor tipped and she collapsed into a faint again. This time she hit her head on a heavily carved chair. When the dizziness subsided she became aware of an expensive perfume wafting about her. She opened her eyes to find she was still lying on the stone-flagged floor, but kneeling beside her with a supporting arm under her head was a woman wearing a fur-collared coat and a crimson silk toque ornamented by a ruby brooch. Sister Delphine was hovering in the background with a bandage and a blue glass bottle of iodine.

'Are you feeling better?' the woman asked, her voice warm and concerned. 'I'm afraid you've cut your head, but it can be easily bound up.' As Lisette made an attempt to rise the woman gave further support around her waist. 'Take your time. There's no need to hurry.' Slowly and together they rose to their feet and then the woman helped Lisette into the chair that had caused the injury. 'I'll leave you now to Sister Delphine's care.'

With a smile the woman turned away and went in the direction of the abbess's study. Lisette looked after her as Sister Delphine began dabbing at her head with iodine, making it sting.

'Who was that?' she asked.

'Madame Josephine de Vincent, a widow. She has been very generous towards our funds and takes an interest in the welfare of our inmates. Since losing her husband she has come to stay temporarily with an elderly aunt, who has not been well.' Sister Delphine finished bandaging Lisette's head and stood back to admire her handiwork. 'Now I don't want you fainting again. You can sit with the old women and mend some bedlinen. Some of them will like having your company too.'

The old women sat in a semicircle around the fire in the linen room and all looked up when Lisette entered. Two of them made concerned little cries and exclamations over her bandaged head, but she assured them it was only a simple cut. Others were less welcoming.

'We don't want her here,' one grumbled to her neighbour, and there were grunts of agreement.

'That will do,' Sister Delphine chided mildly as she gave Lisette a couple of pillowcases to patch and an individual sewing-basket that held needles, pins and all else she would need.

Lisette had only just started to work when Josephine de Vincent entered the room. It was obvious from the reaction of the old women that she always came to see them on her visits to the convent and some smiled their toothless smiles while the more disagreeable ones paid no attention.

'*Bonjour,* mesdames,' she said, raising her voice since they were all deaf, and she received a little chorus of acknowledgement. Lisette guessed that she was in her early thirties and could appreciate now that she was a good-looking woman with long-lashed dark eyes, fine aristocratic cheekbones, a creamy complexion and a smiling mouth. Her glossy black hair was drawn up in the current fashion and no doubt she had a neat topknot under her silken toque. 'How are you all today?'

She went to each of the old women in turn, asking about their aches and pains and showing a genuine interest when they had something special to tell her. Finally she came to Lisette and regarded her with concern.

'Have you quite recovered from your fall?'

'Yes, thank you.'

'When is your baby due?'

'Within the next ten days.'

'Not much longer to wait. Mother Abbess has been telling me about your misfortune. Let us hope the police recover some of your possessions.'

'I hope they will, but I'm not counting on it.'

'I should like to visit you here when your baby is born.'

'That is very kind.'

Josephine then bade everybody goodbye and left. As Lisette resumed her sewing she was pleased with the prospect of having a visitor. Then, unbidden, came the thought of how much better it would be if it were Daniel coming to see his child. Then she shook away the sudden image of him and concentrated on her sewing.

She worked three days in the sewing room. Most of the old women liked to talk and their conversation was well laced with coarse expressions and swear words that came naturally to them. Often they repeated themselves, telling the same stories over and over again as if they had never told them before. Yet as she heard them talk about the hard lives they had had with the loss of loved ones, the betrayals, the poverty, the hunger, the begging on the street and how they had had to sell themselves, she was filled with pity. It made her realize more than ever what a safe and protected life she had led until the day she had run away. Yet even now she did not regret making that escape.

It was not Sister Delphine who moved Lisette out of the sewing room, but another nun, Sister Lucienne. She was a gaunt, sour-faced woman with a sharp tongue and no patience.

'You're too young to be sitting with sewing,' she said crisply. 'It will do you good to be more active. Exercise is needed to bring a baby on time. You can start by scrubbing the passage floors.'

Lisette went to find a bucket and scrubbing brush. One of the middle-aged inmates told her where they were kept.

'You shouldn't be on your hands and knees just now,' the woman said. 'You're big as a house and your belly will get in the way. Who set you on to floors?'

'Sister Lucienne.'

The woman snorted. 'That explains it! She is a hard taskmaster and don't like nobody sitting about. She would have the old women off their haunches if it were possible.'

Scrubbing the passage floors daily was a hard task. Lisette's back ached painfully and her knuckles grew raw. Sister Delphine saw her at her work, but did not intervene. Lisette guessed it was for the sake of keeping the peace, because she had heard from others that Sister Lucienne had a terrible temper and could reduce some of the nuns to tears.

Lisette's pains began early one April afternoon just after she had emptied a bucket of dirty water into a courtyard drain. She gave a gasp at the sharpness of the contraction, dropping the bucket with a clatter and reaching out to clutch at the door jamb. For several moments she could not move. Then she staggered back into the kitchen. Two nuns were baking bread and, seeing Lisette bent double and ashen-faced, they rushed with floury hands to assist her.

What followed was only pain. Sometimes Lisette heard someone screaming and realized it was herself. There was no respite. Outside the window of the birthing room the sky grew dark and then light again by day before the stars came once more. Finally at the following dawn Lisette gave birth to a daughter. She glimpsed her lovely baby as she was lifted from the bloodstained sheets, giving the la-la-la cry of the newborn, her hair as dark as Daniel's.

'Marie-Louise!' she whispered joyfully. Then she slipped away into unconsciousness while the nuns worked franti-cally. She was haemorrhaging and they feared for her life, but gradually they succeeded in stopping the flow and hope returned. They smiled at each other in relief across the bed.

'She'll be all right now,' Sister Delphine said thankfully. 'Praise be to God.'

But Sister Delphine had misjudged the situation. Lisette, already weak and exhausted, developed a high fever and was soon delirious. Again the nuns feared they would lose her, one of them always at her bedside, but somehow she kept the will to live. Finally, against all odds, there came a morning when she recognized her surroundings and saw the sunbeams coming through a high window. Sister Martine, who sat reading, sprang up from her chair.

'You're going to be well again, Lisette!' she exclaimed joyfully. 'How glad everybody will be!'

'My baby!' Lisette appealed eagerly, struggling to rise from her pillows.

'Be calm now. You've been very ill and we almost lost you twice.'

Lisette was looking about her. 'Where is she?' she pleaded frantically.

'Not in this sickroom. We had to get you well.'

'Please fetch her! My darling Marie-Louise! I want to hold her in my arms!' Lisette fell back weakly against the pillows. 'I know she's beautiful, because I saw her.'

'You saw her?' Momentarily Sister Martine looked dismayed, but recovered her smile almost immediately. 'I'll be back in a minute.'

With a swish of her black robe she went from the room at a run. Lisette lay eagerly watching the door. She had felt her heart fill with love in that short, sweet glimpse of her baby. Her arms ached to hold her. All the pain and torment was forgotten as if it had never been.

The door was opening. Lisette gave a joyful cry, but it was Mother Abbess, solemn-faced, who entered and she was empty-handed. Terror gripped Lisette.

'What's happened? Where's my baby? Is she ill? Don't tell me she didn't—' she could not voice the words.

'Your baby is healthy and strong and is in good care. She has been baptized with the name of Marie-Louise, which was your wish. Someone was very careless in letting you catch sight of the child and that will be investigated, although I suppose concern for your life was uppermost in every-body's mind. Naturally it is much harder for a mother to part with a child whom she has seen and normally that never takes place.'

Lisette had been listening with growing horror. 'What are you saying to me? Why shouldn't I have seen her? She's my child! What is this talk of parting? I want my baby now!'

'The morning after you came here you agreed that at this convent we should do whatever was considered best for you and your child. You put your trust in us completely and signed a form to that effect. So we have done the same for you as we have done for other single young women wanting to start life anew, which can prove impossible with the burden of an illegitimate child. You have been set free of the past as you told me you were once before. Marie-Louise has been adopted.'

'No!' Lisette's anguished scream rang out. 'No, no, no! You must get her back! She's my child! Mine!'

In the entrance hall Sister Delphine had just admitted Josephine. As the echo of Lisette's cry reached them she looked startled and concerned. 'Whatever is happening?'

'Lisette showed signs of a full recovery today, madame. Unfortunately, unbeknown to us, she saw her baby after the birth, which is why she immediately started asking for her. Normally, as you know, we remove the child unseen before any bond can be formed, which makes it easier for the mother. I fear from that cry that Mother Abbess has just told Lisette that her daughter had been adopted.'

'The poor, unfortunate girl.' Josephine looked stricken. 'Didn't she understand that whenever possible the fatherless babies are adopted?'

'Apparently not.'

Josephine continued to be deeply distressed, her hands agitated. 'I wonder if it would help in any way if I talked to her. She will be in great need of comfort.'

'I'm sure Mother Abbess would be glad if you did. Lisette is in the room next to the birthing room. We moved her there when another girl began labour pains.'

'I know the way.'

Halfway up the wide staircase Josephine met the abbess coming down and explained her intention.

'That's very good of you,' the abbess replied. 'At the moment, as you can guess, Lisette is inconsolable, crying for her child to be retrieved and given back to her. I'm most anxious that she shouldn't make herself ill again through her distress. She is in a very weak state.'

'If only I had known—!'

The abbess silenced her with a touch on her hand. 'It is all for the best. You and I know how cruel the world can be to a single woman with a child, making her a social outcast wherever she goes. Lisette, educated and intelligent, will be unhampered when she goes forth from here and will be able to gain respectable employment that would otherwise have been barred to her. So encourage her to view the future optimistically when the opportunity arises.'

'I will, Mother Abbess,' Josephine replied quietly. Yet as she continued up the flight she felt she had made the greatest mistake of her life in not doing what she could to prevent the adoption instead of accepting the abbess's decision to let the baby go to others.

Upstairs she knocked on the door and entered. Lisette had thrown herself across the bed in wild sobbing that seemed to be tearing her apart. Hurrying to her, Josephine sat down on the bed and gathered her close, rocking her like a child. 'Hush, hush,' she said soothingly.

Gradually Lisette realized who was holding her and jerked up her head, tears streaming down her face, and she clutched at the lapels of Josephine's coat. 'I never said I wanted my baby adopted! Never! I agreed that the convent should do its best for my baby, but I never supposed that she would be taken away from me! She's mine and nobody else has any right to her! You have influence! You could get her back for me! For mercy's sake, do this for me!'

Josephine could hardly speak in her own distress and smoothed Lisette's tumbled hair back from her tear-stained face. 'That is not possible, however much I wish it were. Marie-Louise has been legally adopted by a good, kind couple unable to have children of their own.'

'You know who they are?' Lisette was stark-eyed with grief, but hope flickered into her face. 'You could explain! Say it's all a mistake that should never have happened!'

'No, that's not possible. I'm only telling you what I know.' Josephine paused. 'The couple sailed with your daughter to the United States yesterday.'

Lisette crumpled up and did not stir.

After that day Josephine came daily to see her. Lisette, physically weak from the fever and loss of blood as well as grieving for her baby, was slow to recover. Seated in a chair with the old women, a blanket over her knees, she sat staring into space, numbed through by shock and anguish. After a while she became thankful for Josephine's visits and learned there had been sadness in her life too, not only in the loss of a beloved husband but brothers and sisters too. Her aunt was her only living relative and the old lady's weakening state was a cause of great anxiety to her.

In turn Josephine was a compassionate listener, encouraging Lisette to talk openly to her whenever they were out of the earshot of others. It enabled Lisette to talk at last of finding Philippe and Isabelle in the summerhouse and how she had fled the château afterwards. She told how she had worked for a lanternist, had served in a department store and then been employed as a housekeeper by a judge before circumstances had brought her to the convent. Only Daniel as the father of her child remained her secret and Josephine did not pry into his identity.

Most of all Lisette liked talking about the happy years she had had with her grandmother in Lyon and Josephine encouraged her, seeing how it drew her mind away from sad thoughts for a little while.

'I can tell that your heart is there,' Josephine said one day with a smile.

'I suppose it is,' Lisette agreed. 'But as I told you, I have to go on waiting for my inheritance. In the meantime, just as soon as I'm well again, I must find employment.'

'I should like to help you,' Josephine answered. 'An acquaintance of mine in Dieppe needs a governess for her young daughter, and I would recommend you most highly if you are interested. I know you would have a good home there.'

'You're very kind.'

'Would you consider it?'

'Yes, of course. I want to get right away from here and if your friend will have me I'll do my best for her child.'

It was the end of May before Lisette was well enough to leave the convent. Although she was much thinner than before her pregnancy she had regained strength. She felt that in losing possession of her child she had been through one of the worst experiences that fate could inflict and nothing else could ever compare, no matter what happened.

None of her possessions had been recovered by the police, but the nuns had given her a change of underwear and stockings as well as a plain blue dress and a paisley-patterned shawl from the charity wardrobe. She also had two silk gowns that Josephine had given her from her own wardrobe.

'I'm not a letter writer,' Josephine said when she and Lisette said goodbye, 'and so I'll not promise to keep in touch. But I do wish you well in the future and I'm sure happiness awaits you somewhere.'

'Thank you for all you have done for me,' Lisette replied. 'I don't know how I would have endured these past weeks without your support and friendship.'

They embraced and then Josephine left, hurrying away. Lisette, watching her go, thought she would turn and wave, but that did not happen. The woman appeared to be in tears.

When Lisette had said farewell to the nuns and those among the inmates whom she had come to know quite well she was ready to depart. Everything had been arranged for her employment in Dieppe. On the morning of her departure Lisette knocked on the abbess's door.

'Here is your jewellery, Lisette.' The abbess had taken it from the safe in readiness and it lay on her desk.

Lisette picked up the softly gleaming pearls and put them around her neck, fastening the diamond clasp. For a moment she rested the spread of her hand against them, feeling their familiar touch. The earrings, the bracelet and the brooch she put into her drawstring purse, which she had made herself from a remnant given to her during her convalescence.

The abbess took up a leather wallet, unclasped it and opened it up to reveal that it was packed full of notes. 'The couple who adopted your baby left this considerable amount of money to help you on your way.'

Lisette recoiled, looking quickly away and shaking her head. 'No! Did they think my baby had a price? Take it! Put it to the convent funds!'

'That was not their meaning, but I will do as you say.' The abbess put the wallet to one side. Then she pushed forward a small purse. 'As I once told you, nobody leaves this convent empty-handed. This purse contains enough to keep you fed for the next forty-eight hours.' She held up a warning finger. 'Don't let your pride stop you accepting it, because it is given in Our Lady's name.'

'Then I accept it gratefully,' Lisette replied and picked it up.

'However, there is something else for you, which I'm sure you will be glad to accept.' She opened a drawer and took out an envelope, which she held out to Lisette. 'Today you were expecting to receive a train ticket to Dieppe from a new employer, but that lady has engaged someone else.' Then, seeing Lisette's expression turn to dismay she held up a hand in reassurance. 'Do not fear. All is well. Madame de Vincent has amended the situation out of her own pocket. You are still getting a train ticket in that envelope, but it will

take you to Lyon instead of Dieppe. It comes with her best
wishes for the future. She has also included an excellent
character reference and a bank draft that will tide you over
until you gain employment.'

'To Lyon!' Lisette felt dazed by such good fortune. 'How
kind of her! I will take the money as a loan until I can repay
her.'

'That is what she thought you would say.' The abbess
gave a nod. 'Whether you return it or not is immaterial to
her, but she wanted to help you in a practical way at this
particular time. I know from the reports I have had from
my nuns,' she continued, 'that you have never shirked any
task given to you here and so at Madame de Vincent's
request I have added a reference of my own. These two
letters should help you gain good employment in Lyon
without any difficulty.'

Lisette took the envelope and held it close to her. 'Thank
you, Mother Abbess,' she said in a choked voice. 'I shall
write my thanks to Madame de Vincent, but in the meantime please tell her that I have never received a more welcome
gift than this ticket that will take me home.'

'She shall be told.'

As the convent door closed behind her Lisette set off once
more along a street leading to a railway station. Nothing
should stop her homecoming now. Nothing! Where else
could she find the strength to go on with her life without
the child she would always love?

Eleven

When Lisette arrived in Lyon she had expected to feel at home from the first moment, but that did not happen. The area around the railway station had never been familiar to her and a number of new buildings had gone up since she was last there, making her hesitate as to which direction she should take. She asked the way from a street newspaper-seller. Then, following his directions, she started off to walk the distance to the Bellecour district where her grandmother's house was located. Soon streets and landmarks became recognizable and her step quickened optimistically until she came to one of the quays where she paused to take in the vista all around her.

Lyon was a city of rivers and bridges, being divided by the Rhône and the Saône into three parts. It was also rich in history, most of which she had learned from her grandmother, although her school had encouraged an interest too. The rivers had always played an important part in Lyon's great silk industry, used for transport. Flanked by quays, the rivers were linked by many bridges to the old quarter of Vaise and to the hill of Fourvière on the west bank and to the newer districts on the east bank. Cradling the city to the north was the old weavers' district of La Croix Russe where once silks had been specially woven for the Palace of Versailles in the days when Marie Antoinette had been at the glittering heart of it and Lyonnaise silk had been sought after everywhere. Lisette smiled to herself as she remembered the old saying that whereas other cities had birdsong Lyon had the clatter of looms.

She walked briskly along, knowing that every step was taking her nearer her grandmother's house. Boats and barges were busy on the water, which was becoming flecked with gold by the setting sun. Here she stood to take in the clear view of the slope of the Fourvière hill rising above the city and where there seemed to be more houses now than she remembered. The ruins of the Roman amphitheatre would still be there and one day soon she would go up there again and sit on the ancient stones to imagine a play being enacted as she had done in childhood.

Standing on a bridge, she gazed down at the water traffic passing below and remembered with a smile how often her grandmother had held her up to enable her to see better. Going on again, she soon came to the Place de Bellecour, which was surely one of the finest squares in all France, and increased her pace until she arrived at a run at the padlocked gates of her old home. There she swung to a halt, dropping her bag, and gripped the bars as she looked through at the house she remembered so well.

Her eager gaze took in every detail. The house's peach walls had faded to the colour of pale sunrays and its green shutters were closed, but it showed no sign of being neglected. Quite the reverse, for the door's brass knocker gleamed, the bushes in tubs were neatly trimmed and the white marble steps up to the entrance must have been cleaned quite recently. In her eyes her old home looked as if it were dozing while it waited for her return.

Her yearning gaze continued to travel over it. If only she had keys! Suddenly it was the only place on earth in which she wanted to spend the night. She could not and would not stay in some cheap lodgings when her room and her bed awaited her here. If only she could get past these padlocked gates she knew where one of the housemaids had hidden a spare house key in order to keep later hours with her beau than had been allowed. She had discovered the housemaid's secret by chance and had never given her away. It was unlikely that the key's hiding place had ever been discovered.

As the house was on a corner she began to scout down the side of the high wall that enclosed it. She was able to tell by treetops, which were taller than in her day, where the garden ended and the stables and coach house stood, but solid gates and a door in the wall were bolted from within, barring the way into the stable yard.

Disheartened, she returned to look again at the padlocked gates at the front of the house. It would be possible to climb them, but she would have to wait until it was dark and then hope that nobody saw her. But she would do it!

In the next half an hour she made some purchases – a loaf, some cheese, two apples, a bag of coffee, a small lantern and a box of matches. Then she went to a bistro not far away and ate a good supper. It was dark when she left and nobody was about when she returned to the gates. She had put her purchases in the bag containing her clothes, and thrust it through the bars. Then she stood to look both ways. She could see a couple approaching and she drew away into the side street where there was no lamplight. When they had gone past she emerged again, knotted up her skirts and the next minute was nimbly climbing up the gates. She swung one gartered, black-stockinged leg over the top, became caught by her petticoat for a few panic-stricken seconds and then she was on the other side. She dropped down on to the drive and dived for cover under the bushes as somebody came from the side street and went by.

She lay there for several minutes, her heart pounding, but when no hue and cry resulted she sat up. Now to get into the house! She darted along the strip of lawn between the wall and the house to reach the rear entrance, which had a porch. First of all she lit her lantern. Then she reached up to slide her fingers along a ledge through dust and cobwebs until, exactly as she had hoped, she found the key. With a sigh of relief she seized it and thrust it into the lock. It turned easily and the door swung open. She was indoors at once and turned the key after her. Here she was in the little hallway where servants had hung their outdoor clothes, the row of pegs now bare.

Holding her lantern, she went through into the kitchen. Copper pots still gleamed on the shelves, saucepans hung in neat rows and a long, scrubbed, white wooden table stood with benches on either side. A big, black range reminded her how red-cheeked the chef had always been from its heat, which made the kitchen such a cosy place on winter mornings.

Suddenly she became aware that the round clock on the

kitchen wall was ticking. That was odd. Maybe the house was inspected periodically and somebody had chosen to wind it up. Letting her lantern-light lead the way, she began to wander nostalgically through the house, memories flooding back. Dust sheets covered everything, but there was also the haunting aroma of beeswax polish. Running a finger along a ledge she saw it was virtually dust free. There must have been a stipulation in her grandmother's will that the house be kept in perfect condition against the day when she would inherit it.

She went through all the downstairs rooms, each panelled in Lyonnaise silk with designs woven in delicious colours that gave such beauty to each salon, and in which all the clocks were ticking. In one salon the chair was still in its place by the wall where she had sat after the funeral before flying in tears to the garden and being comforted by Monsieur Lumière.

Slowly she went up the graceful curve of the wide staircase to the gallery and the bedrooms. In her grandmother's boudoir she stood quite still as if listening for voices from the past and felt a renewed wave of yearning sweep over her for the presence of the woman who had cherished her and given her such a happy early childhood. It seemed to her that the air still held a hint of the perfume that had been delivered specially from Grasse each year and was her grandmother's favourite scent. She sat down on the rose velvet sofa.

'Oh, Grandmère,' she said softly. 'If only you were here now.'

When she went into her own bedroom it seemed much smaller than she remembered. Some of her toys were still in a cupboard and she smiled to see them again, for it was like greeting old friends. She would have liked to spend the night in her old room, but decided it would be safer to occupy one of the servants' bedrooms in the attic. It would allow more time to hide away if anyone came in the early morning to clean the house, and also she would have a better chance to escape discovery by way of the servants' staircase. She tested the taps in one of the bathrooms and the water ran clear and freely just as the water closet had flushed instantly.

It was further proof that the house was visited frequently as the water was not switched off at the mains.

She found clean sheets, pillowcases and blankets in the cupboard where bedlinen had always been kept between little bags of lavender, and took what she needed up to the attic. After making up a bed she lay down on it and let her thoughts wander, but not towards her child. Her pain was still too raw, too agonizing, and somehow had to be kept at bay if she was to retain her sanity. Instead she must concentrate for the time being on other matters, such as seeking out employment again and finding a suitable abode in which to live for the time being. It was then that she slept so soundly that it was mid morning on the next day before she woke to find herself still fully dressed and the sound of someone moving about in the house.

She sprang from the bed and went to listen at the door. A woman was humming to herself on the floor below and there was the swish of a broom. Then a second woman's voice called up the stairs.

'Have you finished yet, Hortense?'

'Almost, but it will do for today. I've done all the polishing.'

'Then come down. I've poured us both a glass of wine.'

Lisette guessed it came from her grandmother's cellar, but she did not begrudge these cleaning women a little refreshment, for they were taking good care of the house. How often did they come? She listened as the woman named Hortense went all the way down the flight to the ground floor, her broom bumping as she went. A door closed after her as she went into the kitchen.

At once Lisette went silently down to the gallery and waited for their departure. It was another quarter of an hour before they emerged into the hall, chatting together as they came, and she kept back against the wall out of sight.

'Four weeks today, Jeanne?' Hortense said.

'Yes, the same time.'

The entrance door banged after them and was locked.

Lisette flew down the stairs and into a front facing salon where she watched through a gap in the shutters as one of the women repadlocked the gates. Then after another word or two they turned in opposite directions. She leaned back against the wall in relief at not having been discovered, for even though it was her house the fact that she had no right to occupy it yet meant that she would have been considered an intruder. The women could have raised a hue and cry and there was no knowing what Isabelle would have done when it was reported to her as guardian of the property. Yet even with four weeks' leeway before the cleaners returned she would not stay any longer. It was not that she felt the house did not welcome her, for its peace was in every room, but she could not live a hide-and-seek existence.

After fetching down the bread, cheese and apples that she had bought the previous evening she made herself a pot of coffee and sat down to eat her simple breakfast. Then, going into the kitchen hallway, she took a bunch of old keys down from a hook. One of them would open the door in the stable yard to the side street and for the short while she was here she would come and go by that route as the servants and tradesmen had done in the past. Outside in the fresh morning air she followed the path by a high hedge that led to the stable yard, shutting it off from the lawns and flowerbeds.

Reaching the stable yard, she went at once to the street door in the wall, shot back the bolt and after several attempts found the right key, but had difficulty in turning it. A drop of oil was needed before she used the key again. Opening the door, she looked out into the side street. There were no windows from other properties looking directly down on to the door and she should be able to remain unnoticed.

Before going back indoors she went into the coach house and saw that her grandmother's carriage, covered by dust sheets, was still there. Propped against the wall was a lady's bicycle with solid tyres, which her grandmother had ridden in the early craze for cycling that they had enjoyed together. Her own smaller bicycle was nearby. Both were hung with cobwebs, but she did not doubt they were still usable. Moving on into the stables, she stood looking at the empty stalls where once fine carriage horses had been fed and groomed. As a child she had loved feeding them sugar and apples. How she would have enjoyed bringing her daughter to pat the necks of the horses as she had done.

Then such anguish followed her thought that she uttered

a strangled cry, driving her knuckles against her temples. She must not think like that! It was where madness lay. But, against her will, despair overcame her and for some time she stood huddled against the stable wall, unable to stop her helpless sobbing. Eventually she recovered enough, in spite of tears still running down her face, to go in search of an oilcan, and she found one on a shelf in the workshop off the stables. When she had oiled the lock of the door in the wall she went back into the house and heated water for a bath.

She soaked in it until the water turned cold. With it she seemed to freeze inside herself, creating a carapace of isolation that would enable her to go on with her life without the child whom she would love until her last breath.

That same afternoon Lisette left the house unnoticed and went to the post office where she sent the letter she had written that morning to thank Josephine for her generous gift. Her next call was at an employment exchange where she awaited her turn to take a chair in front of a very round woman in spectacles. Her character references were carefully read.

'These are excellent,' the woman said, 'and I see you have had experience in bookkeeping and shop work. I have several vacancies for domestic help, including that of housekeeper. There is a haberdashery shop that requires a saleswoman if that interests you. I also have two vacancies for a book-keeper, one of which is at a furniture company and the other at the Lumière factory.'

Lisette caught her breath. 'I should like to try for the Lumière factory. I remember that photographic plates were made there.'

'That is correct. The factory used to be the site of a hatter's before Monsieur Lumière, the well-known photographer, bought it. These plates were an invention of his two sons, Auguste and Louis – both brilliant men, who have been extremely successful financially ever since they were in their twenties and they're only in their early thirties now. They manage the business for their father and must be making a fortune with every shipment that goes out.' The woman gave a decisive nod. 'You would do well to apply there. Monsieur Lumière may leave most matters to his sons, but he takes a paternal interest in the welfare of his workers, who number over three hundred at the present time. Some while ago he introduced savings schemes and pensions for them all, an example that most employers don't care to follow. I'll give you the address of the factory and also that of the furniture manufacturer.'

Outside the office Lisette set off in the direction of the district of Monplaisir where the Lumière factory was located. She remembered hearing in her childhood how brilliantly clever Auguste and Louis had always been. She was confident that neither of them would recognize her after such a lengthy absence during which she had grown from a child into womanhood. She was less certain about Monsieur Lumière. Her surname might stir his memory if ever he should hear it, but she was not ready yet to let anyone know she was back in Lyon.

When Lisette reached the entrance to the factory she was amazed by the size of it. She could see that many new workshops and extensions had been added to the original site and it was a hive of activity. A man on duty at the gates directed her to the office.

Twenty minutes later her interview was successful and she had been shown the desk in the bookkeepers' office where she would work. She had not seen either of the Lumière brothers, but was to start the following Monday at an acceptable wage.

She also left the factory with the addresses of several places of approved accommodation, which had been given to her after she had explained that her present address was only temporary. On her way to view the property she went into a pawnshop, for she guessed she would have to pay a month's rent in advance wherever she went. She handed over her diamond brooch and received the money and the receipt ticket. She was determined to retrieve it at the first opportunity.

Half an hour later she became the tenant of a tiny, two-roomed apartment at the top of a large building in a good residential area and, as she had anticipated, she had to pay four weeks in advance. Her rooms were startlingly wallpapered in roses, but were comfortably furnished, even though everything had seen better days. Yet its two rooms were all she needed and there was a gas ring as well as a small sink in an alcove behind a curtain. A kettle was supplied and a couple of battered saucepans, which she could replace later with two from Bellecour. On the floor below there was a small bathroom leading off the landing, which she had to share with other tenants.

In the early evening, having cleaned her grandmother's bicycle, she strapped her travelling bag on to the back of it as well as a valise she had found in the house and into which she had packed some bedlinen and towels, cutlery and two cups, saucers and plates. The house was well stocked with everything, but she was careful to remove only items that would not be missed by the cleaning women. Then she locked the house up again. She wobbled about unsteadily on the bicycle at first, but soon got into a steady pace.

She arrived at the entrance door of her new abode just as a well-dressed man, tall and dark-haired, was emerging. She wondered if he was also a tenant and for that reason took note of him. He had a square, good-looking face with a long straight nose, the nostrils strongly curved, and a mouth well shaped with a determined fullness to it. She thought he was about thirty. He smiled at her, raising his brown bowler hat, his eyes a remarkable blue.

'Good evening, mademoiselle,' he said. 'I can see you're moving in.'

She gave him an answering smile. 'Yes, I am. Do you happen to know where I can leave my bicycle? I forgot to ask the landlord.'

'There is a shed at the back of the building. Let me take your bike and I'll show you.' He took the handlebars and wheeled the bicycle ahead of her down a narrow passageway. As she followed him he glanced back over his shoulder at her. 'My name is Michel Ferrand. I have an apartment on the ground floor.'

She knew it to be one of the larger and much more expensive apartments with its own bathroom. 'I'm up in the attic,' she replied and then told him her name. They had reached a small courtyard with a shed.

'Your bicycle will be quite safe here, Mademoiselle Decourt,' he said, propping it up against the shed.

They walked back to the entrance together, he carrying her baggage, which he took right up the five flights to her door. There she thanked him.

'It's been a pleasure to meet you,' he replied. Then he went away down the stairs and she unlocked the door to her new home.

Twelve

Lisette had been three weeks at the factory before she saw the Lumière brothers, although they were there every day. Then at last she caught sight of them in the courtyard together where they seemed to be in amiable discussion about one of the buildings, gesturing towards it in turn. Both Auguste and Louis were dark-haired with handsome moustaches and intelligent good looks, and she remembered them well. They did not notice her as she went by on an errand, taking some ledgers to another office.

Those with whom she worked had given her plenty of information about them, some of which she already knew from the past. From the time the brothers had started school neither had ever stopped studying and working, both having brilliant scientific minds. In school holidays and whenever possible they had assisted their father in his studio and with his experiments in photographic developing, their health sometimes suffering through overwork, but still they would not stop, insatiable for knowledge.

They had married two sisters, Marguerite and Rose, daughters of a local brewer, Alphonse Winckler, who was an old friend of their father. The eldest Lumière daughter, named Jeanne, had been the first to marry, her husband a professor. Strengthening still further the friendship between the Lumière and the Winckler families, two of Monsieur Lumière's remaining daughters, Juliette and France, had married the two Winckler sons, Jules and Charles. There was also a ten-year-old Lumière, named Edouard, and there was family speculation that he might end up marrying the brewer's youngest daughter.

'There has always been such domestic harmony in the Lumière households,' one of Lisette's informants, an older woman named Aude, had told her that, 'Monsieur and Madame Lumière, together with their two sons and their wives, the three sisters and their husbands, all meet socially at the homes of either Auguste or Louis for the pleasure of one another's company. It is said that the Lumière family eat more meals together than they ever do apart! What's more, they all play musical instruments and have impromptu concerts. Monsieur Lumière sings and has a splendid baritone voice.'

Lisette made no comment, privately remembering how she had always enjoyed the Lumière musical evenings whenever she had been included in an invitation with her grandmother. In retrospect she believed her deep love of music stemmed from those evenings at the Lumières'. Now, as in the past, Monsieur and Madame Lumière's hospitality reached out to friends from all walks of life, whether they were intellectuals, politicians and local dignitaries or old friends in humbler circumstances from Antoine's early days. Neither he nor his wife had ever harboured any false pride and had brought up their family in the same way.

Lisette recalled how Monsieur Lumière had often spoken of the days when he had sung in a casino and in cafes to make some money when struggling to establish himself as a photographer. She thought to herself that Daniel was presently following a similar path with another kind of entertainment towards an ultimate aim.

She also remembered that Monsieur Lumière had been quick to admit what everybody in the family knew, which was that he had always liked to spend lavishly as soon as he had money in his pocket, a habit that had followed him all through life. Since coming to the factory she had heard that his sons had twice rescued him from bankruptcy and restored the family wealth, but she was sure nothing had ever dimmed their father's charm and exuberance.

'They are a truly exceptional family in many ways,' she commented.

'Indeed they are!' Aude replied on a sigh. 'I wish my family could be on such good terms with one another, but it's quite the reverse.'

Lisette smiled. She thought how much the Lumières

deserved their good fortune and their happiness through their kindness and consideration towards others, including those in their employ. She would have liked to call on Monsieur and Madame Lumière, but it was highly likely that they knew the scandal that she had caused through running away from her wedding. Although she believed that out of the kindness of their hearts they would still welcome her, she had no wish to cause them any embarrassment. Neither did she want any promotion she might gain at work to seem to be through her acquaintance with the family.

She had been back to the Bellecour house several times and taken items that would be useful to her. In one of the chests she had found some bolts of silk and intended to have some new gowns made as soon as she could afford it. Out of her wages she had retrieved her jewellery from the pawnbroker and was thankful to have it in her possession again.

She was enjoying her work and the weeks were sliding by with surprising speed. As she had a quick mind as well as being mathematically inclined, she never encountered any difficulties that she could not overcome and was pleased and proud when she was put in charge of one of the bookkeeping offices. She had seen Michel Ferrand several times since their first meeting, for he stopped to talk when occasionally they happened to meet outside or in the vestibule. He was a lawyer with his own chambers in the centre of town and, judging by his easy, confident air and his well-tailored clothes, quite apart from his expensive accommodation with a manservant to wait on him, he was clearly doing very well in his choice of career. He also knew the Lumière brothers and, although he had not mentioned it, she wondered if he handled their legal affairs.

She had just arrived home one evening and was removing her hat and coat when there was a knock on her door. Opening it, she saw Michel standing there.

'I hope this isn't an intrusion,' he began, 'but I was wondering if you would care to dine with me this evening? Our conversations are so short whenever we happen to meet that I thought we could talk longer over dinner together.'

She was pleased. 'I should like that very much, but I'll need a little time in which to change.'

'Of course,' he replied, grinning with pleasure that she had accepted. 'I'll wait for you downstairs.' Then, before leaving, he nodded with narrowed eyes at the violent pattern of her wallpaper, which he had seen through the open door. 'How do you live with that crazy rose garden?'

She laughed. 'Not very well, but I intend to redecorate one day.'

He laughed too. 'The sooner the better, I'd say.'

When she closed the door she leaned against it for a few moments, smiling to herself. Ahead lay an enjoyable evening with a fine-looking man in a restaurant with white table-cloths, starched napkins and sparkling wineglasses. It would be a return to all she had been used to in the past.

That made her think of Philippe. As far as her heart was concerned it was as if he had never existed. Daniel had been more than successful in driving her unhappy memories away, but unknowingly he had left the scorching memory of himself in their place.

Hurrying to her wardrobe she took out one of the silk dresses that Josephine had given her. It was a rich blue and suited her well. Recently she had followed up her written thanks to Josephine for the ticket by returning the money she had accepted as a loan, but to her surprise it had been returned to her, stamped 'Addressee unknown'. She had then sent it to the convent to be posted on to Josephine and again it was returned to her, this time in an envelope with a covering note from the abbess's secretary saying that Madame de Vincent had gone abroad and her address was not known.

Lisette thought it strange that Josephine had not kept any contact with the convent, having been such a kind benefactress, but there must be a good reason even though it was impossible to guess what it might be.

She puzzled over the little mystery again as she smoothed the blue silk down over her hips. Although bustles had vanished some time ago there was still the fullness of drapery at the back of a gown, which was far more graceful. As for her waist, Lisette was aware that it was fractionally rounder after childbirth, but a slight tightening of her corset made it a hand span as before. The sleeves of the dress came just below the elbow, but she had treated herself to a pair of long white gloves just two days ago, having foreseen that it would not be long before an invitation from Michel was forthcoming. With her pearls and earrings and a cape about her shoulders she was ready.

As she came down the stairs Michel was waiting in evening clothes and his face revealed his appreciation of her appearance even before he said, 'You look beautiful, Mademoiselle Decourt.'

A cab was waiting and he took her to the best restaurant in Lyon, which was everything she had anticipated. An orchestra played and chandeliers glittered. The food was delicious and the wine superb. Michel was also extremely good company and their talk ranged from serious topics to the humorous when they laughed together.

Back at her door she said how much she had enjoyed the evening.

'I hope,' he said, 'that we shall have many more enjoyable times together. Would you care to go for a motor ride on Sunday afternoon?'

Her eyes widened, for there were more such vehicles to be seen all the time and she had often wished to ride in one. 'Oh, yes! I've never ridden in a motorcar! What make is it?'

'It's a Panhard. I bought it two years ago when it was first produced. I'm watching out for a new model, but unfortunately I can't promise that the ride will be without a hitch.'

'I've heard how these motorcars break down from time to time.'

'I'm afraid it is true.'

'I'd still like to go for that ride!' she exclaimed enthusiastically. 'Where do you house the vehicle?'

'In the next street. I don't use it during the week as I prefer to walk to my chambers.'

'Then that's why I've never seen you driving it.'

'So shall we say two o'clock on Sunday?'

'Yes, indeed. I'll be ready.'

It was a glorious summer afternoon when she went outside to find Michel standing by the two-seater Panhard, which was a fine sight with its shining brass headlamps, outside gears, and a steering device shaped like a tiller. He was

wearing a dustcoat and had another for her, which she put
on over her dress before he helped her up into the padded
seat. She had tied a gauzy scarf over her hat and looped it
under her chin. As soon as he had wound the handle and
rattled the engine into life he took the seat beside her and
gave her a grin.

'Here we go!' he said.

They set off slowly at first and on the way they passed
Monsieur and Madame Lumière's grand mansion and close
by were the very fine homes of Auguste and Louis, for all
were near each other and the factory. In one street a number
of urchins ran alongside the motorcar for a while, shouting
and cheering. In another Michel pointed out his chambers and
she looked at the building with interest as they went by. When
eventually they were out in the country he increased speed
and they went bowling along at what was still a gentle pace.

Lisette was enjoying every minute, even though the vehicle
was noisy and shook her and Michel about. She gazed happily
around at the spreading fields and woodland, sometimes
glancing up at the sun-filtered foliage when they passed
through an avenue of trees. Yet inevitably she began to
remember sitting beside Daniel on the cart. Then there had
been no noise of an engine, but only the clop of Prince's
hooves and, she thought, very little difference in the speed.
It was on a similar summer afternoon over a year and some
weeks ago that he had possessed her by the cornfield with
such unforeseen consequences.

Then Michel broke into her thoughts, telling her about a
novel he had recently read and wanting to know her taste in
books as he had his own library in his apartment. 'You are
welcome to anything on my shelves that you would like to
read.'

She was about to say she would be glad of some reading
matter when the motorcar spluttered and suddenly stopped.

'I was afraid this would happen!' he exclaimed, jumping
out to lift the bonnet of the engine.

She smiled. 'You did warn me.'

She alighted to sit on the grassy wayside bank and watch
him as he fiddled with the engine, frowning in concentra-
tion. With his gathered brows and tightened lips she thought

he looked like a musketeer attacking the engine. The comparison made her smile. There was no denying he was an extremely personable man and she hoped that they could continue to share time together without any romantic notions on his part coming between them.

'Sorry about this,' he said, glancing up from his task. 'As we discussed earlier, it does happen sometimes that the engine dies for no apparent reason.'

'Don't worry. It's pleasant sitting here in this lovely sunshine. Take your time.'

He thought how different she was from his past fiancée, who had become so sharply impatient at any breakdown, constantly asking him in irritated tones how much longer he was going to be putting the engine right. Finally one day in the rain she had thrown a tantrum, which had led to the ending of their engagement and he had never had the slightest regret.

There had been other women in his life since then, but Lisette was the first to seriously interest him. Beautiful and intelligent with a seductive figure, she had attracted him at their first meeting and he believed that he was falling in love with her. Now, as he wiped his greasy hands with a cloth, his task done, he gazed at her with pleasure. The brim of her hat shaded her lovely face from the sun, which was outlining her like an aura where she sat on the grassy bank.

'You've been very patient,' he said.

She gave a little laugh, spreading out her arms. 'Who could be anything else on such a perfect afternoon?'

He put aside the greasy rag and pulled a small picnic basket out from under the seat of the vehicle. From it he took a bottle of champagne and two glasses. 'I thought we should celebrate your first drive in a motorcar.'

'What fun!' she declared. 'I love champagne.'

He sat down on the grass beside her and poured the sparkling wine. 'A toast,' he said, raising his glass to her. 'To the future.'

She felt able to drink that toast, wanting the best for him as well as for herself, but not together. That was something she could not foresee in any way. No man could ever get through the barrier around her heart again.

They sat talking for a while before returning to the car.

He drove on until they came to a crossroads where he took an alternative and winding route back to Lyon. By then it was early evening.

'I've had a wonderful time,' she said appreciatively as he drew up outside their apartment building.

'Let's finish the day by having an early supper together,' he suggested eagerly. 'I know a place in the old district that I think you'll like.'

'It's a long time since I was last there,' she said. 'It will be interesting to see it again.'

As a child she had always been a little wary of that old district of the city on the west bank of the Saône. Most of it was mediaeval with black-timbered houses, the doorways deeply recessed and mysteriously shadowed, the stone thresholds worn down throughout the centuries. Some of the doorknockers were moulded into evil-looking faces or mythical creatures that were frightening to a young child. She had always held tightly to her grandmother's hand and was glad that one of the menservants followed behind them every time.

Most sinister of all in this ancient district were the long narrow alleyways that networked the whole area. She remembered how relieved she had always been when they came out into one of the squares and there was daylight again. The attraction, which had overcome all her fears, had been the puppet theatre in the rue de la Bombarde. She would have braved anything to attend those performances that had delighted her so much.

When Michel had parked the Panhard on the edge of the old district they continued on foot along one of the dark alleyways and she told him about those puppet expeditions, which had so scared and delighted her. He promptly took hold of her hand.

'If you held hands then, we had better do the same now.'

She let her hand remain in his, but without any response. They made their way to the Place de la Trinite where the cafe he wanted was located. As the evening was so warm they ate at a table outside and afterwards sat on with coffee as they talked and watched people go by in the square. Three tumblers appeared in gaudy red and yellow costumes and sprang into a performance. Spectators gathered and afterwards threw coins into their caps, Michel giving generously. When the evening was over he saw her to her door and would have kissed her, but she drew back and he did not persist.

'It's been a wonderful day,' she said sincerely.

'I hope it has been the first of many more to come.'

After that they went out together as often as he felt able to ask her. He would have seen her every evening if the chance had been his, but she was a very private person and he could tell that he needed to tread carefully if their relationship was to develop as he wished. Early on when he had tried to make their meetings more frequent, she had turned down his invitations for one reason or another. It was usually because, having made a few friends at her workplace, she liked to meet them socially and, he believed, used them as a convenient excuse not to see him.

One day at her suggestion they took a picnic up to the heights of Fourvière. Autumn was already setting its brilliant colours into the trees and there would not be many more days warm enough to sit out in the sun. There they explored what was left of the Roman ruins. Then they sat to have their picnic and admire the view of Lyon stretching away below them where the Rhône and the Saône threaded through the old city like silver ribbons.

'This is the best view in the world,' she said contentedly.

He grinned. 'I have to question that statement. It's very fine, I agree, but you are seeing it in a nostalgic light.'

'Yes, of course I am,' she admitted frankly. She had told him a great deal about her childhood, but very little about the turns that her life had taken afterwards.

It was not long after the Fourvière picnic that Michel had to go to Paris to represent a client in a court case. It was a complicated affair and, as he had expected, the case went on for several weeks. Letters came from him quite frequently and Lisette always replied, telling him local news and of the friends she had seen. In spite of herself she missed him more than she wished.

She was in correspondence once more with Joanna, who was living in London and having a busy time. She had been a year at the Sorbonne after last seeing Lisette and had followed it with another year learning more in the Parisian studio of an Impressionist artist, but now she was back in her birthplace of London. She had her own studio in Bloomsbury and had held several exhibitions of her paintings. Her work was selling well, and she taught art twice a week to bring in extra funds. Joanna was overjoyed that Lisette had made contact again, wanting to know everything that had happened since the cancelled wedding and imploring her to visit as soon as possible.

On the evening of Michel's return he came charging up the flights of stairs to hammer on the door of Lisette's apartment with a bouquet of flowers and an elaborately trimmed box of chocolates tucked under his arm.

'I'm back!' he declared exuberantly as she opened the door.

She was genuinely glad to see him and invited him in. 'You're in luck! I've made dinner and there's plenty for two. What beautiful flowers!' she added as she took the bouquet from him. 'I'll put them in water straight away.'

'It's good to see you again, Lisette,' he said as he closed the door after him and put the chocolate box on a side table before he took off his gloves and shouldered off his overcoat.

'Yes, it's been quite a long time.' As she placed the vase of flowers on the side table she saw that the box of chocolates was from a shop she remembered on the Champs Elysées. 'Those will be delicious!' she declared. 'Thank you so much.'

Then he caught hold of both her hands, his gaze on her warm and admiring. 'Say that you've missed me!'

She laughed. 'Of course I missed you!' Smilingly, she slid her hands from his. 'It was early autumn when you left and now winter is here. I can tell by your expression that you won your case.'

'Yes, I did,' he declared with satisfaction. 'It was a difficult one, but I gained the right verdict in the end. How are you? Still busy at the factory?'

'Yes, orders from abroad increase all the time.' She went to stir the bouillabaisse, talking to him over her shoulder. 'Do sit down where I've laid my place. I'll set another opposite in a minute.'

'Let me do it,' he said.

She indicated the cutlery drawer and told him there was a bottle of red wine in the cupboard beneath. 'I'm looking forward to hearing about Paris,' she said as she handed him a wineglass and a napkin for the table. 'It's quite a while since I was there.'

As he opened the wine he wondered exactly when that was, for there was still so much about her that he did not know. She had told him that most of her childhood had been spent locally with her grandmother and that after the old lady's demise she had lived with her father and his second wife near Paris, but he was certain she was holding back more than she had revealed. She had never said exactly where she had worked for her living as a shop assistant and then as a housekeeper before coming to take up a bookkeeping post with the Lumières. In a way her reticence only added to her attraction, for here was a woman able to keep an invisible guard about herself, but through which she continually charmed and fascinated him.

He felt she knew all about him, that he had been born in Tours, studied in Paris, and had come first to a lawyer's in Clermont-Ferrand before eventually taking over the chambers of a retired lawyer in Lyon. He had one sister, who was married and lived abroad, and their parents had moved to be near her and their grandchildren.

With any other woman he would have expected to make love to her at the evening's end, but he was certain that if he made one false move with Lisette he would lose her. In any case he had come to realize during his absence from her in Paris that he had fallen in love with her. He had also made up his mind that she was the woman he wanted as his wife and nothing must endanger that ultimate goal.

Over supper, after relating a few of the interesting highlights in the case he had defended, he told her that he and some lawyer friends had celebrated his success by going to a restaurant that she remembered well. She had a momentary nostalgic image of its lights and laughter and elegance, which she had enjoyed any number of times with Philippe and friends.

'I met Monsieur Lumière in Paris,' Michel continued. 'We

both had invitations one evening to a demonstration by the American, Mr Edison, of his invention, the kinetoscope. It's a box-like structure with pictures in it that give the illusion of movement due to the production of curves through a kind of circular movement. Edison was selling these kinetoscopes at sky-high prices.'

'Did Monsieur Lumière buy one of these kinetoscopes?' she asked with keen interest.

'No! He said that he was certain his sons could produce a much better apparatus with pictures that could be projected instead of being enclosed in a box, and he was coming home to get them started on it.'

'I'm sure they will take notice of what he says, because photography is in their blood as it is in his,' she said with a nod. And, she added to herself, as it was in Daniel's too.

When she had cleared away the dishes they sat on at the table with a last glass of wine, the chocolate box open between them, and he felt encouraged enough to say a little of what he felt.

'In Paris,' he said softly, 'I resented every day I had to spend away from you.'

Immediately she saw which way the conversation was turning and thought to halt it by putting her hand on his wrist that was resting on the table. 'We are good friends, Michel. Let us keep it that way. Nothing more.'

He closed his hand tightly over hers. 'Why, Lisette?' There was no turning back now. 'You surely know that I care for you. Do you think we could be more than friends one day?'

She became so pale that even her lips lost their colour and she would have pulled her hand away, but he kept it clamped in his. 'Marriage is not for me,' she said in a stumbling voice. 'There was somebody once, but he has gone from my life and with him all that might have been.'

'But I'm not that man or anything like him, whoever he was. You came to Lyon in order to make a new start in life, didn't you?' When she nodded, he added, 'I guessed as much. Forget the past. It's over and gone. Let me help you with this new beginning.' He took up her hand and pressed it to his lips in a kiss before lowering it again. 'Say you'll look to the future with me. I can pave the way.'

She thought how nothing could make her forget the past, for that would be as if her daughter had never been. Whatever she might have felt for Michel was blocked by what had happened and there was no changing it.

'Don't ask the impossible,' she implored, for she had no wish to hurt him in any way.

'But surely you want a home and children?' he protested. 'I can't believe that you plan to go on working in a factory all your life.'

'I'll not have to do that,' she replied, deciding at last to tell him about her grandmother's bequest. 'I have a house in the Bellecour district that will become mine when I'm twenty-one together with an inheritance.'

He sat back in surprise, but did not relinquish his hold. 'But surely if you are virtually homeless – and you can't consider this apartment to be a home – some claim for accommodation in the house could be made on your behalf in the meantime.'

'The house would be mine now if I married, but as I've already told you I've no wish to be anybody's wife.' She glanced about her, seizing the chance to keep the conversation to a safer level. 'I'm happy enough in this little place, although I would like to get rid of the wallpaper.'

He gave her a long look, understanding that she was drawing him away from further talk of love, and he decided he had no choice at the present time but to follow her lead.

'I'm going to be busy at work for the next few weeks after being away so long, but I'll help you redecorate next Sunday.' He knew better than to offer to have it done professionally for her, which he would have preferred, but he was sure that he had retained some skill in painting walls from his student days.

'Would you? That's very kind! I'll buy the paint in the colour I want.'

'I'll bring brushes and a bucket. We'll need dust sheets to cover your furniture.'

'I know where I can get some.'

It was time for him to leave. Still holding her hand, he drew her around the table as they both rose from it. Then he took her by the shoulders and looked down into her upturned face.

'Grant me as much of your new beginning as you can spare,' he said quietly. Then before she could draw back he bent his head and kissed her softly on the lips. 'Goodnight, Lisette.'

She held the door and watched him leave before closing it. He was all any woman should want and she had become extremely fond of him, but it was not enough. At least, not yet. His talk of children had struck home more than he could ever realize. Nobody she knew suspected that she endured many moments of intense heartache that were usually sparked by the sight of an infant being pushed in a baby carriage or jogged about happily in a mother's arms.

As the months had gone by she had tried to picture every stage of her daughter's growth. By now little Marie-Louise would be toddling about and taking a lively interest in everything. Did she have a favourite toy? Maybe a soft one from which she would not be parted. Perhaps she held it and sucked her thumb until she went to sleep. Such thoughts were both a torment and a comfort to Lisette and she could not let them go.

On Sunday Michel came early to start the redecoration. She had brought dust sheets from Bellecour, going back to the house when it was dark as she always did when she wanted to get something from there. They stripped off the wallpaper, which was already curling over in parts, and prepared the walls. Together they painted them in the soft blue of her choice. When the two rooms were finished and hung with some small paintings from Bellecour she was delighted with them.

'I'm so high up in this building,' she said, laughing, 'that the sky colour will make me feel as one with the birds that I feed on my windowsill!'

Michel did not attempt to kiss her again, except on the cheek, which enabled her to keep their relationship on a level plane. Even when she invited him to dinner in her apartment now and again he never touched her amorously. As if to re-assure her further he began inviting other couples to join them on social occasions, either his married friends and their wives or sometimes bachelors with fiancées. Often a whole party of them would go to a play or a concert and have supper together afterwards. Sometimes Auguste as well as Louis Lumiére would be there too with their wives, Marguerite and Rose, who were both pretty, friendly women, and she enjoyed being with them. As a result of this social round, she and Michel began to be invited everywhere together. Then came an invitation for them to a grand ball on New Year's Eve to welcome in 1895. This time she wore a gown of cream silk that she had had made from one of the bolts that she had found in her grandmother's chest of drawers.

It was a little time after that when she began to realize how much she had absorbed Michel into her life. With it came awareness that her feelings for him were becoming deeper. It was not that she was in love with him, but her affection for him was increasing with every meeting. As a result she told him much more about herself than she would otherwise have done, although she left out how she had taken refuge at the convent and all that had happened there. She also omitted any mention of Daniel and spoke of him as if their relationship had never been more than that of employer and assistant.

Michel was well aware that there were gaps in her life that she still had not covered for him, but he never questioned her, certain the time would come when eventually she would tell him everything.

Thirteen

Michel could not understand why Lisette would not allow him to make a claim for her on the Bellecour house, but in her own mind she had visions of Isabelle arriving in Lyon to contest it and, although it was highly unlikely, even Philippe making an appearance.

'If you would let me know all the facts,' Michel persisted, 'I could easily take up the case for you. From what you have told me I know that your stepmother stopped your allowance simply because you left home to avoid marrying someone you could no longer trust.' It was all Lisette had revealed about Philippe. 'As I have said, I'm not at all sure that she had the legal right to stem it completely. At least let me look into the matter on your behalf.'

'No,' she said firmly, her tone brooking no argument. 'My life is running smoothly at the present time and I want nothing to disrupt it.'

He had to accept her decision.

It was Michel who gave Lisette the news that the Lumière brothers had gone ahead with their father's encouragement and had invented a camera, yet to be wholly perfected, which would take animated pictures and also project them. It filled her with thoughts of Daniel. She wondered how advanced he was now with his invention? Had the Lumière brothers left him far behind?

Then, one warm, late summer day Auguste came into her office on a tour of the whole factory to make an announcement. He had the attention of all the bookkeepers immediately, but he considered what he had to say important enough to summon the clerks from the adjacent office and they crowded together at the back and sides of the room.

'Ladies and gentlemen,' he began. 'Tomorrow when you

leave the factory at the end of the day's work you will see my brother outside. He will be turning the handle of a wooden box mounted on a tripod. It is a very special camera that takes animated pictures and also projects them on to a screen or wall. He will be taking pictures of you that will capture your every movement.'

There was a buzz of surprise and interest. Lisette listened in dismay. So the Lumière brothers were to be first after all! She did not begrudge them their success, but she had never lost her high hopes for Daniel. Almost unaware of it, she rose to her feet.

'I offer my congratulations, Monsieur Auguste, but I have understood from what I have read and also heard that smooth projection has been the great hurdle that has so far been impossible to overcome. May I ask if you have mastered that problem?'

He gave her a sharp look of interest, not having expected anyone to have any real knowledge of the workings of a motion picture camera. 'You are quite correct, Mademoiselle Decourt. It has been an enormous hurdle for many would-be inventors, including my brother and myself, because the resulting jerkiness has made the photographs virtually impossible to watch without eyestrain. I am happy to say that the Lumière camera has solved that problem.'

'I am delighted to hear that,' she continued, but she was still unable to curb her curiosity. 'There has also been the difficulty of printing the pictures on various sensitized papers,' she continued, 'all of which to date have been quick to tear. Is some new material being used?' Then she flushed with embarrassment and corrected herself. 'No, I should not ask such questions, because you must have surely discovered something unknown to anyone else.' She sat down quickly. 'Please forgive my impertinence.'

'There is nothing to forgive, mademoiselle. Your interest is commendable. This past year has been a time of perfecting our invention and the credit for it goes to my brother, Louis. You were not here at the time, mademoiselle, but some while ago my brother was not well and was confined to his bed. As the rest of you will know, he is never idle and nor was he during that enforced rest. Instead he was turning the

problem of a lack of smooth projection over and over in his
mind until the solution came to him. He greeted me from
the pillow of his sickbed with the news that he had solved
the problem that had previously marred a perfect picture!'

There was a spontaneous burst of applause. Auguste
smiled, nodded to them all and then left the office. Afterwards
Lisette found it difficult to concentrate on her work. She
could not stop wondering what the inspiration was that had
come to Louis on his sickbed. Did it mean that the brothers
had outrun Daniel in the great race for perfection?

The next day to the surprise of the Lumière brothers all
their women employees turned up for work in their best
clothes in readiness for the motion picture camera. The rows
of pegs for their hats resembled brightly coloured flower
garlands with all the elaborate trimmings of ribbons, flowers,
feathers and beaded hatpins. Lisette was the exception,
coming in a neat blouse and skirt and plain hat, which was
her normal working attire. She had more on her mind than
the forthcoming motion picture making, for the previous
evening Michel had asked her to marry him. Yet she was not
oblivious to the air of excitement that prevailed in her office
and had to exert her authority to get the correct amount of
work from her bookkeepers done by the end of the day.

'You have surely realized over past months how much in
love with you I am, my dear Lisette,' Michel had said. They
had been seated on a banquette in a secluded alcove, well
hidden by pillars and palm trees, at one of their favourite
restaurants where they had had supper together after the
theatre. She experienced a moment of panic akin to a sensation of being trapped, knowing how easy it would be to
accept him, but sensibly let it pass before she answered in
a calm voice.

'I do care a very great deal for you, Michel,' she admitted
honestly, 'and I truly regret that I'm not able to commit
myself in any way.'

'Is it because you still love the man you almost married?'

'No!' She threw back her head in astonishment that he
should imagine that Philippe should stand between them. 'I
never think of him.'

'Then marry me, Lisette,' he urged. 'I believe you're more

in love with me than you realize. We could have a wonderful life together. There's so much we have in common – a love of books, music, the theatre, the countryside and much more.'

She was uneasy. 'You know my views on marriage.'

'You formed those ideas during the period in your life when you were hurt and unhappy, but now the time has come for you to have a fresh outlook on the future. Be my wife, Lisette. I'll do everything in my power to make you happy. I want you so much.'

He drew her closer and kissed her lovingly as he had done on previous occasions, but this time more intensely with an ultimate purpose. Against her will her whole body yearned to be loved, to surrender to passion, for Daniel had awakened senses in her that had haunted her ever since, but she drew herself away.

'No, Michel! I can't give you any hope.' In her mind's eye she saw again the baby she had never held and yet who had changed her life irrevocably. She knew Michel well enough to know that if he ever suspected that another man had possessed her, giving her a child, he would be tormented by terrible jealousy. She would never subject him to that torture for his sake as well as her own

He shook his head determinedly. 'I can't believe that you want to remain single till the end of your days!'

In her own mind she had already seen her rejection of his offer of marriage as the end of everything between them. 'I'm very fond of you, Michel, but you must look elsewhere for a wife. There is nothing you could say that would make me change my mind.'

'I can't believe that!'

'Then we must make an end to our relationship. It is not fair on you to hope in vain. This has to be goodbye.' Gathering up her wrap together with her beaded evening purse, she pressed a hand down on his shoulder when he would have risen to his feet with her. 'I'll go now. Stay where you are.' Her voice was tremulous. 'The doorman will summon a cab for me. I'll always remember the happy days we have shared.'

As she turned to leave he caught her wrist and compelled her back into her seat beside him, his expression torn and anxious. 'I love you! Nothing can change that! I want you and will always want you. Sooner or later you will agree to be my wife! I'm sure of it!' His voice took on a gentler tone. 'I've seen the way you look at little children. You'll want a family of your own one day, however much you deny it now.'

Although she was very moved by this outburst of his feelings, she doubted that he would ever comprehend that many children, although loved as much, could never fill the gap left by a lost child. She rested her palm lightly against his face. 'You're a good man, Michel. But it can't be.'

He moved her palm from his cheek and buried a kiss in it. 'I'll wait years for you if needs be, but don't condemn me to that, Lisette.'

Now, as she collected her bicycle from the factory shed, her mind was occupied with thoughts of Michel and she forgot all about Louis Lumière and the motion picture camera set up beyond the factory gates. She went cycling right past him before realizing that she must have filled the camera lens for a matter of seconds. Glancing back over her shoulder, she saw the women workers emerging self-consciously from the factory gates, smiles on their faces, while the men, some on bicycles, stared with interest in the direction of the camera. A dog was leaping about as if knowing that something unusual was taking place.

That evening the Lumières gathered in the family home to view the motion pictures that had been taken over the past few days. Madame Lumière was given a front seat beside her husband while young Edouard sat on the floor by her feet and the rest took the other chairs. Auguste and Louis intended to cut out surplus runs of the pictures, but only after the family had viewed them all.

The lamps were lowered and Louis began turning the handle of the camera. There were murmurs of admiration from Madame Lumière and her daughters-in-law at the superb clarity of the pictures. A horse-bus went by. There were boats on the river. Some children ran along, bowling hoops. Next came Auguste sitting with Marguerite at a garden table with their baby daughter, Andrée, between them. None of these strips of film lasted longer than a minute and it took the same amount of time to reload, but that gave the family the chance to chat excitedly during these impromptu intervals about what they had seen so far. Then came the factory pictures, beginning with a young woman cycling right past the camera, her face captured fully for only a matter of seconds. Yet it was long enough to cause Madame Lumière to sit forward abruptly in her seat.

'I'm sure I know that girl!' she exclaimed.

Nobody thought her remark held any significance. It was not often that Jeanne-Josephine Lumière went to the factory, but apparently she had recognized somebody she had seen there. Yet, when the lamplight was raised again, she did not let the matter rest.

'Do run that strip of the factory through again,' she asked her son. When he had obliged she turned to her husband. 'Antoine! I'm sure that was Madame Decourt's granddaughter!'

'Do you mean little Lisette?' he asked in surprise.

'She wouldn't be little now.' Madame Lumière thought for a moment or two. 'I'd say she is at least nineteen, which is surely the age of the girl on the bicycle!'

'But why should she be working in our factory? There was no shortage of money in the Decourt family. I passed the Bellecour house the other day and it is still closed up. Surely you remember that Lisette was not going to inherit it until she married or came of age? So there's no reason for her to be here.' He shook his head. 'I think you're mistaken, my dear.'

Madame Lumière was not satisfied and turned again in her chair to address her sons. 'Auguste! Louis! Do you have a Mademoiselle Decourt working at the factory?'

They were busy with the strips of photographs and neither had been paying attention to their parents' discussion. She had to command their attention again.

Louis glanced up this time. 'Who? Mademoiselle Decourt? Yes, she's in our bookkeeping office. You saw her on the screen a few minutes ago. Michel Ferrand is her beau – he and I were pupils together at the Lycée de la Martinere.'

'Yes, I remember. Now listen to me. I want to see Lisette. Give her permission to leave work early tomorrow afternoon and I will receive her at home. I can guess why she has never been to see me. There was that scandal about her being a runaway bride. Now you will remember to invite her, won't you, Louis?'

'Yes, Maman.' Louis exchanged an amused glance with his brother. There were still times when their mother seemed to forget they were no longer children.

The next morning Louis summoned Lisette to his office to pass on his mother's invitation. When he had explained how it had come about, she hesitated before accepting.

'I have stayed away from visiting her as I was involved in a scandal,' she said frankly. 'Are you sure—?'

Louis cut her short with a reassuring smile. 'You have no need to be concerned. My mother has no patience with gossip. She will expect you at three o'clock.'

From the moment Lisette was shown into Madame Lumière's presence, she was enveloped in all the kindness and warmth of hospitality that she remembered from the past. Her grandmother's old friend kissed her fondly on both cheeks.

'What a joy to see you again, Lisette! You were a pretty child and now you are a beautiful young woman. Oh, how I have missed your dear grandmother over the years, but now you are back in Lyon again.'

She drew Lisette over to neighbouring chairs in front of a low table that had been spread with a lace cloth, ready with cups and saucers as well as a plateful of little cakes and pastries.

'You look so well, madame,' Lisette replied happily, 'and not changed in any way.' Then she added on a sober note, 'I have wanted to visit you, but—'

Madame Lumière smiled and shook her head. 'You do not have to say anything about it, because I guessed why. Yes, we did hear of the scandal at the time, but you must have had good reason for doing what you did.'

'That's very understanding of you. At the last moment an insurmountable barrier arose that made it impossible for me to marry Philippe and so I took the only escape route that seemed open to me.'

'Then I believe, as your grandmother would have done, that you did the right thing. An unhappy marriage is a terrible state to be in.' Madame Lumière began to pour pale golden-hued tea into the fine porcelain cups, adding a thin slice of lemon to each. 'Your jilted bridegroom came looking for you in Lyon and called here to ask if I knew your whereabouts.' She noticed Lisette's startled look. 'Ah! I can see you didn't know that!'

'No, I didn't, although I did think that he might come to Lyon in his search.' She took the teacup that was handed to her.

'Are you aware that he married recently?' Madame Lumière asked cautiously. 'There was an announcement in one of the national newspapers.'

Lisette looked at her in relief. 'What good news!'

Madame Lumière raised her eyebrows. 'I wondered how you would feel about it.'

'I've been so afraid that he would still be looking for me. Now I know that I'm truly out of his life. I hope he and his bride find happiness together.'

The older woman nodded in satisfaction. 'I'm pleased to know that is how you feel. May I ask how you managed to disappear so completely after leaving the château? You were not to be found anywhere.'

'I knew of a travelling lanternist who was leaving Paris and I worked as his assistant for a while. After that I gained employment in a shop and then as a housekeeper before arriving in Lyon.'

Madame Lumière regarded her approvingly. 'Your grand-mother would have been pleased that you've grown up to be self-reliant and that you know your own mind.'

She went on to chat about the past and give news of people whom Lisette remembered, and they discussed other topics that interested them both. Lisette also told of her clandes-tine visits to the Bellecour house.

'You could have been arrested as an intruder!' Madame Lumière exclaimed anxiously.

'I know, but to be so near and yet so far made it impossible for me not to attempt an entry.'

'Be sure to keep away in future,' Madame Lumière advised. 'You're too young to realize yet how swiftly time flies, but the next two years will melt away and then the house will be yours.'

It was then that Monsieur Lumière came into the salon. He still exuded joviality and with his same irresistible charm he welcomed Lisette heartily before sitting down to have a cup of tea himself.

'It's a long time since I found you weeping in the garden on the day of your grandmother's funeral, Lisette,' he said reminiscently, 'and I have to admit that I wouldn't have recognized you on the motion picture as my wife did. But one thing I can tell you,' he added, 'and it is that the camera liked the look of you! That image of you was perfection!'

His wife nodded her head eagerly. 'Yes, it was. The boys must take more moving pictures of you.'

Lisette smiled. 'I feel very privileged to have been photographed already.' Then she made a request. 'Is it possible, Monsieur Lumière, that the plate used to take that last photograph of my grandmother in your studio is still in existence? I lost the photograph when it was stolen with the rest of my belongings from a train.'

'Yes, we keep records and I know that plate will be listed. You shall have a replacement as soon as it can be done.'

She thanked him gratefully. When she left the house an hour later she felt buoyed up and happy to have renewed her friendship with the senior Lumières. A week later she received the new photograph of her grandmother in a handsome silver frame.

Fourteen

After Lisette's reunion with the senior Lumières she received invitations to social events at their home. It was always with other guests, for the Lumières' own family gatherings were kept almost exclusively to themselves. As in the past she looked forward most of all to the musical evenings. These began with dinner at a long table finely laid with good linen and silver, an epergne dripping fresh flowers between candles. Over the good food and wine there would be lively conversation that encompassed everything from local and world happenings to the arts and usually the latest discovery in the field of science. There was also the recounting of hilarious incidents, which set everyone laughing.

Afterwards came the music. France's husband, Charles Winckler, and Auguste both favoured the cello while Marguerite played the piano and others in the family took to the violin, flute or whatever happened to be their favourite instrument. Usually Monsieur Lumière sang a couple of songs and when it was discovered that Lisette had a good singing voice she was persuaded into a solo now and again. It was through this enjoyment of singing that she joined a choir that gave concerts four times a year, and through it she made new friends.

Time thus passed pleasantly into the New Year of 1895. She and Michel did not see each other quite as frequently as before, because she had developed other interests that kept her busy. Even when the colder weather set in she continued to enjoy her trips out with a weekend cycling club for rides into the country, Michel accompanying her whenever his work gave him the time.

She had also joined a local amateur dramatic society, for in acting she was fulfilling a dream that had been ignited

long before in her childhood. It was through going to the
theatre so often with her father and acting in plays at school.
Each time had been a magical experience for her and she
had longed to be able to act before the footlights, but she
had sensed from remarks he had made from time to time
that a career on the stage was the last thing he would ever
wish for her. Anxious not to do anything to disrupt the
harmony between them, which had been so important to her,
she had put away that dream. Yet now it was resurfacing in
a small but satisfying way.

At her request, Michel had not mentioned marriage again,
but she knew he was biding his time. Yet unbeknown to him
she had given the matter serious thought. To have children by
someone of whom she was very fond, even loved, and whose
company she enjoyed, as well as the certainty that he would
be a good parent, would have weighed heavily in his favour
if she had wanted a husband. But as yet freedom was too
precious. Then late one afternoon on a windy, red and gold
October day, Daniel Shaw came roaring back into her life.

He was waiting for her when she came out of the office
building to join the stream of other departing employees at
the end of the day's work. He seemed even taller than she
remembered, clad in a well-tailored greatcoat and wide-
brimmed black hat, a scarlet woollen scarf thrown about his
neck, reminding her in every way of a Lautrec poster she
had seen of a man similarly dressed. He greeted her with a
deep frown and spoke angrily, ignoring the other workers
going by as if nothing else existed except the two of them.

'You've taken a devil of a time for me to find!' he declared
furiously.

She raised her eyebrows incredulously, for his audacious
greeting had taken her breath away for a moment or two.
Fellow workers glanced in their direction with amusement.
She stalked across to him and spoke in a lowered voice in
order not to be overheard.

'I should have thought that the way I left that day was
enough to tell you that we had come to the parting of our
ways,' she said as fiercely in retaliation as he had spoken to
her.

'Not for me,' he replied stubbornly. Then as she began

moving away from him, he called after her in exaperation, flapping his hands at his sides, 'Where the hell do you think you're going now?'

'To fetch my bicycle.'

'Damnation to your bicycle! I've a cab waiting.'

She came to a halt again and faced him squarely amid the flow of people around them. 'Unless you stop being so angry I'm not going anywhere with you!'

He shrugged his shoulders. 'My apologies.' Then a grin touched his well-shaped mouth and he held out a hand to her in supplication. 'I was so relieved to find you at last that I couldn't help cursing all the wasted hours of hunting for you in vain.'

She ignored his hand, thinking to herself that he had behaved like a frantic parent slapping a missing child in relief that it had returned safely. But there was no returning for her.

'Very well,' she said coolly. 'Where is the cab?'

'In the street.'

She fell into step beside him out through the factory gates while he asked her how she was, adding that he had been astounded to discover that she was working for the Lumières. The cab was waiting nearby and she stepped into it. He sat down opposite her.

'Where are we going?' she asked, resting back against the leather upholstery and clasping her purse with both hands on her lap.

'My hotel. There's a quiet salon where we can talk and later we'll have dinner there. The chef is excellent and I've heard that Lyon is becoming quite a magnet for gourmets.'

'I can't stay. I'm dining with someone else.'

'Who is this person?'

She refrained from saying it was no business of his. 'A lawyer friend. His name is Michel Ferrand.'

'You could send a message from the hotel to say that you're not able to come after all.'

'No, I will not,' she said crisply, although inwardly aware of being glad to see him fit and well and full of spirit. 'How long are you going to be in Lyon?'

'I go back to Paris tomorrow. I'm attending the viewing

of the Lumière Cinematograph, which is being presented to the Society for the Promotion of National Industry. Otherwise I'm living in England again these days. I came to Lyon for discussions with the Lumières about my own project. I was lucky enough to be given a tour of their splendid laboratory here on the factory site where they carry out all their camera work and experiments.'

'How do you know the Lumières?'

'I first met Monsieur Lumière at the Edison demonstration some time ago and we have been in contact ever since. I was invited to Louis Lumière's house yesterday evening for a demonstration of some of his animated pictures and also some of mine. That's when I saw you on the screen riding past on your bicycle.'

'So that's how you found me today.'

'I need hardly tell you how astonished I was to see you. I hope you won't be disappointed, but that piece is to be cut out of what the Lumières will be showing in Paris this time. It comes too quickly to set the factory scene.'

'I don't mind in the least,' she said truthfully. 'I'm not looking for fame.'

'What are you looking for, Lisette?'

She escaped answering, for they had arrived at the hotel.

There was no one else in the salon and he helped her off with her coat before divesting himself of his outdoor wear. They sat in comfortable chairs near the fireplace and he ordered wine. In her own mind she was glad it was not champagne, which might have signified a celebration of their meeting again. She supposed that he had sensed the defence she had put up against him.

'Tell me about your camera,' she asked. 'From what you have said already I gather that you have succeeded exactly as you have wished?'

'Oh, yes. It takes pictures as well as projecting them, and has been patented. But Louis Lumière was far ahead of me and everybody else in eliminating flickering. It took time for me to realize that the solution lay in the number of sprockets on the reel as well as some other minor adjustments that I have recently put right. I remember so well the frustration of early days when using reels of sensitized paper, which ripped so easily. Now I am like the Lumières in taking advantage of the recently invented celluloid strips, which are much stronger and have proved very successful.'

'That's splendid news.' She had clasped her hands together in her pleasure at his success. 'I congratulate you. But do you mind very much that the Lumières passed the winning post first with their special camera?'

'I don't begrudge them their success in any way, but –' he added with a wry smile '– I have to be honest and admit that I would have liked to have been the first. They are even ahead in planning the first public showing of animated pictures, which neither I nor anybody else seems ready to do yet. All along it has been touch and go to beat Edison and every other inventor competing in the field, but in a way we were all preceded some while ago by the English photographer William Friese-Greene.'

'You worked for him once. I remember you telling me.'

'That's right. It's quite a while since he patented a working, animated picture camera. He gave a few demonstrations to scientific and photographic associations, but he was unable to inspire any particular interest. I called on him a few weeks ago. Money troubles plague him, but he is forever optimistic as he continues his lonely path. Ever since his wife gave him a prism, he has set his heart on capturing colour in his animated pictures almost to the exclusion of all else.'

'What an ambitious project! Will he ever succeed, do you think?'

'I'm sure he will. In any case, it's bound to come eventually.'

'And you? What path are you following?'

His face lit up with enthusiasm. 'You remember those slide sequences on my lantern that told a story? Well, I want to do that with animated pictures. I've given demonstrations to interest possible investors and had a better response than poor Friese-Green. I've also sold some London property in the heart of the city that I inherited a while ago, which has enabled me to get together all the cinematic apparatus and props that I'm going to need.'

'Where will you set up this new business? Is it to be in England?'

'Yes, on the south coast. Not far from a seaside resort in Sussex. The climate is mild there and is said to have more hours of sunshine than anywhere else in England. A good light is most important. At present I use my camera to take traffic scenes, local events and so forth, but I'm looking beyond that to the future. I've had long discussions with both the Lumière brothers and they believe as I do that animated pictures are going to capture the world.'

'I agree with you.' She smiled as she raised her glass. 'To motion pictures and those who make them!'

He acknowledged her toast and the atmosphere between them became more relaxed. 'There is so much I want to ask you, Lisette,' he said, resting an arm across his knee as he leaned towards her. 'Did all go well with you after you left me? I searched non-stop for you over several weeks and never ceased looking and asking for you wherever I went. It was as if you had vanished off the face of the earth.'

She glanced down for a moment, wondering what he would say if she told him that his child had taken life within her before she had left him that day. 'I found work,' she said, looking up again to meet his eyes with a bright expression that hid her thoughts. 'Then eventually I came back to Lyon and took employment at the factory to see me through until I come into my inheritance. Even then I may continue working for the Lumières, because I could never idle my days away.'

'But now that we've met again perhaps you'll consider doing something else.'

Instantly she was wary. 'What would that be?'

'Come to England and help me follow my aim. I'd like to make my first feature picture with you in it. We could work together as we did with the lantern show.'

She regarded him with amusement, tilting her head slightly. 'That's a last minute suggestion if ever I heard one! You did not know where I was until yesterday, so you cannot have given it any previous thought!'

'That's where you're wrong. I've never stopped thinking about you and wanting you back in my life. Naturally I didn't know I was going to find you in Lyon. But you'll consider my suggestion?'

'No, of course not! I've told you my plans.'

'Does this Michel Ferrand feature in them?'

She had no intention of explaining anything to him. 'Maybe. Time will tell.'

He sat back in exasperation. 'How can you say that after this reunion?'

She sighed. 'It's very good to see you again and I truly enjoyed the time we worked and travelled together, but we have our own lives now – yours in England and mine in France. When I come of age my grandmother's Bellecour house will be my home. I have struck roots again in Lyon after a long absence and have no wish to live anywhere else.' She glanced at the clock on the mantel. 'Now it's time for me to go.'

'Running away again?' he questioned dryly as they rose to their feet together.

'Not at all. You know where to find me now. We can always meet if you should come back to Lyon at any time.'

He glanced at his watch. 'You're dining early, aren't you?'

'I've another appointment afterwards.'

'What's that?'

She sighed impatiently. 'If you must know, I belong to an amateur dramatic society and there is a rehearsal.'

'Good. I'll come along and watch. Where is it?'

She told him and he wrote the address down. In the next moment, taking her completely by surprise, he took her by the arms and pulled her close to him. For a few revealing seconds they looked searchingly into each other's eyes, seeing what had long lain dormant between them. Then she was locked in his arms, arching at the waist as he brought his mouth down on hers in a deep kiss from which there was no escape. Neither did she want there to be. Suddenly she was alive and afire, recapturing moments that she had long ago driven to the back of her mind. They swayed together as they kissed, her arms looped tightly about his neck. It was as if they were trying to assuage with kissing the flare of passion that each felt for the other in that heated, extraordinary matrix in time.

She was breathless when their kiss ended, but he continued to hold her, looking down into her face. 'There's far more between us than you're prepared to admit. That day by the cornfield was only the beginning. Say you will come to England with me!'

But her common sense was returning, already sweeping away what had taken place. 'No, Daniel,' she said, easing herself free of his embrace. 'As I told you, my future is mapped out.'

'I don't think it is. We'll meet again, Lisette. In the meantime, if nothing else, look upon my offer as a business venture that will bring you a new career. Do you really want to bury yourself in a house in Lyon until the end of your days?'

'It is a haven to me, not just a house.'

'Then it always can be. With the ease of travel with channel boats and trains these days you'd be able to visit it whenever you liked.'

'No, I'll not be persuaded.'

He ignored her statement. 'I don't expect to go into production with my cinematograph project for several months yet. So you'll have plenty of time to think about my offer. In any case I'll be back in Paris in December when the Lumière Cinematograph is to be revealed to the general public for the first time. I wouldn't miss that event for anything. It will give me a chance to gauge how successful my own line is going to be.'

He had helped her on with her coat, but when he was about to put on his own to accompany her she stopped him. 'Stay here now. I'm going by cab straight to the restaurant where I'm meeting Michel.'

Yet he still went with her through the revolving door and out to the hotel steps. As she left in a cab she resisted an impulse to look back.

Over dinner she mentioned to Michel that she had met again the lanternist for whom she had once worked, having told him some while ago how she had managed to leave the château without trace. She explained casually why Daniel had been visiting the Lumière brothers, but to her relief Michel showed no interest, having plans of his own to discuss with her. A friend of his had bought a villa in Italy and had invited them as well as several other of their friends to visit him in the spring.

'Let's go too, Lisette,' he urged. 'Tuscany is beautiful. We could visit Florence and see its wonderful treasures.'

She would have loved to go, but he would want to pay all expenses and that would involve her too deeply. Fortunately she had a legitimate excuse. 'There is my work to consider. I could not ask for time off.'

He answered her softly. 'Forget about work altogether. We could go on our own to Italy and make it a honeymoon.'

She wondered afterwards if that was the moment she might have accepted him if Daniel had not burst back into her life that afternoon.

Michel saw her to the door of the hall where her rehearsal was to take place. She entered to find Daniel already there and seated in a chair at the back of the hall. He gave her a wave as soon as she appeared, but did not come to speak to her. He watched the whole rehearsal in silence. Afterwards he took her home, but although he passed comments on the play he said nothing about her performance. But at the doorstep of the apartment building she could hold back no longer. Suddenly his opinion was all-important to her.

'Was I any good on the stage?'

He grinned at her in the lamplight. 'Yes, you were. Keep at it.'

She felt cheered by his praise. 'Yes, I will.'

'You'll meet me in Paris at the Lumière show?'

'I have made a special request to view it and that has been granted. I'm to have three days off from work to be there, but,' she warned firmly, 'I shall be accompanied by Michel.'

He shrugged. 'We can still talk. But don't go marrying him between now and then.'

'What makes you think I've changed my mind about marriage?'

He answered bluntly and without hesitation. 'You've lost the hard streak that bitterness had instilled in you when you were travelling with me. Something has happened to soften you. I'd like to think it was that afternoon we shared, but I believe there's more to the change in you than you're letting me know.'

She stared at him in shock. This man understood her far too well. She needed to get away from his penetrating insights as quickly as possible. 'You're letting your imagination run away with you,' she scoffed lightly. 'Goodbye, Daniel. I wish you a safe journey home to England.'

She entered the gaslit hallway of the apartment building and closed the door after her. Heedless of the cold wind, he remained on the steps until the image of her through the panel of frosted glass had vanished from his sight.

Fifteen

It was after the theatre one night that Michel brought Lisette home and stayed for a glass of wine, saying that he had to talk seriously with her. She steeled herself, guessing that it would be some kind of ultimatum.

'It's high time we were officially engaged, Lisette,' he began firmly, his expression intense. 'You know how much I love you and I've been patient so long. After Christmas, when we're in Paris for the first public showing of the Lumière Cinematograph, let me take you to Cartier's. There you can chose whichever ring you like best.'

She had to admit to herself that their lives had become more intertwined than ever during recent weeks. In her own mind she believed it had come about on her part as a defence against the disruption Daniel wanted to bring into her life and she would not let that happen. As a result it had become difficult to think of a future without Michel, but as yet she still did not want to marry. Sometimes her own unsatisfied desires and his amorousness would have made it very easy to melt into his arms, for he was a highly attractive and virile man, but if she took him as a lover his possessiveness would curtail her freedom as much as if they were married.

'No, Michel,' she stated firmly. 'We're going to Paris to see the show and enjoy being there together as friends, just as we enjoy each other's company here in Lyon.'

'What are you saying?' he exclaimed, throwing out his hands in exasperation. 'You know there's much more than friendship between us, although I hardly see you these days. You're either at work or rehearsing for a new role with the amateur dramatic society or doing charity work at the orphanage or meeting friends and so forth!'

It was true she had become more and more absorbed in

the life of the city. In her constant yearning for her daughter, which never left her, she found that assisting with the children at the local orphanage helped her emotionally, for at least she could give loving care to them. Yet she could not explain the reason to him. She sighed inwardly as he continued to talk severely to her.

'I thought when you agreed that we should go to Paris together that it meant we were moving towards a new phase in our relationship.'

Originally she had intended to go on her own to Paris, but upon hearing of her proposed trip Michel had immediately wanted to accompany her. It was why she had been able to tell Daniel that he would be with her. But now Michel seemed to be reading more into the proposed visit than she wished, clearly believing that at last she was going to let him sleep with her.

From the moment the Lumières had first spoken of the public showing of their animated pictures in Paris she had been particularly eager to attend. She wanted to see for herself how ordinary people would react to this new phenomenon to which she felt so closely linked through her association with Daniel as well as the Lumières. It was the reason why she had worked extra hours in order to have three days off to visit Paris.

'I know I'm defying convention in not having a chaperone wherever I go, Michel,' she answered, 'but I'm one of a whole new breed of educated working women and rules are changing fast to give us the freedom that has long been denied us. You and I have a very good relationship, but, as I've told you before, you will have to look elsewhere for someone – to marry.' She caught her breath, for she had almost said 'to sleep with', but she was sure he did that anyway.

He groaned. Her very elusiveness was a constant incitement to his passion and he was angry with her. 'There's nobody else I want or ever will!'

'That's what you think at the present time, but if I disappeared from your life there would be plenty of women ready to take my place.'

She had learned a great deal about the world since her days of innocence at the château. If she had chosen to take him as a lover there would not have been any fear of pregnancy, for Claudine at the emporium had told her ways to avoid that happening again. Yet her independence was all-important to her and, more and more, she liked being in charge of her own life.

On the twenty-seventh of December, which was the day before the Lumière show, Lisette and Michel arrived in Paris. She was excited to be there again and, as a cab took them to their hotel, she looked eagerly left and right at the passing streets. There had been a time when Philippe might have haunted the city for her, but that was long gone.

All the old familiar sights and sounds seemed to welcome her back. There were far more motorcars about than ever before, but otherwise there was almost no change. Michel had booked accommodation at one of the best hotels and she found that they had adjoining suites. No doubt he still cherished hopes that champagne and excitement would soften her attitude towards him. She checked that the communicating double doors were locked on her side.

For the rest of the crisp, cold day and at her request, they retraced steps that were familiar to her and it was as if she had never been away. To her relief Michel did not suggest again that they visit Cartier, and nothing spoiled their time together. In the evening they dined at one of the most fashionable nightspots and she felt that she was surely glowing with happiness at being in Paris again. Maybe she was, because Michel seemed unable to take his eyes from her. Later he did tap on the communicating door, but when there was no response he did not persist.

The first showing to the general public of the Lumière Cinematographic was to be held at the Grand Cafe on the Boulevard des Capucines. It was the first of the morning performances, with twenty or more to be shown throughout the day with a break at noon and in the early evening. As Lisette was anxious not to be late, she and Michel arrived in good time. Admission was one franc. They paid and were shown to a flight of stairs that led down to the exotic gold and crimson Indian room with its rush mats and ornamentation of elephant tusks and draped silks. A white canvas screen

had been erected and gilded chairs lined up in rows. It was
a small auditorium and Lisette saw immediately that Daniel
was not there. Monsieur Lumière came forward to greet them.

'*Bonjour*, Lisette, Monsieur Ferrand! A pleasure! Welcome!
It's good to see you both here.'

'I'm sure this day will be a great success,' Lisette declared
warmly.

His eyes twinkled. 'Thank you, Lisette. Do take seats wherever you please. We shall soon be starting the performance.'

He was the only member of the family present. It was his
great day and he was full of optimism. He and his sons had
already tasted success with their Lumière camera, for during
the summer there had been successful demonstrations to
scientific and photographic societies. These had been held
in Lyon and Brussels as well as Paris, resulting in high
acclaim, and many orders had been placed by members of
these societies for cameras from the prototype. Yet so far in
the Indian room few of the general public had arrived and
there were many empty seats. The projectionist exchanged
a concerned glance with his assistant.

Lisette and Michel had just settled themselves at the end
of the third row when Daniel arrived. He paused in the richly
draped doorway, seeming to fill it with his height and breadth
of shoulder. He saw her at once and grinned triumphantly.
Then, after exchanging greetings with Monsieur Lumière,
he came across to her, swinging his wide-brimmed black hat
in his hand and with his scarf and coat loosened. Oblivious
to Michel's presence, he seated himself beside her and tossed
his hat on to a spare chair to take her gloved hands in both
of his.

'Lisette! How good to see you!' he exclaimed exuberantly.
'I was sure you would be here! How's life? Have you given
in your notice at the Lumière factory?'

She raised her eyebrows in amusement. 'Of course not! I
worked extra hours to get the chance to come to Paris for
today's show.' Here she placed a hand on Michel's arm. 'You
haven't met Monsieur Ferrand. Let me introduce you.'

The two men shook hands. 'This is a great day for the
Lumières,' Michel said.

'Indeed it is!' Daniel endorsed fervently. 'Being the great

businessmen that they are, they have taken the right step at the right time with this show today. From what I've heard on the grapevine there are plenty of newly invented moving picture cameras about to be launched here and there, and some have had very minor showings. Nothing on this scale.'

'When are you going to hold a public viewing of your moving pictures, Daniel?' Lisette asked.

'In six weeks' time at a hall I've hired in London. But my best work has yet to come.'

'What of your friend, Friese-Greene?' She always felt sympathy for that inventor struggling alone towards his lonely goal of colour.

'The only show he has given to the general public was late on the night when his motion pictures proved to be perfect at last. In his excitement he rushed out of his laboratory into the street, intending to gather in an audience, but the only person around was a policeman and he hauled him in to sit down and watch the result! The constable could not believe his eyes and investigated behind the screen to see what trickery was at work.'

She laughed. 'Perhaps that will happen here today. Do you remember how those lantern slides of a baby crying always outraged women in the audience?'

He grinned. 'Yes, until the baby smiled again. We had some fun with those fast slides.'

'Have you a definite site for your moving picture studio yet?'

'Yes, it's on the outskirts of a resort named Hothampton. You'll approve the site when you see it, I'm sure.'

She became aware of Michel making a restless move beside her, but pretended not to notice. 'I haven't any plans to go to England in the foreseeable future,' she said firmly.

Daniel's face tightened, making a nerve throb in his temple. 'I thought when I saw you here today that you had decided to join me in my enterprise.' Then, as she shook her head, he lowered his voice. 'I hope you haven't made a foolish promise to anyone else since I saw you last. You had made one terrible mistake when I first met you, Lisette. For God's sake, don't make another one now!'

His audacity almost took her breath away and she thought with annoyance that he still expected to sweep everything before him. 'We'll talk later. The show will start any minute now.' Then she turned deliberately to Michel and explained that Daniel had previously offered her the chance to appear in his moving pictures. 'I refused, of course,' she added quickly, seeing his thunderous frown.

Only a few more newcomers had entered to settle themselves. Some women looked nervous, seating themselves on the edge of their chairs, for few of those present, if any, had the slightest idea of what they were to see at this morning's show, except that it was a kind of advanced magic lantern show. Half the seats were still empty when the assistant stood ready to lower the lights. Although Michel seemed mollified, Lisette could sense Daniel's angry tension as keenly as if she were seated next to white-hot burning coals.

Monsieur Lumière moved to stand in front of the screen and gave a short explanatory talk. Then the lights were lowered and the only sound was the click-click of the camera's handle being turned as the screen leapt into life. Immediately the audience gasped with amazement. The pictures really were moving!

The programme had plenty of variety. There were the Lumière factory girls pouring out through the gates in their flower-garden hats and the amusing sight of a toddler, whom Lisette recognized as little Andrée, daughter of Auguste and Marguerite, trying to catch a goldfish in a bowl. In between each episode there was a short pause while the camera was reloaded with the next minute-long film and the audience sat in stunned silence, scarcely able to believe what they had seen. Now they were viewing a garden and there came a burst of laughter from all in the auditorium as a gardener peered into the nozzle of a hose, not realizing that somebody had stepped on the supply, and then a moment later drenched himself. The arrival of a train in a station brought hysterical screams from the women, who threw themselves out of their seats in terror that they were to be crushed until they saw that it had come to a halt and passengers were milling about, even little children too. Afterwards there were more placid scenes, such as those taken in a street with passing traffic and many pedestrians, all of whom had passed the cameraman without as much as a glance of curiosity and which made for a totally natural effect. More of the Lumière entertainment followed and altogether lasted about twenty-five minutes.

As the lights went on again there was a great burst of applause as all rose from their seats in a standing ovation, people exclaiming excitedly. Monsieur Lumière bowed, beaming on them all. His dream for himself and his sons, which had started with his viewing of Edison's kinetoscope, had come true. He accepted the praise and congratulations of the small but excited audience as they left the lounge. Finally only Lisette, Michel and Daniel remained. Monsieur Lumière turned to them.

'Today,' Daniel said, 'has seen the start of something that will encompass the whole world. My sincere congratulations, Monsieur Lumière.'

'Thank you, Monsieur Shaw,' he replied, quietly confident, a twinkle in his genial eyes. Then, after Lisette and Michel had both given their congratulations, he added, 'I think the word will spread out of here to draw another audience back this afternoon and so it will go on and on in ever increasing circles.'

As Lisette with her two escorts passed through the Grand Cafe it was as Monsieur Lumière had predicted. People from the audience were telling perfect strangers excitedly about the marvel they had seen. Outside it was the same. On the pavement bystanders were stopping to listen as dramatic descriptions were given about what had been shown on a screen. Some of those emerging from the Grand Cafe had already purchased tickets to go again in the afternoon, saying that the wonders of the cinematograph could not be fully taken in at one sitting.

Daniel suggested that the three of them have a glass of wine together to celebrate the Lumière success. Michel felt it would be churlish to refuse and suggested a place he knew that was nearby on the same street. When they were seated at a table in the cafe's warm and plush interior, Lisette looked across at Daniel, who was sitting opposite her.

'Now you have seen for yourself that you have every chance of success with your camera too,' she said, smiling.

Heedless of Michel's presence, he answered her blunty. 'But I need you to be in my animated pictures, Lisette.'

She answered calmly, ignoring Michel's sharp intake of breath. 'There are plenty of experienced actresses and would-be actresses who would jump at the chance to get into this new medium. In any case, I have no wish to give up my life here. You discovered the last time we met that I'm now living in the place where I most want to be. There is nothing you could offer me that would make me change my mind.'

'I think there is.'

She was suddenly alarmed at what he might say next and answered quickly. 'Don't try to win me round with hope of fame and fortune. You know that holds no appeal for me.'

Fortunately the wine arrived at that moment. They toasted the Lumières and then to Lisette's relief the conversation kept to a safe plane with Michel questioning Daniel about his various projects and the apparatus used. She was not surprised by Michel's genuine interest, for moving pictures were greatly talked and written about at the present time. It also appeared that Daniel had decided that further persuasion towards her would be useless and without comment had finally accepted her refusal.

Their table was located some distance from the windows and it was not until they emerged into the crisp cold air outside again that they saw what had been happening in their absence. A long line of people had formed all the way from the entrance to the Grand Cafe along the length of the street as far as the eye could see.

'They're waiting for the next Lumirère performance!' Lisette exclaimed delightedly.

'It's begun!' Daniel seized her and swung her around in his jubilation, both of them laughing into each other's faces. 'There'll be no stopping film-making now.'

Later she was to remember it was the first time she had heard the new way of describing the making of animated pictures. She also recalled how he had kissed her in joy as he set her on her feet again. Then Michel had taken her hand

and placed it firmly in the crook of his arm as he reminded her that they had planned to spend the afternoon in the Louvre.

'Where are you staying, Lisette?' Daniel asked as they were drawing away. 'We must meet again before I leave tomorrow.'

Michel had hailed a cab. 'I'm afraid that will not be possible,' he replied, answering for her. 'We are fully booked for the rest of our stay.'

Lisette did not care for him deciding matters for her. In truth she would have liked another meeting more than she was prepared to admit even to herself, but in Michel's presence there would be no chance to talk freely to Daniel. It was better for them to part now.

'Goodbye, Daniel. As always I wish you good luck with your enterprise.'

Then, as she waved to him from the cab window, he gave her a broad wink as if they shared a secret. She smiled to herself. Maybe they did. She almost believed that somehow or other he would try to see her again before he departed. Yet that was unlikely to happen, for he did not know where she and Michel were staying and there were many hotels in Paris.

As the cab passed the Grand Cafe she saw that not only was there a great number of people waiting outside, but also another enthusiastic audience was streaming out. She was seeing how it would be in the future at every venue where these moving pictures were shown.

'The Lumières are going to make another fortune,' Michel remarked, 'because – as Monsieur Lumière told us – apart from making films they are already manufacturing the cameras to sell at an affordable price. There will soon be a worldwide market for them.'

In the Louvre they came to the almost deserted gallery where the Mona Lisa hung on the wall, allowed only a moderate amount of space among other pictures. Michel glanced at Lisette, who was gazing at it somewhat absently.

'You have the same kind of smile on your lips, Lisette. As if you're amused by some secret that I know nothing about.'

'Why ever should you think that?' she asked evasively.

She had visited the Mona Lisa several times in the past with her father, and her thoughts had not been with the glorious masterpiece, but were dwelling instead on Daniel's audaciousness. Neither could she crush down a hunger to see him just once more.

That night she and Michel were quite late back to the hotel, having been to the opera and had supper afterwards. He kissed her with barely controlled passion at her door, his embrace crushing her against his taut body.

'Lisette,' he implored, 'let me stay with you a while longer.'

'No, Michel,' she answered determinedly, afraid that his feelings would make him thrust himself into the room with her. 'We'll say goodnight here.'

He was too afraid of losing her through any false move and forced himself to let her go unhindered into her room. As she closed the door she leaned against it in distress. She would have to end her association with him. It was not right that he should keep hoping that she would change her mind, which she knew for certain now – after meeting Daniel again – would never happen.

She gave a start a few minutes later as the gilded telephone gave a little ring. It could only be Michel phoning her from his room. With a sigh she took up the telephone receiver from its elegant cradle. But it was Daniel who spoke.

'Come downstairs. I'll be waiting in the lobby.'

Afterwards she wondered why she had not refused, but instead she snatched up the cape she had discarded and left the room. The lift was at an upper floor and she did not wait for it, but almost ran down the curving flight of red-carpeted stairs, her cape rippling out behind her. She sighted him before he saw her and paused, questioning her wisdom for a moment in coming to meet him. He was waiting amid the potted palm trees and the marble columns. Music from the orchestra in the restaurant was drifting through a pair of open doors. Then she took a deep breath and continued down the flight at a slower pace.

His face lit up when he saw her and he came forward to meet her as she reached the bottom stair.

'However did you know I was here?' she asked.

He gave a quiet laugh. 'I phoned the five most expensive

hotels in Paris. I was sure Michel would have booked in at one of them.'

She smiled, shaking her head. 'I should have known you would find me again.'

He took her hand. 'We don't want to talk here. I know just the place.'

It was a cafe in Montmartre, not far from the Moulin Rouge, with its walls hung with paintings given by artists in lieu of payment for drink and food. Although noisy with chatter and laughter, its alcoves with the wooden tables and benches nevertheless gave individual privacy. Daniel ordered wine for them both and continued to hold her hand across the table.

'I had to talk to you on your own,' he began. 'You're not seriously involved with that fellow, are you?'

'If you are referring to Michel, the answer is no,' she replied frankly, 'but neither do I intend to complicate my life with anyone else.'

'Meaning me?' He had laughter in his eyes.

'Most especially you, Daniel!'

He raised his glass, the red wine glowing. 'Let's drink to your change of mind.'

'No,' she replied. 'We'll drink instead to your success.'

He shrugged, still smiling as he drank with her before setting his glass down again. 'You could easily travel to England with me tomorrow. After all, you must have a friend who would pack up your belongings and send them on to you.'

She sighed, sitting back in her chair. 'Think sensibly now. The last time we met you saw for yourself that I have settled in the one place in the world where I most want to be. It won't be long now before I inherit my grandmother's house and my independence will be permanently secured. There is nothing you could offer me that would make me change my mind.'

He gazed at her seriously for a few moments before he spoke in a lowered voice. 'What of my love for you?'

She stared at him incredulously. 'How can you say that? You're trying another tactic to make me change my mind!'

He shook his head seriously. 'Think back to that night in

Paris when I came out of that bistro to see a crazy girl wanting to hitch a lift on my cart. I knew in the same instant that you were someone I was going to want in my life.'

'That's not true!' she declared fiercely. 'You couldn't wait to get rid of me the very next morning. It's why you mended my bicycle so that there would be no delay in my departure!'

'You were too mixed up to know what you wanted at that point and I have to admit that maybe I wasn't ready for a change in my life. But through finding each other again in Lyon we have been given another chance.'

'I don't see our meeting again in that light.'

He leaned forward and spoke forcefully in a lowered voice. 'Tell me honestly, Lisette. Do you really believe in your heart that we can part in an hour or two and go separate ways for the rest of our lives?'

She was unnerved. 'All you want of me is someone to act for your camera!'

He sat back and thumped his clenched fists on the table in exasperation. 'Damnation to that! I needed a means to get you to come away with me and I thought that was the only way I might manage to do it. Although it will be the camera's loss you need never let it see your face if that's what you want! All I know is that I can't live the rest of my life without you!'

Her expressive eyes gave away her own feelings for him. 'I don't think I would want that to happen,' she admitted quietly.

Suddenly they smiled slowly at each other. 'I love you, Lisette,' he said softly, taking up her hands and kissing her fingers, his unswerving gaze holding hers. 'I have done from the start. Spend the night with me. We can stay here. No questions will be asked.'

Her eyes had widened, but more with anticipation than surprise. She accepted now in her own mind that he was the reason why she had been determined to get to Paris for the Lumière premiere. Certain that he would keep his word and be there, she had wanted to see him again with a longing she had been unable to subdue. Just one more time, she had told herself, and then that would be an end to it. Michel's presence was to have been her protection, her insurance against Daniel's persuasion to get her into his motion pictures, and above all a barrier against any amorous advances on his part. Instead she had thrown that defence away and was allowing herself to be swept away by her own passionate feelings, which she seemed unable to stem.

She found her voice. 'I believe my whole life has been directed towards this moment.'

'I know,' he said softly. 'For me, too.'

'I have something to tell you, Daniel.'

'What is it?' he asked, his eyes full of love.

'Later,' she said.

They rose from the table and he put an arm about her waist. He took a key from the landlord's wife and together they went up the narrow staircase to a garret room, which was warmed by some ugly pipes passing through it. There was a wide iron bedstead with clean sheets and a harlequin-patterned cover, a few sticks of furniture and a faded rag rug on the floor, all softened visually by a candle-lamp. Lisette turned in the circle of Daniel's arm and they kissed long and deeply.

They made love most of the night in the candle-lamp's glow, their naked bodies glimmering and constantly entwined in passion as well as in more restful moments when they murmured love words or else dozed briefly. It was all as she had remembered between them, enriched by the maturing of her love for him in these blissful hours.

It was early morning with the clatter of Paris stirring again as she woke to Daniel's caresses.

'You're so lovely,' he breathed. 'Every single beautiful part of you is beyond belief.'

She cupped her hand against his face. 'Hold me now. It's time for me to tell what you have a right to know.'

'Yes?' He scooped her to him. 'You can tell me anything, my lovely Lisette.'

'Think back to when after making love I left you that day by the cornfield. It wasn't long afterwards that I discovered I was pregnant.'

For a matter of seconds he stared at her in astonishment, leaning back to look full into her face, before he spoke with quiet joy. 'We have a child! A boy? Or a girl?'

'A daughter. I named her Marie-Louise, but she was taken away from me for adoption.'

'Adoption?' His eyes narrowed in shock and he almost shouted. 'You let her go? Why?'

He listened intently as she told him all that had taken place. Then she turned her head away from him in her distress, not knowing how he would react. 'I think of her all the time,' she said brokenly. 'Her adoptive parents took her to America.'

His arms enclosed her more tightly and his voice was heavy with sadness. 'Oh, my love! If only I had known where you were! Then you would never have gone through that terrible time and our child would have been with us now.'

'Forgive me, Daniel,' she implored.

Gently he tilted her face to his. 'It was no fault of yours! You would never have let our child go if it had been within your power to prevent it. I should have been with you! Then it would never have happened.'

They clung to each other in consolation until he took her again with such tenderness and adoration that she wept with joy at his loving.

Back at her hotel Daniel saw her into the spacious lobby. The hour was still early and there were only a few people about. They faced each other.

'I'll be waiting for you,' he said.

She nodded. Both of them were aware that she had made what was to her a momentous decision. Then he kissed her long and hard before returning to the waiting cab that had brought them to the hotel. He continued on to the railway station.

Turning, she crossed over to the desk and collected her key. Then she went to the lift and rode up in its glided cage to reach her room. Entering, she passed the bed where the sheet was still turned down for her from the night before and went to the window to look out at the avenue below, which was swinging into life.

She and Daniel had made their plans, although his disappointment was intense when she had refused to leave for England with him that day. Neither could she give him a definite date as to when she would join him.

'I'll lose you again!' he had protested wildly.

'No, you won't.' She had put a finger against his lips to calm him. 'But I have commitments I must fulfil before I leave Lyon. There is the month's notice I must give the Lumière management, the solo I'm to sing in the choral society concert next month and six weeks later I have the lead in a new play for the amateur dramatic society. I can't let these people down.' She had taken his anxious face between her hands. 'Then I'll come to you, but not to be idle.'

'What do you mean?'

'I'll want to work. I can either do your bookkeeping or – if you buy one of these recently invented typewriting machines – I can type scripts for you. Anything as long as I'm useful to your projects.'

Neither of them had mentioned film acting again. He knew it was work she did not want. 'There will be plenty to keep you occupied,' he had promised. All that mattered to him was that she should be with him.

Leaving the window, Lisette removed her evening clothes and took a hot bath. Afterwards she packed, for although she and Michel were to have another day and night in Paris it would not be fair to him to stay any longer.

At eight thirty Michel came to take her down to breakfast. He was surprised to see her luggage standing ready. 'What's this?' he asked. 'We're not leaving today.'

'But I am, Michel,' she replied quietly.

He turned pale in a burst of anger. 'It's that motion picture maker, isn't it? He's the reason!'

'I think he has always been between us. Ever since I first met him. In a couple of months when I'm free of all my obligations I intend to join him in England.'

'You can't do that! You would be throwing away all you've wanted ever since you came back to Lyon.'

'I realize now that Daniel was all I ever wanted.'

Michel accompanied her back to Lyon, but his attitude towards her was icy and both of them were silent most of the time. At her door he bowed very formally over her hand, but turned away without speaking. She knew he would never forgive her.

*   *   *

It was late March before Lisette had fulfilled all her obligations. The Lumières in their generous way gave a farewell party for her and other friends did the same. She received a number of gifts to take with her. To her surprise and pleasure Michel called on her with flowers two days before her departure.

'I wanted to wish you well, Lisette.'

'I'm so glad,' she replied genuinely as she took the flowers from him. 'Does this mean that we are still friends?'

'Yes. It also means I'll be waiting for you when you find that England is not the place for you.'

She shook her head. 'I'll be back to visit, that's all.'

He smiled. 'We'll see. Time with tell. *Au revoir*, Lisette.'

On her last day in Lyon she went to the gates of the Bellecour house and stood looking through at it.

'I'll come back when you're mine,' she promised in a whisper. 'You'll always be my true home no matter where I go in the world.'

She did not want any of her friends to see her off on the train when the morning of her departure came, saying that she did not like farewells in railway stations. She had a special reason for wanting to depart alone, because unbeknown to anyone else she was not going direct to the coast as everyone supposed. Instead she took a ticket to the little town where she had given birth to her daughter. It had been Daniel's suggestion that they should try to get some clue to their baby's exact whereabouts. He had wanted to call on the convent himself, but she had thought it better that she should go there alone.

Memories flooded back as she lifted the heavy knocker on the convent door and banged it twice. A nun she had never seen before opened the door to her.

'Yes, mademoiselle?'

'I should like to see the abbess.'

'For what purpose?'

'It is a private matter.'

The nun narrowed her eyes. 'She is at her devotions and cannot be disturbed. I can deal with anything you wish.'

'No, thank you. I'll wait.'

The nun stood aside for her. As Lisette entered she saw to her relief that Sister Delphine was passing through the hallway and called eagerly to her. Immediately the old nun smiled and came forward, recognizing her as she came nearer.

'It's Lisette! How are you, child?'

'So glad to see you! I'm on my way to England, but I could not leave without coming to ask about my baby. Is there any news of her?'

Sister Delphine waved the other nun away, indicating that she herself would deal with this enquiry. They sat down together on the hall seat and she took hold of Lisette's hand. 'You were told at the time that when a baby is adopted from here there is no follow up as the responsibility of the convent is at an end. Be content in remembering that your daughter went to a good couple and take comfort from that. Do not torment yourself any further by cherishing false hopes of some enlightment.'

'Has nothing been heard from Madame de Vincent? She seemed to have some knowledge of the couple who took my baby.'

'We have never received a word from her.' Sister Delphine patted Lisette's hand, trying to comfort her, even though the young woman's stark expression showed that she had seen her last hope destroyed.

With a heavy heart Lisette left the convent, trying to face the harsh fact that the child she kept in her heart and mind was lost to her for ever.

Sixteen

There was rough weather on the April day when Lisette crossed the Channel. She did not go below deck, wanting to see for the first time the white cliffs of Dover at close hand. If she still had doubts about her wisdom in leaving France, especially since she had only to wait until her twenty-first birthday in January next year to inherit the Bellecour house, she crushed them down. She wanted to be with Daniel whatever the cost to herself in homesickness, which she guessed would be inevitable.

As she sat in her deckchair, wrapped in a plaid rug that had been provided by one of the stewards, she watched other hardy passengers lurch their way along as they held on to the rails. She thought about the joyful letters from Daniel that she had received, many showing the haste with which they had been written as if he hardly had a moment to spare, which was probably the truth of it. He had given many successful cinematograph shows in London and elsewhere, receiving the same acclaim as had the Lumière films in Paris. Yet he was not alone in his venture. In the short time since that great Paris occasion many other operators had started making motion pictures and presenting the results, not only in England but also in the United States and many other parts of the world, even as far away as China. Some used Lumière cameras while others had similar inventions of their own. It was like a great flowering all over the globe.

When the steamer docked Lisette tucked the wind-blown strands of her hair back under her hat and then saw Daniel waving to her from the dockside. She was soon through the customs shed and in his arms.

'Welcome, my love!' he exclaimed happily after they had

kissed. 'These past weeks of waiting have seemed like for ever.'

'It has been the same for me! But now I'm here to stay!'

They took their seats side by side on the train that would take them to London. Being on their own in the first class carriage he was able to ask the question that was uppermost in his mind.

'Did you gain any news of our child?'

She shook her head sadly, her eyes stark, and told him all that had taken place. 'It is as if a door has been slammed for ever in our lives,' she concluded almost in a whisper.

He held her tightly in his arms. For the moment there was no need for words. Then the train began to move and they were on their way. At her wish they began to talk of other matters, filling in gaps that their letters had not covered in detail.

'You wrote that you had some screaming from the women patrons at your shows, but you didn't say what frightened them,' she asked. 'Was it a train as in the Lumière show?'

He shook his head, laughing. 'No, my audience thought they were going to be drenched by an ocean wave! I took the sequence off the beach when a high tide was hurling spray all over the promenade! One woman in the audience shrieked even more piercingly than the rest and put up her umbrella!'

She laughed delightedly. 'What else has happened since then? You promised me some good news about your productions when I arrived.'

'Yes, after the first London show a music hall manager contacted me and now there's a short programme of my films included in the programme every night. Not only is it profitable, but it's brought me publicity and a demand for film programmes from other music halls. I have even had a fairground proprietor wanting to show my animated pictures in a side-show, so there's another outlet for my comedies. At the studio we're working all day when the light is good. I was right to choose the present site of my studio on the south coast, which really does average more hours of sunshine than anywhere else.'

'You called the resort Hothampton in your letters, but I looked for it on several maps and could not find it.'

'I was referring to the location of the studio. The patch
of land there still has the name of Hothampton, which was
for a short time the name of the resort before it reverted to
its original name of Bognor, which I believe has Saxon
origins. Some other movie makers have started up in Hove
along the coast for the same reason of good weather. The
whole industry has taken off like a rocket!'

'I know that already from the Lumières' success. The
brothers are sending their cameramen all over the world now
to film foreign places and ceremonial events.'

'That's another praiseworthy move on their part! Patrons
will love it. They'll be seeing parts of the world that would
never otherwise come their way in everyday life.'

Now and again as the train rattled along Lisette looked
out of the window at the passing Kent countryside. There
was a gentle, dewy look to it, for spring had taken hold with
an abundance of wild flowers on the grassy banks on either
side of the tracks and the many orchards held clouds of pink
and white blossom.

When they arrived at smoky, noisy Victoria Station they
took a cab to Brown's Hotel where they stayed for a week.
As she had hoped, Daniel took her to see the sights. They
watched the changing of the guard at Buckingham Palace
where the absence of the Royal Standard showed that the
elderly Queen was away. Daniel thought she was probably
at Windsor Castle, but next year would be the Diamond
Jubilee of her reign and he planned to take film of the event
and Lisette would see her then.

'I've already booked hotel accommodation for that time,
because London will be jam-packed,' he said.

He took Lisette to the Tower, Westminster Abbey, the
Houses of Parliament, various art galleries and on a river-
boat trip to Hampton Court, all of which helped to satisfy
some of Lisette's eagerness in all she wanted to see. In the
evenings they went to the theatres and the music halls, having
supper at nightspots afterwards, and always making love
passionately before sleeping, their arms about each other.

The week went by quickly and back at Victoria Station
they took a train to the south coast. It was warm and sunny
when they arrived at the resort where Daniel went to a nearby

garage to collect his motorcar. He had left it there before
leaving by train for Dover, not wanting to risk any engine
trouble that could have delayed his meeting her. Although
he had bought it new only six months before, the motorcar
already showed signs of hard use with a number of dents
and scratches on its otherwise gleaming paintwork. Lisette
guessed it had been used many times for transporting cameras
and tripods and other equipment. It took quite a lot of cranking
up before the engine started, but then he leapt into the driving
seat at Lisette's side.

'This is like being in the cart again,' she said happily as
they drove along, 'although these seats have better padding.
What happened to Prince? Where is he now?'

'I found him a good home before I left France. He will
be treated well to the end of his days.'

'That's good to know,' she commented, remembering how
hard Prince had been ridden that day when Daniel had been
searching for her.

They were driving through the resort and he was taking a
route that enabled her to see the charm of the many Georgian
houses, which had been built by the founder of the town over
a century before. Then they followed along by the promenade, where she saw the stretch of golden sands and the sea
lying like a glittering throw of turquoise silk. She inhaled the
clean salty air with pleasure. Beyond the resort they followed
a country lane until he drew up outside a large thatched cottage
that he had rented furnished for the time being.

'What a dear old house!' she exclaimed. 'But where is the
studio?'

'It's a short drive away. I'll take you there tomorrow. Ah,'
he added as a youth in a yellow and black striped fustian
jacket came hurrying from the cottage to unload the luggage,
'this is Tom. When he's not assisting in the house he helps
out at the studio.'

'Afternoon, *mad-e-mois-elle*.' He had little idea how to
pronounce the address correctly, but Lisette appreciated his
effort and nodded to him with a smile. Then at Daniel's side
she entered the cottage.

'Good afternoon, madam.' The housekeeper, a pleasant-
looking, neatly-dressed woman in a dark blue dress and

white apron had been waiting in the oak-panelled hall to greet her. 'I hope you had a good journey.'

'Yes, thank you, Mrs Pierce.'

'I'm sure you would like a cup of tea and some toasted crumpets too,' the woman suggested, taking Lisette's outdoor clothes. 'I'll bring them to the sitting room.'

Lisette did not often drink tea and had no idea what a crumpet was, but she was prepared to adjust herself to whatever came along in these new surroundings. There was a faint aroma of new paint, which caused her to guess that Daniel had had some refurbishment done in readiness for her coming. The sitting room was low-beamed, causing Daniel to dip his head in some areas, and the antique furniture was dark and well worn, but two comfortable looking wing chairs flanked the fireplace. She went across to sit in one of them and hold her hands to the flames of the logs burning brightly on the hearth, for the afternoon had cooled.

'I like this house, Daniel,' she said, looking up at him where he had come to stand beside her. 'It feels like a home.'

He bent down and kissed her. 'I'm glad to hear that,' he said softly, 'because I want you to be happy here.'

The tea and crumpets arrived. Lisette, accustomed to pale tea with a lemon slice, found the contents of the teapot far too strong, but the buttery taste of the crumpets pleased her, although she thought they were probably very fattening.

Afterwards Daniel took her upstairs to her bedroom, which had a four-poster bed and where a young housemaid was unpacking a trunk. The girl, blue-eyed and round-faced, her fair hair pushed into a mob-cap, sprang to her feet at once.

'You are Daisy Robertson,' Lisette said. 'Mrs Pierce told me your name.'

'Yes, miss.' The girl had a pretty smile. 'I'll come back later.'

She scurried away, closing the door after her.

Lisette looped her hands behind Daniel's neck, smiling into his face. 'I'm so glad I came. This is such an adventure. We have the whole world to conquer. When do we start?'

He grinned as he went to turn the key in the lock. 'Not

quite yet,' he said, coming back to sweep her into his arms and across to the bed. They fell laughing on to it together.

Later he left her to go to the studio and check on what had been done in his absence. 'I'll not be long. We'll go through some scripts later if you'd like.'

'Yes, I would.'

He was gone far longer than she had anticipated, returning with his chief cameraman, whom he introduced as Jim Baker. He was a short and smiling freckle-faced fellow with carrot-coloured hair, who shook her hand heartily.

'Glad to have you on the team, miss,' he declared warmly. 'All has gone well in the boss's absence and orders for our productions keep flooding in.'

'I'm delighted to hear it,' she replied, liking him. 'Daniel has told me that there is to be another public cinematograph show very soon.'

'That's right! Every night next week at the Queen's Hall – that's the resort's local assembly rooms. On the Guv'nor's instruction I've been using the camera around the resort and the surrounding district. People like to see themselves on the screen. The programme will end with a couple of short comedies. They're always popular and tomorrow – if the light is good – we'll be making another.'

He talked on enthusiastically for another ten minutes before leaving and even then he paused to look back at her. 'Our cameras would love you, miss. I hope the boss will persuade you to change your mind.'

As the door closed after him Lisette turned to Daniel with her eyebrows raised enquiringly, a smile playing about her mouth. 'And what exactly did he mean by that? Or can I guess?'

'Naturally I told him that although you had done some amateur acting you have no wish to appear on the screen. But now he has seen you he would prefer you to be in front of the lens instead of out of its range.'

'Ah!' she said merrily. 'He doesn't know yet how good I can be at sound effects behind a screen instead of being on one. He might like me to be in charge of them at the Queen's Hall performances! Just as in my magic lantern days!'

He grinned at her joking, hugging her to him. 'No! But

one day we'll have coordinated film and sound without any assistance. Colour, too.'

She leaned back to look searchingly into his face. 'I can anticipate colour, because already the Lumières have tried hand-tinting every frame of a film. I'm told they have created one animated picture where a dancer's dress changes colour all the time in a butterfly dance. Everything in this new industry is advancing so quickly. But sound?' She frowned uncertainly.

He grinned at her confidently. 'It will come eventually. How that will happen I've no idea, but I have already tried the experiment of filming a woman singing while recording her on a phonograph. Naturally the coordination was not perfect, but it's a beginning. Meanwhile, those working at capturing good sound on mechanical instruments are working as hard in their field as those of us in the animated picture industry.'

'I think it's all wonderful!' she declared. 'Now, where are those scripts you were going to show me?'

They sat by the fire and went through some of the scripts together. Most of them were comedies, but Daniel's true interest, yet to be tried, was in short, simple dramas that could be easily followed and understood.

He wanted to be early at the studio next morning and Lisette intended to go with him, but when she awoke it was half past seven and he had already breakfasted and gone. As it was a brilliantly sunny morning she supposed that work would start early and he would want to make the most of the daylight hours.

When she was bathed and dressed she went downstairs to find Mrs Pierce prepared to fry her a full English breakfast. Although she had enjoyed many such breakfasts with Daniel when they were touring she had long since reverted to croissants and jam. Here she substituted toast and marmalade.

When she was about to set off on foot for the studios one of the film crew arrived in Daniel's car to collect her. 'I'm Mike, miss,' he said, reaching down a hand to help her up into the seat. 'Have you seen any picture making yet?'

'Not yet. I've been looking forward to today.'

They talked as he drove her along the lane until he turned

through an open five five-barred gate by a sign that announced SHAW STUDIOS in large letters and underneath in smaller ones 'Hothampton Meadow, Bognor'. A great mediaeval barn and a number of converted farm sheds and stables had been adapted entirely to the new use of movie making. It was a busy scene. Carpenters were sawing and hammering, painters were at work on some scenery, and a boy was filling buckets with water from an outside tap, which he was placing in a long line by the barn wall.

'That's a fire precaution carried out routinely whether we are in production or not,' Mike explained, indicating the buckets. 'Celluloid film is highly inflammable and there have been disastrous fires in two or three places that have made many people wary of attending performances.'

Daniel had seen her and was already coming across in her direction, but then Jim Baker, a pencil tucked behind one ear and a script in hand, waylaid him. Leaving the motorcar she went to join them. Jim greeted her warmly.

'Good to see you here, Miss Decourt.' Then he turned again to Daniel. 'The steamroller will arrive at eight o'clock and the prop man has half a dozen of those life-size cut-outs in case of damage.' He squinted up at the sky. 'I think today is going to be good to us.'

Seeing that they were too busy talking over the project in hand to notice her leave, Lisette withdrew quietly to make a tour of the studio buildings. The only one newly built was an office with Daniel's name on the door. He had told her that there was an adjoining room to his office where he and Jim would view whatever they had taken during the day and it was also where the splicing and editing were done.

In the vast interior of the ancient, oak-beamed barn she stood to look around at what she had been told were called 'sets'. It was like being backstage in a theatre with canvas scenes of a drawing room, a kitchen, and other interiors stacked against the walls. There was furniture too, a bed, cupboards, tables and so forth, which would be used with the various sets. As she stood there two of the film crew had started to pull forward a low-wheeled wooden platform to draw it outside through the barn's great open doors.

'What's that for?' she asked, moving out of the way.

One of the men answered her, able to tell by her French accent who she was, but neither he nor his companion paused in their task. 'It's needed for all sorts of things. Sometimes as a floor for an indoor scene with a backdrop, but mostly for pushing forward a cameraman to follow a scene or drawing him backwards. Today Jim Baker wants to take some shots from a high angle. So we're going to erect a stepladder on it for him.'

She decided she would not miss that, but continued her tour, opening the door of one shed and seeing what she first thought were beer barrels before realizing that they were the metal containers that kept the reels of highly inflammable celluloid safe from a chance accident. Seeing a middle-aged woman unlocking the door of another smaller building Lisette introduced herself.

'What goes on under this roof?' she asked with interest.

'Come in and see for yourself,' the woman invited pleasantly. 'I'm Mrs Leigh. My husband is one of the carpenters here.' She led the way in and Lisette followed, seeing immediately that it was a wardrobe room, for there were two sewing machines and a long table for cutting cloth.

'So you are the studio dressmaker!'

The woman nodded. 'That's right. I have to make any special costumes that are needed and repair whatever gets torn or damaged in any way.' She opened in turn the doors of two enormous wardrobes to display the assortment of garments within. 'The chests of drawers here are also full of shawls, purses, fans, socks and all sorts of other things that get needed from time to time. I'm always on the lookout for second-hand clothes that can be washed and mended and used by the actors. The budget for my department is very small. So if you have anything you don't want to wear any longer—?' She left the question hanging in the air.

'I'll remember what you've said.'

'Good. Everything helps. If you'd like to go into the shed next door you'll find Ethel Davis in there. She works with me when she's not dealing with make-up.'

Lisette found Ethel setting out theatrical make-up on a dressing table by the window. She was a young, bright-eyed woman and pleased to talk.

'I apply the make-up to both the actors and actresses.' She unscrewed the lid of a large jar filled with some greenish-white cream. 'This is what is used on the face, and there has to be plenty of dark make-up to accentuate the eyes of both men and women.' She picked up one of the lipsticks. 'This helps to give the heroines the look of having rosebud lips like the Gaiety Girls on those postcards and the pretty girls you see on chocolate boxes.' She glanced up at a clock on the wall. 'Mr Arnott will be in very soon – he's in the comedy being filmed today.' Then she looked towards the window. 'I can see he's coming now. He's a real belly laugh on the screen, but he's as miserable as hell in ordinary life. I've noticed that with other comedians.'

Lisette met Arthur Arnott on the doorstep. He was a rotund little man with a round-cheeked, impish face that looked as if it should be well-used to laughter, but there was no gladness in his eyes and he introduced himself very solemnly, giving a bow.

'My pleasure to make your acquaintance, Miss Decourt.'

She left him to Ethel's attentions and when she had seen everything she returned to the gateway where the steamroller had arrived in the lane. It was hissing and steaming, giving out its aroma of tar. Its driver, sitting high in his seat like a king on a throne, was wiping his hands on a greasy rag and listening attentively as Daniel told him precisely what he had to do. By now a stepladder had been mounted on the wheeled base that Lisette had seen earlier and Jim was high on it with his camera ready at the angle needed to follow the action when he would be pushed or pulled according to what was needed.

Arthur soon arrived in his chalky make-up and wearing a top hat and a checked suit that was short in the sleeves and legs, which added to his comical appearance. Immediately work started, but there were various hitches and delays before eventually, after several retakes, the film was completed. Throughout it had brought loud bursts of spontaneous laughter from those assisting, for it was as if before a camera Arthur became completely transformed. Here was a defiant little man with an amusing strut, taking a leisurely stroll in the middle of the lane and deliberately ignoring the steamroller approaching behind him. Sticking his nose up in the air, he strode ahead, refusing to get out of its way and, if any attempt was made to pass him, he dodged leisurely one way and then the other. The driver, coaxed by Daniel, shouted and gesticulated wildly in fury, giving his best while keeping his vehicle on its unremitting course. At the right moment Arthur nipped out of the way and a dummy was thrown down in front of the rollers to be replaced by a flat cut-out of Arthur on the far side as the driver drove on. When the film was spliced Arthur would appear to spring up again unharmed while the driver stood up to shake a furious fist after him as he ran away into the distance. A fade-out would swallow him up.

Applause greeted Arthur as he returned from his final spurt of speed, but he did not acknowledge it, changing once more into the gloomy individual unknown to the cameras.

Work continued throughout the day and set a pattern for the following weeks, everybody at the studio getting a day off on Sundays if there had been enough good weather for maximum filming during the week, otherwise it was work as usual. On free Sundays Lisette and Daniel drove out into the country where they walked through the woods and followed the gentle grassy slopes of the bow-backed Sussex Downs. She loved the views that stretched as far as the sea, pierced by the distant spire of Chichester Cathedral

The public performances at the Queen's Hall had been a great success and there had been non-stop performances to accommodate all who wanted to attend. Afterwards the programme moved to a hall in Chichester where it received the same approbation, Jim having used the camera on scenes and events there too.

With the coming of the warmer weather Lisette sometimes went swimming, hiring one of Mr Jenkins' bathing machines located west of the pier. Why they were called 'machines' she did not know, for no machinery was involved. They were just huts on large wheels with a door at each end. One entered at the rear and there was a bumpy ride down the beach until the machine was hub-deep into the sea. There the horse was unhitched and led back up the beach while the occupant, now in her bathing costume, could emerge directly and modestly into the waves. When her swim was over the procedure was reversed, the horse being hitched to the opposite end of the machine to draw it up the beach again. Daniel was never able to swim with her on these occasions, for bathing was segregated, but there were warm nights when they went down to the sea away from the resort and discarded their clothes to swim naked together in the moonlight-flecked water.

Daniel had become aware that soon it would no longer be a novelty for people to see themselves and local vistas on the screen. So, except for special occasions or important sports events, he concentrated throughout the summer on turning out innumerable one-reel comedies, for which there was an insatiable demand.

With the sea being so near there were plenty of opportunities for comic actors to fall in and out of boats, get large artificial crabs pinching their toes, become entangled in fishing nets, be buried in sand up to the neck and also be chased by irate husbands for spying on lady bathers through a telescope. He often found new talent among comic actors who performed in the resort's small theatres, one in particular called the Olympian Gardens had given him three good comic actors, but if he was unable to attend the shows he relied on Lisette to go alone and report on any possible talent.

Filming continued into the autumn, but the shorter daylight hours soon slowed down production almost to a standstill. Then Daniel, leaving Jim in charge to carry out whatever work was possible on brighter days, left home to gather in orders for his animated pictures from London and elsewhere in the country. He was often away for weeks at a time, during which he also kept a lookout for a possible new site for his studio

Lisette knew he had become dissatisfied with its present position, partly because the farmer who owned the land had refused to let him rent a neighbouring meadow for expansion, which was becoming necessary. Another reason was that he had tried in vain to get gas lamps installed for extra illumination, oil lamps being only a feeble help on a gloomy day. The local gas board had refused his application as the studio was considered to be too far out of the resort for the cost involved. At the same time electricity was beginning to replace gas lighting in major cities in the United Kingdom and in other parts of the world. Daniel saw it as the solution to winter filming.

During his absences Lisette, although she missed Daniel, was never lonely. She had met a fellow countrywoman, named Veronique Desgrange, who was married to a local businessman, and through her Lisette had met two other Frenchwomen living in the district. The four of them met often in one another's houses. Otherwise Lisette was kept busy reading scripts, for would-be scriptwriters had started sending their work to Daniel. She also wrote some herself, although hers were dramas and not comedies, for she knew that eventually Daniel would move into drama and she would have her work to show him when the time came.

It was a December afternoon, shortly before she was expecting him home again, when Tom brought her two letters that had come in the post. One was from her Paris lawyers, which she guessed would be about her inheritance due in January, and another was from Joanna, which she opened first. They had corresponded ever since Lisette had written to her after settling down again in Lyon, although Joanna knew nothing of Marie-Louise's birth or the trauma that Lisette had suffered afterwards. Lisette was pleased to read that her friend was holding another exhibition of her paintings, which seemed to sell well. There followed the usual invitation to visit, but as yet Lisette felt unable to accept, for she was in charge when Daniel was away and all too busy working with him when he was at home and in action at the studio.

She was about to open her lawyers' letter when Mrs Pierce entered the room and made a surprising announcement.

'I've come to give in my notice, madam.' The woman's face was grim and her hands were folded firmly in front of her.

'Whatever has happened to bring that about, Mrs Pierce?' Lisette asked with concern.

The reply came stiffly. 'It is what has *not* happened and I'm at the end of my patience in waiting for it. When I heard you were coming here from France I naturally expected a marriage to take place soon after your arrival. That has not taken place and I see no sign that it ever will.' Her next words came in a rush of embarrassment. 'There is a great deal of gossip in the neighbourhood about you and Mr Shaw living in sin. For the sake of my own good name I cannot stay any longer under this roof.'

Lisette regarded her steadily. 'In that case you must leave immediately, Mrs Pierce. I would not want your conscience to be troubled for a moment longer.'

Mrs Pierce looked taken aback. 'I'm willing to work out my month's notice.'

Lisette shook her head. 'Certainly not. Do not be afraid that I'll refuse you a reference, because I have found no fault with your work. I will write it now for you to collect as you leave.'

The letter was written. Lisette was putting it ready on the kitchen table when Daisy came to her in tears.

'Do Tom and I have to leave too, madam?'

Lisette raised her eyebrows. 'Tom spends more time working at the studio than he does here in any case. As for you, Daisy, of course I don't want you to leave.' Then she added dryly, 'Unless your mother has expressed doubts about your being here.'

'Oh, no!' Daisy's whole face showed her relief. 'She's glad I'm here. As you know, madam, she has a boarding house in the resort, but she was a housekeeper once until I came along. She has always said those were her best days. Is there any chance of her applying for Mrs Pierce's place?'

'She may not wish to do that.'

'Oh, I think she would, The house we live in ain't ours, only rented, and it's not all honey having summer visitors with their howling kids that wet the beds and families that get bad-tempered and quarrelsome when it rains and they can't enjoy themselves on the beach. Then in winter it's travelling salesmen that drink too much and try to have their way with my mother and me too, if you get my meaning. People take advantage of a woman on her own and sometimes they slope off without paying their bills. Please would you just see her, madam?'

Lisette smiled. 'Yes, Daisy. If she is willing, tell her to

come tomorrow afternoon. In the meantime I'll take over the cooking.'

She returned to the sitting room where she opened the letter from her lawyers and received an unexpected shock. It informed her that recently they had been working on her behalf to try to regain some of her late father's bequest to her, which, unbeknown to them, had been siphoned away by her stepmother through a loophole in his will. The vanished money had gone in costs for the upkeep of the château where major alterations had taken place. This was quite a separate matter from her late grandmother's bequest, which would come to her intact and which no outsider could touch.

Lisette crumpled the letter in outrage at her stepmother's deviousness. Then, springing to her feet, she paced up and down in her frustration at being powerless to take any action. Isabelle in her greed had taken revenge by the only means open to her.

Underlying Lisette's rage was her bitter disappointment that now she would not be able to use her father's money to help Daniel to build a new studio when he found a new site that was suitable. He had made it clear a while ago that her grandmother's bequest was solely for her, but he had not known what she would inherit from her father and it was that money that she had planned should make her an equal financial partner in his enterprise. But now she foresaw endless arguments over his determination not to risk her income in any way.

That night she could not sleep, this knowledge hanging over her like a heavy cloud. At three o'clock she went downstairs and unburdened herself in a long letter to Daniel, too upset to wait until he was home again.

As a result of her disturbed night Lisette was still somewhat distracted when Daisy's mother, Maisie Robertson, arrived at the time arranged for her interview. She was in her early forties, a pretty woman, round and smiling with the same large blue eyes as her daughter, her light brown hair curling up under her feather-trimmed red hat. Everything about her was neat and clean.

'I'm a widow,' she began, 'and have been since before Daisy was born, I started in service as a scullery maid and then rose to parlour maid and eventually I became house-keeper to two elderly spinsters. I can't give you a reference from them, because I left in a hurry for reasons of my own. But I was with them for four years, which should show you that I was satisfactory, although you would have to take my word on it as I have no proof to offer.'

Lisette had been hearing echoes of her own interview with old Judge Oinville in the woman's words. She wondered what hardships Maisie Robertson had endured after leaving the spinsters' employ, but at least her baby had not been taken from her.

'My late father was a local fisherman here at the resort,' Maisie continued. 'We had fallen out in the past, but when he was ill towards the end of his life he let me come home to nurse him. With the little bit of money he left me I started renting the boarding house and taking in lodgers. At this time of year without the summer visitors business goes down and its mostly commercial travellers, who only stay a night or two, so I could easily shut the house and come on a month's trial if you wished. I'd like to get back into service in a proper home and Daisy has been real happy here with you. If you should decide that I suit you, I would give up the boarding house and move into the rooms that Mrs Pierce occupied.'

'But there is no guarantee that Mr Shaw and I will be living here permanently,' Lisette said. 'In fact there's every chance that he might move the studio elsewhere at any time.'

Maisie Robertson gave a quick reply. 'But you'll still need a good housekeeper and a reliable maidservant wherever you go, madam.'

Lisette gave a smile. 'In that case you may come for the month's trial as soon as possible.'

When Daniel returned home two weeks later with a wad of orders for his productions he was surprised to find that a new housekeeper had replaced Mrs Pierce.

'What was the reason for her leaving?' he asked Lisette as they sat at dinner.

'Her conscience troubled her. She felt unable to remain under the same roof as a couple living in sin,' Lisette replied. 'But Daisy is still with us and it's her mother who has taken over the housekeeping duties.'

He merely raised an eyebrow, but made no comment. At
the end of the meal he went into the kitchen. The past housekeeper had cooked well, but her replacement was even better.
'That was an excellent dinner, Mrs Robertson,' he said.

She beamed, partly with pleasure, but also because she
liked good-looking men with a virile look about them.
Turning back to the dishes in the sink after he had left again,
Maisie discussed him with her daughter.

'Why don't she marry him, Daisy?' she pondered aloud.
'He wouldn't have to ask any other woman twice.'

'He wouldn't want anybody else,' Daisy replied. 'Anybody
can see that.'

'Maybe he hasn't asked her. So many men like to have
their cake and eat it too.'

'Or perhaps he's asked her and she has refused him. She
is a very independent lady, as you'll soon find out if you
haven't noticed already.'

Maisie paused for a moment, a dripping plate held in mid-
air as she waited for her daughter to take it. 'She's French,
of course. Foreigners often have different ideas about things.
In any case the two of them are sort of stage people anyway,
being connected to entertainment as they are.'

'I suppose so.'

'Therefore the same rules of marriage don't really apply
to them. I know that from some of the actors and actresses
from the Olympian Gardens and the theatre at the end of the
pier that stayed with me during the summer months.
Sometimes there was scarcely a wedding ring among them
and they were always in one another's bedrooms.'

Daisy had heard it all before and wanted to know something far more important. 'Your month's trial will be up soon,
Ma. Have you thought yet whether you want to stay on here?'

'Yes, I have. I've weighed everything up in my mind.
Miss Decourt is always busy reading and writing scripts or
at the studio, and she has found no fault with my work
or me. There's no more scrubbing floors here with a
village woman coming in daily. I'll have comfortable accommodation in those two rooms off the kitchen near my own
bathroom. There's a good regular wage and time off. What's
more, you could live here too if Miss Decourt agrees. There's

that storeroom next to my rooms, which would make a nice little bedroom for you if the trunks and valises in there were stored elsewhere.'

'Oh, Ma!' Daisy exclaimed with relief. 'I'm so glad you like it here.'

She had her own reason for being pleased with her mother's decision. It meant an end at last to all the extra chores she had had to do at the boarding house when her day's work was done at the cottage, because her mother was a stickler for having everything spick and span. Although she would have preferred not to continue to be under her mother's watchful eye, always having to say where she was going and kept to a strict nine o'clock curfew, the advantages outweighed the disadvantages.

Although neither Daniel nor Lisette referred again to the reason for Mrs Pierce's departure he had not forgotten it. It was in his mind again that night as he began to make love to Lisette in their wide bed. Then passion obliterated all else.

It was during Maisie's trial period in late November when Daniel was away again for a few days that Joanna came to stay, having given up expecting Lisette to visit her for the time being. They embraced each other joyously. Joanna had put on weight about the hips and breasts, but her waist was still small, giving her the ideal hourglass figure that was what most women wanted.

It was as if they could never stop talking as day followed day and yet still Lisette felt unable to tell Joanna about her lost child. It was only with Daniel that she could share her deep feelings for Marie-Louise.

'You must love this Daniel Shaw very much indeed to give up living in your beloved France,' Joanna declared as they sat talking. 'Do you feel that you're starting to put roots down into English soil?'

'Roots?' Lisette echoed smilingly. 'I'm not sure yet. You must remember that I still have roots in the Bellecour house and maybe they will never let me break free.'

Joanna shrugged. 'Don't ever let that house come between you and Daniel,' she advised seriously.

Lisette laughed lightly. 'That could never happen.'

'Shall you marry him?'

'It's most unlikely. I was still helping him with magic lantern shows when we last discussed the state of marriage, the restrictions of which did not appeal to either of us.'

They began talking of other matters. Lisette enjoyed every moment of Joanna's visit and it amused her to see how her friend was fascinated by everything to do with the studio and motion picture making. When some snow fell and lay for several days, which was unusual in the south, Jim was able to use its brightness with the weak November sunshine to make three new comedies, all of which had comic policemen in various ridiculous situations. Joanna did not miss any of the action, arriving before filming started and staying until the end of it, laughing and clapping her hands at all the antics like an excited child. When one of the comic actors had to fall into a pond, breaking the ice at the end of a scene and losing his policeman's helmet, Joanna was the first to reach him with a warm blanket.

Daniel came home before her visit ended and they soon approved of each other, he liking her frankness and lively sense of humour, she admiring his good looks and able to see that he was obviously very much in love with Lisette. As it was his first evening home after an absence she tactfully retired early to her room. She went on the pretext of being tired and wanting to finish a book, giving them the chance to talk on their own after his being away.

While they sat together by the fire Lisette brought him up to date with all that had happened at the studio. Then she discussed her depleted inheritance with him.

'My father made a new will after marrying Isabelle, which was the right thing to do, but it was the only time he did not use the lawyers that had served him all his life. I suppose, being so much in love with her, he failed to see how the will was too much in her favour.'

'She must have had a clever lawyer working on her behalf.'

'I don't care about the money for myself,' she burst out, 'but I wanted so much to help you financially when eventually you build a new studio. You must let me draw on my grandmother's bequest for it when the time comes!'

He answered her firmly. 'I told you some while ago that your inheritance was your own and that I would make sure of being fully prepared financially when a move is made.' Then he grinned widely. 'Let Isabelle enjoy her ill-gotten gains. You'll always be able to afford some jam on your bread and butter or –' he added with a laugh '– in your case a croissant!'

He had coaxed her back into a smile.

'I've shown Maisie how to make them,' she said light-heartedly, 'and she's become such an expert that every time her croissants could have come straight from Paris.' She gave an amused little laugh. 'That in itself makes me glad that we shocked Mrs Pierce away.'

The gentle joke she had made remained in Daniel's thoughts as they went to bed that night, but soon their mutual passion eclipsed all else. Yet in the morning he remembered once more what had been said and kept it at the back of his mind.

Seventeen

On New Year's Eve Daniel and Lisette welcomed in 1897 with a party, combining it with a celebration of her twenty-first birthday. Joanna came specially for the occasion and had been invited to bring her current beau, a pleasant young man named George Scott Moncrief, who was tall and lithe with an open-air look about him and a lively sense of humour. He had recently inherited a great estate somewhere in Bedfordshire, which Joanna had already visited several times.

'Perhaps I'll end up as the lady of the manor,' she whispered jokingly to Lisette, who wondered if her flippant attitude concealed deeper feelings.

He had brought Lisette a large bouquet of hothouse flowers, but Joanna's gift was a small painting of a girl with flowing hair, who stood looking out to sea. It was by a Nordic artist named Edvard Munch, purchased when she had had a few days in Paris to view two new art exhibitions.

'I bought it privately from the artist himself,' she said. 'It saved him losing a percentage to the gallery, because although he is the handsomest man I've ever seen he is as poor as the proverbial church mouse. His studio was even more chaotic than mine with paintings stacked everywhere. I adore his work, but although he's a brilliant artist he hadn't sold anything at the exhibition. He looked quite ill and tired. I told him to go home to Norway and breathe in some clear mountain air.'

'You always were good at giving advice,' Lisette replied in amusement.

'But you didn't heed it when I tried to tell you that Philippe was not the one for you.'

'Did you ever suspect what was going on between Isabelle and Philippe?'

'No, but I always thought his eyes were too close together for him to be straightforward.'

Lisette burst out laughing. 'That's not true! He had wonderful bedroom eyes, although I just thought them handsome at the time.'

Then Maisie came into the room, bearing a cake with lighted candles, which brought a burst of enthusiastic applause from everyone. Daniel made a short speech in praise of Lisette, which everybody clapped and cheered. Then she cut the cake.

Both she and Daniel liked the Munch painting immensely, for it had dramatic and mysterious depths, commanding notice from where it was hung on the sitting room wall the morning after the party. Something of Joanna's exuberance seemed to linger about the painting after she had gone, adding to its drama.

Spring brought a renewal of work at the Shaw Studio. Lisette, knowing how much Daniel was yearning now towards stronger productions, continued to encourage him by finding good scripts and stories that eventually he could bring to the screen. He took a big step in producing a one-reel murder mystery after a pair of rival movie makers in the north captured on film, entirely by lucky chance, the actual arrest of a murderer, a scoop that had put them on the map. Daniel's murder mystery had women screaming in the audience, although no violence was shown beyond the shadow of an attacker on a wall. Yet the resulting publicity was good and agents began ordering it for various circuits.

Then soon it was June and as the Queen's Diamond Jubilee drew near, red, white and blue decorations began to burst forth everywhere with bunting and flags strung across all the streets. Every shop window had a patriotic display, usually with a large photograph of the Queen as a centrepiece and often of her family too. On the eve of the celebration Daniel, Lisette and Jim with his assistant, Sam, set off for London, which they found ablaze with flags and even more patriotic displays. Crowds thronged the streets to see the decorations, hundreds wandering up and down the Mall, which was lined on both sides with tall flagpoles displaying the Union Jack.

Daniel had shown foresight in booking hotel rooms so far

ahead, for now it would have been impossible to find accommodation anywhere. Many people were camping along the processional route, some having been there for several days to ensure that they would have a good view when the Queen passed by.

The day itself dawned gloriously bright, warm and sunny. Special stands had been erected for the press and for those taking animated pictures. Jim set up his camera with Sam on a stand in the Mall while Daniel chose to be by the steps of St Paul's Cathedral where the service of thanksgiving would take place, Lisette with him. Her task, as with Sam's, was to hand Daniel fresh reels as he needed them and put those used into cans.

At St Paul's the enormous waves of cheering that greeted the procession were heard long before it came into view. Then to the stirring music of naval and military bands came the dazzling sight of many splendid uniforms with shining breastplates, plumed helmets, tall bearskin caps, and colourful turbans, while glittering harnesses jingled as row upon row of magnificent horses went by. Regiments were represented from home ground to every corner of the great British Empire, which covered a quarter of the globe. Daniel, steadily turning the handle of his camera, wished he could be capturing everything in colour instead of in black and white.

Then the cheering reached new crescendos as in the midst of all the splendour there came an open carriage bearing the little old lady. She was holding a black and white striped parasol to shade her face. It was Queen Victoria herself.

'How tiny and round she is!' Lisette exclaimed.

The Queen's health did not permit her to mount the many steps up to the cathedral, filled now with the choir in their white cassocks, and the thanksgiving service was conducted on the stairs while she remained in her carriage. When the service was at an end she rode on again, waving her little white-gloved hand to the roaring crowd.

Daniel was well pleased with all he had taken of the great occasion. 'That was history!' he declared triumphantly. 'Captured for ever!'

He left on his own to meet Jim and Sam for the homeward

journey as Lisette had previously arranged to stay a few days in London with Joanna.

She had had her trunk conveyed from the hotel to Joanna's address and had only her purse to carry. She managed to get on a horse-bus to take her most of the way, but the thronging crowds caused so many hold ups that eventually she alighted to walk the remaining distance. Hansom cabs were in such demand that there was no chance to hail one anywhere until she was almost at her destination and then it was too late. Joanna's address was a tall house at the end of a Georgian terrace. Before Lisette had a chance to ring the bell the door was flung open by Joanna with an exclamation of joy.

'I've been watching for you, Lisette! Come in!'

They embraced each other affectionately, both talking at the same the time while Joanna took Lisette's coat from her and then dumped it with her hat on a chair.

'Did Daniel get some good motion pictures of the Queen?' she wanted to know. 'I watched the procession from a friend's balcony along the route. I doubt if London has ever seen anything more spectacular.'

She swept Lisette into a large drawing room. It was unlike any other that Lisette had ever seen. Sofas and chairs were swathed in silks and brocades of rich scarlet, purple and wine reds, woven with gold and silver thread. Enormous soft velvet cushions with gilt tassels tumbled everywhere and Persian rugs covered the floor. Silken drapes of violet and burgundy hues were looped at the windows and on the olive-green walls were half a dozen large paintings. The great marble fireplace had two bare-breasted caryatids on each side supporting a wide mantel and a vast gilt framed mirror.

'What a gloriously exotic room!' Lisette exclaimed, twirling to take in all the details of this gigantic cave of colour. 'I love it! Is the rest of the house like this?'

'No. This was specially done for me. My mother nearly fainted when she saw it!'

'Well, it is very different from anything I know she would have chosen. Are the paintings here yours?' Lisette's gaze had been drawn to them and she would have gone across to look more closely if Joanna had not caught her arm.

'You can look at them later and everything else I have in

my studio upstairs. Now we're going to have some champagne to toast the Queen. As I believe I told you, I have two servants and a cook, but I gave them the time off to see the procession and join in the festivities that will be going on everywhere tonight.' She went to a side table where a bottle of champagne was waiting in an ice bucket with two glasses and she opened it expertly.

'I knew you wouldn't be living in a garret,' Lisette remarked as she sat down, 'but this house and three on the staff suggest to me that you've been modest in your letters about your success.'

Joanna shook her head, pouring the champagne. 'I'd like to say that my work is in demand as soon as the paint dries on the canvas, but that's not the case.' She raised an eyebrow. 'I thought you would have guessed that my father is the one who pays the rent on this place as well as the servants' wages and other incidentals.' Then she giggled. 'He thinks Bloomsbury is a den of sin, and although – as he says – I mix with weird arty people of whom neither he nor my mother approve, at least I could have a decent house!' She handed Lisette a glass and sat down opposite her. 'It's really so that their friends will not guess at my Bohemian way of life.'

'Nevertheless your parents were always generous to you. Did they ever refuse you anything?'

Joanna made a pantomime gesture of sticking her finger in her cheek and tilting her head as if pondering. 'I don't believe they ever did!' she admitted on a laugh. 'Although I did have a struggle to get their permission to study with that artist in Paris for a year.' She laughed mischievously. 'Their misgivings were well-founded, although thankfully they never knew it. That artist taught me a good deal more than how to paint!' Her eyes twinkled merrily and she raised her glass. 'Here's to us! And may the Queen keep Eddie, the Prince of Wales, off the throne for a long time yet!'

They drank the toast. Then she fetched the champagne bottle and topped up their glasses before setting it down on the floor beside her.

Lisette sank back luxuriously against one of the cushions. 'Although I haven't seen you since you came to our New

Year's party it could have been yesterday that we last met and it has always been the same.'

'You're right. Friendship takes no heed of time or distance.' She took a sip from her glass. 'But I've never quite forgiven you for making me wait months and months before you finally wrote to tell me the reason why and how you escaped from your wedding that night.'

'You know it was only because I didn't want to involve you in my troubles.'

'Yes, I do.' Joanna paused deliberately, twirling her glass by the stem. 'I came face to face with Philippe a few weeks ago.'

'In London?' Lisette asked in surprise.

'Yes, it was one of those crazy, unexpected meetings that come out of the blue. There was a special exhibition at the National Gallery and just by chance we both stopped to look at the same picture. I think it was sheer astonishment on his part and mine that made us converse, because later I wondered why I hadn't cut him and gone by.'

'He was never interested in art when you and I knew him, except to flatter me by praising those watercolours I used to do.'

'Then his wife must be the art lover. He introduced her to me. Her name is Ellen and she's an American from Boston. She was expensively and elegantly dressed. A pretty woman about his age, but with a firm mouth and chin that suggested to me she would not allow any waywardness from him.'

'Do you think he's met his match?'

'Who can say? The meeting lasted only a matter of two or three minutes.' Then her eyes danced. 'But here's the really interesting part. Behind his wife's back he must have watched to see which way I went, because after about five minutes he was suddenly by my side again with no sign of her. That's when he asked about you and wanted to know where you were.'

Lisette blanched. 'You didn't tell him anything?'

'No, of course not! I gave him the perfect answer. I told him he should ask your stepmother for information as he knew her so well! He went crimson with rage and stalked off!'

Lisette flung back her head and laughed. 'You could not have said anything that would have enraged him more.'

'He deserved it! Would you like to hear some news about your stepmother too?'

'Not particularly,' Lisette replied dryly, 'but I can see that you're going to tell me.'

'I met Lorraine from school when I was last in Paris and she told me. Isabelle has married again. An elderly and very wealthy Italian this time, who has homes in Tuscany, Switzerland and Nice, which should give her plenty of scope for amorous intrigues. The château has been closed up with a caretaker in charge.'

'What of my little half-brother?'

'All I heard from Lorraine was that she had seen him once with Isabelle and he is a healthy, fine-looking little boy.'

'I'd like so much to see him again, even though in retrospect I have wondered if he was my father's child.' She let her shoulders rise and fall on a sigh. 'But that hasn't stopped me remembering how I loved him as a baby.'

She wished she could have found the strength to tell Joanna of her own baby, but it was still too painful to share with anyone except Daniel and she believed it would always be the same.

'How is George?' she asked as Joanna refilled her glass.

'Oh, that's all over.' Joanna flapped a hand in dismissal. 'I was very fond of him, because he had a great sense of humour, but he was too much hunting, fishing and shooting for me. I embarrassed him and everybody when I cried during a shoot when they were bringing down all those lovely birds. Now I have someone else.'

'So who is this new man?'

'He's Russian,' Joanna answered enthusiastically, 'and totally beautiful from head to toe. His name is Boris and his surname in unpronounceable.'

'Why is he here in this country?'

'He's on some diplomatic business for the Tsar. It was he who called in one of his fellow countrymen, who is a designer for the stage, to do this room as a gift for me.'

'Shall I meet him?'

'Yes, he's taking us to a gala performance at Covent Garden

Opera House this evening and afterwards we'll be going on to a party. All my friends want to meet you.'

'What a fun way to end this auspicious day!'

Boris was exceptionally handsome, tall and broad-shouldered and extravagantly mannered. He bowed deeply when he kissed Lisette's hand. 'I am honoured, mademoiselle.'

His English was poor, but he spoke French fluently and the three of them conversed in Lisette's own language until they arrived at the party to which they had been invited. Then in between dancing and supper and dancing again he drank himself insensible, but was still beautiful even in his cups. He was left on his host's sofa when Joanna and Lisette went home again.

It was already dawn as the hansom cab carried them through the streets that were empty now except for a number of revellers here and there making their way homewards, still waving flags and wearing patriotic headgear. On the way the cab passed maidservants coming up steps from basement kitchens with jugs or lidded containers to meet the milkmen, who were on their rounds ladling out milk for the households.

'It's a pity Boris doesn't stick to milk instead of alcohol,' Joanna remarked on a sigh. 'That lovely creature will kill himself with it before long, although he'll be back in Russia by then.'

'Shall you be very sad when he leaves England?'

'Yes, for a little while, but I can forget everything when I'm painting. It's as if I lose myself in another world. I'm going to start a portrait of you before you go home to your movie maker.'

Lisette liked Joanna's work. The portraits were strong and yet sensitive, while her landscapes were sweeping, capturing the feeling of space and the open air. In the studio Lisette sat for her against a background of looped grey silk. Yet the two of them were so busy, going to exhibitions and other events by day and partying every night with Boris escorting them, that the portrait was only just finished when the day came for Lisette's departure.

Joanna carried the packaged painting when she went with Lisette to Victoria Station to see her off on the train.

'Now you will come down to the coast again very soon and stay with us, won't you?' Lisette said through the open carriage window.

'I promise,' Joanna said. She stood waving until the train had carried Lisette's fluttering handkerchief of farewell out of sight.

Daniel approved of the painting and had just finished hanging it above the fireplace in the sitting room when Jim arrived in search of him.

'That's fine portrait of you, Miss Decourt,' Jim said admiringly as he stood back to study it carefully. 'There indeed is a face to launch a thousand cameras.'

Daniel grinned. 'How right you are, Jim.'

It seemed to Lisette that the look they exchanged had more to do with her than an admiration of her likeness. Yet she had forgotten about that moment when Daniel mapped out his next project as they sat together in the firelight.

'It will be a story with romance and drama,' he said, full of enthusiasm. 'For the time being comedies will still be made, for those bring in the money, but this time I'm aiming to tell a full story!'

'Your first epic!' she exclaimed, delighted

He grinned. 'That's what it will be!'

'The title?'

'"Out of the Flames."'

'Splendid! What comes out of the flames?'

'Love, of course. It's time to put romance on the screen.'

'I agree!' she exclaimed delightedly.

'There's something else I want to tell you.'

'Yes?' Her eyes were still sparkling from what she had heard already, but as his expression became serious she realized that he had something else on a different line to say to her. Yet his next words were totally unexpected.

'I think we should marry, Lisette?'

She straightened up in her wing chair. 'Why?' she exclaimed in astonishment. 'We decided long ago that neither of us needed marriage in our lives.'

'That was when you were in flight from a man you had no wish to marry and I had not fully overcome a setback in my past.'

'But I don't understand. Whatever has happened to make you change your mind?'

'I have good reason.'

She felt the old fear of being trapped and took refuge in being slightly scornful. 'Don't tell me it's the gossip? I knew there was tittle-tattle long before Mrs Pierce left us and it is still rife.'

'You know me better than that,' he replied soberly.

'Then why do you want to change everything? Surely we're happy as we are! What difference would a marriage certificate make?'

'Suppose we should have a child?'

She was taken aback and averted her eyes from him. It was not chance that she had not become pregnant. 'We had a child,' she exclaimed emotionally. 'One who can never be replaced!'

'Do you think I don't realize that?' He moved across to sit on a footstool beside her and gently turned her face to him again. 'For that child's sake we should be husband and wife. If ever she should come looking for us in years to come it would lift the stigma of illegitimacy from her to find that her parents are married to each other.'

Her eyes were agonized. 'How could she ever find us?'

'One day she's going to see her birth certificate and discover the truth if she has never been told, which is most likely. Maybe it will happen when identification is needed for a passport or perhaps for a marriage, but sooner or later she will discover her true identity.'

'But she's not three years old until May!' Lisette exclaimed in exasperation. 'How can you look so far ahead?'

'Because I love you and will always love you to my last breath. That's why I want the pain in you to heal by your looking to the future instead of being held back by the past. Marry me, Lisette. The time is right for us now.'

She sat very quietly, looking down at her hands resting in her lap. 'You really believe that, don't you?' she said softly.

'With all my heart.'

It was a long time before she finally raised her head and her eyes, warm and loving, gave him his answer. He stood to draw her up from the chair into his arms and kissed her.

Three weeks later they left for France. Lisette wanted to marry in Lyon. An invitation had been sent to Daniel's sister and her husband in Edinburgh, but they declined as he was not well. They sent a very handsome wedding gift which was an elegant silver set of a Georgian coffeepot, teapot, milk jug and sugar basin. Lisette was delighted with it

On the way to Lyon she and Daniel broke their journey for a week in Paris where she met her lawyers and signed some papers concerning her inheritance. As they left the lawyers' chamber again she linked her arm in Daniel's and he grinned into her face.

'I told you that you would always be able to have jam with a croissant.'

She laughed. 'Now I want to go shopping to prove it!'

At the House of Worth she chose a wedding dress and jacket in blue velvet with a fashionably large hat trimmed with ribbons, veiling and silk roses. Daniel had a discreetly splendid suit for the wedding day that had been made by his Saville Row tailors and in the Champs Elysèes she bought him a silk cravat with a trace of blue in it that matched her bridal attire.

When they arrived at the Bellecour house it had been fully opened up at her instruction with fresh flowers in all the main rooms, and temporary staff installed to take care of everything during their stay. Then there began a renewal of friendships for her in the community and introductions for Daniel, who only knew the Lumières. The brothers were continuing their immense success. One of their cameramen had stood in a gondola in Venice and turned his camera slowly around to take the whole panoramic view, which was again a 'first' for the brothers and had already become known as 'panning' a scene.

Two days before the wedding Joanna arrived to be brides-maid. She had chosen her own gown in burgundy silk and a beautiful hat as large as Lisette's with abundant trim-ming. She was so excited to meet the Lumière family, whom she declared were the source of the entire movie industry, that the brothers gave her a tour of the factory and they answered her many questions with patience and a smile at her enthusiasm.

The wedding day dawned bright and sunny, but cold. Multi-coloured sunbeams, coming through a stained glass window, fell full on to Daniel and Lisette as they stood side by side for the service in the church she had always attended as a child. Monsieur Lumière himself took a motion picture of the bridal couple coming out of church, which would be presented to them before they left Lyon again. Joanna departed the day after the wedding with a promise that she would see Lisette and Daniel again soon.

When the time drew near for their departure, Lisette felt the same fierce wrench at the prospect of leaving the old house as she had done previously. Secretly she wished they could have gone on living there with Daniel engaged in work less hectic than movie making, but it was in his blood and nothing could change it.

On the eve of their leaving they went into the blue salon where she opened the bureau and drew forward a sheet of paper. Picking up a pen, she held it out to him.

'You write the letter,' she said.

He gave a serious nod, looking deep into her eyes. 'Do you know now what you want to say?'

'Yes. Do you?'

He nodded. 'I've been giving it a great deal of thought ever since we first discussed it.'

He sat down at the bureau and she rested a hand on his shoulder as together they composed a letter to their daughter. Then they both signed it before he folded it into an envelope. He rose to his feet and took her gently by the shoulders.

'Now we have done everything in our power,' he said quietly. 'Everything else will depend on the convent and meanwhile we must be patient through the years ahead.'

Her head drooped as tears gathered in her eyes. He drew her forward and held her close to him.

They broke their journey to Paris as Lisette had done in the past to visit the convent. To Lisette's relief the abbess was available and agreed to see them. As Daniel's surname was unknown to her she had supposed them to be a couple wanting to adopt, but she recognized Lisette immediately and welcomed her. She listened compassionately as Daniel explained their mission.

'So you see,' he concluded, 'it is our earnest hope that one day our child will want to trace us and perhaps discover that she was born here.'

The abbess gave a little sigh and her sympathetic gaze rested on their anxious faces. 'It is good news that you have found and married each other,' she said, 'but the situation is the same as when you last called here, Lisette. No,' she added as Lisette asked if there had been any communication from Josephine de Vincent. 'We have never heard from her since she left here the last time. Yes, I will take your letter.' She held out her slim-fingered hand to receive it. 'This is not the first time I have had a similar request, but I cannot say there will ever be a result. I have been here twenty-nine years and to date I have never had an inquiry from any of the many children that have been born here.'

It was a depressing statement of fact and Lisette was downcast as they left, until Daniel spoke optimistically to cheer her. 'There's always a first time for everything, and maybe our daughter will surprise Mother Abbess one day by arriving in search of us. We must never give up hope. Remember that sooner or later Marie-Louise will become curious about her origins.'

Lisette managed a smile in an effort to be more cheerful. 'If she has your determination and my stubbornness she should be able to find us wherever we are!'

He grinned. 'That is true!'

The next day they returned to England and the routine of movie making.

As preparations went ahead for *Out of the Flames* Lisette was surprised when Daniel told her that he had chosen a young actress named Betsy Grey to play the heroine. Previously the girl had only appeared in comedies. She was a pretty little thing, but Lisette did not think her acting ability was nearly strong enough to sustain this particular role. It was also known that the girl was nervous about the conflagration scene when she had to be in a burning building, all of which had been arranged with the resort's fire service.

Lisette challenged his decision as they sat with coffee one evening after dinner, for during a rehearsal that day Betsy had dissolved into tears several times at having to repeat a scene yet again.

'I admit Betsy looks the perfect heroine,' she said, 'with her big eyes and naturally rosebud mouth, but you should face the fact that she isn't a good enough actress for this very important role. Your reputation as an exceptional movie maker will stand or fall by this new venture.'

Daniel inclined his head towards her attentively. 'I agree with all you've said. But everything is set up now and where else would I find another actress at such short notice?' He looked persuasively at her. 'Of course, you could always step in.'

She was undeceived, seeing that this was what he had been aiming for over some months. She also remembered the conspiratorial look that he had exchanged with Jim, who had made the remark that her face could launch a thousand cameras. The two of them had been plotting for a situation like this all along!

'Since you need a replacement so urgently,' she conceded, amusement in her eyes, 'I'll take the part. But it's for once only.'

Yet she knew full well that he would keep finding roles for her from now on.

Eighteen

As Lisette had guessed, Betsy Grey was thankful to be replaced, especially as she was given a minor role that was more suited to her talents.

Before rehearsals started Lisette met the young actor, Ronald Davis, who was her own age and would be playing the hero to her heroine. He had only recently joined the studio and was tall, broad-shouldered and handsome with romantically long-lashed dark eyes and a swashbuckling look about him. Lisette thought that women in the audiences would love him on sight. He seemed to think the same, for he exuded self-confidence even though it was his first time in the motion picture business.

'I've been in repertory on stage for two years,' he had told her, 'and so I've played a variety of parts. I was in a major production at the Theatre Royal in Brighton when Mr Shaw saw me and offered me this new experience. Acting in such a very different medium should be an interesting interlude.'

He gave the impression that he had been playing the lead in the major production, but she had been with Daniel at a performance and seen that he had had quite a minor role. In fact it was she who had pointed out to Daniel that he had the looks of a romantic hero.

'Perhaps you will never want to return to the stage,' she suggested. 'With time, many more people would see you on the screen than in a theatre.'

He preened. 'Yes, I should like to be seen as much as possible.'

Lisette thought him insufferably conceited, but she had seen during rehearsals that he could act, sometimes quite sensitively, which was what mattered.

On the day that filming started Lisette emerged from the

make-up room with her eyelashes very black and her lips as rosebud as was possible with her generous mouth. She was wearing one of her own summer dresses and a straw hat with ribbons, which was from the wardrobe room. Tom, who had long since left her domestic employ to work full-time at the studio, gave her a courtly bow copied from one of the actors.

'You look very fine, madam.'

Daniel gave a nod. 'I agree,' he said with a grin as she came towards him. 'Every inch the demure maiden. Now we'll get to work.'

Jim, who always wore his cap back to front in order to keep its peak from getting in the way as he filmed, had set up his camera on its tripod in the lane. He gave her a smiling wink as she passed him. This was his day of triumph. He was getting her before his lens at last.

She went along the lane to take her place at a five-barred gate. There she leaned an arm on it as she gazed into the distance. Today there were sheep in the field, a peaceful scene under a porcelain blue sky flecked with wispy clouds like sugar strands and the soft, undulating line of the grassy downs lay in the far distance. Momentarily letting her thoughts slip, she realized how much she was beginning to feel at home in England.

Daniel's shout through his megaphone broke into her reverie. 'Camera! Action!'

After a few moments, as rehearsed, she moved away from the gate and started strolling leisurely in the direction of the camera. As she passed Ronald, apparently without noticing him, he moved into the lane and gazed after her as if already smitten by love at first sight.

'Cut!' Daniel snapped. Instantly Jim stopped turning the handle of his camera and they exchanged a grin of satisfaction.

For the next scene they all moved into the neighbouring hamlet where at Daniel's prompting through his megaphone Lisette came out of a bakery in time to see Betsy getting her purse snatched. Then she watched in apparent admiration as Ronald gave chase, fought Betsy's attacker and brought him to the ground. With the cooperation of the resort's police force, a Black Maria was driven on to the scene. Then an actor, dressed as a policeman, jumped from it with truncheon and handcuffs to arrest the villain and bundle him into the vehicle. Lisette, watching the action, thought it was as well there was no sound as she could hear the policemen laughing in the vehicle and guessed they had come along to enjoy the action.

Throughout the week the filming of *Out of the Flames* continued with an unwinding of the plot, which included a scene of Betsy shyly giving Ronald a photograph of herself in the hope that she would fix herself firmly in his memory and he would want to see her again. The casual way in which he slipped the photograph into his pocket would confirm to audiences that his heart was already lost to the girl he had seen in the lane.

Most animated picture directors wanted acting on screen to be slightly larger than life for the meaning of everything to be fully understood by audiences, but Daniel believed otherwise. When taking close ups, he wanted expressions to be subtle and all movement to be totally natural. Even when a dramatic indoor scene was to be enacted he warned both Lisette and Ronald not to exaggerate their gestures in any way.

It was to be filmed as every indoor scene had to be: in the open air. On the wheeled platform a backcloth of a sitting room had been set up with plywood walls, one inset with a door, on either side. The furnishing consisted of a rag rug, two chairs and a table laid for tea. The plot had brought Lisette and Ronald to the point of his declaring his love. The breeze fluttered the tablecloth and played with Lisette's hair as she poured the tea, but Daniel said the audience would be too enthralled to notice, especially when Ronald took up Lisette's hand and kissed it, his handsome eyes very eloquent. But then the photograph of Betsy fell from his pocket and Lisette viewed it with an anguished gaze.

The sequence of the quarrel then took place, both Lisette and Ronald enjoying the enactment of the clash between them, she in tears at his deceit and he throwing his arms about in protest at being unjustly accused of unfaithfulness. In a final gesture he tore up the photograph to show that it belonged to the past, but when Lisette refused to be convinced and turned her back on him, he rushed off the set in a fine show of despair. All those standing around clapped enthusiastically.

Two days later Jim set up his camera again. Everybody was on site early at the derelict house that was to be burnt down in the climax of the movie. The resort's fire brigade arrived on time, brass helmets and the clanging fire bell well polished and flashing back the sunshine. Word had spread beyond the studio that the brigade was to be involved in the filming and local people from both the neighbouring hamlet and the resort gathered to watch the spectacle, not realizing that their presence would add to the realism of the scene. There was some delay when the chief of the brigade, resplendent in the silver helmet that denoted his rank, felt that he should rescue the heroine.

'We always keep the public well back and out of danger,' he insisted. 'No bystander would get past us.'

It took Daniel quite a little while to persuade the chief that for once the situation had to be otherwise. The previous day's shots had been of Lisette at one of the upper windows of the doomed house, crying out for help with arms outflung. Behind her and out of sight one of the crew had wafted the smoke of some smouldering rags around her as if the house were already on fire. Then Ronald had been filmed running towards the house to rescue her. Now all was ready for the climax of the film.

Two firemen set light to the building and the spectators, whose numbers were increasing all the time, cheered. As the flames took hold Jim began turning the handle of his camera. Then, before it became too dangerous, Lisette and Ronald slipped into the front entrance to be ready for him to carry her out in his arms. But when Daniel's voice boomed through the megaphone, telling them to emerge, Ronald held back.

'Let's wait a few more seconds!' he suggested eagerly. 'It will build up the suspense.'

'No!' she answered impatiently. 'If we delay now the fire brigade will ruin everything by charging in to rescue both of us!'

The sudden crashing down of a timber beam upstairs ended any further idea he had of remaining longer. Snatching Lisette up in his arms, he rushed out of the building in a burst of genuine panic that was most effective and the camera captured it all.

The next morning, Lisette, in bridal attire, her veil flowing from a garland of flowers encircling her head, and Ronald in his best suit were filmed coming out of the resort's ancient church in a final fade-out. The whole film would last a new, revolutionary fifty minutes. Its subsequent success put an end to a great many debates in the press and elsewhere as to whether a screen could hold an audience's attention in the same way as action on a theatre stage.

Work continued every day at the Shaw Studio and the months slipped past. Lisette was not in everything that was filmed, because knockabout comedies were still being made as well as minor productions in which she played no part. During these times she dealt with scripts, some of which came by post from would-be scriptwriters. One of her former tasks on site had been keeping her eye on continuity, making sure that nothing was changed in clothing or props or anything else when the filming of one scene took longer than a day, but now an observant young woman had been employed for that duty.

In the spring of 1899 Daniel launched another major production, which came about by chance when a jumbled collection of dusty, neglected looking garments from an attic were among the items to be sold at a local auction. Mrs Leigh, always on the lookout for anything the studio could use, examined them with interest. Afterwards she reported to Lisette, who had taken charge of many behind the scenes matters to save Daniel from unnecessary work,

'We could use those silks for all sorts of costumes,' the dressmaker said eagerly.

Lisette went to view the garments the day before the auction and realized they were genuine Chinese kimonos. At the auction itself nobody was seriously interested in the garments and Lisette managed to get them for a surprisingly low price. Mrs Leigh and Ethel promptly went to work mending and washing and ironing what proved to be some lovely silks. They caused Lisette to remember a script that she had read not long after coming to England. She found it in a file. It was the story of a Chinese girl loved and abandoned by an English lord touring China, but rescued by the true love of a mandarin. Daniel, confronted with the need for a Chinese atmosphere and the virtual impossibility of getting any Chinese actors, baulked at first from giving the script serious consideration. But Lisette was persuasive and soon the production of *Passion Flower* was set into action.

The carpenters had made rickshaws and Mrs Leigh some Chinese coolie hats. With the absence of any Chinese actors the entire cast had black lines drawn by their eyes to give them an oriental slant, except Ronald, who was playing the English lord. He had shown signs of temperament before, his head turned by the flattering attention he received from women who came to watch him act whenever the opportunity arose, but this time he was being extremely difficult.

'I should win the heroine!' he declared fiercely, his cheeks flushed with indignation. 'Casting her aside will put me in a bad light with audiences.'

He had an ally in Lisette, who agreed with him. Already he was an asset that she did not want the studio to lose to another company. Immediately she did some rewriting of the script to make the mandarin the villain while the English lord became the hero. It was a relief to her when both Daniel and Jim agreed that after all it would be a better ending for more reasons than one.

Daniel was having no problem with the outdoor scenes supposedly set in China. The local owner of a fine estate had collected and planted many exotic trees from warmer climes and, having met Daniel on several occasions, gave him permission to film there. The owner and his wife and all his family, including aunts, uncles and cousins, gathered on his veranda and watched rickshaws pulled by coolies and dramatic scenes enacted that could have been taking place in China.

For important indoor scenes Daniel went to nearby Brighton where the Royal Pavilion, once owned by the Prince Regent, had an exotic Chinese interior. Although Daniel had never visited the palace, for it had been closed for many years and was not open to the public, he had read about it. So he made his request to those in charge of the building and such was the enthusiasm for motion pictures that he was given special permission to film inside for one day only.

It was generally known that Queen Victoria had no liking for the Royal Pavilion and, although its furniture and other items had long since been crated up and sent into storage at Buckingham Palace, a few oriental pieces did remain in situ. When the dust covers were removed and shutters taken down from the tall windows a surprising amount of light flooded into the exotically beautiful rooms, highlighting the Chinese decor, which was exactly what was required for the Mandarin's palace. With the glow of every oil lamp from the studio combining with the exceptional brightness of the day, Daniel was able to film amid the richness and splendour that the passing of time had not decayed.

By the time *Passion Flower* was being shown all over the country with acclaim from audiences everywhere, Daniel had produced two more fifty-minute motion pictures. As Maisie's preparations for Christmas filled the air with the appetizing aroma of newly baked fruit cake and mince pies, Lisette was astonished that another year should have gone by so swiftly.

The arrival of the New Year heralding the twentieth century was celebrated with parties everywhere. As 1900 was toasted in champagne, Lisette hoped fervently that this new century would be peaceful and prosperous. Privately she added the wish to become pregnant for Daniel's sake. For herself it was enough that she cherished the memory of the baby that had been taken from her, but she knew that he wanted children and it was more for his sake than her own that she had not taken any preventative measures since their marriage. She felt it was a cruel irony that conception should have taken place instantly in her first coming together with Daniel, but now that she had prepared herself for motherhood it was being denied her.

The jubilation over the arrival of the twentieth century was dashed away the following year when the beloved Queen died and the whole country went into mourning, even schoolchildren wearing black sashes to mark their respect. Daniel's cameramen filmed the London funeral that gathered all the crowned heads of Europe, and this was duly shown all over the country.

As the months and years went by Daniel's motion pictures continued to be successful. Now that Lisette was taking the leading role in all his most important works her face as well as her name was becoming known to audiences. She was surprised and pleased when she began receiving mail that praised her acting. Now and again one would come from the United States where some of Daniel's productions had been shown. Yet these were always a poignant reminder of her child growing up so far away, making her wonder yet again whereabouts in that vast land she might be.

Always in May on her daughter's birthday she tried to imagine how the day would be celebrated. During the early years there would have been other toddlers to share a birthday cake and later when Marie-Louise was a little older there would be games at the parties with her playmates. But what would there be on Marie-Louise's forthcoming seventh birthday in this year of 1902. Perhaps a Punch and Judy show – or didn't they have those in America? Maybe a visit to the circus? Perhaps even a magic lantern show specially for children?

She never shared these thoughts with Daniel, even though he would have been sympathetic and consoling, for she did not want him to concern himself about her when he was often harassed by delays and other complications at work. His interest in the United States was in what his American counterparts were producing. This interest had been sparked off when he had seen an American movie combining glamour and comedy when a row of pretty girls entered a rocket, which had promptly landed in the eye of the moon, which had a human face. At first most filming had been done in New York, but now the motion picture companies were all moving to California where they were building studios in what had been a large country estate known as Hollywood. He thought them fortunate to have both the right weather at all times and the space to further their productions.

He was away on one of his business trips when Lisette found herself feeling tired and even exhausted after a day's filming. It still took a little while for her to realize that at last she was pregnant. Daniel had planned that his next film should be the story of Robin Hood, but now he would have to find someone else to take her role of Maid Marion.

She had decided to wait and tell him her news when he returned, although they did have a telephone installed in the cottage now and she could have told him on one of his calls. She knew he would be overjoyed, but she felt only trepidation herself, for whenever he had spoken of his hopes for a family she had never disclosed her most secret fear. It was that she would find that she could never love another child as she had loved her daughter, for she was desperately afraid she would resent the usurper taking Marie-Louise's place.

Yet as the spasms of morning sickness began to ebb all her doubts and anxieties seemed to go with them. She became quite tranquil in her mind, even beginning to hope with a quietly joyous anticipation that it was a brother for Marie-Louise that had taken life within her.

It was the night before Daniel's return when a thunderous knocking on the front door awakened her. Throwing on a robe, she came to the head of the stairs in time to see Maisie, similarly clad, opening the door to Tom.

'There's a fire!' he shouted. 'At the studios! I saw it from home and my dad has sent for the fire brigade! Tell Mr Shaw to come at once!'

'He's not here,' Maisie gasped, but he did not hear her, already off at a run back to the scene of the fire. She looked up over her shoulder and caught a glimpse of Lisette as she ran back into the bedroom. 'Don't you go, madam! Let me see what is happening!'

Lisette was already throwing on her clothes. She was downstairs and out of the house before Maisie or her daughter knew it. The glow lighting up the sky told her at once that a fierce fire had taken hold.

She ran to the motorcar, but the winding handle defeated her, failing to give life to the engine. Leaving it, she began to run. By now Maisie and Daisy, fully clothed, had come out of the house and set off in her wake. The fire engine, its bell clanging, overtook them as well as others that had emerged from houses and cottages to flock towards the fire, many only in dressing gowns and slippers.

By the time Lisette arrived on the scene the hoses were already playing on the flames of the barn-studio, but it was not only there that the fire was raging. She clapped a hand over her mouth in dismay. Every building on the site was burning. Through the smoke she saw Jim and another man rolling away canisters in which reels of finished films were stored and she hoped they had managed to save others. Everywhere else people were forming bucket chains. She rushed to join one of them where people were trying to douse the flames of Daniel's office.

She lost count of time. It was like being caught up in a nightmare of noise and heat and smoke. All she knew was that after a while it felt as if her arms would fall out of their sockets as bucket after bucket was sloshed from hand to hand. Once Maisie tried in vain to drag her out of the chain, shouting that she must think of her baby, but when Lisette paid her no attention, seeming not to hear her, she joined the line herself, Daisy at her side.

All around there was the sound of collapsing timbers and the shouts of those trying to master the flames. A fire brigade from Chichester joined the local one, but their hoses failed to save the ancient barn, warning shouts scattering people in all directions as it finally caved in with a vast firework display of golden sparks

Gradually all in the chains began to drop their buckets, able to see there was nothing more they could do, for every building, large or small, had become a furnace or a blackened, smoking shell. Lisette stood staring in dismay until Maisie came to put an arm around her and lead her away. It was dawn. A man with a lorry gave them a ride home.

Later that day Lisette miscarried. When Daniel returned that evening, Maisie having managed to leave a telephone message about the fire at his hotel, he went first to the site of his burned-out studio, not knowing that other distressing news awaited his return home.

Nineteen

Daniel did everything in his power to comfort Lisette over her miscarriage, but she became hollow-eyed in her grief until she realized how much he needed her support in the great financial loss that he had suffered. Then she put her own deep sadness aside to concentrate on helping him. The insurance would cover a great deal of what Daniel had lost, but he could not rebuild on the same site, for the farmer, who had always been difficult, had curtailed their agreement over the renting of the land, which meant a court case and all the expense that would be involved if Daniel should contest the matter.

It had been established that arson had caused the fire, each building having been doused with an inflammable liquid, but no obvious culprit could be traced. Lisette suspected the farmer himself or perhaps one of his farmhands doing his bidding, but it was impossible to prove anything.

Without Daniel's knowledge Lisette wrote to her Paris lawyers and instructed them to sell all she owned, including the Bellecour house and the land that her grandmother had bequeathed her. It was a heart-tearing wrench to let the house go, but Daniel needed immediate financial help and at least she could do that for him.

The lawyers replied that they were carrying out her instructions over the sale of the land, which had soared in value over the past two years, but instead of selling the house, which was a valuable property, they advised renting it to reliable tenants and that would provide her with a sizeable regular income. In view of the high price that the land was expected to fetch she accepted their advice over the house, thankful in her heart not to be parting with it, and gave them permission to arrange the tenancy.

When notification of the completed sale of the land reached her she could scarcely believe the amount raised. Immediately she went to Daniel, the letter in her hand, and found him seated at his desk.

'Look!' she exclaimed joyously, thrusting the letter in front of him. 'Our financial troubles are over! You can have the studios that you want wherever you wish to build them!'

He took the letter and read it through before looking up at her, frowning incredulously. 'You've let tenants into the Bellecour house!' he exclaimed on a note that showed he was far from pleased. 'Were you out of your mind? That meant everything to you! And that land? Why didn't you discuss it with me first?'

She saw that he was not going to react with total pleasure as she had expected. Quite the reverse. There was only one way to save the situation and in any case it was time that she told him what had been in her mind for so long.

'It's been my hope that one day I could become your partner in business as well as in marriage,' she said quickly. 'You can't deny that I have learned all the ins and outs of the animated picture industry, from judging scripts to acting, and I've even operated a camera on several occasions.'

'Yes. I know. But—'

She interrupted him. 'Hear me out before you say any more!' she implored. 'This is just the time, now that you will be starting up all over again, for a legal agreement to be drawn up for a partnership between us. I want to buy into Shaw Studios! Don't say you won't accept me!'

He turned in his chair and put his arms about her hips to draw her close, burying his face against her for a few moments before raising his head to meet her eyes again. 'If a partnership means that much to you, then of course I accept you, but one day you must have your old home back for you alone.'

She took his face between her hands and kissed him. 'One day,' she repeated.

On his travels Daniel had seen three or four sites suitable for studios and he and Lisette went to view each one together. One was already sold with house building in progress, but they both reached the same conclusion about a favourable

site on the outskirts of London. There would be easy communication and enough land for later expansion. He would
continue filming outside in good daylight, but as soon as he
could get electricity installed the vagaries of the weather
would no longer be such a problem. Meanwhile, the additional erection of a large glass studio would allow work to
progress most of the time by keeping out wind and weather.

Lisette had the task of finding the right house for their
new home and settled on a pleasant, newly built residence
with a large garden not far from the studios. It was well-
proportioned with spacious, elegant rooms on three floors,
a large kitchen area and a wine cellar in the basement. There
was also a housekeeper's suite that met with Maisie Jones's
approval. This time there was an attic room that made
comfortable accommodation for Daisy and would give her
privacy away from her mother. Yet it was Daisy who was
the least happy over the move. She had left behind her first
real beau, a farmer's son, and she doubted that he would
keep his promise to write to her. Yet a few letters did come,
although inevitably they finally trickled away. By that time
the son of a local butcher was taking her out and Maisie
encouraged it. The joints and steaks that were delivered were
the best to be had anywhere.

By now Daniel's studios were busy all the time and apart
from using some of Lisette's exceptionally good scripts he
was buying work from other quality writers, which increased
the variety of his productions. Ever since the Lumières had
created the demand for animated pictures there had been film
agents springing up everywhere, competing with one another
to secure contracts for as many motion picture releases as
they could grab, but from the start Daniel had kept a firm
hand on his business interests and was able to dictate his
terms.

He was among the first to insert captions into his films to
aid a complicated plot and had a number of favoured actors,
both male and female, that he liked to include in his cast.
He continued to produce comedies, but for longer productions he concentrated on historical themes, which had become
increasingly popular with audiences, and mostly Lisette took
the lead. In three years she played Joan of Arc, Eleanor of

Aquitaine, Nell Gwyn and Queen Elizabeth, among other
important roles. Always she threw herself into her work, her
acting gaining a new sensitivity that had originated from the
emotional crisis of her miscarriage. In close-ups her face,
unmarred now by the heavier make-up of the past, conveyed
the finest changes of expression and, if tears were necessary,
her violet eyes could brim at will. She sometimes felt that
she had had a deep well of tears within her ever since Marie-
Louise was taken from her.

Before it became known that she and Daniel were part-
ners in Shaw Studies there had been a number of unsuc-
cessful attempts by other movie makers to tempt her away
from his productions into their own. She had also turned
down stage roles that she had been offered by London
producers until Daniel thought it would be good publicity
for her to be seen in person by the public. As a first step he
made an event out of a premiere of her latest movie at one
of the leading London theatres that alternated motion pictures
with musical comedies and plays.

When the movie ended to thunderous applause the audience remained in their seats, knowing that they were to see
her. Then Daniel, handsome in white tie and tails, introduced
her from the stage.

'Ladies and gentlemen, it gives me great pleasure to present
the star of the evening, Lisette Shaw!'

When she appeared in a long, sparkling gown there was
a standing ovation, during which she was presented with a
bouquet of red roses that Daniel had ordered specially, but
others had had the same idea. Bunches of flowers were
brought to the stage in such numbers that it was impossible
for her to hold them all and she stood as though in the midst
of a flower garden. The applause followed her off the stage.

'You called me a "star".' she said later. 'What made you
think of that?'

He shrugged on a happy grin. 'You dazzled. What better
term could I have used?'

Afterwards the publicity that he issued always referred to
her as the star of Shaw Studios. Eventually the term became
generally used in the animated picture industry.

Three months after her premiere appearance, Lisette

appeared in a London production of *Hedda Gabler*. It was
the ultimate test of her acting ability, but she carried the role
well. One newspaper critic wrote that it was not just on the
screen that she could wring hearts and she received similar
favourable reviews from others. But she was glad when its
run ended and she could return to the medium that she liked
best.

'Movies are my life now,' she said, her fingers linked
behind Daniel's neck as he held her to him. 'Just as they are
yours.'

But he was concerned about her. She looked extremely
tired and had lost weight, the demanding role she had played
having taken its toll.

'You need a holiday before we talk of any more work for
you. Why not visit Joanna in Monte Carlo while she is still
renting that villa there? You can leave this winter weather
behind and enjoy some sunshine. She has invited you to visit
several times.'

Lisette closed eyes blissfully for a moment. 'A holiday in
the sun. What a tempting thought! But could you come with
me? She has always included you in her invitations.'

He shook his head regretfully. 'Not at the present time,
but maybe I could manage a few days when you're ready to
come home again.'

She knew he meant what he said, but doubted that he
would have the time to spare if he should be in the middle
of directing new work.

'I shall break my journey south to call at the convent,' she
told him. 'I know that there can't be any news of our daughter,
but the abbess is old and if she should be replaced through
ill health at any time I want to know about it. Then I could
make sure that her successor was fully informed about our
letter and it would not lie forgotten in a drawer.'

Privatley he wished Lisette would not to go there, knowing
how it evoked painful memories for her, but he would not
interfere. Since her miscarriage she had begun to pin such
hopes on that letter and he would have liked to be able to
share her optimism to the same degree.

It was raining hard when the train from Paris brought
Lisette to her destination. Taking a seat in a waiting cab, she

told the driver to take her to the convent. He turned to look back over his shoulder at her.

'Are you sure that's where you want to go, madame? There's nothing left of the convent since the fire.'

She thought her heart stopped in shock at his words. 'What do you mean?' she asked falteringly, the colour draining from her face.

'Six months ago a fire started in the kitchen and took hold quickly, spreading throughout the building. Those old timbers burned like matchwood.'

'What of the inmates?' she gasped, horrified.

'A few suffered minor burns, but nothing fatal. They've been dispersed to other convents, the surviving nuns going with them. One nun was crushed under a falling beam as she tried to save the abbess, who was probably dead already as she had been trapped in her study, which was like a furnace.' He was like many bearers of bad news in feeling important from the drama of it, but when he realized the effect his information was having on her he spoke more gently. 'I can see you're shocked, madame, but it could have been a lot worse. Do you still want me to take you there or is there somewhere else you'd like to go?'

She passed a hand across her forehead, trying to gather her thoughts together. 'Take me to the hotel in the square.'

It was where she and Daniel had stayed overnight when they had visited the convent together and now, as on that occasion, there was no train to suit a continuation of her journey until the next morning. Her trunk had been sent ahead to Joanna's address, but she had come prepared with hand baggage, never supposing that the purpose of her visit would be totally in vain.

In the morning she did let a cab take her past the scorched ruins of the convent before going to the railway station. Already the site had been partially cleared. Tears filled her eyes at the sight as she grieved for the two women that had lost their lives there and forced herself to accept that the last hope for a reunion with her daughter had gone for ever.

It was warm and sunny when Lisette arrived in Monte Carlo. She knew from Joanna's letters that a host of royal personages and other distinguished visitors had arrived at the start of the season to enjoy its pleasures, including gambling at the famous casino. A cab from the railway station took her to a peach-tinted villa with dark green shutters that had a view of the Mediterranean and was set in a tree-shaded flower garden on a slope of a hill. Joanna, wearing a paint-daubed smock, her bright curls tied up with a ribbon, came running to meet her with open arms.

'Welcome, Lisette! How wonderful to see you again! This is going to be like old times!'

They hugged each other in greeting and then Joanna held her by the shoulders at arm's, length to look at her with concern.

'You've been ill,' she stated.

Lisette shook her head, evading her friend's direct gaze, 'Not at all. I've been working hard and it's left me in need of a rest.'

'It's more than that. You and Daniel aren't splitting up, are you?'

'No! No!' Again Lisette shook her head. 'The truth is I received a shock yesterday and I'll tell you about it later.'

Joanna looked concerned, but did not pursue her questioning. She knew Lisette well enough to see that something very serious had given that stark look to her eyes. 'I read your *Hedda Gabler* reviews in the English newspapers, but I had just arrived here then and couldn't return to see your performance. I never realized when we were at school that you would reach your full potential as an actress. Yet I do remember when you played Lady Macbeth during our last term there that your fear and confusion after the crime moved me to tears.'

Lisette showed surprise. 'Did I really have that effect on you? I never knew. But I was always sure that you would become an artist of renown. I hope you'll let me see all your latest work.'

'There's plenty of time for that. Now I'll show you to your room and afterwards we'll sit out in the shade and have a glass of wine and catch up with each other's news.'

It was the start of a companionable time that slipped by with no notice taken of the passing of one week and then another. Lisette told Joanna at last of her baby's adoption and it took all her will power not to break down completely when she spoke of the burnt-out convent and the destruction of her hopes.

'My life has twice fallen apart through a fire,' she said quietly. 'The first caused me to miscarry and the second has severed the last chance of my ever finding Marie-Louise again.'

'Oh, my dear friend!' Joanna exclaimed in distress, her own eyes filling with tears. 'How desperately sad you must be! I wish so much I could help you in this matter.'

'Your friendship is a help in itself,' Lisette replied gratefully.

Daniel had written consolingly to her after she had sent a letter telling him of the convent fire. She wrote regularly to him, but after his first reply his letters were as usual short and obviously hastily scrawled. She could picture him dashing them off whenever he remembered. She knew it would not be a case of out of sight and out of mind, but he was engrossed in preparation for another movie and that would be taking up every minute of his days.

She had plenty of leisurely time to herself, for Joanna had a very capable and fierce-looking housekeeper in charge of everything and it was advisable to keep out of her way. So, seated in the shade of a tree. Lisette read from Joanna's collection of books, kept up with the news in the papers, and jotted down ideas for future productions to discuss with Daniel when she was home again, all of which kept her out of the way while her friend was at work in her studio.

She also went for a daily stroll, always pausing to gaze out at the magnificent yachts in the harbour where the sea flashed diamonds that dazzled the eye in the glorious weather. It was also enjoyable to observe the fashions. The S-shaped figure still relied on corsetry, but silhouettes were softer, although continued to be crowned with large, gloriously trimmed hats with flowers and ribbons in abundance, some with floating veils, which with pastel-hued parasols gave additional protection to complexions from the sun. By day Lisette kept to a delicate veil, which helped her to remain incognito most of the time. Yet she recognized many well-known people and although portly King Edward was staying at his favourite resort of Nice she saw him several times, always with a beautiful woman at his side.

Sometimes Joanna's elderly uncle, a charming old gentleman who resided in Monte Carlo, took them out to dine and to the casino afterwards. It was during these occasions that smiles and stares told Lisette that there were animated picture goers among the well-dressed and the bejewelled, who knew her from the silver screen.

The evenings spent at the villa were quite different when nobody cared who she was, which was a relief. After Joanna had put aside her brushes and palette for the day a motley crowd would descend on her, spilling out on to the lawn with food and drink to sprawl on the grass or in comfortable wicker chairs. There were intellectuals, artists and some whose occupations were a mystery, but who wore the oddest clothes, and other interesting people who liked to get into deep discussions about one topic or another. None of Joanna's former beaux were among them. Sometimes there were parties at other venues that could vary from an artist's studio to a luxurious hotel suite or a magnificent mansion overlooking the sea. As in London, Joanna's friends and acquaintances came from all walks of life, but here she did not have a current lover.

'Has there ever been anyone with whom you would have liked to form a permanent relationship?' Lisette asked one morning when Joanna was sketching her in the garden.

'There was someone once,' Joanna answered quietly, her pencil becoming still in her hand, 'but he was married and the scandal of a divorce would have ruined his political career. So that was that.' She shrugged her shoulders and resumed her sketching. 'We have to take whatever life brings along.'

The peace and quiet of the days did much to help Lisette recover from the shock over the destroyed convent that she had received and, even though heartache remained, she lost the gaunt look that she had had on arrival. She had also regained some of the weight she had lost over past months. Soon, feeling well and rested, she was ready to go home again, but there was no chance of Daniel coming to Monte Carlo for a few days as she had hoped. He had written that he was too busy, but knowing that she intended to go shopping in Paris for a day or two on her way home, he asked her to select the best settings for the historical movie he aimed to film in France. She was not surprised by his request, knowing that he had long wanted her to play Marie Antoinette.

'I shall miss you when you leave at the end of the week,' Joanna said with a sigh. 'It has been fun having you here. I shall also be sorry when my rental of this villa is at an end, but I have to get back to London in good time for my next exhibition.' Then she smiled broadly, clapping her hands together. 'Let's go on our own to the casino this evening. We'll try to break the bank and then we can each go home with a fortune!'

That evening Lisette put on a favourite cream silk gown with a low décolletage and added a diamond pendant and earrings that Daniel had given her. With a gossamer wrap about her shoulders she came downstairs to meet Joanna, who was striking in purple with sequins, and together they set off in a hired carriage.

No sooner had they mounted the steps of the casino and passed through the marble-pillared entrance into the red and gold gaming rooms than people they knew greeted them on all sides and there were pauses to chat here and there. Then they took the only two vacant chairs at their favourite roulette table, although it meant that they were at opposite ends. Lisette lost a little and won a couple of times before the seat next to her was vacated and somebody else took it. She did not look to see who it was, concentrating on placing her chips. Then as the roulette wheel began to spin the newcomer spoke to her.

'It's a long time since we first met on a train, Lisette.'

She felt a shiver of apprehension pass down her spine, for she would have known that deep, articulate voice anywhere. Her eyes wide, she turned her head sharply to look full into the face of Philippe Bonnard. Then, making her catch her breath, she felt a swift surge of the long forgotten love that she had once felt for him. It was part of the shock of seeing him again, but then reason returned and her acting ability took over. Appearing perfectly composed, she regarded him with a cool smile, even though a kind of dread lingered in the pit of her stomach as if some danger lay in this encounter with the past.

'Yes, it has been some years, Philippe. You look well.'

'I'm in excellent health.' A narrow moustache now enhanced his handsomeness. 'You, Lisette, are more beautiful than ever. This is such a pleasure to meet you again. I'm staying in Nice, but came here with friends this evening to try our luck at these tables. I have seen you on the silver screen several times.'

'Have you?' she commented evenly.

'Allow me to congratulate you on becoming such a fine actress.'

'Thank you, Philippe,' she answered. The roulette wheel had stopped and she had lost again, but it was of no importance. She gathered up her silver-threaded evening purse to move away from him to another table with some alternative play. She had wondered very occasionally in the distant past how she would feel if ever their paths crossed again. Now that had happened. Although all animosity towards him had long since melted away his presence had cast a cloud over her and she did not want to be drawn into further conversation with him. Yet he had risen to his feet with her before she could say goodbye.

'Yes, we can't talk there,' he said as if she could not have had any other reason for leaving the table, and he took her elbow possessively to guide her away to a quieter place where they could sit down together, but she drew to a halt. They stood facing each other out of earshot of others in a buzz of background conversation and the clear voices of the croupiers.

'I heard a while ago that you had married, Philippe,' she said, 'and wished you well.'

'That was generous of you, Lisette.'

'Is your wife at one of the tables?' she enquired, glancing about.

'No. Ellen is in the States at the present time, visiting her family in Boston. Her father has not been well and she wanted to spend some time with him.'

'I hope she will return with good news. Now I must rejoin Joanna. Did you see that she is here?'

He nodded, but showed no interest. 'Where are you staying in Monte Carlo? Which hotel?'

'None of them. I'm staying with Joanna at a villa that she is renting.'

'Ellen and I went to one of her exhibitions when we were in London. I asked Joanna about you then, but she was quite hostile towards me, even though my wife had just bought one of her paintings. Frankly, I thought it damned expensive for a few daubs of colour. Did Joanna never tell you that she and I had met again?'

'She mentioned it,' Lisette replied.

He shrugged in amusement and grinned with all his old charm. 'I thought it might have slipped her mind. She never did like me. I remember you were quite an artist in your own right with your watercolours. In my opinion, they were much better than any of her present paintings. Do you still paint?'

'I don't have time these days.' She looked beyond him to where Joanna had risen from the roulette table and was beckoning fiercely to her. 'I must go. I see that Joanna is ready to move on to another table.'

He raised his hand in a gesture of appeal that she should spare him a few more minutes. 'Now that we have met again as – I hope! – old friends with the hatchet well and truly buried, I'd like to hear about your career and what guided you into acting. Have lunch with me tomorrow.'

'I was planning on packing tomorrow. I'm leaving for Paris the next day.'

'Paris? Shall you be involved in animated picture work there?'

She fielded his question. 'I'm planning to shop,' she said truthfully. Then to avoid any more questions she added, 'I shall certainly pay a nostalgic visit to the Grand Cafe and see the Indian room where the Lumières set the motion picture ball rolling. Then I'll go home.'

'You call England home?' he said in surprise.

'I consider that I have two homelands – France where I was born and England where I live.'

'Then if you're already in a nostalgic mood about the Grand Cafe I think you could extend a little of it towards me for old times' sake and spare two hours to lunch with me tomorrow.'

She frowned. 'Over past years I have never been the least nostalgic about you, Philippe!'

He was not daunted, a wide smile playing about his mouth while his eyes danced good-humouredly. 'I can understand why, but I feel that at least you should tell me how you managed to disappear from the château on the eve of our wedding and then vanish completely from the face of the earth!'

She was wryly amused by his curiosity. 'Yes, I did manage that rather well, didn't I?'

'Then you will meet me?'

She hesitated briefly. 'Very well. But now I must get back to Joanna.'

Arrangements were made. They would meet at one of Monte Carlo's best restaurants. She had her own special reason for accepting his invitation, for she was hoping that he would be able to tell her the whereabouts of her half-brother and even have some news of him.

'So until tomorrow,' Philippe said, bowing over her hand. Then Lisette turned to find Joanna waiting a little distance away with a grim expression on her face.

'Why have you been wasting time with him?' she demanded fiercely as Lisette approached. 'He belongs to the past.'

'Of course he does, but in a way I'm grateful to him.'

'Grateful?' Joanna exploded in disbelief. 'After the way he treated you!'

'But if he hadn't had that *affaire* with Isabelle I would never have met Daniel.'

'You're being very forgiving.'

Lisette laughed. 'Why not? A great deal of water has flowed under the bridge since he was all I wanted in life.'

'Was he drunk this evening? He was at my exhibition.'

'There was wine on his breath, but he was not drunk and had his wits about him.'

'Let's forget him now and choose another table. I'm on a winning streak.'

Joanna led the way. Lisette, following, realized she still had to break the news that she had accepted Phillippe's invitation to lunch. She knew that Joanna would not be pleased.

Twenty

A s Lisette lunched with Philippe she thought it was as if the clock had been turned back, for they talked as easily as if there had been no time between. Yet there was one great difference. She saw him now as the philanderer that he would always be and not a trace remained of her own passion for him. When he had first spoken to her in the casino that momentary flash of what she had once felt for him had been a trick of memory and nothing more.

A violin was being played and there were potted palms everywhere that gave some privacy to conversation. He gave her news of mutual friends and acquaintances and, as she had hoped, was able to tell her about her half-brother.

'Maurice is in the same class at boarding school as my godson, Robert, and they are good friends. So whenever I do my godfather's duty by taking Robert out to luncheon during the school term time, I let Maurice tag along too. He does not get home often as the château is only opened up for Isabelle's infrequent visits and he usually has to go elsewhere during vacations. It's my belief that Isabelle doesn't care to be seen with a tall, sixteen-year-old son. I suppose she still thinks she looks like a belle of twenty, but the reverse is the case. Not that she ever speaks to me these days. She blamed me entirely for your running away.'

Lisette had no interest in hearing about her stepmother. 'Do you see any Decourt family resemblance in Maurice?'

He narrowed his eyes, regarding her with a cynical smile playing about his mouth. 'He's not my son, if that's what you're asking.'

'Of course not! I know that!' she answered impatiently. 'You had only been back in France a matter of weeks before the christening, but there may have been others before you.'

'You're right. I happen to know that I wasn't her first indiscretion and certainly not her last, but whether Maurice is like your father or anyone else I couldn't say. He is quite a scholar at school, according to Robert, who has nothing else in his head beyond sport and girls.' Then a waiter came to remove their plates and another swiftly set cups for their coffee. Philippe sat back in his chair until they were gone and then he leaned forward again to ask her the question that he had been waiting to voice throughout the meal. 'Now tell me, Lisette. How did you manage to disappear?'

She stirred cream into her coffee. 'Take your mind back to that last evening when we went to a magic lantern show,' she began.

He listened intently as she gave an account of her escape, adding how afterwards Daniel had employed her as his assistant and that eventually they had married after he had moved into the motion picture world. She gave no mention of anything that had happened in between. 'Now I'm going home to work, although I enjoy my career so much that even though I get very tired sometimes acting is never a chore to me.'

He looked at her shrewdly. 'Are you acting now? Pretending that there is still no bond between us? Nothing of our love still left?'

She regarded him steadily. 'Philippe, be sensible. I was very young and gullible in those days while you thought that marrying an heiress would settle your gaming debts for the rest of your life. There was no real love between us.'

'You're being very blunt and extremely cruel.'

'Cruel?' she echoed with wry amusement. 'I didn't enjoy seeing you and Isabelle in the summerhouse.'

His eyebrows shot up and he gave a little gasp. 'So that was when you found out!' Then he gave a hoot of laughter. 'That must have made you grow up!'

His shallowness exasperated her. She no longer had any patience with him and was glad the meal was at an end.

'I think we've talked enough about the past,' she said firmly, 'and now I must get back to the villa.'

'Give me a few minutes more,' he said very seriously. 'I did love you in spite of everything. Losing you was the greatest shock I had ever received and I soon realized what a fool I had been.'

She looked steadily at him with a slight smile. 'I happen to believe that, Philippe, but it is a long time ago now.'

His serious expression did not lift, but he signalled to the waiter and settled the bill. Outside the restaurant he saw her into a cab and as she rode away she heaved a sigh of relief that she would not be seeing him again.

Next morning Lisette said goodbye to Joanna at the villa and they exchanged promises to meet again soon in England. At the railway station Lisette had reserved a private compartment on the train, because it had happened in the past that fellow passengers had recognized her and she had been pestered by their attention.

She took a window seat and put ready the book she had brought to read, but first there was the newspaper she had just purchased. As she opened it she happened to glance out of the window and saw a little fat man in a straw boater was staring at her. She supposed he had recognized her and she looked away quickly, not wanting to offer any encouragement for him to come closer. She began to read an article about Germany's increasing military strength.

The locomotive hissed out steam as a sign of departure. Then, just as the wheels began to move, the door of her compartment was wrenched open. For a second she thought the little man in the boater was brashly invading her solitude, but it was Philippe throwing himself into the opposite seat! She gave a gasp of annoyance.

'What on earth are you doing here?' she demanded, crushing the newspaper down on to her lap.

He had tossed his grey bowler up on to the rack and he sat grinning triumphantly at her. 'I'm coming to Paris with you.' He held up a hand, foreseeing a protest. 'Hear me out! I could tell from what you said yesterday that you would like very much to see Maurice again. I'm going to ask for permission at the school to take him and my godson out to luncheon tomorrow, which will give you the chance of a reunion with Maurice.'

'That would be wonderful!' she exclaimed, feeling overwhelmed by this thoughtfulness from such an unexpected source.

'Don't raise your hopes too high. The school only allows limited outings in a term, but it should be all right. I suggest we meet at the Grand Cafe. Shall we say at noon?'

She nodded gratefully. 'I realize you have interrupted your stay in the sun to do this for me.'

He shook his head. 'Not entirely. It's high time I was back in Paris. There is building work going on in our home, making it uninhabitable, but Ellen will have expected me to be there all the time to ensure that everything is being done to her satisfaction.'

'So you've been playing truant,' Lisette remarked dryly.

He gave a careless shrug of the shoulders. 'Ellen does not approve of gaming. I had to take the chance while it was available. You were far more tolerant.'

She ignored his comment. 'So is the house the one where you were born or are you and your wife residing somewhere else now?'

He crossed his long legs, leaning back comfortably against the upholstery and smiling at her. 'No, it's the same house that you went to some years ago when you and I were going to make it our home.'

She remembered it vividly. A fine mansion with a gloomy interior. It did not surprise her that his wife wanted extensive alterations. 'What about those portraits of your ancestors on the walls of the hall and staircase?' she asked in a moment of curiosity. 'Have they been moved to the gallery?'

He laughed and shook his head. 'No such luck! Americans are crazy about their ancestral roots and Ellen was delighted that I had so many likenesses of my forebears. It also pleased her that the house itself is over a hundred years old, which is relatively new to us, but ancient to her. At the present the paintings are all being cleaned and restored.' This statement seemed to jog his memory. 'Damnation! I haven't checked that they'll be ready in time for Ellen's return at the end of the month. She will expect the work on the extension completed, the decorating done and the portraits rehung by the time she appears. Then she plans to oversee the finishing touches. The house will probably end up looking like Versailles in its heyday, but not in the same good taste.'

She was afraid he was going to start criticizing his wife and she put an end to that line of conversation by offering him her refolded newspaper. 'Read the prediction in this article and tell me that all this sabre-rattling by Germany doesn't mean that there's going to be a war. It looks very ominous to me.'

He took it from her, glanced at the headline of the article she had indicated, and shook his head. 'Not in our time,' he said confidently. 'The Kaiser has inflated ideas of his own importance, twirling his moustache and liking to be seen in that ridiculous helmet.'

She remembered seeing the Kaiser in the movie that Jim had taken of Queen Victoria's funeral procession. The German emperor was the son of an English princess, would he consider going to war against his own mother's country? Yet power-mad rulers cared only for their own ruthless ambitions and it seemed to her that everything was very much in the balance. It was a sobering thought.

The journey passed. She and Philippe lunched together in the dining car. She noticed as she had done the previous day that he kept reminding her of various good times they had had in the past, almost as if he thought those memories would eliminate all that had parted them.

When they arrived in Paris Philippe's chauffeur was waiting with the car. After taking her into her hotel Philippe waited until she gave him a farewell nod from behind the gilded grid of the lift as it took her from his sight. Then he went to the reception desk and spoke to the clerk there before signing the register. He had made sure that the suite he had booked for himself would be on the same floor as hers.

As soon as Lisette had refreshed herself after the journey she took a cab to the House of Paquin where mannequins paraded for her. Not having been in Paris for some time she was restocking her wardrobe and chose four daytime gowns and two for evening. Before returning to the hotel she went to a wine merchant whom her father had patronized in the past, and bought a truly superb cognac as a gift for Daniel, knowing how much he would enjoy and appreciate it. Then, having had such a full day, she decided to dine quietly at the hotel, choosing to wear a black evening gown that she

had worn to several of Joanna's parties and which had been
unpacked for her.

The head waiter bowed to her as she entered the restaurant, which sparkled with chandeliers and crystal on damask.

'Good evening, Madame Shaw.'

Then he guided her to a table where Philippe in white tie
and tails rose to greet her.

'How did you know I would be dining here this evening?'
she demanded impatiently as she sat down in the chair being
held for her.

'I didn't, but I hoped you would, and in any case I have
dined here several times during my stay.'

'Your stay? Here in this hotel?'

'Yes, it's the best in Paris. Where else would you expect
me to take a suite? I told you my own home is uninhabitable at the present time.'

'But you said that your wife expected you to be living
there throughout the alterations.'

'I do what I please, Lisette.'

She smiled wryly. 'Oh, yes, Philippe. I know that very
well.'

He grinned at her persuasively. 'Come on, Lisette. This
should be an evening of celebration for you. I've arranged
with the school that I take the boys out to luncheon tomorrow.'

She caught her breath, her eyes bright with joy. 'Oh, thank
you, Philippe!'

He held her gaze for a moment, highly pleased by her
reaction, and seeing that all boded well for the rest of the
evening. After dining they talked for a while before he saw
her to the door of her room and bade her goodnight. He felt
as if he were playing a salmon at the end of a fishing line.
Only when the right moment was reached would he be able
to land his catch.

In the morning Lisette set out for the House of Worth on
the rue de la Paix where she ordered several more beautiful
garments such as only a Parisian couturier could produce.
Then it was time to meet Philippe and the two sixteen-year-
old boys. As the doorman swung open the door to the Grand
Cafe she saw the three of them rise to their feet from where
they had waited for her. She saw at once that Maurice was

indeed her father's child. It was not only because of his fair hair, height and sturdy stance, but because he was so like a portrait of her father as a young man, which had hung above the fireplace in the library.

Maurice watched Philippe go forward to greet her. His mother had never mentioned her, but he had known from others that he had a half-sister and had even seen one of her movies. He had calculated that Lisette was thirty-two, but she looked very young and slim as she came towards him and was even more beautiful than she had appeared on the screen.

'I'm so happy to see you again after so many years, Maurice,' she said gladly as he bowed over her hand.

'I'm honoured, madame,' he said stiffly.

'Call me Lisette,' she said eagerly.

He had not been looking forward to this meeting, but the warm friendliness that emanated from her caused him to smile broadly and relax, unaware that he was tilting his head exactly as his father had done when particularly pleased. 'Yes, I will, Lisette.'

For no reason at all they both laughed as if already a bond had been formed between them. Philippe had warned him that if he should wish to see his half-sister again he must never mention this meeting to his mother and already he knew he would keep silent.

At luncheon Philippe again showed unusual thoughtfulness by having booked a separate table, giving Lisette and Maurice a chance to sit by themselves and get to know each other. This was a personal sacrifice for Philippe as his godson bored him utterly. Every time his gaze wandered from the nearest pretty women to their table he saw that Lisette and Maurice were talking animatedly and laughing together.

She was pleased to discover that Maurice was quick and intelligent with various interests that included archaeology. The previous year he had been to the tombs in Egypt with a small party from school, led by the headmaster, and on another occasion he had worked at a dig on the site of a Roman villa. Tennis was his sport and he hoped to go mountaineering during his next vacation.

'I'm keen on photography as well,' he said confidentially, 'and my stepfather gave me a very good camera on my birthday last year, but motion pictures interest me most of all. We're not supposed to go to movies during term time, but I have managed it sometimes.' He grinned broadly. 'I skipped lessons once to see you as Joan of Arc.'

'Did you get into trouble over it?'

'Yes, but it was worth it. You are a splendid actress.'

'Thank you, but remember that I have an exceptional director in my husband, Daniel. It was also his idea to release "Jeanne d'Arc" with French subtitles for France.'

'I should like to hear how he decides to direct various scenes. Where does he start?'

She answered his questions as fully as she could and there was always another query to follow about the movie world. So many of his facial expressions, his way of raising an eyebrow, reminded her so much of their father that she suddenly broke off what she was saying. 'Oh, Maurice! You are so like our father!'

He looked surprised. 'Am I? What sort of man was he? Mother has never talked to me about him. She just fusses over my stepfather and I have to call him Papa. But then she has never spoken about you either.'

It saddened Lisette that Maurice had grown up knowing almost nothing about the man who had been so proud of him. So she did all she could to fill in some of the very wide gaps, telling how their father had introduced her to Paris and all its arts and treasures out of his own enjoyment of everything beautiful and of historical interest.

'He read a great deal, which is why there's such a fine library at the château, some of the books he collected being very rare. I know from what my grandmother told me,' she continued, 'that he was also a keen sportsman in his youth, although by the time I went to live at the château he had put on weight and his favourite sport was betting on the races at Longchamps.'

'I've never seen a photograph of him, although there is a painting of him when he was young that hangs in one of the corridors near the servants' quarters. I don't think my mother wants to remind my stepfather too often of her previous marriage. Unfortunately for her I'm sometimes around.' He made a cheerful grimace and shrugged his shoulders, causing Lisette to guess that he had become used to it over the years.

'I should like so much to keep in touch with you, Maurice,' she said. 'Do you think we could correspond with each other sometimes?'

'Yes, I would like that, Lisette. Please let me know all that is new in the movie world and be sure to tell me when you are coming back to France again.'

'I will do that,' she promised.

The luncheon came to an end. When the two boys had been delivered back to school Lisette expressed her thanks to Philippe. 'I appreciate so much what you did for me today,' she said warmly.

'Does this mean that all in the past is forgiven?' he asked quietly.

'That happened a long time ago,' she answered.

'I needed reassurance.' He took up her hand and kissed it. 'Let me take you to the opera this evening. I have two tickets for the best box in the house. It's "The Marriage of Figaro". Remember that we went to a performance together with friends when all was well between us? It could bridge those unfortunate times in between and banish them for ever.' Before she could reply, he added. 'Surely this is not too much to ask?'

She knew it to be emotional blackmail, but she was in a happy mood and the theme of the opera would match it very well. She agreed to go.

They sat in the best box and she enjoyed every moment of the performance. Afterwards they had supper together in the gilt and sparkle of Maxim's. Back at her hotel he saw her to the door of her room as he had done the night before.

'No, I can't lunch with you tomorrow or see you at any other time,' she said, refusing his invitation. 'I have some motion picture business that will keep me busy all day.'

It did take the whole day, for she was taking note of an important historic location for Daniel's film about Marie Antoinette. She started early in the morning by taking a cab out to Versailles. Only a very few of the palace's great rooms were open to the public, for much of it was used as offices, but she was able to go into the Hall of Mirrors. Reflected by its many mirrors, she gazed up at the murals on the ceiling that had been darkened by time and neglect. This once magnificent hall, as with everywhere else on view, was devoid of its glorious chandeliers, its draperies and all the fine furniture that had once made the great palace the jewel of France. She hoped that one day her countrymen would be enlightened enough to restore it to its full beauty.

Afterwards she went down to the lake and into the park's secluded glades where in the heyday of royalty before the Revolution open-air balls, banquets, masquerades and theatrical productions had been held. Coming upon Marie Antoinette's charming little summerhouse she looked through its windows. She remembered her father bringing her here and then showing her the nearby leafy grove where the tragic Queen had been given the warning that the mob was marching on Versailles. How terrified the poor woman must have been as she fled back to the palace.

When Lisette arrived back at the hotel she was quite tired after a full day's sightseeing at the palace and throughout its vast park, but as she kicked off her shoes and lay down on the suite's chaise longue she was well satisfied with her day. She felt that having reabsorbed Marie Antoinette's surroundings she would be able to play far better the role of the tragic Queen.

It was just as she was about to order a light supper to be brought to her suite that the telephone rang. It was Philippe issuing an invitation that took her by surprise.

'A magic lantern show?' she exclaimed with amusement. 'I thought the movies had put an end to them long ago.'

'This lanternist is said to be the best ever, which is why his shows can still attract audiences. Surely you'd like to see the performance and judge for yourself whether he comes up to the standard that you remember?'

She was tempted. It would be interesting to compare this lanternist's technique with Daniel's and see what new ideas were being presented. 'I think I would,' she replied.

The venue was a large private mansion with marble pillars, floors and statuary, A party of about a hundred well-dressed guests was in full swing with an orchestra playing for dancing. In a side room a long buffet table was heaped with various delicacies. The hostess, her face highly painted, her diamonds sparkling and her cleavage well revealed, welcomed Lisette as effusively as if they had known each other for years.

'I expect she has seen you on the movie screen and thinks she knows you,' Philippe said by way of explanation, taking a glass of champagne from the tray of a waiter and handing it to Lisette before taking one for himself. She thought he was probably right.

They went to join other guests helping themselves at the buffet, for Philippe was hungry and so was she, having had nothing since breakfast, except for an apple that she had taken with her to Versailles. Already she had felt some effect from the champagne, but not as much as Philippe, who had most certainly been drinking heavily in the hotel bar before meeting her after she had descended in the hotel lift. As they ate he also constantly emptied his glass for a refill and wanted hers topped up too. She thought he was feeling some regret that she would be leaving in the morning, for they had had a pleasant time together.

'Let's dance,' he said, taking her hand as they left the buffet, and he twirled her on to the floor. They had always danced well together and even though he was quite drunk he did not miss a step.

'What time is the magic lantern show?' she asked, noticing that an ormolu clock showed it was almost midnight, She was regretting that she had come, for he was holding her far too tightly and watching her with drunken amorousness through his lashes.

'It's on now,' he answered. 'It's a continuous performance.'

'Why didn't you tell me?' she said in exasperation. 'We'll take a quick look and then go.'

'What's the rush?'

'You seem to have forgotten I'm leaving for home early tomorrow morning. My train to Calais goes at nine o'clock.'

He put an arm about her waist. 'We'll fill up our glasses once more and then we'll go and watch the pretty pictures.'

He did not see that she left her refilled glass on a side table as a door was opened for them into a darkened salon. Black velvet curtains were keeping out the light and these

were parted for them to enter by a footman and then closed
again. The air was heavy with the perfume of the women
and the smoke of cigars as well as a certain exotic aroma
from Egyptian cigarettes.

She did not glance at the screen until they were seated,
but immediately she realized the type of show that it was.
A young woman with large and very beautiful breasts was
being undressed by her lover through a series of deftly
changed colour slides. He was wearing a costume such as
Romeo might have worn and was kissing every part of her
that became blatantly exposed. This was being accompanied
by the music of a violin being played somewhere behind the
screen, although it could hardly be heard above the giggles,
little shrieks and guffaws from the audience with the occasional burst of applause.

Lisette sighed in exasperation at her own foolishness in
having been trapped into viewing this lascivious rubbish. She
should have known that nothing as straightforward as an
ordinary slide-show would interest Philippe who – judging
by the salacious pleasure on his face in the light reflected
from the screen – had clearly known what to expect from
this performance. Romeo had now thrown off his clothes to
reveal his own masculine magnificence and copulation began
to take place in what was obviously going to be a variety of
gymnastic and very exposed ways.

She had seen such slides before when Daniel had gone
through other lanternists' collections that he had bought at
auction, for he hated to see antique slides broken up or thrown
away and watched out for any coming on to the market. He
saw them as the true forerunners of all animated pictures,
and felt they should be preserved as part of motion picture
history, whatever the content.

She had to admit to herself that this lanternist was skilled
and she watched with professional interest for another five
minutes before putting aside Philippe's arm, which he had
draped about her caressingly, his fingers stroking her. As she
rose from her chair. the velvet curtains were again pulled
aside for her while the footman's gaze remained glued to
the screen. She went swiftly out of the room.

Philippe came hurrying after her and caught her arm,

swinging her round to face him. 'I thought marriage would have driven prudishness from you!' he exclaimed bitterly.

She gave him a tired look, not bothering to answer. 'I'm going back to the hotel. There is no need for you to leave.'

'I'm coming with you.'

They rode back in silence, but she sensed the rage building up in him. He had thought that with enough champagne she would soften towards him, perhaps even be stirred to amorousness by the slides as had been happening with some of the couples revealed by the glow from the screen.

They collected their keys at the reception desk and went up in the lift without speaking. Yet he saw her to her door as he had done previously and unlocked it for her.

'Goodnight, Philippe,' she said, drawing back over the threshold, disturbed by his mulish expression. 'I shall not be seeing you in the morning, because I'll be having an early breakfast in my suite. Thank you again for arranging the meeting with Maurice.'

He did not appear to have heard what she had said. 'I loved you, Lisette!' he burst out furiously. 'You should never have run away from me all those years ago! And I'm damned if I'll let you leave me now!'

He threw himself forward, bearing her with him, and slamming the door behind them. She cried out as she fought him, kicking and hitting out, but she was no match for his fired up strength. He was trying to get her through to the bedroom, determined to have her at last, but the chaise longue was nearest and he threw her down on it, crushing her with his weight. The struggle continued as he clawed at her skirts, but his hand fell away from her thigh in the sudden exploding brilliance of a photographer's flash powder coming like a bolt of lightning from the re-opened door.

'What the hell—?' Philippe roared, falling back awkwardly, and she sat up, both of them staring in horror at the intruder, who stood poised to take a second photograph. With him was a little man whom Lisette recognized instantly. It was he who had stared so penetratingly at her from the station platform when she was leaving for Paris!

'Get out!' Philippe staggered forward, but threw his arm up across his face, momentarily half blinded by the second flash before he charged forward to throw both men back into the corridor. But the little man was quick moving and with a powerful thrust adroitly sent him staggering back while speaking politely in surprisingly cultured tones.

'Pray forgive the intrusion, Monsieur Bonnard, and my apologies to you, Madame Shaw, but Madame Bonnard needed evidence for a divorce and now she will have it.'

Both men departed swiftly, closing the door after them. Philippe sank down on to a chair and dropped his head into his hands. 'Oh, my God,' he repeated over and over again.

Lisette, feeling as though all her strength had ebbed from her, managed to get up from the chaise lonque, aware of shaking uncontrollably from the shock of Philippe's attempted rape and the aftermath.

'Go now, Philippe,' she said through clenched teeth, clutching the back of a chair for support.

He nodded in a drunken daze, but did not move. 'I never thought she would set a private detective on me.'

'On us,' she corrected flatly. 'That little man was in Monte Carlo and no doubt he has recorded all the other times we have met.'

Yet Philippe's thoughts were only for himself and the bleak future ahead of him if the divorce went through. 'Oh, my God,' he began again. 'She's rich as Croesus. I can't let her chuck me out!'

'Then use your charm on her,' Lisette said sharply, ice in her voice. 'You have found it useful enough in the past. Go!'

He nodded. This time he rose to his feet and reeled towards the door. He left without a backward glance in her direction.

She rushed to close and lock the door after him before leaning back against it in overwhelming wave of despair. How would she explain everything to Daniel? She was terribly afraid that it would open a gulf between them.

Twenty-One

Lisette delayed her journey home by twenty-four hours in order to consult her lawyers. She guessed that Philippe had checked out of the hotel as she did not see him again.

When she arrived home she telephoned Daniel at the studios. He was glad to hear her voice, although he thought she sounded very tired, and he promised to get home as soon as it was possible to have an early dinner with her. Yet two hours went by and Maisie was keeping the food hot as she had so often before, wondering why she still believed that he would be on time Eventually he threw open the front door and called out happily, 'I'm home, Lisette!'

It surprised him that she did not come to meet him after her lengthy absence. Daisy, taking his hat and coat, told him she was in the drawing room.

He found her standing by the fireplace and she turned to face him as he entered. His immediate thought was that she was not looking radiant as he had expected, but was pale and heavy eyed. Her smile trembled as did her clasped hands that she was holding in front of her at waist level.

'My darling! What has happened to you?' he asked in concern, coming across to take her in his arms and kiss her.

'Something quite dreadful has taken place.'

His immediate thought was that some serious calamity must have overtaken her friend. 'Is it Joanna?' he asked with concern. 'Has something happened to her or anybody else? An accident, perhaps?'

She shook her head. 'Nothing like that.' She hesitated in her misery of what she had to tell him, not knowing how to start, although she had gone over it all so many times in her own mind. 'It's something entirely different.'

He was relieved. Since nothing fatal had occurred he took a guess at the cause of her distress. She had mentioned going to the Monte Carlo casino several times in her letters and he believed now that she had lost a great deal of money at the tables and was worried about how to tell him.

'Come and sit down.' Taking her by the shoulders, he guided her to a brocade-upholstered sofa in the bright flicker of flames in the fireplace. 'I can see that you're tired from the journey. Was it a rough crossing? I'll get you a cognac.'

'I've brought you a bottle from France.' She indicated where it stood on a side table.

He was a cognac connoisseur and when he picked up the bottle he whistled appreciatively as he studied the label. 'What a splendid gift! Thank you, darling!'

She watched him open a rosewood cupboard where he took out two tulip-shaped glasses. When he had poured the cognac he handed one glass to her and then sat down in the opposite chair, holding up his glass to examine the cognac's superb colour. Then he inhaled its aroma, assessing its force and elegance. Yet all the time he was watching her out of the corner of his eye, able to see she was in a high state of tension, and he cupped his glass in his hand to warm it while giving the golden liquid a little swirl.

'Take your time and do this nectar justice,' he advised, wanting to calm her. 'It will do you good. Shall I tell you what has been happening at the studios since my last letter?'

She nodded, thankful for a reprieve to gather her thoughts together. While she sipped the cognac he chatted, elaborating on what he had told her in his hastily scrawled letters. He was enthusiastic about his investment in a small London music hall, which had been closed for a number of years and was almost derelict, enabling him to purchase it at a bargain price.

'I'm going to call it the Royal Picturedrome. It will be adapted for showing motion pictures with music hall turns performed on stage in between the movies instead of the other way round. It's high time that motion pictures took first place.' He leaned forward in his enthusiasm. 'The theatre is being renovated throughout and I intend to have a grand opening.' He grinned. 'I hope you chose something splendid in Paris to wear for the occasion.'

'Yes, I did,' she answered tonelessly.

'Now,' he said encouragingly, 'what is it you want to tell me?'

She was not to know how much her first words were to chill him through. 'By sheer chance and after all these years I met Philippe Bonnard again at the casino in Monte Carlo.' She paused, gathering the courage to carry on. 'I think that for both of us it was as if momentarily the clock had turned back to the happier times he and I had known before the night of your magic lantern show. The great difference was not that we were older, but that this time I was not wearing rose-coloured spectacles. Yet when he invited me to luncheon the next day I accepted. It was in the hope that he would be able to give me news of Maurice, my half-brother.'

He listened frozen faced and without interruption as she gave him a full account of all that had happened.

'The divorce will create a dreadful scandal,' she concluded wearily, 'as divorces always do, especially since so many people will know my name. The case will come to court in Paris.'

She kept her eyes lowered, not knowing whether he was showing anger at her stupidity in letting herself become involved again with Philippe or jealous suspicion that she had softened towards the man she had once loved after the lapse of years. Then, although Daniel spoke very calmly, there was a sharp edge to his voice.

'Let's go over what happened once more.' He put aside his glass and began to tick each meeting off on his fingers. 'After meeting Philippe at the casino you lunched with him. Then he travelled with you to Paris where you booked into the hotel where he was staying and later you dined together that evening. The next day you both lunched with the two schoolboys and in the evening you and he had supper at Maxim's after going to the opera. Last night you went with him to a lewd slide show and afterwards in your suite the two of you were photographed in each other's arms.' He paused deliberately, his throat tight with angry jealousy. 'I don't think Madame Bonnard will have the least difficulty in getting her divorce.'

A terrible silence fell between them before she spoke, her voice almost inaudible. 'It all happened because I was just so grateful to Philippe for arranging the meeting with Maurice.'

'But,' he answered fiercely, 'this was the man you once said you never wished to see again for as long as you lived.'

His harsh tone seemed to cut through her, but she jerked her head up on an unexpected rush of anger to meet his rage with her own. 'He did not become my lover!'

Springing to his feet, he began pacing up and down. 'I don't doubt your word! It's just that I wish I could get my hands around his scrawny neck!'

She felt an hysterical urge to laugh. 'It's not in the least scrawny. If it had been I might have managed to strangle him myself!'

He stopped his pacing and their eyes met and held. She saw his fury ease at her absurd declaration and he came forward to snatch her up into his arms. 'I never want to lose you,' he exclaimed in torment.

She took his face between her hands. 'You never will!' she promised fervently.

They drew apart as Daisy came to say that dinner was served. When she left them to eat on their own Lisette told Daniel about her visit to her lawyers. She felt calmer now that she had told him everything else.

'The last of those who served my father have all retired, but the grandson of one of them, Monsieur Monier, will handle everything for me.'

'Does that mean you will not have to make an appearance?'

'He is hoping that I can be spared that, but if Madame Bonnard is vindictive my presence will be demanded.'

'Do you know anything about her?'

'Only that she is beautiful, very rich, and clearly was very generous to Philippe. He was in total panic when divorce was mentioned by the private detective. So I suppose she paid off all his gambling debts as well as everything else.'

'Have you any idea when the case will come to court?'

'Monsieur Monier thought it would be in about three months. Fortunately my countrymen are far more tolerant and far less hypocritical about amorous matters than people here in England and the divorce will cause me less harm there. But if an account reaches English newspapers, my name, known to so many people now through our movies, will become a target for scandal. It could change the attitude of audiences towards me. Some would boycott any movie I appeared in.'

'That's true,' he admitted evenly.

'I know that two-thirds of the film is already in the can and it will be a financial loss to have to change the leading actress at midstream, but you'll have to give the role of Marie Antoinette to someone else. I believe this movie is going to be your best yet and I don't want to ruin it for you.'

He raised his eyebrows. 'You have been working everything out, haven't you?'

'I've scarcely slept these past two nights and have thought of nothing else except this dreadful situation.'

'No wonder you look exhausted. Be sure you sleep well tonight. I want you on the set tomorrow and in costume for the wedding scene of *The Tragic Queen.*'

'I can't do that! I've told you! You must get another actress!'

'You said yourself that this is to be my best movie yet and you are the only one I want to play the part.'

She held his gaze steadily. 'In spite of everything?'

He nodded. 'Everything? There was nothing.'

That night he would have denied himself and held back from making love to her in her present exhausted state, but as he slid into bed with her she embraced him amorously, arching her body against his. Then he took her with such passion that she was reminded of when they had first made love. Then she had wanted him to drive Philippe out of her mind and heart. Now he had the same purpose with her.

The making of *The Tragic Queen* went ahead. Some of the action was filmed on location when Daniel and Lisette, together with Jim as well as the leading actor, three assistants and a motor van full of equipment, went to Versailles. They were not permitted to take any film indoors, but were allowed two days in the park. Fortunately the weather was warm and sunny and not a moment of filming was wasted. In costume, Lisette and the actor playing Louis VI strolled in the park, descended the great flight of steps to act out a scene among the potted orange trees. Then she and Ronald Davis, who was playing Count Axel von Ferson, the love of the Queen's life, danced together in the open-air ballroom where once cascades of water had added beauty to the scene. Again on her own she sat in the grove while the camera captured her horror as one of the assistants in costume came to give her the terrible warning. After two days all that Daniel wanted had been taken and while the others returned to England he and Lisette went to see Monsieur Monier at his Paris chambers.

'Yes, as I informed you, Madame Shaw,' the lawyer said, 'the date of the divorce coming to court has been set for the fifth of September. Unfortunately I have not been successful in sparing you attendance. You will have to be there.'

Lisette nodded resignedly. It was a day to dread, but she would have to face it. Worst of all was that she and Daniel, in spite of their efforts, could not seem to recapture the old harmony between them. It was fear of losing her on his side and bitter regret on hers that she had ever met Philippe again.

Before leaving Paris they arranged to meet Maurice, with whom Lisette had been in correspondence ever since Philippe had arranged the luncheon for them. Her half-brother had been eager to meet Daniel from the start and Lisette was glad that most of the conversation passed between them, because she felt intensely weary and was thankful not to take part.

Yet when filming of Daniel's epic continued in England she showed none of her inner weariness and was unaware that with her emotions at their peak she was giving the performance of her life in her role of the Queen. The final scene was filmed when she sat in the cart on the way to the guillotine, her hands roped together behind her back. There were women in the crowd of extras instructed to shout abuse and shake their fists, who had tears in their eyes at her tragic appearance. They had to wipe them away before Daniel shouted, 'Action!'

Inevitably a report appeared in the British newspapers that

the well-known animated picture actress, Lisette Decourt, had been cited as co-respondent under her married name in a forthcoming French divorce case.

When the time came for Lisette to return to Paris and attend court Daniel would have gone with her, but she was adamant that he should not come.

'You know the truth of what happened,' she said in appeal. 'I don't want you to hear any twisted version of what took place.' Her voice faltered. 'I could not bear it.'

He had to accept her wish. Joanna went with her instead and Lisette was thankful for her friend's support throughout the ordeal. It was also a comfort to her that Maurice turned up to show his loyalty to her.

In court Philippe looked thin and haggard and did not once glance in her direction. His American wife, a handsome woman with a commanding air, gave each of them a single vicious glare and afterwards avoided looking at either of them for the rest of the case. Lisette was given the chance to deny everything of which she and Philippe were accused, but the fact that she was an actress made her denial and her accusation of attempted rape less convincing to those who still thought theatrical people were of dubious reputation. Yet some of her admirers were there too, Englishwomen who happened to be on vacation or in Paris for some other reason and they gave her sympathetic glances in court and applauded her outside as she got into the hired motorcar with Joanna. Nevertheless, Ellen Bonnard won her case and the divorce was granted.

Daniel arrived the same day. He put his arms about Lisette.

'Now I'm taking you home,' he said. She did not see the conspiratorial look that he exchanged with Joanna, having told her his plans before she had left England with his wife.

'I wish you all the best,' Joanna said with a smile, going off on her own to journey back to England.

'Why aren't we travelling with her?' Lisette asked.

'We're going to Lyon. You told me yourself that your tenants had given up the house some time ago and I have had it put to rights again. Most important of all, you need a rest after all you have been through.'

Her reaction was to weep with thankfulness. Being in her

childhood surroundings again would be a time of healing for her after all the anguish of past months.

The gates of the house stood open for them when they arrived. A maid, watching out for them, swept open the door for them and bobbed a curtsey.

'Welcome, monsieur and madame!'

The house had been redecorated in its original colours and some damaged furniture had been restored. Items of value, which had been stored for security during the tenants' occupancy, were back in their rightful place. Lisette flitted though all the downstairs rooms before returning to throw her arms around Daniel's neck, her face radiant.

'It's so good to be here with you!'

'It will not be long for me, but you can stay until you feel able to come back to the cameras.'

Daniel stayed two weeks and during this time he and Lisette were able to renew their friendship with the Lumières and to hear of the brothers' latest achievements.

The evening before Daniel left she asked a favour of him. 'Would you let me rest for a while from acting? I still feel emotionally wrecked by all that has happened. Here I can be peaceful for a while. It will give me the chance to do more writing instead.'

He agreed that it would be good for her to stay for a while and had reasons of his own to be glad she had made her request. 'Stay as long as you wish. There are two movies waiting to be made as soon as *The Tragic Queen* is in the can and I'm keeping it back for the Royal Picturedrome's premiere.'

She stayed on for another month and settled to writing, having had several plots in her head for some time. When she left Lyon the house was closed up again, but with a non-resident housekeeper to keep it in order and the same two cleaning women from the past. Lisette felt that now she had what amounted to Daniel's blessing on the house she would be free to come and stay whenever the mood took her.

Daniel had a special reason for holding back the premiere of *The Tragic Queen,* which he had not disclosed to Lisette. He wanted to be sure that there would be no backlash against her after details of the divorce had been published in the

London papers. He was counting on the fact that – on the whole – the public had short memories, some new calamity or event forever diverting interest. So he encouraged Lisette to spend more and more time at the Bellecour house where she could settle peacefully to writing, which she enjoyed. It would give her the chance to come up with more original plots with scripts such as those of hers he had previously filmed successfully.

From that time onwards Lisette travelled between London and Lyon at quite frequent intervals, but her every home-coming to Daniel was like another honeymoon, for they were always starved of each other, even after the briefest of part-ings. Then, when he felt she would be safe from public ostracism, he finally set the date for the grand premiere.

When he had first taken Lisette to see the theatre it had still been in the early stages of restoration, the air cloudy with brick dust and stinking of whitewash.

'I'll come again when it's finished,' she had said, coughing as she left the building with him.

Now with the premiere only a few weeks away, Lisette returned home again from France with another new script and, surprising herself, more than ready to act again if Daniel should need her. She knew that the restoration of the theatre had proved more costly than originally anticipated, but she had complete faith in his project. It was why she laughed with delight when she entered the theatre with its vast red-carpeted foyer and elegant staircases. The auditorium was an orgy of crimson and gold with cherubs ornamenting the proscenium arch, and handsome velvet curtains that when parted revealed a screen larger than any she had seen before.

'It's like a palace in a fairy tale,' she exclaimed, clapping her hands in approval. 'Audiences will love it!'

'So you see it as I do,' he said, pleased that she shared the same vision. 'People need to be transported out of their everyday lives when they come to see a movie, and entering these surroundings will take them halfway there before the entertainment has even started.'

She nodded. 'And, most important of all, this theatre will fulfil your aim to put motion pictures on an equal footing with the theatrical stage.'

But the chosen date for the grand premiere had to be postponed. King Edward was taken ill and died, plunging the country into mourning for a monarch who had enjoyed life, the racetrack and beautiful women. With the suffragette movement gaining momentum people remembered again the woman who had thrown herself in front of his horse at the races, giving her life to bring publicity to the cause.

Out of respect for the late King and on the more mercenary level of not wanting the gaiety of the evening to be dampened by patrons wearing mourning black, Daniel waited several weeks before the grand opening of his theatre took place. Then he ensured that there was plenty of good publicity to attract his first audience.

On the opening night gilt-edged programmes, which could be kept as souvenirs, were to be given free. He let it be rumoured that there might be a royal presence, although the court was still in mourning and neither the new King, George V, nor his wife, Queen Mary, were known to have any great interest in the theatre and were far less likely to attend a picture house. Nevertheless the rumour took hold and Daniel was rewarded on the opening night by a foreign princess and her ladies taking the royal box. Every other seat was sold and outside a crowd of spectators gathered to watch arrivals with several policemen on duty to keep order. Unfortunately there were a few religious extremists in the crowd carrying banners against Lisette's appearance that proclaimed 'A Harlot in the role of a Harlot!' and 'Close this house of Sin!'

Daniel was concerned about Lisette having to face hostility from this section and telephoned her at home to give a warning, but she had already left. He kept a watch on those arriving, greeting people whom he knew and welcoming all the others. Nobody was being hindered by the demonstration outside and the flow of arriving patrons was like a river.

It was when Lisette arrived and stepped out on to the red carpet there came a great wave of shouting. It was not only from the extremists, for a swarm of suffragettes, taking advantage of this chance of publicity, had been biding their time out of sight and now came thrusting into the crowd with banners of their own. There was pandemonium.

'Votes for women!' they shrieked. 'Franchise for all!'

Police whistles blew. People pushed and shoved. One of the policemen seized Lisette as she was almost knocked to the ground in the seething throng and he shielded her with his body as he pushed a way through to the entrance where he thrust her forward into Daniel's arms.

'Are you all right?' he demanded anxiously.

'Yes,' she said breathlessly. 'But what about the patrons caught up in the scrum outside?'

'I'll make it up to them. Free tickets for future performances.'

Police reinforcements had arrived. Order was soon restored and a number of suffragettes were arrested as police shins were kicked and helmets knocked off. Inside the picture house people had taken their seats and in the orchestra pit a pianist played popular music of the day. When the lights were lowered the programme began with some news items followed by two comedies interspersed with music hall turns. During the first one the film broke, which happened quite frequently in any performance, but it took only a minute to repair and the show continued. Last of all came *The Tragic Queen*.

It ended to a standing ovation and when Daniel led Lisette on to the stage the applause trebled in volume. Bouquets were presented to her. They both made short speeches and were applauded again. Afterwards the audience left without meeting any trouble outside

'Now we've launched our Royal Picturedrome,' Daniel said with satisfaction, 'the next one will be far bigger in every way.'

For the time being she was content with what they had, but she knew that Daniel would always strive towards greater achievement.

Twenty-Two

Although Daniel's major interest continued to be movie making as it always would be, he kept a lookout for the right location for a larger animated picture house and found the site after three years. His success with his original venture had attracted investors and the new edifice was to be built grandly on the site of an old factory in the heart of London. Other entrepreneurs were beginning to follow his example and all over the country various buildings were being adapted as permanent picture houses, although few were purpose-built as his would be and most had other uses when movies were not being shown.

There were almost always minor hold-ups at most performances. Frequently a film would break, often more than once on a reel, even on the best of projectors such as those that Daniel and others of his standard used. It was generally accepted as a normal happening and it was fortunate that most audiences were remarkably good-tempered about it. It was only if the delay in mending the film extended beyond a few minutes that those in the cheaper seats began to stamp their feet and whistle their impatience until eventually everybody else joined in too.

Lisette was present at one exceptionally long delay that was not caused by a breaking film. She was with Daniel, who was checking up that the individual musical scores he was sending out to accompany his epic movies were being played as under contract. These days there was always a pianist to underline with music all that was happening on the screen and it was a skilful task, but on this occasion the woman pianist had been taken ill at the last minute and the relief pianist could not be contacted.

As the audience began to show noisy impatience while

they waited in vain for the programme to start, Lisette did not hesitate, but went swiftly to take the pianist's empty chair. A satisfied sigh swept over the auditorium. She began to play and the screen leapt into life. It was just as if she were playing again for audiences at the magic lantern shows, except that this time she had to keep glancing up at the screen, ensuring that she was keeping pace with the action and that the music was appropriate. Thunderous music for drama, romantic tunes for love, and gentle pieces that brought women in the audience to tears when tragedy struck. Yet the performance was not trouble free, being interrupted twice by breaks in one of the motion pictures, but she played on even though the stamping, whistling and shouting drowned her music. So she started to sing a popular song of the day, thumping away on the piano keys. Immediately the riotous noise faded away as everybody listened for a few moments in surprise and then joined in. After a second song the whole audience applauded her and the return of the screen action at the same time.

'It was a good idea of yours to grab attention by singing,' Daniel said reflectively, as they drove home after the performance. 'It might suit the action in some scenes to have a tenor or a soprano standing at the side of the screen and singing an accompanying song.'

'Yes, that could be interesting. I started to sing because I began to be afraid that the vibration caused by the stamping would bring down plaster from the ceiling!'

'It was a sensible move, because the audience was getting irate and you immediately soothed them.' He grinned. 'Yet even without your lovely voice nobody would have walked out. Any motion picture audience would stamp all night rather than not know how the film ended.'

She gave him an amused glance. 'You're right, of course. It's as if the screen casts is brilliance like a magic spell over them.'

'If any of those in the auditorium had guessed your identity you would have been autographing those picture postcards of yourself for them throughout the breakdown.'

He was particularly pleased that recently her photograph had begun taking its place among the picture postcards that were eagerly collected of the lovely Gaiety Girls, their title taken from the theatre where they appeared in musical shows of the highest standards. Lisette was among several stage and screen actresses being included for their beauty, and Daniel saw it as more welcome publicity.

It was while plans for his new building were still being discussed with the architect that Lisette began to feel unwell, suffering inexplicable attacks of dizziness and nausea. She said nothing to Daniel, for he was presently so busy that he was in and out of the house at all hours and she did not want him to be distracted from his project by concern about her. Then gradually it occurred to her that she could be pregnant, for there were other signs that supported this possibility. She was thirty-seven and nature was relenting at last and giving her one more chance to bear a child.

She felt almost delirious with happiness, but decided not to say anything to Daniel, who in any case was away again, until a doctor had confirmed her pregnancy. This time she was not plagued by her old fears of the past that she could never love another baby as she had loved Marie-Louise. That nightmare was completely gone and she had total peace of mind. She seemed to be going around with a permanent smile on her face, her heart ready to welcome and love that baby within her. She began looking at infant clothes in shop windows and studying perambulators in the stores.

Then, not long before Daniel was due to arrive home again, she went to see Dr Sarah Pomfret, a young, newly qualified woman doctor, whom Lisette had met socially and liked very much. Dr Pomfret had recently set up her own practice in the neighbourhood, but was failing to get male patients, some men even leaving the waiting room when finding out that it was not a man they were to see. Lisette believed the reason was that men saw female doctors as being on a par with the suffragettes in failing to be traditionally subservient to the male sex.

Dr Pomfret gave Lisette a thorough examination before returning to her desk where she wrote up her notes while her patient dressed herself again. As Lisette resumed her seat in front of the desk, her face radiant with expectation, she was surprised that Dr Pomfret did not return her smile. Instead the woman shook her head.

'You are in the best of health, Mrs Shaw. However, I'm very sorry to have to disappoint you, but you are not pregnant.'

Lisette stared at her in disbelief. 'But all the signs—?'

'Although you are only in your thirties it is not unusual for the change of life to begin at your age.'

Lisette left the surgery in a daze of total disappointment and almost in disbelief that fate should have delivered yet another blow to hopes she had cherished. It seemed to her that she had plunged from the pinnacle of happiness into an abyss of despair and as the days went by the began to be more and more depressed. Such dark moods overwhelmed her that she felt totally lost and afraid.

Daniel was sympathetic when she told him of her disappointment on his return home and he was deeply concerned to find her so prone to tears and showing no interest in anything. He waited a while before broaching the subject of her next role, hoping to stimulate her interest, but she shook her head.

'I'm not ready to think about acting again yet!' she said, bursting into tears.

He went at once to put his arm around her. 'You don't have to do anything that you're not ready to do.'

He was extremely worried about her. The pills that Dr Pomfret had prescribed to lift her depression were having no effect and there was such a sad look in her eyes. He believed that Lisette was mourning all over again the babies she had lost through adoption and that ill-fated miscarriage, but she showed no desire to confide in him as in the past.

Then, quite unexpectedly one day at breakfast when he was glancing through his mail, Lisette made an announcement. 'I have to get away, Daniel. I'm going home to Lyon. I need to be there as never before.'

Startled by the coldly determined note in her voice, he looked across the table at her with a concerned frown.

'I have thought that a change of air and surroundings would be good for you,' he said, 'but you've shown no interest whenever I've broached the subject. Now that you feel ready for change I'll come with you. Allow me a day or two to make some arrangements.'

She looked at him almost as if she did not know him. 'No, Daniel. You are far too busy. You have to be here to see that all is well with the building of the motion picture house and you're just starting that new epic. You can always join me later when it is easier to get away.'

He allowed himself to be persuaded, for it could not have been a more difficult time for him to be absent from all he had in hand. 'Yes, it will be best if I join you at the first possible moment. In the meantime three or four weeks in Lyon should help you to feel well again.'

'Yes,' she agreed. 'I may stay longer. All I know at the present time is that I need to go back to my roots.'

When the day came of sending luggage ahead of her departure, Daniel stared in dismay when he saw three large trunks and the other baggage that had been put in the hall ready for transport.

'You look as if you're moving out,' he said half-jokingly, but with a ring of concern behind his words.

'I told you that I don't know yet how long I'll be staying,' she said vaguely.

He thought to himself that he would soon fetch her if she were too long away.

With the April sun streaming down through the opaque glass of Victoria Station he embraced her tightly, giving her a lover's kiss. Yet she did not respond, as if her thoughts were already centred on her beloved house in Lyon. Neither did she wave to him as the train left the station, although he stayed where he was until she was gone. It was as if she had put him out of her life as soon as he was out of her sight and he was deeply anxious about her as he returned to where he had parked his motorcar.

The morning after Lisette arrived in Lyon she went into the garden with a box of seedlings from her greenhouse in London, having long thought that she would like some flowering plants from her English home to be planted in her French garden. She had also brought some lupin seeds, which she had collected the previous autumn, having always liked lupins for their abundant colour in shades of pink to deepest blues and purples, although her English gardener had resented their presence. She believed it was because they grew mostly in the gardens of humble country cottages in England and that gave them a lowly status in the eyes of expert gardeners interested in more exotic blooms.

As a child here at Bellecour she had had a little patch of the garden for her own and under her grandmother's guidance she had grown pansies and other small flowers as if it were a doll's garden for her toys. After fetching a trowel and a watering can as well as a small mat to kneel on she chose a sunny spot for the seedlings and afterwards the lupin seeds were duly planted in anticipation of a fine show the following year. Without acknowledging it to herself, she was convinced she would still be in Lyon to see the first shoots of the lupins and all else she had brought come into flower.

With her task done she noticed a cluster of little weeds that had come up since the Lyonnaise gardener's last visit. She promptly cleared them out before getting up from her knees and inspecting the other flowerbeds to check that there were no more.

She was far from ignorant about gardening in general, always having had discussions with her London gardener as she did with his counterpart here in France, but with her writing and her acting she had never had time to do any gardening herself. But now circumstances were different.

When the gardener made his next visit he was far from pleased to hear that lupins had invaded his domain, especially in places he had intended for something else.

'If they take well in this soil lupins can spread everywhere, madame,' he complained bitterly. 'It will be the devil's own task to keep them down.'

'Well, we can judge what is best to be done when they flower next year,' she said calmly.

After that she went daily into the garden to carry out some small task or another. When April and May gave way to June she went daily to deadhead the overblown roses from the bushes that had added their beauty to the garden. With a watering can she made sure in the evenings that the beds were well dampened after a hot dry day and she took delight in forestalling the gardener by keeping the beds free of weeds. He grumbled to the household staff that she was only leaving him the lawn to mow.

Her gardening had proved to be therapeutic in every way, for she always forgot everything as she dug and planted and watered and trimmed. A kind of euphoria had settled upon her as if her mind had shut out all else she had ever known. After a while she began visiting and entertaining, but only close friends of long standing. Madame Lumière was relieved to see that Lisette was losing the dreadful haunted look that she had had for several weeks after her arrival in Lyon.

Yet not once did Lisette settle to writing a new plot or script and the only time she sat at her bureau was once a week to write what she thought of as a duty letter to Daniel. He had long since stopped asking her when she would be returning home, for she never gave him an answer, except to say that it would be useless for him to come intending to fetch her, because she was not nearly ready to leave yet.

Her great concern at the present time was for France and she read the newspapers avidly. Talk of war was growing all the time. The Kaiser had reached the status of a giant ogre threatening Europe, for it was no secret that his army had grown to be thousands strong. In Lyon as elsewhere in France and other parts of Europe reserves were being called up and Lisette would pause in the street to watch them march by. How young most of them were!

Yet still she felt no desire to return to England. It was as if having gone back to her roots they had struck again so deeply that this time it was impossible for her to wrench herself away. She knew that Daniel would have been disappointed that she had not returned to England for the grand opening of his motion picture house, but she was sure all had gone well. It was then that she admitted to herself that her old home had become a refuge that she never wanted to leave. Another month slipped by and Daniel's letters no longer came.

It was early one morning when the post brought a letter from Joanna that had the devastating effect of shattering Lisette's tranquillity completely. She was so totally unprepared for what she read that her hands began to shake uncontrollably.

You really should come home as soon as you possibly can. Daniel is being seen constantly in the company of a very fine-looking woman about his own age. According to what I have heard she has even moved in with him! How can anyone blame him when you have been away for months and show no sign of ever coming back to him? Is it really over between you? If not, then don't delay, Lisette. If you still love him come home the moment you receive this letter or else it will be too late.

Stunned, Lisette lowered the letter to her lap. Joanna would never have written in that vein unless she truly believed that Daniel had turned seriously to someone else. In the past it had sometimes crossed her mind as to whether he was ever unfaithful to her on his business trips, no matter how much he loved her. But she had always dismissed the thought, totally sure of him and deliberately ignoring the fact that there were so many pretty young women wanting to act in animated pictures these days. Yet it had to be admitted that Daniel, with the luck of so many men, had become even more attractive and handsome in maturity than he had been in his youth. Now an older and obviously experienced woman had manipulated her way into his life. And perhaps his heart!

She heard a low, tortured moan of pain and realized that it came from herself. She recalled now that Joanna had once advised her never to let the Bellecour house become too important in her life. Although she had smiled away the advice at the time, just as she had ignored Joanna's good sense on other occasions, it was what had happened and she had let it shut out her marriage. Never again! Whatever happened she would sell the house. It belonged to the past. Not to a future with Daniel if that could still be saved!

Delaying no longer, she jumped to her feet, and went to tug a bell pull. A maidservant appeared almost at once.

'I'm returning to England!' Lisette exclaimed. 'Today! Now!'

'What shall I pack, madame?'

'Nothing. Just get my cream silk travelling clothes ready.'

Had that happened only this morning? It seemed a lifetime

ago, as if she was already too late to win Daniel back from this unknown woman who had filled the gap that her own absence had created. She had travelled non-stop from Lyon to Paris and then changed trains to continue on to Calais and take the Channel crossing.

Now here she was in a cab being driven home through the night traffic. The sun had set and the London streets had become lamplit. Ahead lay the daunting task of seeing if she could still salvage her marriage from whatever had taken place. During these past months she had forgotten that she still loved Daniel with all the force and power of their early days together. Joanna's letter had jerked her back to reality and fired her up in a determination to banish this other woman from his life and to try to mend all that had caused them to drift apart. If only she was not too late! She thumped her fists on her lap in frustration at every slight delay whenever other traffic slowed the cab down.

Finally the cab drew up outside her home where lights were glowing in most of the windows. As she stepped out of the cab she let her gaze roam over the house. How could she have stayed away so long! It was as if she had awoken from a dream only to find herself in a nightmare. She pushed open the ornamental iron gate and went up the path to ring the doorbell, even though she had a latchkey in her purse. She had no wish to burst in upon Daniel and this unknown woman without warning, which could be acutely embarrassing for all three of them. At all costs she wanted to retain her composure and her dignity. A manservant whom she did not know answered the door.

'Is Mr Shaw at home?' she asked.

'Yes, madam. Whom shall I say wishes to see him?'

'I'm Mrs Shaw,' she said, entering and ignoring his glance of surprise. 'You're new here. What happened to Richardson?'

'He retired, madam. My name is Jenkins. Shall I announce you?'

'Yes, Jenkins. Where is Mr Shaw?' She discarded her gloves and removed her hat as a gesture of having returned to stay.

'He's with a guest in the drawing room.'

She steeled herself. 'Is that the lady who is staying here?'

'Yes, madam.'

Glancing in the hall mirror, she automatically touched her hair back into place where her hat had flattened it. So it was just as Joanna had written and Daniel had moved his mistress into the house! Fury threatened to choke her. As soon as she had challenged them and could estimate the damage done, she would banish the woman from the house and establish herself once more in her own realm. She could not believe that Daniel, seeing her again, would have forgotten how he had always loved her. If all that had been between them failed at this crisis in their lives she would let her heart break, but not yet. Not now. Her whole future was at stake!

She followed the footman to the drawing room where he opened the door and announced her.

She had a lightning image of the scene before her. The woman, clad in a crimson velvet gown, was sitting opposite Daniel with her back to the door as they played chess at the games table. They both looked up simultaneously as Lisette was announced, the woman startled and turning pale as she glanced over her shoulder. Daniel sprang to his feet with a wide grin of total delight illumining his whole face at the sight of Lisette framed in the doorway.

'Darling! You're back again! Why didn't you let me know? I would have met you!' He swept forward to seize and kiss her before spinning her round to face the woman who had risen from her chair. 'Look who is here, Lisette!'

Lisette caught her breath in astonishment. It was Josephine de Vincent, whom she had not seen since their farewell at the convent so many years ago. Then suspicion and anger soared in her again at this betrayal by someone who had been her friend. If Josephine had shown any pleasure at the sight of her then she could have dismissed all suspicion, but that was not the case. The woman, her face wracked by guilt, was in total distress

Lisette drew in a deep breath. 'I'm very surprised to see you of all people, Josephine,' she said coldly, detaching herself from Daniel's arms.

'I'm sure you are, Lisette,' Josephine replied in a shaking voice, gripping the back of the chair as if needing support at this climactic moment. 'I was planning to come to you in

Lyon and tell you everything that you should know, but now you are here instead.'

'How did you meet Daniel?' Lisette's voice rasped.

'When I was looking for you after my arrival in England. Having seen you on the screen I had recognized you instantly and went to the Shaw Studios. That was three weeks ago. Daniel kindly offered that I should stay here instead of in a hotel and I accepted gratefully. You and I have much to talk about, but how it will affect our friendship I do not know.'

'I thought friendship meant trust and contact, but you abandoned the nuns at the convent even as I believe you have betrayed me.'

'How could I keep in touch with them when any contact with the convent would have reminded me constantly of the worst mistake I have ever made in all my life? I wanted to try to forget and to make amends in whatever way I could.'

Lisette sank down on to a nearby chair. 'I don't know what you are talking about,' she said in angry bewilderment. 'You were a benefactor at the convent and they always spoke most highly of you.'

'They never knew how bitterly I regretted being instrumental in the adoption of your baby.'

Lisette's face drained of all colour and she sat very still. 'Are you telling me that you were responsible for my baby being taken from me?' she uttered in a horrified whisper.

It was Josephine's turn to look puzzled. 'Isn't that what you were talking about when you spoke of betrayal? I thought you meant that at some time you had guessed what had happened.'

Suddenly Lisette realized that this was all about the adoption of her baby at the convent and not the possible ensnaring of her husband.

'What are you trying to tell me?' she demanded, reaching for Daniel's hand and finding his warm, reassuring clasp.

Josephine pressed her palms together and linked her fingers nervously as she prepared herself for what she had to say. 'First of all it is a terrible confession that I have to make to you. I knew the couple, Arnaud and Rose Dubois, who adopted your baby. They were good friends of mine.' She paused. 'No doubt you will hate me for the rest of my life, but it was I who recommended your baby to them, knowing how desperately they had always wanted a child. They were already in their late forties and had never been able to have any children of their own.'

'How could you have been so cruel to me?' Lisette burst out in torment.

'I did it in all innocence!' Josephine exclaimed, lifting her linked hands up and down in anguish at what she was confessing. 'The abbess had mentioned to me that little Marie-Louise was to be adopted and I thought immediately of my friends. I knew that with them your baby would have a good home and be cared for with love.' She paused, looking in appeal for understanding at Lisette's stony face. 'Then, when you recovered from the aftermath of the birth, I learned that you had intended all the time to keep your baby, but it was too late for me to do anything about the adoption. The abbess had arranged it and my friends had already sailed for the States where Arnaud was taking up a diplomatic post at the French Embassy in Washington. It is where they began a new life with your daughter.'

'Did you ever have news of her again?' Lisette implored, hardly able to endure what she had been told.

'Yes, I went to live in New York for some years where I married and was widowed again in a very short time. I visited Arnaud and Rose quite often in Washington and was able to see how Marie-Louise was growing up to be a lovely girl and very like you, Lisette. Sadly, Arnaud died some years ago and then when Rose was taken very ill I went to be with Marie-Louise and help her with the nursing. It was after her adoptive mother's funeral that Marie-Louise found the documents showing her true parentage.'

'How did she react?' Lisette's voice was barely audible, and she closed her eyes in fear at what she might hear, tightening her grip on Daniel's hand.

'At first in dismay that she had never known she was adopted,' Josephine continued. 'Then, when I explained that I had been instrumental in her adoption, she began questioning me about her true parentage. She wanted to know everything about you both. I told her the whole story.'

Lisette looked at Josephine with the first faint light of

hope in her eyes. 'You know where she is?' she asked breath-lessly.

'Yes, I do.'

'Do you think she would let me write to her?'

Josephine exchanged a meaningful glance at Daniel, letting him reply.

'There's no need to write,' he said, joy in his voice. 'She's here. In our home. Reading in the library. If you hadn't come home as you have done you would have found us on your Bellecour doorstep next week.'

Lisette dropped her face into her hands, overcome momentarily by all she had learned during the last few minutes. Then, raising her head again, she stood up.

'Come with me, Daniel,' she said.

'Wouldn't you like to meet her on your own as I did at Josephine's suggestion?' Lisette shook her head. 'No, we are a family now. That's how I want to welcome her.'

At the library door Daniel turned the handle and opened it for Lisette to enter first. Their daughter was curled up in a wing chair, her kicked-off shoes left on the carpet, her dark curls bent over the book that she held.

'Marie-Louise,' Lisette said softly.

The girl looked up quickly. A lovely young nineteen-year-old with lustrous blue eyes in a finely boned, expressive face, her chin touched by a tilt of determination inherited from her natural father. Never taking her gaze from Lisette she put the book aside before she unfolded herself and rose to her feet. She and Lisette were of similar height. Neither made any move. In the long look they exchanged much passed between them. Then the girl spoke.

'*Maman* Lisette,' she whispered emotionally.

Lisette nodded, beyond speech or action in her joy. It was as if all the love she had felt when seeing her daughter for the first time had flooded back into her heart with abundance, filling at last the hollow that had been there all through the years. Then simultaneously she and Marie-Louise moved towards each other, smiling and then embracing, both in happy tears. For Lisette all the years fell away. This was a new beginning.

Daniel left the room, closing the door quietly behind him.

He knew from a long talk he had had with Marie-Louise that she wanted to stay with them. Although the bond she had had with her adoptive parents would always remain, she was already at ease and contented in his company, as she soon would be with Lisette.

Josephine left for France the next day, having made her home there again, and when she went it was with Louise's forgiveness.

Daniel was glad that he would not be leaving Lisette on her own when his military duties took him away from her. With war threatening to break out at any time he had already been contacted by the Ministry of Defence to become a news-reel cameraman at the battlefields. He had also been given the responsibility of recruiting a team ready to film what-ever this war should bring about. Jim would have been the first to volunteer to accompany him, but a foot injury some years ago would keep him out of uniform. It meant that Lisette would be in charge of the studios with Jim as her right-hand man.

Daniel was sure he would get leave home from the war sometimes and then he would be able to sort out any prob-lems that might arise, although he was confident that Lisette would be able to cope with anything that came along. After all, entertainment would be needed as never before to lift the spirits of servicemen on leave as well as those of anxious civilians at home.

Then a short while after Lisette's reunion with her daughter and far away in Sarajevo a fanatic shot an emperor in his carriage and it was the spark that plunged Europe into war. Flags flew, marching bands played and recruitment sergeants ignored the age of volunteers and signed up every one of the men who queued to enlist, even the still growing boys whose mothers thought they were at their lessons in school. Lisette received a letter from Maurice telling her that he had enlisted with the French Flying Corps and she said prayers for him.

Daniel gathered his camera team together. They had to go through military training like everyone else and then he was given the rank of captain.

Throughout this time Lisette and Marie-Louise became

close. The girl marvelled that her birth parents should be so young and lively in their outlook on life when her adoptive parents, much as she would always love them, had been old in their opinions and in their ways. With Lisette and Daniel she felt free to express her views and ideas, however outrageous, such as she never had before.

'Could I have a part in a Shaw film?' she asked one night at dinner, looking expectantly at Daniel. 'I don't mind being in a crowd and milling about in the background.'

Daniel grinned widely. 'I don't think anyone would ever be able to keep you in the background for very long.' It was his last night at home before leaving for France in the morning and he was in the mood to grant her anything. 'Lisette is in charge now. If you have her permission to start acting you have mine too.'

Lisette gave a pleased nod. 'A second generation Shaw actress. I like that idea.'

'Then my screen name shall be Marie-Louise Shaw!'

The girl saw how she had pleased her father with this announcement. In her heart she was deeply afraid of what he would face in the trenches, for this dreadful war had taken hold in terrible ways. She thought she understood him well enough now to know that he would never hold back with his camera, but would be at the forefront of any charge. Then, if filming proved impossible, he would sling his camera strap over his shoulder to take gun and bayonet to play his part.

Lisette stood with Marie-Louise when the time came for Daniel to depart. A military car had come for him and the driver had jumped out to salute and hold the door open. Daniel and Lisette gave each other a long look. They had made love the previous night with all the passion that the years had never diminished and now he was leaving to face untold dangers in the field of war, his last kiss still warm on her lips.

'You have to come back to us, *Papa* Daniel,' Marie-Louise said sternly to hide her heartache that this newfound father was going away. 'How else can I learn to be a true star of the silver screen without your tuition?'

He smiled. 'Just try to be as good an actress as Lisette.

You can learn more from her than you ever could from me.'

Marie-Louise ran a few steps after the military car as it drew away. Then she came to a halt and continued to wave her farewell to him. Daniel's last sight of Lisette was of her deliberately holding both arms out to him in the classic way of the heroine in motion pictures welcoming home the hero. It was her own private message to him.